PENNSYLVANIA'S FINEST

A NOVEL

By
Michael Banas

PENNSYLVANIA'S FINEST

CHAPTER 1
The Hippocratic Oath

It was a hot June day in the City of Brotherly Love as the senior class of the University of Pennsylvania School of Medicine gathered at the corner of 34th and Spruce Street. It was graduation day for one hundred and sixty students, each having just completed four years of intense medical training. Every student in line represented the dreams and aspirations of a proud family in attendance. Within an hour, they would all be medical physicians.

The venue was the Irvine Auditorium, which sat majestically in West Philadelphia since 1929. The interior of the great hall was filled with honored guests, relatives and academic staff. Just outside the Irvine, a serpentine line of students formed, each being adorned with a cap and gown. Excitement filled the air amid the graduating class, with each student anticipating a bright future.

Philip Michael Drummer stood out in line by nature of his height. He was 6 foot 5 inches tall with a lean build and thick crop of black hair. Brown eyes adorned a tanned complexion, which was intermittently freckled in a pleasing pattern. A kind demeanor combined with a caring attitude made him one of the most popular students amongst the graduating class. Phil, as his friends called him, was a product of Northeastern Pennsylvania, having grown up in the anthracite coal region. He represented generations of hard workers who toiled endlessly for the betterment of future generations. Phil Drummer was that future generation, suddenly poised to graduate from Penn Medical School.

Phil turned around and smiled at his adjacent classmate by nature of the alphabet. Laura Eichler graduated in the top ten of the class. She was smart, good looking and headed to Harvard for a Dermatology residency. She was destined to excel.

"Are you ready to become a doctor?" asked Phil with a smile.

"Definitely," said Laura. "Can you believe four years have gone by so quickly?"

"Hard to believe," nodded Phil who fondly remembered meeting Laura on their first day at Penn together. She was a lot like him, having been raised in a small town and possessing unassuming qualities. They became great friends, having toiled through many a lab and lecture next to each other. Phil had only great memories of her.

"Your family make it in time?" asked Laura. She knew that the trip for Phil's family represented a major journey.

"You bet," replied Phil. "They rolled into town bright and early this morning."

At that moment a booming voice at the head of the line yelled, "Class of 2010 look sharp. Congratulations and lets go!"

Phil then smiled at Laura and turned towards the Irvine while straightening out his cap and gown. The line slowly lurched forward as the long procession proudly rolled through the lower Penn campus into the Irvine Auditorium. A ray of brilliant sunshine then blessed the class from a blue summer sky above.

Phil's first impression of the Irvine Auditorium was the majestic sound of the Curtis pipe organ. This organ boasted 11,000 pipes and was built in 1926 for the Philadelphia Sesquicentennial Exposition. The organ was then donated to the University of Pennsylvania, which subsequently incorporated it into the Irvine's original construction. A deep tone from the organ echoed through the hall and provided a regal aura. Sound waves vibrated through Phil's body as he continued a procession further into the cavernous building. The coolness of the air-conditioned building was well received by all members of the class.

Phil looked up into the balcony for his family. It was a Drummer tradition to always sit in the balcony when possible. He soon spotted them. First on the right was his dad looking ill at ease in the crowd. Next to him sat his older brother Joe, dressed in a smart business suit. Finally his Aunt Emma completed the trio, craning nervously forward in an attempt to see her favorite nephew. Phil gave a short wave to the group, being unsure if they actually recognized him as he took his seat.

The commencement ceremony soon started and progressed in a fashion similar to all commencement ceremonies. The Dean of the school gave a speech mostly touting the greatness of Penn Medical School. The Dean of Student Affairs then lectured upon the talent and greatness of the class sitting before him. Lastly the guest speaker paid kudos to the great Penn Medical School before pontificating upon the sacred life of a physician. The event was academia at its finest with each speaker exalting the prior, thereby justifying their earthly existence.

Phil's mind wandered during the lectures. He spotted Amy Bryson who was sitting one row ahead of him, with an attentive gaze fixed upon the speaker. Her silhouette was one of classic beauty that was well known to Phil, since their one-year romance had just ended in an abrupt fashion. Amy was unfortunately headed to Texas for a residency in family practice. The logistics of a long distance relationship in conjunction with waning emotions precipitated the breakup that occurred just three weeks earlier. As Phil stared at the dark haired beauty he began to reminisce upon the good and bad days of their torrid affair. He was happily recalling the many good times when Laura Eichler suddenly elbowed him in the gut.

"Stand up Phil, time for the Oath," she whispered.

Phil snapped out of his daydream and stood up with the rest of the 2010 class. The Dean of Students then asked the class to repeat after him in a very serious tone. Absolute silence gripped the auditorium in a manner that temporarily froze time. Then in a tradition dating back to the origins of medicine, the ancient Oath of Hippocrates was recited.

Phil began swearing to several Greek gods including Apollo and Panacea. However upon hearing the phrase "To consider dear to me, as my parents, him who taught me this art" he lost all concentration. Memories of his deceased mother jolted him with a somber thud.

Martha Drummer was 58 years old when she died of breast cancer. A mother of two, she always enjoyed the simple pleasures of life. Phil was a senior in high school when she was diagnosed with cancer. He was a junior in college when she succumbed to the disease. She endured multiple operations over a period of three years without a negative comment or complaint. She died on a rainy Sunday morning with her family at her side.

Phil recalled her intense love for life, which was anchored by God and family. Her strong moral compass helped steer the Drummer family along a path of joy and happiness. She could always find the best in everyone, no matter how deeply it was suppressed. Although only educated through high school, she fiercely encouraged her son's education and commitment to a medical career. Phil knew that the very moment he was experiencing, his moment, actually belonged to her.

His mind returned to the Oath hearing "I will not give a lethal drug to anyone if I am asked," and again his mind wandered.

"Why would anyone give a lethal drug to a patient?" he thought. Then he remembered the callous attitude of some of surgeons that cared for his mother. Pompous in nature, they frequently spoke with lack of care and patience, babbling words that were foreign to his family in general. They feigned compassion, but their body language spoke otherwise. He quickly made a personal promise to never act in this manner.

The oath rambled on and finished with, "If I keep this oath faithfully, may I enjoy my life and practice my art, respected by all men and in all times; but if I swerve from it or violate it, may the reverse by my lot."

"Whoa," thought Phil. "This Hippocrates guy didn't fool around."

Then, at that very moment, Philip Drummer became a medical doctor. He turned to congratulate Laura and they joyfully hugged each other, knowing that their young medical careers had just begun.

The inner bowels of the Curtis pipe organ then erupted and the applause of the adoring throng was drowned out by the organ's majesty. Phil slowly walked down the aisle towards the exit as the sun shone through stain glass windows in a mystical fashion. Looking up to the balcony his father and brother were proudly clapping. Aunt Emma was waving her hands and about to become airborne. She then steadied herself to take a photo of the pomp and circumstance with a camera that still used old- fashioned film.

The scene just outside the Irvine Auditorium was chaotic. Students were hugging each other and trying to find family members. Phil exited to the left as his family exited to the right. He spotted them over the crowd and began to slowly work his way through the swarm. Suddenly he walked into the midst of the Riles family. Frederick Riles III was a fellow classmate of his at Penn Med. They were never good friends but both were heading into the same surgical residency starting that July. Fred Riles came from a fine pedigree in Boston. His father was a prominent general surgeon on the staff at the Massachusetts General Hospital. From the moment Frederick Riles III was born, he was destined for this exact moment in time.

"Congratulation Fred," shouted Phil to his classmate over the clamor.

Fred Riles was thin and wiry in stature. At six foot tall he weighed at best 160 pounds. Nervous in attitude he was always smartly dressed and well spoken. Wearing wire rim glasses, a conservative theme exuded from his frame. A formal bearing and Boston accent helped to identify him as a product of the finest New England schools that money could buy.

"Thanks Phil. Congratulations to you," responded Fred.

At that moment Frederick Riles II M.D., stepped between the young graduates. "This must be Dr. Philip Drummer," said the older Riles in a calculated and pleasing tone. "I had dinner with your soon to be chairman last night, Dr. Barnes, and he told me all about you. Sounds like it is going to be a great intern class next year."

Phil had never met the older and often mentioned Frederick Riles II. However, he knew that he trained at the Philadelphia General Hospital some twenty five years ago, and since then kept close ties with the current chairman of the program, that being Dr. Michael Barnes. It was obvious to Phil that the younger Riles had his path paved into the Philadelphia General surgical program well in advance.

"You know Dr. Barnes and I trained together," said the older Riles not allowing Phil to introduce himself. "We had many a crazy night at the old PGH," said Riles now chuckling aloud. The term PGH referred to the Philadelphia General Hospital, where Phil and Frederick were scheduled to begin an internship that July.

"It's a pleasure to meet you Dr. Riles," said Phil extending his hand. "I've heard a lot about you."

Dr. Riles shook his hand and smiled while moving his head right to left. His teeth were over bleached and blinding white. "Good luck young man. Stay away from those young nurses," said the older Riles. He kept shaking Phil's hand while looking around at the Riles family members. They all nodded in approval.

"Thank you sir," said Phil as he pushed on realizing that the younger Riles had nothing further to say in the vast shadow of his dad.

Phil then worked his way through the crowd to meet his family, which was standing aside near the curbstone of Spruce Street. Phil went to his dad first.

"Congratulations son," said his father extending his hand with a firm grip. "Mom and I are proud of you."

Phil's dad was a hard worker who came from a long line of hard workers. His own father was sent over from Eastern Europe as a teenager and worked the mines in Northeastern Pennsylvania. Phil's father briefly worked in the mines but was thankfully able to make a living above ground. Hard work was his father's best friend.

"Thanks dad," said Phil understanding his dad was a man of few words. "Thank you very much."

He then turned to his brother Joe who was two years older than him.

"Congratulations doctor," said his brother as the two shook hands. "I believe I am technically the first one to call you doctor."

Joseph Drummer was the smartest of the Drummer boys having excelled throughout school with a love for mathematics. He joined IBM years ago and worked in the Hudson Valley region. He was always sharply dressed in a manner that all successful businessmen were.

"Thanks Joe D.," replied Phil. "Thanks again for bringing everyone down to the city."

"No problem," said his brother Joe. "We do a lot of business with the Philadelphia General and I know the route well."

Lastly Phil turned to his favorite Aunt who smiled broadly at him with her hands clasped together at her breast. Before he could say anything Aunt Emma burst forward hugging him.

"Your mother would be proud of you," she said with tears in her eyes. "So very proud."

Aunt Emma Gibson was the slightly older sister of Phil's mother. The two sisters were inseparable growing up, being the only girls in a family of eight.

"I know Aunt Emma, I know," said Phil pretending to be short of breath from the bear hug grip still in effect. "Mom would be proud of all of us."

Then without much fanfare the Drummer family turned and began walking home. They slowly proceeded up Spruce Street deeper into the core of West Philadelphia. Phil's apartment was just off campus eight city blocks away. Their journey was slow and relaxing, through the

Penn campus. Several rest stops were made for Aunt Emma, who was not accustomed to the heat and humidity of Philadelphia.

Dinner that night was a homemade tray of lasagna since it was another Drummer tradition to never eat out at a restaurant. Soon afterwards the Drummer family departed to return home. Later that evening Phil took a slow, pensive walk through his neighborhood. Record setting summer heat gripped the area, with the evening humidity still high. His stroll took him to just outside the Philadelphia General Hospital complex, which shone bright amid the dark skyline. Phil appreciated a hum of energy and activity emanating from the complex, as weary interns and residents passed by. His orderly mind tried to redefine his sense of presence just outside the institution. Behind him was medical school, filled with years of written tests and boring didactic lectures. Directly in front of him stood the great PGH, one of the true paragons of medicine in the world. Generations of physicians had learned their trade within the walls of the PGH, each then passing down their knowledge to the generation that followed. Phil knew that it was his turn to enter the hallowed halls and learn the true art of medicine. Only then, after five years of training, would he be able to carry a surgeon's torch of knowledge. Knowledge that permitted him to enter a human being's physical dimension and reverse a disease process with expertise.

Sleep did not come easy that night for the newly anointed physician. As Phil lay awake listening to the street noises below he thought of his aunt and father, and how proud they were of him. His dad's parting advice echoed through his mind as he unsuccessfully tried to sleep. "Work hard and remember where you came from," was his parting counsel, and mantra for life. Phil then made a promise to himself during the early morning hours, that being to honor this code throughout his career at the PGH. Unfortunately the fitful night continued, as the harsh reality of a pending surgical internship bore down on the young doctor.

CHAPTER 2
Internship

PHIL DRUMMER WAS about to begin a surgical internship at the Philadelphia General Hospital. This internship was a time honored, rite of passage for a surgeon, entailing a full year of intense training at a medical center. Upon satisfactory completion of this first year, an intern was then permitted to take the next step up the educational ladder, with that step becoming a resident. In the simplest of terms, an intern dwelled at the bottom of a vast educational food chain within the confines of an academic teaching hospital.

During internship the newly crowned physician was called a house officer, because he or she basically lived in the hospital, venturing home only a few nights a week in order to sleep. Interns were required to "take call" every other or every third night. The basic rule of a call night was simple, that being to never leave the hospital setting during your shift. For instance a Monday night call would require reporting to work Monday morning at 5:30 a.m., then toiling through the day and night caring for patients. No sleep was guaranteed during this shift. Monday night would simply blend into Tuesday morning. Work would then continue through Tuesday evening until about 6 p.m.

Then the weary intern would wander home, eat and collapse into bed. Every other night call meant that the process would simply repeat itself the following Wednesday morning. The intern's creed during this punishing year was also quite simple, that being "Eat when you can and sleep when you can."

Adding to the misery of the year was the job description of an intern. Basically put, the intern carried out the most vile and distasteful functions necessary for a medical center to function. Atop their daily list was the dreaded chore of starting intravenous lines and drawing blood. Also included was wound care, dressing changes and emergency room management. Every patient admitted would require a physical exam, which had to be meticulously logged into a computerized system, in compliance with hospital regulations. Adding to the computer crunch were daily patient progress notes, again being the responsibility of the intern. The intern quickly learned that life on the bottom of a totem pole was cruel, especially when their lowly position was considered a privilege to possess.

The intern was only one small cog of a teaching institution's surgical team. On the top of the pyramid sat the elder professor, or attending surgeon. This physician was usually a middle-aged surgeon who for multiple reasons decided to work and teach at a medical center. Most attending surgeons had a research interest, and this intellectual itch could only be cared for within the confines of a teaching institution. An unwritten agreement existed between the attending and resident staff, allowing the residents to do a fair share of the work, while in return receiving the knowledge passed down by the attending. This symbiotic relationship formed the basis of a teaching hospital, having been in existence for hundreds of years.

Below the attending was the chief resident, who was in the fifth and final year of surgical training. The chief resident was the so called "right hand man" of the attending, carrying out their most trusted chores, in return for permission to perform their surgical procedures. This resident position was coveted, since it represented the end point of a five year battle to the top. Between the chief resident and intern lay multiple layers of junior residents, who were completing their second, third and fourth years of surgical training. They formed the vast mid level management position of surgical teams throughout the hospital network.

Unfortunately all residents were not created equal. There were good chief residents and bad chief residents. There were lazy junior residents and motivated junior residents. Lastly there were competent interns and incompetent interns. Every surgical team had its own inner dynamics depending on the personalities involved. This surgical team, put together randomly by an administrative scheduler, was ultimately responsible for the smooth and safe care of thousands of patients a year. Trusting patients who travelled from near and far to the prestigious Philadelphia General Hospital, in order to place their health in the system's capable hands.

For whatever reason the residency calendar began and ended on July 1st of a calendar year. That day marked the yearly move up the ladder for each resident. Like clockwork the medical student became an intern and the second year resident became a third year resident. July 1st marked the promotion of each physician, along with the challenges associated with it. Therefore, July was a dangerous time to be in a teaching hospital. In July, a tired and nervous intern would be starting your IV and performing your rectal exam. In July, a new second year resident would be controlling your medications overnight in the surgical intensive care unit. In July, a newly crowned chief resident would be performing your surgery for the first time in their career. Therefore, a good general rule was to avoid being a patient at a teaching hospital during the month of July.

July 1st was near and Phil Drummer was getting nervous. Several days after graduation, he reported to The Philadelphia General Hospital for mandatory paperwork.

The PGH was a short walk from Phil's apartment complex at 42nd and Spruce Street. The hospital complex itself was massive in scope, encompassing six city blocks in one direction and three in another. It represented one of the first hospitals in the country and sat adjacent to the University of Pennsylvania campus and medical school.

The hospital infrastructure consisted of a sprawling hodgepodge of buildings. Each building was connected either by a direct hallway, underground route or above street walkway. If desired, a physician could enter the complex at 40th street and exit on 34th street, without ever leaving the confines of the facility. The center was a mixture of ultra-modern wings and outdated open hospital wards. Pavilions were frequently named after a physician who spent an entire medical career at PGH, thus gaining immortality by the passage of time.

The Department of General Surgery sat on the sixth floor of the Kirby Pavilion, which was named after a general surgeon from the 1800s who also practiced Veterinary Medicine. Doctor Kirby was famous for curing a patient and then examining their mule team prior to leaving the hospital. The Kirby building was an ancient complex, left standing only for architectural and budget constraint purposes.

The department's main office was dank, tight quartered and depressing. Only scattered windows let in filtered light, which struggled to get past adjacent taller buildings. An outdated heating and air conditioning system frequently malfunctioned, producing variable ranges of temperature within the facility. Upon entering the office Phil took two steps and stopped at the receptionist's desk.

"May I help you?" asked the young secretary, with a smile.

"Hi, I'm Doctor Drummer", responded Phil with an eye on the attractive woman. "I'm going to be a new intern in July and am reporting for duty as ordered." Phil smiled with his subtle attempt at humor.

"Doctor Drummer, yes we have been waiting for you," replied the secretary now with an added gleam to her eye. "Please have a seat and I'll see if Doctor Barnes is available."

As the secretary arose Phil admired her physique and the fact that she called him doctor. She turned the corner and walked down the hallway with a calculated, curvaceous gait.

Phil sat down and looked around the waiting room. Some information posters hung on the wall and a small coffee machine sat in the corner. A single low table was to his side and had a few medical magazines on it. "Wow," thought Phil, "What a dump." The Surgical Department at the PGH was known worldwide as it historically trained the best of surgeons. Its residency was a coveted position sought annually by hundreds of over qualified medical students from across the land. "This is the best they can do?" thought Phil.

At that moment the young secretary turned the corner smiling with a middle-aged woman. The secretary sat down neatly keeping her eyes on Phil at all times. The older woman was one of the many residency coordinators Phil had seen in the past. She was not as thrilled to see Phil but offered her handshake with a welcoming smile, while taking Phil back to her office.

She informed Phil that Dr. Barnes was unavailable and in surgery that morning. Then for the next 30 minutes she succinctly informed Phil of his required duties prior to starting work on July 1st.

Phil was given a PGH employee handbook laying out the bylaws of the hospital. He was informed of the necessary paperwork to be completed regarding personal information. He was instructed to report to the occupational health department regarding necessary immunizations. Also necessary was a trip to hospital security for a photo ID and security clearance. Lastly he was asked to report to the Information Technology department for clearance and instructions regarding the hospital's computer system. Phil coldly felt like he was starting a job, which by the end of the lecture, was true.

"Any questions?" asked the coordinator.

"Yes," said Phil, "When do I meet the other interns from my year?"

"June 30th," was the matter of fact response. "Doctor Barnes will be hosting a reception that morning in the conference room at 6:00 AM."

Phil smiled wondering why general surgeons always meet at the crack of dawn. Perhaps some curse was thrown upon the profession by a sadistic Greek god ages ago.

"We will send you a confirmation email and text regarding the reception," said the now inpatient coordinator.

"Great," said Phil. "I hear we have a wonderful intern class."

The coordinator smiled, not wanting to prolong the meeting. "Any other questions?" was her next terse line.

"No, but thank you for the help," said Phil politely as he got up remembering his dad's advise never to burn any bridges. He then extended a parting handshake in saying goodbye.

"Nice meeting you Doctor Drummer," said the interested young secretary as Phil walked out.

"A pleasure meeting you," said Phil with a wave goodbye. "See you on orientation day."

Phil then spent the final few days of June preparing for internship. He uneasily smiled for an I.D. photo at the hospital security department. He stoically received a booster shot for hepatitis prophylaxis at the student health office. Then, he happily received a laptop computer from the Information Technology office.

On the eve of orientation day, Phil sat alone in his apartment. He was attempting to hook up his new computer to the hospital web site when a knock rattled his door.

Upon opening the door Phil greeted his friend and apartment mate from across the hall. Jim Turner was a veterinary student at the University of Pennsylvania. He was born and raised in central Pennsylvania having grown up on a dairy farm. After college he worked as a vet surgical assistant for ten years, then decided to apply to vet school. At 32 years of age he was the oldest, and seemingly most brilliant student in his class. Turner was polite, somewhat portly and a bit reclusive. He was a technophile and was some way or the other connected to every satellite over North America. His quirky passion was drinking a large glass of whole milk at every meal. When on the farm it was straight from the cow, when in Philadelphia he would settle for the pasteurized brand from the nearby Acme market.

"Are you ready?" asked Jim with a down home grin on his face.

"You bet," said Phil extending his hand for Jim to enter the apartment.

Jim entered the small corner apartment on the seventh floor of the Greycliff apartment complex. Phil's apartment consisted of a galley kitchen, small living room and a single bedroom. Turner and Drummer shared the same floor for the past two years and formed a great friendship during this time. Having both grown up in Pennsylvania they had a common bond.

"Just trying to hook up to the hospital hub on the new computer," said Phil, "Having a problem getting recognized." Phil knew this would peak Turner's interest and immediately help rectify the computer glitch.

"A new laptop?" said Turner as he rapidly approached Phil's desk. Then with geek like envy Jim Turner eyed the laptop while saying, "The latest and greatest, nice."

"Compliments of the PGH," replied Phil knowing that Turner would immediately offer his help to solve the connection problem, which he did. Within twenty minutes Phil's computer was up and running, seamlessly communicating with the innards of The Philadelphia General Hospital. The final preliminary step leading into his internship was now complete.

Phil smiled proudly at the laptop like a new father in the nursery. The crisp computer screen was bright and inviting. He leaned back in his chair with his hands clasped behind his head saying, "Life will never be the same."

High fives were happily exchanged between the two Pennsylvania products, who then proceeded to watch a Phillies baseball game well into the night, unaware as to how prophetic Phil's words would soon be.

CHAPTER 3
Orientation Day

SURGEONS BY AND large are antisocial creatures. They start a workday too early and end too late. They practice their trade behind a mask in a sterile environment, closed to the public. Their schedule is overbooked and subject to instant change. They thrive on physical and mental challenges and the associated adrenaline rush. This frenetic schedule over time produces an individual who is brash, productive and confident. It also creates an alpha wolf who only socializes with the pack to exert dominance. Therefore surgeons do not enjoy meetings or gatherings. They prefer to be moving and producing as opposed to standing and conversing.

Surgical orientation began at 6 a.m. on June 30th. Phil woke up at 5 a.m. being unaccustomed to the early rise. The streets of West Philadelphia were empty as he walked through the Penn Campus. Orientation was in the department of surgery office that morning.

Upon entering the department office Phil thought he was there on the wrong day. The office was dimly lit and not a soul was in sight. In the cramped office the smell of coffee permeated the air giving Phil hope that his calendar was correct. After a brief pause the door opened behind him and a tall, somewhat confident young woman walked in.

Cathy Finley was a slim 5'8" tall with brown hair and brown eyes. She wore fashionable glasses and minimal make up. Her facial features were individually plain but together created an attractive appearance. Born and raised in New England she was well educated and cultured. Having spent two years earlier in the Peace Corps, she would be the oldest intern of the group at age 27. Phil immediately recognized her from a group email sent to him by the surgical coordinator.

"Hi," said Phil extending his hand. "You must be Cathy."

"Yes I am Cathy, Cathy Finley," was her response while firmly shaking Phil's extended hand. "You must be Phil Drummer."

"I am. It's a pleasure to meet you," replied Phil hoping she was somewhat normal in light of the year ahead. "Brown medical school, right?" asked Phil.

"Yep, and you are from Penn," replied Cathy looking around for anyone else in the room.

"Right," said Phil "I love the city so much I didn't want to leave." An awkward moment went by, allowing Phil to appreciate the lameness of his comment.

At that moment the door again opened and Frederick Riles III entered the room. Frederick was sharply dressed in pressed pants and a starched shirt. He wore a bow tie and had a professorial appearance despite his young age. His shoes were well polished and comfortable in appearance. He walked with a sure gait cultivated over time. He stepped up directly to the two other interns.

"Hi, Frederick Riles," was his polite introduction to Cathy with a bow. They shook hands extending greetings. Fred smelled manly of expensive cologne.

"Another Penn boy," said Drummer patting Riles on the back.

The department door opened again with a member of the cafeteria staff entering the room. Dressed in white pants and a short sleeve shirt the dietary worker wore a hair net over his head. He carried a tray of donuts and pastries that did not look fresh at all. He was whistling a jazz tune and moving as if the young interns did not exist.

"Cookie! What's up?" said Phil recognizing the cafeteria worker.

Cookie was a popular member of the cafeteria staff. He worked at PGH for the past 15 years serving up breakfast, lunch and dinner to the resident staff. He was a 36 year-old thin male with a fantastic smile despite lacking a few teeth. He was a tremendous worker always on the move. Outside of the hospital he was Terrance Jones, a proud father of four.

"Hey doc," replied Cookie. "Got some good chow for you here." He quickly moved across the room depositing the tray of goodies on the table. "Enjoy."

"Thanks my man," said Phil shaking Cookie's hand. Cookie obliged.

"Gracias," said Riles attempting to belong, but Cookie did not respond as he left the room.

For the next 15 minutes the three interns shared some donuts and coffee wondering why they arrived so early. Two secretaries then wandered in with a smile as they reported to their work area. The young receptionist who met Phil several days earlier wore her favorite skirt and blouse outfit, a fact that caught Phil's attention even in the early hour.

The time was 6:30 a.m. when Dr. Michael Barnes, the Chairman of the Department of Surgery entered the room.

He approached the group from the opposite side of the room with a broad smile on his face. He walked quickly.

"Sorry I'm a tad late," said Barnes who then employed the oldest excuse known to the medical profession. "We had a bit of an emergency downstairs but things have finally settled down. It's a pleasure to meet you all."

Behind Barnes was Chief Resident Pete Larson. Larson had one year left in his residency and knew the PGH system well. He was planning a plastic surgery fellowship in Southern California the following year. He had sandy blonde hair and was a tad overweight for a soon to be plastic surgeon. He appeared fatigued.

"Welcome to the Philadelphia General Hospital," said Barnes with his arms extended in a welcoming fashion. "I know that some of you are Penn grads and know the hospital well. For those of you who are new to the PGH, we welcome you. You are in for a fabulous year here in Philadelphia." Barnes smiled and looked around the group waiting for a response. The three interns just nodded back at him.

"We are missing someone?" inquired Barnes just realizing that one fourth of the class was absent. "A Dr. Polk I believe. Has anyone heard from him?"

The three interns just shook their heads nodding no.

"Hmm" mumbled Barnes. He then paused for two seconds then continued by saying, "Well let's get started anyway. I would like to introduce Chief Resident Peter Larson. Doctor Larson has excelled here at the PGH over the past four years and has accepted the esteemed position of Chief Surgical Resident. He will be in charge of your schedule and clinical rotations."

Pete Larson stepped forward in a fashion not becoming of an esteemed resident. "Welcome, just call me Pete. I was hoping that all four interns would be here," said Larson looking at his watch. "I guess however that we can begin."

At that moment the door opened and in walked a disheveled and portly young man with brown hair and brown eyes. His shirt was wrinkled and he wore thread worn khaki pants. He looked a bit confused.

"Hi, Rick Polk here," said the intern. "Sorry I'm late. I got lost and ended up in the morgue." Polk was laughing while approaching the group.

Polk then exchanged introductions with the group as Dr. Barnes watched patiently. Phil shook his hand realizing immediately that a portion of a jelly donut was smeared onto his palm. Polk had a comical appearance that was somehow relaxing to the group.

"As I was saying," started Larson regaining control of the group. "There are four surgical rotations for the interns. Each rotation will run three months. Night call will vary from rotation to rotation. The four rotations are general surgery, cardiothoracic surgery, trauma service and specials. The specials rotation will consist of equal time with the urology, orthopedic, plastics and gynecology teams. Any question?"

"What's the overnight call schedule for each," mumbled Polk with a pastry stuffed in his mouth.

Larson responded, "Cardiothoracic is every other night in the hospital. General surgery and trauma is every third night in the hospital. The fortunate intern on specials rotation will take call from home, only coming in for emergencies."

Chief resident Larson paused then continued. "Drummer will start cardiothoracic with me, Finley on general surgery, Polk on trauma and Riles on specials."

Phil gasped while Riles let out a sigh of relief. Cardiothoracic was the toughest three months of all and Phil had the pleasure of starting there first.

"Any other questions?" asked Chairman Barnes.

The interns were quiet, each with a deer in the headlights look, as they pondered the news bestowed upon them.

"Well then enjoy the breakfast in front of you. Get to know each other and again welcome to the PGH," said Barnes with a smile. "See you all tomorrow, bright and early."

Then Chairman Barnes quickly turned and vanished around a corner. Chief resident Larson's beeper went off and he headed towards a phone. Prior to picking up the phone he looked at Phil saying, "Drummer, tomorrow, 5:30 a.m. in the cafeteria."

Then as unceremoniously as it began, the intern orientation was over.

Phil had a heavy feeling in his stomach. It was 6:40 a.m. and Larson quickly vanished down a hallway.

"Wow," said Polk. "That was pretty short. The elevator ride up to this floor took longer." Polk laughed a deep chuckle that echoed from his stomach. Looking around he grabbed another pastry.

Cathy Finley then spoke, "I hear that CT is tough." She was referring to the cardiothoracic rotation that Phil was about to begin.

Before Phil could answer Riles chimed in, "Yes and we all know who runs that ship." He smiled looking at Phil, waiting for him to clue in the crowd.

"Doctor Richard Knight," said Phil shaking his head. "Dr. Richard Knight," he repeated again quietly.

Riles smiled as if he knew the rotation schedule ahead of time. He slowly nodded his head up and down with a smirk.

"I haven't heard nice things about him," said Cathy.

"No," said Phil. "He is one mean old dog," recalling his medical student experiences with Dr. Knight. "I can't believe I have to spend the next three months with him."

"We all do," said Polk. "What's the big deal? Take it like a man." Polk had powder from his third pastry around his lips. He wiped his mouth with his sleeve.

An awkward silence then hit the group. Riles broke the silence excusing himself first. Then Cathy Finley spoke of a necessary trip to the bookstore and departed.

Polk and Drummer remained.

"Man I moved into a dump across the river yesterday," said Polk shaking his head. "It looked good over the internet, but wow, what a hole." Polk then wiped his mouth with his sleeve while mumbling, "Cockroaches everywhere."

Phil was still a bit numb as Polk then slapped him on the back prior to leaving the office. Unaware, he now had pastry powder on his shirt.

"Doctor Richard Knight," Phil whispered to himself. "Doctor Knight."

As Phil wandered out of the office he didn't even notice the young secretary smiling at him so early in the morning. He slowly wandered back to his apartment, realizing the horror that lay ahead of him the following day.

CHAPTER 4
The Doctor is In

PHIL'S ALARM CLOCK went off the next morning at 4:30 a.m. It was a sweltering hot day in the city. The Greycliff apartment complex was deathly quiet at that time of the morning. Phil sat silently at his kitchen table during breakfast, looking out over West Philadelphia from his seventh floor apartment. The intersection below was Walnut and 42nd street. The eclectic intersection hosted a Vietnamese grocery store, laundromat, pawnshop and pub. Not a soul was in sight at that time of the morning. Phil sipped some black coffee with his cereal. Occasionally, a city bus roared through the intersection.

He realized that morning was the beginning of his career as a doctor. Years of hard work got him to that point, yet he was again starting at the bottom of the ladder. By and large the medical profession was a relentless climb upwards. After being a senior in college the next step was that of a first year medical student. After reaching the top of the medical school ladder the bottom wrung of internship was next. Then after climbing the residency ladder the next step was to the bottom of a fellowship program. Phil knew quite well that he was at the low point of a new level of training that would challenge his inner core.

The walk from his apartment to Philadelphia General was quick and calm. There is a quiet peace to the city and a college campus at 5 a.m. Some local corner fruit stands were setting up shop for the day. An occasionally homeless person rolled over on their asphalt bed as Phil walked by. The humidity was already thick in the early morning July air.

Phil arrived in the hospital cafeteria at 5:20 a.m. always aware of his dad's advice to show up early. Chief resident Larson was eating breakfast at a table not looking up as Phil sat next to him.

"Good morning," said Phil.

"Morning," mumbled Larson reading the sports page. He shook his head and then moaned about the Chicago Cubs loosing yet another game the night before. Larson unfortunately belonged to the Cub's Nation.

Larson raised his head and looked around the cafeteria. "Have you seen the two medical stupids?" he asked Phil.

Phil nodded in the negative understanding that Larson meant the two third year medical students assigned to their rotation that summer. Phil remembered his three-month rotation in surgery and shuddered.

Just then a sharply dressed female approached them with a short white coat on signifying her status as a medical student. Melissa Bankart was an insecure, timid and at times emotional young woman starting her surgery rotation. Despite being a third year medical student she was unsure that the field of medicine was for her. Larson looked at her and immediately sensed doom.

"Good morning I'm Melissa Bankart," was her introduction in a cracking voice. Larson and Drummer introduced themselves.

Several steps behind Bankart walked her fellow Penn classmate Charles Roden. Roden was good natured, confident and intelligent. He loved being a medical student and excelled in the classroom and on the clinical rotations. His physical presence that morning emitted a calm determination.

"Charles Roden here. Just call me Chuck," was his relaxing introduction to the group.

"All right this is it," said Larson. "This will be the team for the next three months. The rules are work together, work hard and never go home until all the work is done. We round together every day at 5:30 a.m. Usually have about 15 patients on the floor. Then to the OR at 7:30 a.m."

Medical student Bankart already appeared white and ill at ease. Medical student Roden was smiling and nodding his head.

"Doctor Drummer will take in house call every other night and the medical students will spend every third night in the hospital. Any questions?" asked Chief Resident Larson.

It was too early in the morning for the team to speak.

Larson went on, "As you know Doctor Knight runs a tight ship. His post op patients usually spend one night in the intensive care unit. Then the next day, after being extubated, they travel to the step down unit. Usually two days on step down and then a final day on the floor. He wants all of his patients out of the hospital by post operative day four."

The surgical team nodded as they looked at each other. They were unaware of the multitude of postoperative complications that would easily derail the four-day plan.

"Just don't cross Knight. Be on time always and just be quiet. I'm sure you have all heard about him. Don't rock the boat or you will end overboard."

Larson paused, still no response.

"Here is how rounding works," restarted Larson. "The medical stupids get here early and stock the supply pack." He then handed Roden a large red plastic bucket with a shoulder strap on it. It was filled with tape, dressing gauze, bandages and antiseptic supplies. "You two idiots carry the bucket and change all dressings on rounds. Keep the bucket filled and hide it wherever you please. But have it on your shoulder every morning at 5:30 a.m."

He continued to look at the two medical students. "You are also responsible for a computer print out of all the morning lab values. Put them on a clipboard in room number order. When I ask for the lab value at the bedside I expect you to have it ready."

Medical students Bankart and Roden each exhibited distinctly opposite body language at that moment in time. Melissa Bankart wanted to vomit and Charles Roden wanted to run up the steps to start rounding.

Larson didn't care and went on, "Drummer you examine the patient and document a note in the computer system that morning. Try to make physical contact with the patient every morning even if it means putting your stethoscope onto their chest."

Phil nodded being comfortable with the hospital's computerized medical record system, which was recently mandated to exist by the federal government. He was aware that every bit of clinical data was collected by the system to assure compliance with accepted treatment protocols.

"Got it?" asked Larson. He paused and then stood up quickly. "Lets go!" and with a quick step perfected over time, Chief Resident Larson led the inexperienced team out of the cafeteria towards the stairwell.

"Never take the elevator," yelled Larson as he burst into the stairwell. Medical student Roden was all smiles as they double-timed it up six flights of stairs to the car-diothoracic floor.

"No surgery yesterday so the ICU is clean," said Larson. Lets start in the Step Down Unit. He then pulled out a crumbled piece of paper with all the in house patients of the cardiothoracic team listed. Larson turned right and rocketed down a hallway with his long white coat flying in the breeze.

Larson took a hard right into room 721 and the team followed in pecking order. In the bed was a frail 71 year-old pasty white female who two days earlier had a cardiac procedure performed by Dr. Knight. She was sound asleep under the covers in the air-conditioned room.

"Good morning," shouted Dr. Larson clicking on the lights in the room. Mrs. Townsend lurched forward being startled by the care team assault.

"How do you feel today?" blurted out Larson snapping his fingers at Phil who quickly took out a stethoscope and put it on her back. Drummer tried to listen to her lungs and air exchange but only could hear Larson start again. "Are you having any pain?"

Mrs. Townsend blinked her eyes and moaned putting her hand to her sternum, which was the source of her pain. She weakly said "just a bit," and cleared her throat.

"You are coming along well" said Larson now taking the tape off her chest tube which was coming out of the right side of her pleural cavity.

A chest tube is routinely inserted between the rib cage and lungs after any procedure that enters the chest cavity itself. The tube is connected to a closed suction system and removes any unwanted collection of fluid, blood or air after the operation. The chest tube allows the lungs and heart to function properly in the postoperative state.

The tube is routinely removed one to two days after the surgery.

Larson was preparing to remove the tube at bedside.

"We are going to remove this tube from your chest," said Larson as he clamped the one-inch tube from its suction canister. He motioned to Drummer as he cut the suture holding the chest tube in place. Phil knew the drill and grabbed each end of the suture, which was still in the patient's chest wall but now free of the chest tube.

Mrs. Townsend's eyes were large as she was instructed to take three slow deep breaths and hold her breath after the third one. Chief Resident Larson then counted from one to three as the trusting patient slowly inhaled and exhaled. After the third inspiration he loudly said, "Hold your breath now!"

The patient obliged and with a flick of his wrist Larson yanked the long tube out of the patient's chest cavity. Phil immediately tied the sutures together not allowing any air to enter the chest cavity. Mrs. Townsend let out a scream, as did third year medical student Bankart.

General surgery training is a rite of initiation and third year medical student Melissa Bankart just received her baptism. Accidental or not, Chief Resident Larson's follow through brought the two foot long by one inch wide chest tube fanning across the room. Medical student Roden had seen this before and side stepped at the last second. However Melissa Larson held her ground that early morning. Unfortunately the exiting tube was filled with clotted blood and bodily fluid. The follow through sprayed the young student across her shoes and stockings with the mixture of chest cavity contents. She stood in shock looking down at her outfit. The outfit she so carefully picked out last night for her first day of surgery.

Larson didn't even break stride. "Get a dressing on that!" he barked at Roden who responded with the supply bucket. "She needs a chest x-ray this morning," was his order to Drummer. Larson then rocketed out the door without another word to the patient. The team followed after medical student Bankart cleaned off her shoes. Both she and Mrs. Townsend had a tear in their eyes.

Rounds continued at a frenetic pace for the team. Larson was a veteran of the rounding process and never broke stride. Phil was a bit overwhelmed with the process and orders given to him. Medical student Roden handled it well as he continually dove into the supply bucket. Medical student Bankart never recovered from the chest tube event, and contributed little to the team that morning.

After rounds it was 7:30 am. Larson notified the team that Dr. Knight was again out of town that day and no surgery was scheduled. Therefore the day was going to be light. He gave a laundry list of floor work for Phil to do that morning. He asked the medical students to help Drummer. He then asked the students to look up the physiology of chest tubes that night and give him an oral presentation the next morning on rounds. Chief Resident Larson then disappeared into the inner core of the medical center. His only other duty that day was to await a call from Dr. Knight regarding the status of his in hospital patients. Fortunately everyone looked well that morning.

Phil and his medical students spent the next several hours carrying out floor scut work. They entered a daily progress note into the computer for each patient. Chest x-rays were ordered and labs were double-checked. After lunch the students headed to the library to learn about chest tubes and their function. Phil headed to the intern call room.

The intern call room was located in the basement of the Philadelphia General. Decades ago it was a wing of the city morgue. However a renovation twenty years ago moved the morgue to a more modern facility. The surgical interns were then given the space to set up a series of call rooms connected to a central lounge. The walls were cinder block with overhead exposed piping throughout, which gave a gritty industrial look to the facility. Lovingly called "The Hole," it represented the personal space in the hospital for the interns, both surgical and medical.

Phil entered the call room finding fellow interns Rick Polk and Cathy Finley laughing aloud in the lounge. Polk was reliving a favorite Seinfeld TV episode in which Kramer finds the Merv Griffin set in the trash. Finley remembered the episode well since it involved an Easy Bake Oven as a prop. Polk had tears of laughter in his eyes when Phil walked in. Immediately Phil felt welcomed by the two.

"And who do we have here? A surprise guest?" said Polk pretending to be Merv Griffin. "Cathy please move down and let Phil have a seat," laughed Polk. Finley did not oblige but continued to laugh.

"Seinfeld again?" said Phil.

"Yep," replied Polk, "Check it out." He then pointed to the DVD player and connected small flat screen TV in the room. Next to the TV sat a DVD collection of all nine Seinfeld seasons. "1990 to 1998" said a proud Polk extending his hand gracefully over the set.

"Wow, it is really going to be a long year," said Phil sitting down next to the two. Polk then picked out a disc and put it into the player. For the next 20 minutes the three interns watched a Seinfeld episode uninterrupted. They laughed together as a bond began to develop between them. Polk even treated them to a bag of microwave popcorn midway through the episode. Phil had a good feeling about his two fellow interns.

That night Phil felt good about himself. The first day of his surgical internship went by without a hitch. He split a pizza pie with vet student Jim Turner. They watched a Phillies game on TV followed by the local news. The lead story talked of a heat wave taking hold of the city. The bleach blonde weather girl predicted that the upcoming week would be sweltering hot, with the temperature steadily rising each day.

CHAPTER 5
Doctor Richard Knight

DOCTOR RICHARD KNIGHT Jr. was an old school surgeon. He trained at the PGH thirty years ago and never left West Philadelphia since. At fifty-five years old he was at the peak of his career. His life was surgery. He was a talented cardiothoracic surgeon who honed his skills over the past three decades. Well respected amongst colleagues his name was always mentioned in any discussion of best surgeons. Like all successful surgeons his life outside of medicine was a mess.

He was unhappily married for twenty-nine years and had three children. His children respected him and grew up only catching glimpses of his presence. His wife loathed him but tolerated his vile nature in exchange for opulence. In public they presented a striking couple. Living in a tony neighborhood they enjoyed the arts and commonly graced the society pages. In private their relationship was respectfully cold. Mrs. Knight understood her position and therefore tried to dwell on the positive aspects of life.

Knight was a fit man at six foot two inches tall. He attended undergraduate school at the University of Pennsylvania, on a football scholarship. Against Princeton he intercepted a fourth quarter pass and ran it back for a game-winning touchdown. He was captain of the football team and always dated the best looking cheerleader. By the end of his collegiate career he had developed an insatiable appetite for women, which was a byproduct of his good looks, intelligence and swagger.

His hair remained full and he kept it trimmed short. He worked out daily at five o'clock in the morning. Medicine then consumed the remainder of his day. Outside of medicine he enjoyed three passions. One was driving a black Porsche very fast. The second was Russian vodka. The third was young women. He frequently mixed the three passions together in no particular order.

Knight's medical routine was rigid, having been chiseled in stone over time. He performed surgery every Tuesday and Wednesday in operating room number four. He demanded the same surgical team for every case, while performing three cardiac by-pass procedures per day. His patients were by and large from the well-to-do list of the Northeast. He played classical Russian music throughout every case.

It was 7:15 a.m. and Phil Drummer was about to enter into Knight's world. Having completed rounds that day Larson and the surgical team hustled to the OR suite. Larson moved quicker than usual. The medical students sensed fear.

"Just pay attention and do what he says," were Larson's final words of advice to the team. "Get the patient prepped on time and never be late to the OR. The knife hits the skin at 0745 hours sharp. No exceptions." Larson paused briefly before stating, "And turn off your cell phone before going into his O.R."

Phil and the students just nodded and then split up heading to their respective locker rooms. Phil quickly dressed into his surgical scrub outfit and darted down the hallway with Chuck Roden to operating room number four. They put on surgical masks and then headed into the room.

Larson was already in the room. On the table was an elderly female patient lying supine, completely nude. The anesthesia team had just completed placing a breathing tube down the patient's windpipe in a process called intubation. Larson was rapidly positioning the patient and the overhead operating room lights.

"Get scrubbed up," yelled Larson to Phil and Roden. Within minutes they were back in the room putting on their surgical gowns.

"Start painting the patient," was Larson's next line as he left the room to wash his hands in the scrub sink area. The scrub nurse quickly rolled a table in front of Phil containing a skin cleanser called betadine. Phil's job was to prep out the patient's chest and leg area with the betadine. It was the final step in a process that sterilizes the skin prior to an incision.

Phil began the cleansing process on the chest and Roden started on the leg. Phil looked at the paralyzed and intubated patient on the table. It was strange to him that he had no idea who she was. Her face was pale and her skin was pitted from acne decades ago. He was unaware that her name was Mrs. Stiles and she was the heir of a department store fortune.

At that moment the door opened and in walked Dr. Knight with his hands wet from a surgical scrub. It seemed to Phil that a rush of cold air accompanied the surgeon. Phil and Roden continued their task.

"Good morning Doctor," said surgical scrub nurse Frey as she gowned and gloved the doctor.

"Good morning Ella," replied Knight in a cordial tone. Ella Frey was his favorite scrub nurse who knew his every move.

Larson then stormed into the room with a quick pace.

"You're late," said Knight to Larson.

Larson looked at the clock responding, "We are going to make it." It was 7:40 a.m.

Phil continued his prep but then felt a monstrous presence behind him. A second passed and Knight shoved him away with his body. He grabbed the betadine stick and without looking at Phil screamed, "You're not painting the god damn Mona Lisa!" Knight then finished the prep within 5 seconds as he poured betadine over the patient's chest.

Over the next two minutes a flurry of activity occurred over the surgical patient. Sterile drapes were quickly placed in two layers above and below the patient. Suction tubing was set up, as was an electrocautery for bleeding control. A headlight was turned on which Knight wore brightly above his eyes. The anesthesia team administered intravenous antibiotics. Larson headed to the patient's chest area on the opposite side from Dr. Knight.

Phil and Roden drifted to the left of Larson down the surgical table. Surgical scrub Frey stood to the right of Knight ready with the scalpel.

"Bypass team ready," barked Knight looking at the clock.

"Ready," said a portly man in the corner of the room sitting next to the cardiac bypass apparatus.

"Start time 0744 hours," said Knight looking at Larson with a smirk in his eyes. "Begin."

With a quick swipe of his arm Knight cut lengthwise down the middle of the patient's sternum. Blood quickly welled up which Larson suctioned.

At that same moment a circulating nurse flipped a switch and Alexander Borodin's Symphony #2 in B Minor commenced over the speaker system. The harshness of the opening violins embodied a macabre atmosphere. No one spoke further as Dr. Knight proceeded rapidly with his trade.

Three minutes later a somewhat bemused Medical Student Bankart wandered into the room. She had never been in an OR suite and had trouble finding the female locker room. She was directed to OR number four, and timidly walked in.

At that very moment Knight had completed his saw cut of the patient's sternum. He asked for a self-retaining retractor and placed it quickly between the patient's split sternum. He looked up at Bankart as he slowly and methodically clicked open the patient's chest cavity with the retractor. His headlight shone brightly into Bankart's eyes and she squinted.

"Who the hell are you?" said Knight looking back down at the patient's beating heart.

Larson responded, "That's our other student." Melissa Bankart stepped forward about to introduce herself.

"You're late. Get the hell out of my room," was Knight's matter of fact response. He continued to peer into Mrs. Stiles' chest cavity.

"I'm sorry but I couldn't find any open lockers," said Bankart, "then I...."

"Get out!" said Larson sharply. He understood that setting off Knight that early in the morning would lead to a very long day. He then tilted his head looking at the door. "Go to the library and look up that info we talked about earlier."

Bankart defiantly sighed and turned away, and then began walking towards the door. Before she left the room she could hear Knight saying how they don't make medical students like they used to. She wandered into the hall wondering what to do next.

"When I was a student we got here two hours before the case," mumbled Knight as he prepared the heart for the bypass machine. "We had to admit the patient the night before," he paused looking up at Phil and Chuck Roden. His headlight again blinded the two. "Then the morning of the surgery we had to start the IV fluids, wheel the patient down to the holding area and get the patient into the OR on time." He paused, and then said with a touch of sadness, "Those were good times. Good, good times." No one dare spoke.

Twenty more minutes went by as Mrs. Stiles' heart was stopped and she was placed on the heart bypass machine. Knight identified the three separate areas of critical stenosis that compromised the blood supply to her heart, thus prompting the surgery.

"We are going to need a vein," he then said to Larson. "Go get it and send one of those idiots up here to help me."

Larson quickly slid down the table to the patient's leg and asked Drummer to help Knight. He knew better then to send a medical student to help Knight.

"My physician assistant is away this week so I'll need your help here," was Knight's comment to Phil. The statement appeared sincere, which generated a deep concern in Phil's stomach.

Knight then poured a bucket of ice into the patient's chest. He then took Phil's hand, positioned it under the heart saying, "Don't move." He then deftly began a coronary bypass procedure.

A coronary bypass treats a blocked artery by rerouting the oxygen rich blood supply around it. The arteries of the heart are on the peripheral wall and easily visualized. It was common practice to use a vein taken from the leg to bypass the blocked vessel. A surgeon would stitch the vein both above and below the blockage, thus allowing the laws of physics to reroute the blood along the path of least resistance. It was also common to use an artery from the chest wall to bypass a blocked vessel. This oxygen rich artery was released from the nearby chest wall and then sutured below the blockage. The arterial pressure immediately pulsed blood beyond the blocked coronary vessel. This artery was called the internal mammary or IMA for short. Knight frequently used the artery and then some veins for a bypass procedure. The operation was the most common procedure that Dr. Knight performed. It was titled a coronary artery bypass graft and for short was called a CABG or "cabbage."

Within 15 minutes Phil's hand was getting numb. It was tucked under the heart in a chest cavity full of ice. Knight was working on the patient's internal mammary artery while Larson was harvesting a vein from the leg. In another ten minutes the IMA bypass was complete, supplying much needed blood to the patient's main coronary artery.

Larson then handed up to Knight a long stretch of saphenous vein that he harvested from the patient's leg. This vein provided Knight with a means to complete the final two bypasses required on the patient. He cut the vein in half anticipating the need for only two more arterial jumps. Knight then hooked up a syringe with liquid saline solution to the vessel, and forcefully injected the fluid. He was checking for leaks. One by one Larson's sutures popped off the vein graft, spewing saline out the sides of the graft. The end result looked like a garden hose with multiple puncture holes in it.

Knight just looked up at Larson blinding him with his headlight. "You're a senior resident?" He sighed shaking his head. "And you want to be a plastic surgeon?" laughed Knight. "I'd hate to see your first boob job."

Larson knew better than to respond. He asked nurse Frey for another suture to repair the leaks. Knight then deftly repaired the leaks, as Phil's hand continued to freeze up in the ice solution.

While Borodin's Symphony #2 continued Knight rapidly finished the case. During the third and final graft bypass, Phil's numb hand twitched and the heart moved. It caused Dr. Knight to stop his suturing of the graft.

"You're giggling the god damn heart," barked Knight not lifting his head from the surgical field.

"Sorry but my hand is numb," said Phil. Larson immediately rolled his eyes upwards and took a deep breath. Nurse Frey gently shook her head back and forth. Medical student Roden continued his struggles trying to suture close the patient's leg, unaware of the comment.

Knight lifted his head and looked at Larson sarcastically. "Where did you get this candy ass?" Larson didn't respond. "Nurse Frey please be sure to get Mrs. Drummer a scrub dress for the next case." Knight shook his head and returned to work mumbling, "They just don't make them like they used to." Phil didn't move his hand for the remainder of the case.

The surgery on Mrs. Stiles was a success. Two more surgical procedures were performed that day. During the second case Phil was caught off guard as the overhead classical music was abruptly stopped. Knight and Nurse Frey quickly stepped back from the table. Knight put his bloodied hand on his heart and stared stoically forward as did Nurse Frey. Chief resident Larson also stepped backwards, placing his hand on his heart. Phil and Chuck Roden just looked at each other, bemused by the sudden actions of the surgical team.

At that moment, which was exactly noontime, a local radio station was turned on overhead in the room. Kate

Smith's rendition of God Bless America was loudly piped into the room. No one said a word throughout the song. Dr. Knight stared directly ahead, as did nurse Frey, both not moving a muscle. When Kate Smith stopped singing, Knight simply stepped forward and said, "Resume." The Russian music then returned overhead, and the case restarted. Phil later learned that this was a long standing tradition at high noon in room four, always observed by Knight, without exception.

Before Phil knew it the third case was over and it was 4 PM. Knight took off his gloves and looked at the surgical team saying "Get him to recovery. Lets round in thirty minutes." Knight then left the room. Everyone sighed.

"Good job gentlemen," said nurse Frey proudly.

"Not bad," said Larson realizing what a benign day it was in the OR. "I thought it was going to be a long one when he threw Bankart out of the room." Larson was helping move the patient off the OR table and reiterated to the team saying, "Never get here late."

Thirty minutes later the team met Dr. Knight in the recovery room. All heart patients spent about three hours in the recovery room followed by an overnight stay in the surgical intensive care unit, or SICU. Knight and Larson quickly checked all three patients labs and ventilator settings. The patients routinely stayed on the ventilator, with a breathing tube in their windpipe overnight. The breathing tube was commonly removed the following morning in a process called an extubation. All three patients looked very well that evening, bringing a smile to the face of Dr. Knight.

At 6 PM Dr. Knight left the building, telling Dr. Larson to keep an eye on all the patients. It was Larson's ultimate responsibility if any complication occurred that evening.

Phil was exhausted. It was a long, stressful day. Larson found medical student Bankart on the surgical floor trying to look busy. He then went over the patient list with the team.

"All right, lets do it again tomorrow," said Larson. "Good job today. See you at 5:30 sharp tomorrow AM." Then the team broke up. Larson went home to his wife and two young children. Medical student Roden went to the library to look up some information on the heart lung bypass machine. Medical student Bankart went home to cry and call her student advisor.

Phil suddenly realized that he was on call that evening. He would not be going home. His shift was to continue through the night. The thought of a cafeteria dinner entered his mind just when his beeper went off. He recognized the Emergency Room phone number coming across his pager. He answered the call.

On the other end of the line was PGY-2 resident Randy O'Keefe. "Drummer, get your butt down here now, we got troubles!" was the message from O'Keefe. He then hung up on Phil. It was the beginning of a long call night for surgical intern Drummer.

CHAPTER 6
The Cabbage Patch

TAKING OVERNIGHT CALL in a teaching hospital is never pretty. Phil was exhausted from a full day of work that started at 5:30 AM. He now was commencing a work shift that would take him through the night. There was no guarantee for sleep. Then at 5:30 AM the following morning, the cycle would start again. There would be no complaining. Every physician above him in the residency program survived the test of internship. Now it was Phil's turn to answer the call.

Phil worked his way down to the ER. The emergency room at PGH was a melting pot of every possible disease entity in the Delaware Valley. It was a madhouse of activity that in some crazy way was able to triage, treat and discharge 80,000 patients per year. The rallying cry of the emergency room resident was to "treat and street" the patient. This motto emphasized quick, efficient care followed by a dismissal of the patient out the door onto the street.

In a large urban setting a few million inhabitants used the emergency room as their primary care provider. The ER was conveniently located in town and within walking distance for the majority. There were no appointments necessary. State of the art medical care was offered twenty-four hours a day. The facility was open and fully staffed 365 days a year. Medical insurance was unnecessary and therefore not a concern for many. The inner city emergency room was therefore a win-win situation for the populace surrounding it, except for the wait.

The hospital's non-urgent care waiting room represented the modern day equivalent of the nether world. Located next to the walk in entrance along 34th street the room was long and narrow with an austere theme. A wall of glass windows allowed the patient to look directly out onto the street in order to occupy their mind. A never ending series of wooden chairs and sofas were scattered throughout the room in no particular order. A few vending machines graced the room's corner, providing nourishment without regards for nutrition. As a rule anything could happen in the non-urgent care waiting room. Children ran around and played while their parents awaited care. At times outside arguments and disputes spilled into the waiting area, prompting an all out security alert. Laughter and frivolity existed in small social pockets throughout as flat screen TVs provided the obligatory background chatter. Patients slept and occasionally died while curled up on a sofa, waiting for their proverbial number to be called.

That evening doctor Drummer walked directly into this world as he made his way to the ER. Having taken the stairwell down to the ER he unexpectedly strode into the non-urgent waiting area. All eyes in the room immediately converged upon the young doctor. Like a young gazelle away from the herd, Phil quickly strode towards the emergency room's locked door leading into the treatment area. Behind a glass partition next to the door sat a clerk with a smirk on her face. Phil peered into the glass with an apprehensive look upon his face, having heard previous horror stories of demise occurring in the public waiting zone.

"May I help you?" asked the clerk.

"Hi, I'm Dr. Drummer and I need to get into the ER," replied Phil looking back over his shoulder. He had heard stories of violence and unrest in the waiting area.

The veteran clerk of 33 years had Phil right where she wanted him. "May I see some ID?" Her head slowly rolled from right to left while talking. A nurse behind her smiled at the new intern.

"Yea," replied Phil fumbling for his ID badge, which was fixed to the collar of his white lab coat. He held his face close to a conversation slot in the glass partition.

Just then Randy O'Keefe stuck his head into the clerk's station. "Let the kid in Mrs. D.," was his polite request. "It's his first night."

"He looks kind of suspicious," said Mrs. D waiting for a response. She then said, "And he is just too young to be a doctor."

"And way too cute," said the younger nurse behind Mrs. D.

Before O'Keefe could respond Mrs. D. reached under her counter and pressed a button. The door buzzed and Phil walked through into the perceived security of the medical system.

"Troubles," said O'Keefe walking quickly into the ER proper. "A drunk in bed six needs some suturing."

O'Keefe quickly pulled back a curtain turning into the bed six treatment room. On the gurney was a middle aged, red headed man with a bloody bandage across his face. His right arm was in a temporary splint. He was moaning a low groan.

"Hit in the face with a bottle," said O'Keefe. "Going to need a lot of work," was his next statement as he lifted the bandage off the patient's face. The patient winced as the gauze was lifted. Underneath the bandage was a jagged laceration starting just to the side of the patient's right eye, coursing across his cheek and ending with a large split in his upper lip. Blood was oozing out of the wound. Phil immediately smelled a strong mixture of cigarettes and alcohol. The patient smiled at him.

"Wow," said Phil realizing that he had never sewn up a wound this big. "Might need a plastic surgeon."

O'Keefe laughed and looked at Phil. "Are you kidding me? Every plastic surgeon around is in their Porsche heading home for a drink and dinner. No one will turn around for this guy." O'Keefe paused as he started to draw up some novocaine into a syringe. "He's a staffer anyway."

Phil nodded as he approached the patient. He knew the term staffer meant an uninsured patient. They subsequently were a member of the resident team or house staff service. As an unwritten rule no attending would come forward to treat an uninsured patient unless a critical condition existed. Phil and O'Keefe were now the patient's main treating physicians.

"Hi, I'm Dr. Drummer," said Phil.

"Pleased to make your acquaintance," said the drunk politely. He smacked his lips together as a bubble of saliva and blood formed.

"What happened?" asked Phil.

"I fell," said the staffer.

"Out of a second floor window," said O'Keefe. "He remembers being hit in the face with a beer bottle before the fall. O'Keefe paused. "A witness said he actually jumped."

"She's a liar," yelled the patient staring towards the ceiling. "A dirty, no good, cheating liar!"

Phil shook his head while looking at the wound. "Why did you jump out of a window?"

"I was trying to prevent a murder," replied the patient in a matter of fact tone. A rancid belch then followed the patient's comment.

"A murder," said Phil now with sudden interest. "Whose murder?"

"Mine!" said the drunkard with a cackling moan of a laugh interrupted by a deep bronchial cough. Phil and the medical team then burst into laughter upon hearing the smooth punch line.

"Whew, good one," said O'Keefe while gathering his composure. "He also broke his wrist and the Ortho boys will be around." He then looked at Phil. "I've got an acute abdomen down the hall if you need me. Just take your time and line up everything well, especially the lip."

"Right," said Phil and in an instant second year resident O'Keefe was gone. Phil was now alone with the bloodied patient who was staring at him with glassy eyes and a smile on his split lip. Phil noticed some missing teeth in his smile.

Over the next two hours Dr. Drummer worked carefully on his patient. A nurse assisted his progress, which was slow and methodical. Halfway through the repair the medical team took a break after the patient vomited all over his chest. Only once did Phil request O'Keefe's input, but was informed by the nursing staff that he was busy with another patient.

At the completion of his work Phil proudly took the sterile drape off the patient's face saying "All done Mr. Kern." Only then did he notice the patient fast asleep in an alcohol stupor.

Phil took his gloves off as he walked out of the room. His lower back was sore from leaning forward during the procedure. He looked at the nurse saying, "You better have a dentist check him out. He has a few teeth missing."

The nurse nodded as she cleaned up the equipment and patient. Phil looked back onto Mr. Kern, proud of his work. O'Keefe appeared suddenly behind him with a partially chewed muffin in his mouth. It was 8 PM.

"You have go to the OR," said O'Keefe in a matter of fact fashion. "The guy with the acute abdomen needs some immediate work."

"What?" said a now tiring Phil. "I haven't even had dinner yet."

"Follow me," said O'Keefe quickly spinning away and heading behind a nursing station. He entered a small narrow room with a sink, refrigerator and pantry cabinets.

"Remember the intern creed," said O'Keefe opening the refrigerator. A large sign was taped to the refrigerator door stating All Food is for Patient Consumption Only. "Eat when you can, sleep when you can and never touch the spleen." He smiled, ignored the sign and handed Phil a cold roast beef sandwich.

Phil then helped himself to a cold Ginger Ale and roast beef sandwich. The feast lasted all but three minutes. O'Keefe then gave him a small cup of vanilla ice cream from the freezer. "Compliments of PGH," said O'Keefe with a smile.

"Obstructed bowel going to the OR now," was O'Keefe's next line. "Elderly man with increasing abdomen pain and distension. CT scan shows a large bowel mass. Probably a large tumor."

Phil shook his head as he listened to O'Keefe. He felt much better already with the food in his system.

"Dr. Brown needs a set of hands to help him with the case. Room two," said O'Keefe heading out towards the nursing station. "When you are done with the case call me to round in the SICU."

"Right," said Phil again to another order from the junior resident. Phil then hustled up the stairwell to the OR. He changed into surgical scrubs quickly and headed to surgical room two. Looking into the room a thin elderly man lay supine on the table being prepped out for surgery. Phil then spent the next three hours in the room helping to remove a large cancerous tumor from the patients descending colon. It was the first time he saw metastatic tumor lesions, which were scattered all over the patient's diseased liver. Despite the expert care provided to the patient, his prognosis was dismal.

After the case Phil paged O'Keefe and was told to meet in the SICU at midnight to check Knight's patient's with him. He had 30 minutes of down time and headed to the intern call room. Upon entering the hole he came upon intern Polk lying on a sofa watching TV.

"Hey Rick, why are you here?" asked Drummer.

"Air conditioning broke down back at the apartment," was his response as he put his greasy hands into a bag of half eaten potato chips. "The landlord is a bum, no where to be found."

"Nice and cool in here," replied Phil heavily plopping down onto a chair next to Polk.

"I'll just stay here until it is fixed," said Polk. "I'm on call tomorrow night anyway."

Then for the next fifteen minutes the two interns discussed their first few days on the job. Polk loved the story about the drunk jumping out the window. He smirked upon hearing Knight stopping the case to listen to Kate Smith singing.

"I hear Knight is a nutcase," said Polk. "How about his P.A.? I hear she is some good looking arm candy for the old man." He was referring to Dr. Knight's physician assistant.

"She is away on vacation this week," said Phil now getting comfortable and a bit sleepy in the chair. "I've seen her up on the floor in the past, good looking woman."

"How old is she?" asked Polk.

"I'd guess about thirty," replied Phil as he put his legs up on the coffee table between the two interns.

"He must pay her a ton of cash to care for all his needs," was Polk's response as Phil sensed the conversation about to go into the gutter. "Can you imagine that old man …"

At that moment Phil's beeper abruptly went off spoiling Polk's developing metaphor. It was Randy O'Keefe from the SICU requesting Phil's presence. The interns parted ways as Rick Polk settled in on the couch under a white sheet. The caffeine from the large iced tea he was drinking didn't seem to have any affect on his level of consciousness.

For the next two hours Phil rounded with Randy O'Keefe in the SICU. In the early morning hours the SICU was serene, with a welcoming ambience. Overhead room lights were low and room monitors gently shone bright. Time was marked by the methodical beat of ventilator machines doing their job. A few nurses sat quietly at their stations while charting data into the computers.

Phil and O'Keefe checked each patient's vital signs and ventilator settings. All three post-op patients from that day looked well. Mrs. Stiles was able to open her eyes while still on the ventilator. She had no idea what time it was, but was impressed by the youth of the medical team caring for her. Everyone was stable throughout the SICU, which was a good thing at the PGH.

"Lets check labs," said O'Keefe sitting down at the nursing station. "The troops are looking good." Phil was amazed at the confident command that the junior resident had over the unit.

The two young physicians then logged into the computer system to check the patient's recent blood values. Each patient had a recent set of electrolytes drawn per routine. The electrolytes checked standard parameters such as sodium, potassium, chloride and glucose. Also drawn was a hemoglobin and hematocrit to monitor their red blood cell count.

"The cabbage patch is alive and well," quipped O'Keefe as he quickly scanned all of the lab values on the computer screen. "Everybody is rock solid."

"Cabbage patch?" asked a fatigued Phil realizing it was now two o'clock in the morning. "Never heard that term before."

"Yea," said O'Keefe with a smile. "This is the famous Dr. Knight's cabbage patch and surrounding you are the cabbage patch kids." O'Keefe paused to then log off the central computer system.

O'Keefe continued, "This place is Knight's little garden. He drops off about six coronary bypass or cabbage patients a week, and we have to care and nourish them through." O'Keefe leaned back in his chair and put his hands behind his head with a professorial look. "They are his children. Some children are strong and others weak." He then started gently rocking back and forth on the chair. "When they thirst, we hydrate them. When they bleed we transfuse them." He paused and then said more seriously, "And when they code we resuscitate them."

"How frequent is that?" asked Phil referring to the term code, which meant a heart stoppage, or cardiac arrest.

"Not that often, but when it does occur you better hope it's not on your shift and the patient survives," replied O'Keefe. "Farmer Knight doesn't like one of his kids checking out early. Makes him look bad. Makes him angry."

Phil was too tired to respond.

"Hit the rack," said O'Keefe. "Its quiet, let's call it early tonight."

Phil agreed and wandered back to the intern call room. Polk was asleep on the couch under his sheet, snoring loudly. Phil turned off the overhead light and TV. He then headed into one of the small side rooms where a single bed sat alone. He crawled under the fresh sheets pulling them up to his neck area. Immediate ease and comfort came upon him. Within seconds he was fast asleep. His beeper remained quiet for the next three hours.

Then, at about 5:15 AM a door sound followed by a bright light woke him up. It was well rested medical student Roden heading into the hole area. He rustled into a closet and pulled out the team's rounding supply bucket. He then stuck his head into Phil's room.

"Hey get up," said Roden in a whisper. "Dr. Larson wanted me to make sure you were up for rounds." Phil blinked at Roden gathering his senses.

Dr. Drummer then arose without fanfare to continue his shift. He brushed his teeth and kept the same surgical scrubs on that he slept in. Putting on his white coat he left the call room and headed upstairs. Polk was still asleep on the sofa and appeared not to have moved at all overnight.

The remainder of that day was somewhat of a blur to Phil. He experienced an intern's persona that day, which combined confidence and fatigue. Such a post call mixture characteristically energized an intern with an associated sense of élan and bravado. Phil appreciated the euphoric rush that morning, having passed his first night of intern call with flying colors.

The team quickly rounded in the SICU and Phil felt a connection to Mrs. Stiles. She was extubated that morning and taken off the ventilator. Her voice weakly thanked

Phil for his care. In the OR that morning Dr. Knight queried Phil on his patients and he responded assuredly.

Knight took the team through three CABG procedures without a hitch. Phil expertly helped him at the head of the table throughout all three cases. Knight was in a good mood and each case went smoothly. He even took some time to teach medical students Bankart and Roden some anatomy. All was well on the cardiothoracic team that day.

Per protocol the team again rounded in the SICU now seeing a total of six patients, which had been operated on over the past 48 hours. Phil looked at his clock realizing that it was now 6 PM and his shift was over. The team broke up and Phil headed home.

Upon exiting the hospital the evening sun blinded Phil. He had been indoors for 36 hours. The humid air felt good on his skin. He walked home with his surgical scrubs on, oblivious to the world around him.

Dinner was a box of macaroni and cheese. It was soon 8 PM and Phil answered a few emails while watching a Phillies game on T.V.

At about 9 PM Phil got into bed. He tried to do some reading but his eyelids were heavy. He put the book down and turned off the light.

Phil then thought of what just happened over the past work shift. During that time he held the ailing hearts of six patients in his hand. He sutured the face of a drunkard and then helped remove a cancerous tumor from the bowels of a patient he didn't even know. He tended to Knight's cabbage patch and enjoyed it. He wondered how Polk's first call night was going as he quickly fell into a deep sleep. He dreamt of being home as a youth playing baseball with his older brother.

At 4:30 AM his alarm loudly woke him. Only then did Phil realize that another call shift was about to begin.

CHAPTER 7
Weekend Off

THE FIRST WEEK of Dr. Drummer's medical career went by quickly. It was a blur to all of the surgical interns. Before Phil knew it Friday night arrived and he was walking home after another marathon shift. The summer heat and humidity continued to grip Philadelphia. The cool lobby of the Greycliff apartment felt good as Phil walked in from the outside.

Upon entering the elevator Jim Turner waved to hold the door from across the lobby.

"Thanks," said Jim getting into the elevator car. Turner was carrying a copy of PC World magazine under his arm. Sweat marks stained the armpits of his polo shirt. Turner's body habitus did not respond well to the stifling summer conditions.

"No problem," said Phil as the elevator door closed behind the two. "First week over and I've got tomorrow off," was Phil's next comment with a relaxed smile on his face.

"How was it?" asked Turner.

"Unbelievable," replied Phil as the elevator made its way to the seventh floor. "I'm exhausted after one week."

Exiting the elevator the floor mates turned to the right. Their apartments were near the end of the hall opposite each other. Approaching them from the far end of the hallway was fellow seventh floor resident Maria Cruz.

"Here comes your girl," whispered a giddy Turner. "Bom Chicka Wah Wah," was his next line.

Maria Cruz was a student at the Wharton School of Business at the University of Pennsylvania. She was completing her final year of study in Philadelphia, with plans to return to Chicago the following year with an MBA degree from the prestigious Wharton. Of wealthy Brazilian descent her physical features were defined and stunning.

"Hello gentlemen," was her energetic introduction. She stopped directly in front of Turner and Drummer with a smile. Her white teeth fit perfectly with her full lips and dark complexion. Her posture was perfect as she looked slightly upwards at the taller men.

"Hi Maria," was the combined response.

"Ready for tomorrow?" said Phil referring to their planned jog through West Philadelphia.

"You bet," was her reply. "Nine o'clock as usual?"

"Yep," said Phil realizing that the Brazilian women were the most beautiful women in the world.

"How about you Jim?" was her next question of obligation.

Turner nervously swayed side to side. Despite being 32 years old his experience with women was minimal. Socially awkward by nature he just shook his head back and forth responding "Nah, not a runner."

Maria quickly turned back to Phil where her true attention lay. "O.K. see you then," was her perky reply. "Late for a study group," was her next line as she slid quickly between Turner and Drummer. She smiled looking back at both men heading down the hall.

"Wow," said Turner. "What's up with you and her?"

"It's a work in progress," said Phil. We have gone to a few movies together so far. Nothing serious."

"You haven't spent the night down the hall yet?" was Turner's next question as they approached their apartment doors.

"No not yet, not quite yet," was Phil's response as he unbolted his door with a smile. The two in unison then peered back down the hallway to get a final glimpse at Cruz.

"Phillies at seven?" asked Turner.

"Yep," replied Phil. "How about Touchdown Tuna Noodle Casserole tonight?"

"My favorite," said Turner referring to a quick casserole dinner dish that they enjoyed together. "Be right over."

That night Turner and Phil ate dinner together. They discussed at length Maria Cruz who was a reality to Phil and a fantasy to Turner. They spent a good deal of time comparing Phil's medical training regimen to that of a veterinarian.

"Your patients never complain," laughed Phil. "If you run into a complication you can just euthanize the poor animal."

"Not true," replied Turner. "My patients don't complain but they can bite."

"So do mine," said Phil. He then paused as the two laughed. He continued, "I would love to walk out of the OR and tell the family that Grandma Jones didn't do well in surgery and we are going to have to put her down."

"Don't forget to ask them for a donation to the SPCA after that line," said Turner. "It's the best time to get a donation."

Turner then continued, "All kidding aside, I wouldn't take my sick dog to the PGH this time of year." He sighed and continued, "The worst possible place for medical care is the PGH in July or August, a bunch of rookies take care of you."

"I agree," responded Phil, "That's a well known fact. A teaching hospital is a dangerous place in July."

"I had a relative get knocked off about thirty years ago in that slaughter house one July day. A simple surgery turned into a funeral," said Turner in a matter of fact fashion.

"No kidding, what happened?" said Phil.

"Don't know. I've only heard second hand but its family folklore now. A simple surgery gone bad," said Turner getting up and stretching. It was getting late and the Phillies were wrapping up another win.

"Another brew?" asked Phil referring to the Moosehead beer they were enjoying.

"Nah, have to get up early to watch you and Maria run tomorrow," replied Turner. "The highlight of my day."

The young physicians then parted ways and Phil felt obliged to check on Knight's cabbage patch kids. He sat down at his computer and logged into the PGH system. Knight's patient list came up and Phil recognized everyone's name immediately. He felt that they were his patients. He checked everyone's evening lab values and knew that Dr. O'Keefe was on duty that night. All labs were within normal limits and Phil felt good. The cabbage patch was secure.

After logging off the system Phil called his dad and updated him on week one. He then spoke to brother Joe D. who enjoyed the noontime Kate Smith story. Post call sleep again came very easy that night.

The following morning Phil and Maria Cruz exited the Greycliff lobby at nine o'clock sharp. Surprisingly the humidity had eased and the air was breathable.

"Regular route?" asked Phil.

"Yea, only four miles today." replied Maria as they stretched out in preparation for a run. "Late night studying." was her next comment to Phil.

The duo then commenced a run towards center city. They ran directly down the middle of the Penn campus. Phil noticed how the undergrad males kept their eyes on Maria. She wore her dark hair in a tight ponytail and ran with a bounce in her step. The black sports bra she wore complemented her tanned skin of Portuguese descent. A light sweat glistened on her skin.

"What are you up to tonight?" asked Phil as they passed the Wharton School.

"Just some studying," replied Maria a bit short of breath.

"Going out with a few interns tonight to the pub," said Phil. "Want to come along?"

"Is there going to be a lot of alcohol involved?" panted Maria.

"Yes," said Phil.

"Then I'll definitely go," replied Maria with a smile and quick look at Phil.

Phil laughed knowing that Maria enjoyed a few drinks as much as he did. Having gone out socially with her several times before he knew she had a steady beau back in Chicago. However Phil felt a definite connection between them and knew the Windy City was far away.

The duo ran past PGH and headed across the Schuylkill River. Beneath the bridge passed a crew team practicing their strokes. The morning sun was starting to rise high, as was the temperature. At 20th street the runners turned around and headed back West. They were home in another 20 minutes having completed a four-mile loop. They walked the final two blocks to cool down from the heat.

A runner's high set in as they walked back to the Greycliff complex. Both runners looked forward to their date that night.

Later that evening Phil and Maria headed down to the Irish Pub in center city. Downtown was alive with activity. The warm weather brought out all of the city students and local denizens. Upon entering the crowded pub they spotted Rick Polk and Cathy Finley sitting in a corner booth. The couple headed through the thick crowd towards the booth. Phil again noticed how all the males in the room focused their direct or indirect attention on Maria.

"Welcome," said Rick Polk loudly while standing up and waving to the waiter for a round of drinks.

"Hello doctors," said Phil to his fellow interns.

Phil then introduced Maria and the four sat down each to enjoy a mug of cold beer.

"First week down," said Polk raising his glass to toast the interns. Each person then held their mugs up clanking them together in salute. "Here's to fifty one more weeks," shouted Polk.

"I wonder how Fred's call night is going," said Cathy Finley over the crowd. She was referring to Fred Riles who was taking intern call that night.

"Can't be that hard," said Phil. "He is taking it from home."

"I think that guy has a black cloud over him" said Polk being the first to down his beer. He reached for some pretzels and again hailed the waiter for a refill.

Phil knew Polk was right. A black cloud meant that seemingly bad things happened to a person when they were on call. Certain interns could handle the pressure and persevere in a quiet way. Others couldn't handle the work load and carried on as to how horrible their call night was in comparison to others. Their whining usually brought the black cloud analogy to their name.

"He had a black cloud as a medical student," said Phil. "I'm sure he will have one as an intern."

"How is it going with Dr. Knight?" asked Cathy.

"Interesting guy" said Phil choosing his words carefully. "You have to stay alert around him. Larson keeps warning me about his bad side but I haven't seen it yet."

"I hear he is a maniac," said Polk. "I've only been in town a few weeks but it seems everybody knows the guy." Polk took another drink from his mug now starting to stare more obviously at Maria.

"You remind me of Rachel Goldstein," said Polk looking at Maria.

"Who?" asked Maria with a smile.

"Rachel Goldstein, you know Jerry's girlfriend on Seinfeld," said Polk. "The one who made out with him in the balcony during Schindler's List."

"Ignore him," said Phil as the table broke into laughter. "He is stuck in a Seinfeld time warp."

"What is everyone's favorite Seinfeld episode?" asked Polk looking around the table.

Before Phil could change the subject Maria blurted out, "The Merv Griffin set episode."

"With the Easy Bake Oven!" said Cathy. "I had one as a child."

"Exactly" said Maria while fist bumping with Cathy. "Everyone had an Easy Bake Oven back then."

Phil shook his head not believing the women at the table were Seinfeld fans. "O.K. which one is your favorite" said Phil to Polk.

Polk leaned into the table. He paused looking around as if to give out a secret. The group leaned in as he spoke.

"The Phil Rizzuto bobble head doll episode." was his response.

"What?" was the combined response in disbelief.

"It had it all," said Polk. "Don't you remember?" He paused to gulp some beer. "It is officially called The Pothole Episode. I'm sure you remember Kramer adopting a highway and then changing the lanes from four to two."

"That's when Jerry's girlfriend had the toilet explode on her at the end right?" asked Maria.

"Yea," said Polk now becoming very interested in the Brazilian beauty next to him.

"Do you remember what Seinfeld's girlfriend dunked in the toilet to drive Seinfeld nuts?" asked Polk with a gaze directed at Maria.

"Of course a toilet brush" said Maria quickly while smiling and looking around the table. The group broke out in applause. Polk had met his match that night.

"Wow, the girl of my dreams," said Polk shaking his head and leaning back in the booth.

Over the next hour the group shared intern stories. Phil informed them of Knight's passion for Russian music and fast cars. Cathy Finley told the crew how much she enjoyed general surgery. Polk informed everyone that he was considering moving into the call room area for the entire year. He continued to experience problems with his leased apartment and was trying to get out of his contract.

Later that evening Phil was making his way towards the bathroom when his eye caught a strikingly attractive female sitting across the room. He noticed the woman tracking his movement, and then excusing herself from a group of friends while getting up. She then approached Phil in a noticeable fashion. Her figure was striking and she moved with confidence. Phil continued along his route quite aware that their paths were going to cross.

Phil then came face to face with a mature and beautiful woman as she extended her hand to him. "Hi, I'm Jennifer Ranier," was her introduction. "Everyone just calls me Jenna." She wore spiked high heels and stood only four inches shorter than Phil. Her hair was a sandy bleach blonde and ironed straight to shoulder level in the latest style. Her wrists, earlobes and ankles were adorned with silver jewelry that set off a smooth tanned skin. Her eyes were icy blue and her petite nose complemented her full lips in a pleasing fashion. What struck Phil the most of all was a perfume of intoxicating nature, subtle yet stimulating to the senses.

"Hello Jenna, Phil Drummer here," was the reply. Phil remembered Pete Larson mentioning her name. She was just as attractive as he described. Phil guessed she was about thirty years old. The combination of alcohol and perfume pleased him.

"I'm Dr. Knight's physician assistant," said Ranier with a smile and look directly into Phil's eyes. She continued to hold his hand saying, "I was on vacation last week so I missed meeting you."

"Oh yea," said Phil. "Dr. Knight did say you were away." Phil noticed she let go of his hand yet still stood close enough to him to feel a near physical contact. She leaned forward to talk over the crowd and pushed her hair back behind a shoulder.

"I hope the first week went well," said Ranier. "The rotation can be tough for an intern at times."

"Not bad for the first week," answered Phil as he leaned and talked into her ear. "Dr. Larson kept us all on track. It was actually fun."

"Wow," said Ranier stepping even closer to Phil. "I've heard the CT rotation called everything but fun. Hopefully it will stay that way."

Phil just smiled as someone behind him accidently bumped him even closer to Ranier. He felt her pink halter-top touch his chest. Phil searched his mind for a conversational item as Jenna continued to look directly upwards at him. "Come to the Irish Pub often?" was his line.

"Yea," said Ranier with a smile while putting her hand lightly on his shoulder as someone bumped her from behind. "Here with a few of my friends from the social work department at the hospital."

Phil smiled back at the beautiful blonde in front of him.

"Well, just wanted to say hello," said a smiling Ranier. She paused for a moment looking up at Phil. "See you next week."

"It's a deal," said Phil again searching for words.

Ranier then turned away and walked back to her group. Her perfume smell remained in Phil's olfactory system for some time. Upon returning to his table Polk was alone while the women visited the restrooms.

"Who's the babe?" asked Polk

"Jennifer Ranier," was his response. "She is Dr. Knight's P.A."

"Nice rack on that gal," said Polk. "Knight must be pulling some overtime with her."

Drummer just shook his head. Pete Larson had informed him all about Jennifer Ranier. She was Knight's P.A. for the past four years. A talented girl who knew every move Knight was going to make in the OR. She made his life easier on a professional level and therefore everyone enjoyed having her around. Outside of the O.R. she was well known to be Knight's mistress. She lived in a swank center city apartment and drove a Mercedes all funded by

Knight. Her fine perfume and jewelry also came from the same benefactor. It was rumored that Knight's wife even knew about her, yet silently permitted the tryst in order to satiate the beast.

"She sure did smell nice," mumbled Phil looking across the bar at Ranier. "Really nice."

The reverie continued between the interns well into the night. Polk kept the party going, being no stranger to a barroom. Cathy and Maria held their own very well, even ordering the final round of spirits. Upon breaking up for the night, the interns made a drunken pact to see each other through the year. They agreed to always help each other in times of need, no matter how difficult the situation. They confidently departed, guaranteeing that the internship would be completed together, without pause. The name of fellow intern Frederick Riles was never mentioned in the agreement.

Phil and Maria took a cab to West Philadelphia, and then walked through the Penn Campus together. The evening was hot and humid, as predicted. The couple held hands as they walked through the Greycliff lobby, taking the elevator up to the seventh floor. Neither hesitated as they walked arm and arm past Phil's door, then turning left down the hallway towards Maria's apartment. They spent the night together, content in each other's arms, not concerned about what tomorrow would bring, enjoying a bliss that only a young couple can experience.

At 3 A.M. a full moon shone through Maria Cruz's apartment as she slept in her young doctor's arms. Phil lay awake staring at an overhead ceiling fan that slowly rotated back and forth, cooling the couple. Philadelphia was quiet below, yet he couldn't sleep. A relentless visual image of the older Dr. Knight embracing Jennifer Ranier had seized his mind. In an attempt to battle this mental disturbance, Phil held Maria's body closer and tighter, realizing how great she felt in his arms. Despite his best efforts, a mental torment continued throughout the night. Soon thereafter, Phil Drummer arose from bed, only to start another call shift at the PGH that hot Sunday morning.

CHAPTER 8
Knight's Machine

THE MONTH OF July passed quickly for Phil and his colleagues as Dr. Knight's cardiothoracic team began to function in a coldly efficient manner. Phil and Larson began to anticipate each other's moves while creating seamless acts of compassion at every bedside. Medical student Roden was always prepared with a seemingly bottomless supply bucket. Melissa Bankart soon deftly began side stepping all flying chest tube fluids. In fact she pulled some tubes on her own while soiling the walls in grand fashion. Soon, it was the last Wednesday of July as the team began to wrap up morning rounds.

"Good job team" said Larson. The patient census was down due to Knight being on vacation the prior week. Rounds finished early and it was only 6:45 am. "My treat for some coffee," said Larson as he headed down the seventh floor hallway.

The CT team followed quickly behind. They were a seasoned group of one month. They passed a group of medical interns standing outside a room. In the middle of the group was a professorial appearing physician pontificating to the group. The medical rounds and ongoing lecture appeared dry and winded. Fatigue was in the eyes of the surrounding cast of residents and interns. A medical student on the crowd fringe swayed back and forth appearing to fall asleep standing up.

"Medical drones," said Larson as they proudly passed. "All talk and no action," was his next slur. The team rocketed past the elevator and per protocol took the steps double time down to the cafeteria. Fresh coffee was passed out amongst the group.

"One month down," said Larson. "Congratulations."

"Hard to believe," replied Phil. "Went by fast."

Larson paused sipping the bitter cafeteria coffee. "Knight's back today from vacation. Traditionally a bad time for the house staff."

"How so?" asked Roden.

"He had to take the obligatory beach vacation with his wife," replied Larson. "One week with the old lady makes the man cranky." Larson paused looking into the distance, "It usually takes about a week for him to settle back into a sense of normalcy."

"So the take home message is watch your step," said Phil.

The medical students nodded their heads and understood. Roden then spoke, "Today is Melissa's birthday."

Melissa Bankart blushed and pushed Charles Roden's shoulder.

"Happy Birthday," said Larson. "Sorry you have to spend it in the OR today.

"No problem," said Melissa. "At least I'm not on call tonight.

Larson then checked his clock. "Let's roll, better get Knight off to an early start today."

The team arrived in the OR suite earlier than usual. Upon entering the room nurse Ella Frey greeted them with her usual warm smile. Ella was happy when Dr. Knight was back in town. She was oddly comfortable in his presence.

On the table was a 57 year-old patient named William Brown. Mr. Brown was a black male with a long time history of uncontrolled diabetes. Over the past three decades he smoked and drank with the best of them. Last night while walking past the PGH he experienced chest pains and collapsed. The EMT squad brought him to the ER and the cardiology team admitted him. An emergency cardiac catheterization was performed identifying critical blockages of his arteries. Emergency surgery was recommended and Knight was the only CT surgeon in town. The other cardiac surgeons were at the shore enjoying quality time with their wives that week. Mr. Brown had no insurance. His friends called him Willie.

The pre-op process was ahead of schedule as Knight roared into the room. He moved quicker than usual with aggression in his step.

"Good morning Dr. Knight," said Ella Frey.

"Good morning Ella," barked Knight.

"How was vacation?" was her next question to Knight as he picked up the patient's chart. Nurse Frey had a smile on behind her surgical mask.

"It was horrible," said Knight not lifting up his head up from the chart. "I'm going to write a book titled "The Shore, Its Overrated, Overpriced and Overcrowded." Knight paused and then looked up saying, "We evolved from the ocean, why does everyone try to swim back in?"

Ella smiled. She knew that Knight abhorred the New Jersey shore.

Before Nurse Frey could continue her questioning Knight spoke, "How did I get stuck with this staffer?" He was referring to Willie Brown on the table. "For God's sake he is a piss poor piece of protoplasm who is going to try and cag on my record." The word "cag" was hospital slang used in place of death or dying.

No one spoke because they all knew the answer. A hospital could not deny care to a local indigent who nearly dropped dead on their doorstep. It was by luck of the draw that Knight was the only CT surgeon in town.

"This case is going to screw up my whole schedule today," barked Knight. "I had to push back my normal schedule to accommodate Mr. Brown here."

Larson and the CT team kept quiet and moving while prepping the patient. No one dared speak as Knight continued, "I can't wait until the government mandates a national health care program." He paused then spoke again, "Once that occurs Mr. Brown would be deemed too expensive for the system. Surgery would be denied. He would then be put in a ward with ten other men and fed soup and crackers until he died. Just like they do in Europe." Knight paused as he walked toward the intubated patient at his mercy.

"Where the hell is Ranier?" yelled Knight.

"She is back in the sterility room looking for your favorite needle driver," said Ella Frey. "The team who picked your instruments last night didn't put it into the tray."

"Idiots," said Knight shaking his head slowly. "I've been doing the same case for the past 25 years here and they still can't get it right." Knight turned to walk out of the room saying, "I can train a pack of monkeys to do a better job than the night shift team."

Then as Knight left the room to begin scrubbing P.A. Ranier entered the surgical theatre through an opposite door.

"Found it," was her energetic comment as she opened up Dr. Knight's prized needle driver and placed it onto nurse Frey's table.

Throughout the past several weeks the cardiothoracic team enjoyed Jennifer Ranier's presence. She calmed Knight in moments of tension and helped move all the cases along. She worked well with scrub nurse Ella Frey while assisting both Knight and the residents. On the floor she helped to expertly manage the postoperative patients in the cabbage patch. The entire house staff appreciated her presence and her most pleasing presentation. In homage to her looks, Dr. Polk constantly referred to her as "easy on the eyes."

Phil Drummer also enjoyed her presence in the operative suite. She frequently stood next to Phil at the surgical table, with a constant physical contact between their bodies. Phil noticed that Ranier had an ability to lean one way or the other to maximize that contact for the benefit of the patient, and seemingly himself. She wore a pair of purple clog shoes and firm fitting scrub pants that complemented her physique. A surgical mask that covered her mouth and nose, accentuated her energetic blue eyes. She wore a tight surgical cap that only allowed a few strands of blonde hair to escape and dangle free. Most pleasing of all was her scent, the scent that Phil first appreciated a few weeks ago, which had an unmistakable texture of sensuality.

"Keep moving," yelled Larson. "Don't push his buttons today. Remember beach vacation," was his next comment as the team headed to the scrub sink to join Dr. Knight.

At 0740 hours Borodin's Symphony #2 started five minutes ahead of schedule. Under protest Dr. Richard Knight began his self-proclaimed charity work on Mr. William Brown. All was going well until he went to harvest the patient's internal mammary artery.

"Look at this piece of crap," was his comment to the crowd. He cocked his head back while looking through his magnification loops at the patient's internal mammary artery. "This IMA is as hard as a rock."

Phil and Ranier were on the other side of the table and didn't speak.

"This guys been smoking since second grade and now I'm supposed to resurrect his arteries," said Knight. He was referring to intense plaque build up in the patient's artery making the outer wall rock hard. He then went to pass a suture through the vessel wall and the tip of the fine needle bent somewhat. "Look at this, my needle is bending. You see something new every day," yelled Knight sarcastically as he applied more pressure onto his favorite needle driver.

At that moment the suture needle skipped off the hardened arterial wall and Dr. Knight's right hand follow through was more forceful that usual. In a split second the needle driver in his right hand drove the sharp needle into the index finger of his left hand which was holding a pair of pick up tweezers. Dr. Knight immediately felt the intense pain of a needle stick that all surgeons feel throughout their career. That sharp down to bone searing pain that is over in a nanosecond yet lingers for a long time.

"Ah!" yelled Knight as he threw the needle driver and suture onto the floor. "Betadine," was his cry as he took off the double gloves on his left hand. Within a few seconds nurse Frey was pouring antiseptic betadine directly over Knight's left index finger as the entire OR team looked at him. Knight then squeezed his left index finger tip between the adjacent thumb and long finger. A fine drop of blood oozed out of the puncture site. Knight shook his head is disgust.

Then like all surgeons Knight's mind registered one word, with that word being "hepatitis". "I knew it," said Knight as nurse Frey reapplied two sterile gloves to his left hand. "I knew the only thing I would ever get out of this case was a lawsuit or hepatitis." Knight looked up to the anesthesiology team and spoke again, "Send his blood for a hepatitis panel and HIV."

Then Dr. Knight continued, yet his mind remained focused as it always did on a needle stick. As a surgeon needle sticks were common as a resident and young practicing surgeon. As a surgeon's skills matured the needle sticks became less frequent yet still occurred. The fear was always of the HIV positive patient suffering from AIDS. However the bigger fear among surgeons was that of hepatitis, especially hepatitis C. This virus was prevalent in the populace and transmitted by blood-to-blood contact. Many patients with the disease were unaware of their infectious state. Therefore they do not appear physically ill to their treating medical team. There was no complete cure for the disease and it frequently progressed to liver failure, being the most common cause for liver transplants in the country.

Unknown to Willie Brown was the fine print in the surgical consent that his brother signed prior to the case. A clause just permitted by the PGH legal team had recently been inserted regarding a needle stick. It permitted the involved surgeon to draw the patient's blood during the surgery and send it off immediately for testing. It was a controversial clause since it theoretically did not protect the rights of the patient. Certainly the legal argument could be made that the patient actually acquired the disease from the surgeon's blood that they were exposed to during the incident.

"What an occupation," said Knight. "We work ungodly hours for less and less money. The government is breathing down our necks. Plaintiff lawyers are flooding television reruns of Gomer Pyle with lawsuit commercials as we speak." He then paused and shook his head continuing to work on the IMA, "And I have a good chance of getting a fatal blood borne disease from Mr. Brown who will then die on my behalf." The martyrdom speech then finished with the statement, "Of course his family will then sue me for not saving his decadent life."

"Not much of a family," said Ranier knowing she would be allowed to speak. "His brother had to be tracked down by hospital legal to sign the consent. He looked like a street person. No other family in site."

"I'm not sure what the transmission rate is for a closed bore needle stick," said Larson. "I know it is lower than an open bore needle." Larson was referring to the type of needle Knight stuck himself with. A surgical suture needle, or closed bore needle, is solid tipped since it only has to pass through tissue. A needle used to draw blood from a vein has to be hollow inside. This is referred to as an open bore needle.

Knight looked up at Ranier and Larson garnering some solace from their well-crafted comments. Suddenly a voice from the lower end of the table was heard.

"It's the rule of 3's," said medical student Roden.

The entire surgical team looked towards Roden at the end of the table. He was helping Phil harvest a vein for the coronary bypass.

"Who the hell is he?" said Knight implying that Roden's physical presence over the past month didn't register with him.

"The third year medical student," said Larson looking directly into Roden's eyes pleading him to stop.

Before anyone else spoke third year med student Roden continued, "It's the rule of 3's," he said again. "With an open bore needle stick the rate of transmission of hepatitis B is 30%, hepatitis C 3% and HIV 0.3%." Roden looked up from the field with an innocent look on his face. "I just read it yesterday in a journal."

Knight stepped back from the table and paused looking directly at Charles Roden. "But if I get hepatitis from this staffer the rate is 100% and my career is over!" he shouted. "Who the hell are you to be lecturing me?"

Roden and the rest of the team froze up. No one moved. The circulating nurse turned down Borodin ever so softly to appreciate the coming attraction.

"I'm the chairman of cardiothoracic surgeon you miserable student. I probably wrote that article you read," was his next shout. The only movement in the room was nurse Frey shaking her head as she looked at the student. The anesthesiologist's face slowly arose above the surgical drapes at the head of the table. No one wanted to miss the ensuing ejection.

"Get the hell out of my room," barked Knight as Roden stepped back from the table. Melissa Bankart stepped into his place to assist Phil harvest the vein. "I'll give you such a bad grade you will be doomed to a career of popping pimples as a dermatologist." Knight's face began to turn a dark red as he turned back to the chest cavity.

Roden quickly exited the room looking back through the glass partition at the scrub sink. He was intelligent enough not to say another word.

Then as if the Greek Goddess of Chaos reached her hand into the room a chirping sound went off.

"What the hell was that?" said Knight quickly, again stepping back from the table. The chirp went off again. "Turn the music down," said Knight.

Again the chirping sound went off as all eyes looked at medical student Melissa Bankart. Attached to her waist beneath her surgical gown was a cell phone that she forgot to take off prior to the case. Unknown to her the caller was her father wanting to wish her a happy birthday. He lived in Cincinnati and was very proud of his daughter who was a medical student at Penn.

"Is that a cell phone?" yelled Knight. The phone chirped again. "Is that a god damn cell phone?" said the red faced Knight stepping towards Bankart.

"Yes," said a timid voice from Bankart. "I forgot to turn it off."

Knight motioned to the circulating nurse, "Help this student answer her phone nurse. It may be something critically important." Knight hated cell phones and text messaging. "Thanks goodness for cell phones to keep us all connected. That way we will never miss another emergency."

The circulating nurse reached into the back of Bankart's scrub gown and felt her cell phone attached to her waist. She lifted the phone out and looked at its face. The caller ID said "Daddy" but the scrub nurse knew better than to speak.

Knight then grabbed the cell phone with his bloody hand. He cranked his right arm back and fired the phone across the room. It hit the opposite wall and upon impact shattered into several pieces. It continued to chirp and Knight strode over to the main phone component. He then stomped on it with his shoe until the chirping stopped. Mr. Bankart's cell phone in Cincinnati immediately registered a lost call signal. A moment of angst seized him as he unsuccessfully attempted to recontact his daughter again.

He looked at Larson, "Get her out of here. You know the rules."

Chief resident Larson nodded his head to the right looking at Bankart as she quietly left the room. She joined Roden outside the room where a small crowd of surgical personnel was forming.

Knight continued with the surgery. P.A. Ranier stepped down the table to now help Phil. Larson remained at the head of the table to help Dr. Knight. The Russian music was turned back up to its normal level.

Within five minutes Knight yelled again as Phil quickly looked up. Phil immediately saw a pulsating stream of blood spraying all over Knight's chest and surgical mask. He had inadvertently transected the internal mammary artery while trying to reroute it to the heart.

"Crap," yelled Knight. "Tie that thing off," he said to Larson as he stepped back from the table. He turned around and the circulating nurse quickly wiped the blood off his mask and forehead area. Knight turned back to the table shaking his head. "We are going to need a lot of vein," was his next comment to the team. "I don't think God could have saved that artery."

And so it went for the rest of the case. Phil and Ranier harvested extra strips of vein, which were peppered with holes. Knight swore like a sailor while patching up the leaks. He struggled suturing each bypass graft together. Each stage of the procedure failed to go smoothly and the case finished two hours behind schedule.

It was noontime before Knight began wiring Mr. Brown's sternum back together. Per protocol Kate Smith was piped in over the intercom and began singing her rendition of God Bless America. Phil was sure Knight would continue on with the case and ignore tradition. However, like a true warrior, Knight stepped back from the table and put his bloodied right hand on his heart. All activity stopped at the moment in room four. Together the team paid respect to their beloved country. Phil looked at Knight and an odd sense of revere came upon him. He realized that the man standing in front of him had tremendous talent and drive. Although beaten down by the case he proudly stood tall in a moment of silence. He wondered what thoughts were going through Knight's head.

Phil then looked across the table and saw Ranier staring directly back at him. Her eyes were fixated on his and Phil appreciated a smile behind her mask. Phil smiled back at her. He noted a fine line of sweat across her forehead that permeated her cap. The visual connection continued between the two as Ms. Smith completed her compelling rendition of the song.

After the case, Knight reminded the team that they had three more cases to go. It was going to be a long day for the team with a late finish. Thankfully for all, the next three cases went well as a string of blue bloods returned to the table. The medical students remained banished from the OR for the remainder of the day.

Post op rounds in the SICU started that evening at 7 PM. The CT team along with Knight and Ranier checked on each patient. Everyone was stable. Knight and Ranier then met with each patient's family in a waiting area. Positive reports were given to each family. No family members were present for William Brown.

Knight's final words to Larson mandated him to keep a close eye on everyone over night. Then, like a tornado heading out of town, he and Ranier quickly disappeared down the hallway.

"That's the real Dr. Knight," said Pete Larson as they headed down to the call room. "He smashed that phone into a million pieces."

"That first case was jinxed from the start," said Phil as the entered the call room area. "A curse was upon it."

Both physicians entered the call area and dropped down onto adjacent couches. Although young in age, each physician was physically exhausted. Sitting in a chair next to them was intern Polk eating a bowl of ice cream.

"Don't you ever go home?" asked Phil.

"You are in my new home," replied Polk. "Why live anywhere else, and by the way, please wipe your feet the next time before entering." Polk then explained to them that he walked out on his slum landlord and moved into the call room the previous night. "I'm here to stay," was his proud exclamation. "Please don't call it The Hole anymore. Its new name is The Richard Polk Lounge," he paused and then said, "Adds a little class."

Phil and Larson then relived Knight's morning melt-down with Polk. Second year resident O'Keefe entered the room midway through the conversation.

"He kept yelling that the staffer would die on his shift," said Phil.

"That's his main concern," said O'Keefe. "No cabbage patch kids can die. Period."

"If any of his post op patients die it increases his mortality rate" said Larson. "At the end of the year every surgeon's mortality rate is calculated by the hospital and available for public consumption." Larson paused as the interns tried to understand. "Then about every two years The Philadelphia Chronicle runs an article reviewing all of the CT surgeons mortality rates. Every surgeon in the city is then compared to one another. It makes all of them nuts," said Larson.

"Wow," said Polk, "Kind of like their batting average."

"Yea," said O'Keefe, "and Knight likes to lead the league in hitting. So do whatever is necessary to keep his patients alive. "

"Definitely," said Larson. "I've seen him send out some very sick patients to nursing homes. As long as they take one step out of the hospital before dying, he is O.K. with it."

"Once a patient is physically outside the hospital walls a death is not a mortality on his name," said O'Keefe.

"And that keeps his batting average up," said Polk in a rare serious tone.

A shutter went up Phil's spine. He thought of Willie Brown lying up in the SICU. The concept of keeping the cabbage patch watered and disease free now made more sense. Knight was obsessed with maintaining a low mortality rate at all cost.

"Why else would he be named a top doctor in the Philadelphia magazines year after year?" said Larson. "He has created an institutional machine that spit shines his patients which in turn fuels his ego."

"It also gets him the pretty girl," said Polk with a smile.

Phil leaned his head back on the couch while staring at the ceiling. He thought of the pretty girl that Polk was referring to. He then tried to rationalize his role as a simple cog in Dr. Richard Knight's complex machine.

CHAPTER 9
A Fatal Move

THE SURGICAL INTENSIVE care unit at the PGH was a lesson in dynamics. Better known as the SICU this beehive of activity functioned for the sole purpose of stabilizing post-operative patients. Within the SICU a collision of technology, communication and intellect merged to preserve human life on an hourly basis. Additional variables of stress, interpersonal conflict and fatigue contributed to the milieu. Lastly, a blend of intuition and experience completed this tested recipe for success.

Most post-operative cardiac patients spent 48 hours in the SICU. New patients would be transported to the SICU from the surgical recovery room area. Upon arrival all patients would still have a breathing tube down their trachea or windpipe. They would immediately be hooked to a ventilation machine to provide oxygen. Multiple intravenous lines or IVs would be started to hydrate the patient and administer a slew of medications. The patient would also be hooked to a series of monitors to constantly record their vital signs. Computers constantly recorded the patient's heart rate, blood pressure, oxygen saturation and temperature. A SICU nurse with special training in intensive care directed this intimidating orchestration. This nurse intimately communicated with the resident house staff, whose orders were carried out for the benefit of the patient.

A new SICU patient would be sedated while on the ventilator. This would permit the patient to tolerate the breathing tube down their trachea. Sedation would allow the patient to understand sentences and physically respond to questions with a nod of the head or gesture of the hand. Narcotic medications were also administered to lessen the pain of the surgical procedure. A morphine drip was the norm. An avalanche of lab values was generated on each SICU patient. Blood work was obtained every twelve hours to monitor the patient's electrolytes, hemoglobin and clotting factors. Foley catheters and chest tubes generated numbers for urine output and chest cavity fluids. Arterial catheters or A-lines were placed inside the patient's arteries to constantly monitor their oxygen supply and blood pressure.

To the uninitiated this scene was overwhelming. To the SICU nurse it was commonplace. Each nurse was assigned one to two post-operative patients per shift. They expertly cared for the patient while following medical orders and interpreting data. Their hub was the computer. Each nurse had a mobile computer station consisting of a display screen and keyboard. The station was on a sleek stand with wheels allowing it to pass from room to room. The computer gathered all of the patient's data and presented it in an orderly fashion. The simple act of clicking on a patient's icon would generate every possible piece of medical data regarding that patient. This would include his past medical history, medications and social history. Intraoperative records would be visible along with reports of all radiology studies. Blood values would be available in table or graph form to identify trends. Abnormal blood values would be set off to the viewer with bolder print and asterisks. The computer also contained all physician orders regarding post-operative care and management. Orders included medications and dosages, ventilator settings and catheter care. This computer hub represented the glue that held the complex nature and multiple facets of the SICU together

The SICU at PGH was composed of twenty rooms each containing one bed. The rooms were set adjacent to each other on a single floor in a circular fashion. In the middle of the circle was the nurse's station. This station was a massive expanse of countertops and chairs surrounded by computer screens, fax machines and printers. Sprinkled amongst the machinery was a never-ending blend of nurses, residents, medical students and physicians. Each played a role in caring for the postoperative patient during their brief but critical stay in the SICU.

Willie Brown and the three blue bloods arrived in the SICU late that evening, on the last Wednesday of July. Each patient was assigned a specific room and care team. Each patient was stable having done well that day in the operating room. No problems occurred overnight as all four patients were closely monitored by the staff.

The following morning Dr. Knight and the cardiothoracic team commenced rounds at 7 AM in the SICU. As Dr. Knight walked into the SICU theatre he appeared to represent the second coming of the Lord. Approaching the unit from a long hallway he slowly walked with a gang of white coated house staff behind him. In tow was chief resident Larson along with Drummer and the medical students. Physician assistant Ranier accompanied the group. Upon entering the SICU junior resident O'Keefe and two nurses joined into the group. Upon approaching Willie Brown's room a respiratory therapist and wound management nurse joined in. Knight never broke stride as his gang grew with every step. He stopped outside of Willie

Brown's room and while looking at Chief resident Larson he began to speak.

"Begin," was Knight's only word as the crowd went silent.

"Mr. Brown did well last night," said Larson. "Oxygen saturation was fine and we got him off the vent at 2 AM." Larson was referring to the patient having his breathing tube removed. "His labs are rock solid and we will get him out of bed today. Probable step down unit tomorrow." Larson then stopped.

Knight then looked at the SICU nurse who was just starting her shift that morning. She reported no nursing problems overnight. Knight nodded his head as he slowly stepped into the room. The large group followed.

Upon entering the room William Brown looked up at the medical team and smiled. Although the room itself was large the medical team stood in tight formation shoulder to shoulder behind Dr. Knight. Mr. Brown had not officially met Knight in person.

"Hello Mr. Brown, I am Dr. Knight," Knight paused and then continued, "I performed your surgery yesterday."

"Pleasure to meet you," said Mr. Brown with a respectful bow of his head. "Thank you," was his next comment with his voice raspy and weak.

Chief resident Larson then quickly listened to the patient's chest with a stethoscope stating his lungs were clear. His vital signs were then reviewed. The nursing staff reported his current medications and fluid output. Mr. Brown was deemed stable and as quickly as the group entered into the room, they turned around to leave.

"I hear you like the 76ers," said Mr. Brown as the group was turning.

Knight turned back to face the patient. "Pardon me," he said.

William Brown pointed to Larson saying, "The doctor told me you like the 76ers," he paused and continued, "You know they are my team." Willie Brown was referring to the Philadelphia 76ers basketball team. Earlier that morning Dr. Larson informed him that Dr. Knight was a fan of the team and courtside season ticket holder.

Knight uncomfortably shifted in front of the patient looking at Larson with a glance. He did not like any personal information being given out about himself. He was a very private person.

Knight then spoke with reservation, "That's right, I'm a long time fan."

"Should have a good team this year," said the weak Mr. Brown. "I love the boy they drafted from Villanova. He is a Philly product you know, from Overbrook High School."

Knight immediately knew of the first round draft pick selection of the 76ers that year. He nodded saying, "I know, good choice." Knight then turned away but Mr. Brown kept talking.

"Do you mind if I call you the Messiah?" said William Brown.

Knight's posse smiled and laughed but before Knight could respond Mr. Brown continued, "Maurice Williamson was old school, I remember watching him play in the Spectrum." Mr. Brown then hummed a slow "Hmmm, Hmmm" while shaking his head side to side. "Lit up the Lakers for 35 points that night." Willie Brown was referring to the iconic Maurice "The Messiah" Williamson who played for the 76ers some thirty years ago. "You're my Messiah," said a smiling Willie Brown as he gave a thumbs-up sign to Knight.

Then, as Mr. William Brown started to win over the affection of the group, Dr. Knight was able to speak, "Sure

Mr. Brown, you can call me the Messiah." He then smiled leaving the room.

As the group left the room they could hear Willie Brown saying loudly, "The Messiah is in the house, hallelujah!" followed by a painful bronchial cough. Everyone had a warm feeling in their heart except Dr. Knight who was worrying about Mr. Brown's hepatitis panel. As of that morning the intra-operative blood work had not been reported back.

Knight's team then visited the three other post-op patients that morning. He spent a noticeably greater amount of time at the blood blue patients' bedsides. All three patients represented a true cross section of Knight's private practice. They all were Philadelphia Main Line well to do residents who through word of mouth and connections made it to the famous Dr. Knight. All members of the blue blood team were doing well that morning.

That morning rounds ended at 7:45 AM. All was well in the SICU. Each post-operative patient was stable with plans for transfer to the step down unit the following morning. The step down unit represented a less monitored floor and final bridge to the cardiac seventh floor. Each step brought the patient closer to Knight's goal of a stable transfer out of the Philadelphia General Hospital. The Big Knight Machine was humming on all cylinders that morning.

The remainder of the day was quiet for the interns and residents of the PGH. Phil was on call that night and settled into the Polk lounge to watch a Phillies game. The namesake of the lounge was present, sitting in an oversized ottoman chair that he bartered from the local Salvation Army. Intern Polk called it his throne and dubbed PGH his kingdom.

"Hard to believe one month is over with," said Polk.

"Going by fast," replied Phil who was lying on a couch with his feet up. The Phillies game was in the third inning.

"I think we are all doing fine except for Fred," said Polk referring to fellow intern Frederick Riles III. "He has been looking miserable lately."

"Yea," said a tiring Phil Drummer. "I don't think the Specials Rotation is doing him too well." Phil knew that Riles was not getting along with the upper levels of the surgical residency. Despite not having to take in house call for the first few months, Fred Riles was struggling to make it through the year. This was in part due to the hard time the upper level residents were giving him, being well aware of his pedigree and easy path into the PGH program.

"Cathy is doing great," said the king from his throne.

"Great gal," said Phil referring to Cathy Finley. Phil knew she had her act together. She was a hard worker, never complained and was genuine to everyone.

"What are the odds of you hitting the sheets with Jenna Ranier?" was Polk's next matter of fact line. He didn't take his eyes off the T.V. set while articulating.

"What's it to you?" said Phil.

"I have my dreams," said Polk. "My parents always taught me to dream big."

Phil didn't respond while shaking his head, but did realize the subtle nature of Ranier's actions around him. She certainly smiled at him tenderly and always stood more erect in his presence. As time went on her bodily contact in the operating room lasted longer. Phil then suddenly wondered if her tendencies were obvious to Dr. Knight, prompting a cold feeling to come upon him.

"I don't think the big man would take kindly to you snaking on his woman," said Polk.

"Believe me, I have no intentions of going in that direction," replied Phil, trying to convince himself. "But she is a beautiful woman."

"I give you to December at the latest," said Polk again in matter of fact fashion. "The dirty deed will be done by New Year's," was his blunt prediction. "Let's bet on it," said Polk looking at Phil with a dare in his eyes.

Phil just smiled and shook his head. He knew better not to continue this line of thought with Polk. As the evening progressed fatigue set in upon each intern. By the eighth inning they were both asleep in their respective positions, missing a late inning come back by the Phillies.

All was quiet later that evening in the SICU. Second year resident O'Keefe was on the job that night. It was midnight as he checked all the labs on each cardiac post op patients. Like a seasoned pro he made subtle changes to I.V. fluids and medications based on his knowledge base. Nothing was out of the ordinary as he pulled up Mr. William Brown's blood results. The quiet comfort of the SICU prevailed as the nursing staff went about their business. Per protocol the SICU lights were dimmed at night, providing a warm ambience to a high tech environment.

Mr. Brown was resting comfortably in SICU bed number three. Up to that point, his life was a happy but unfortunate series of events. He was raised never to have known his father. His mother died of a heroin overdose when he was just ten years old. A loving but infirmed grandmother then raised him along with an older brother. High school lasted a total of two years before trouble began with the law. An ill-conceived burglary attempt resulted in some prison time where he discovered Jesus. The good Lord brought Willie back onto terra firma but alcohol fueled continued instability. Middle age produced a happy drunk that was kind and charismatic. He was on his way to the liquor store the evening he collapsed in front of the PGH.

Bad luck seemed to follow Willie Brown throughout his whole life. His bad luck was about to run out that early August morning.

As second year resident O'Keefe hit Mr. Brown's icon on the computer screen a series of events occurred in nanoseconds. Upon depressing the enter button on his keyboard a series of lab values were retrieved from the blood lab. These values included the electrolytes of Mr. Brown. The electrolytes represented four critical factors in the blood stream. Standard electrolytes reported included sodium, potassium, chloride and bicarbonate. Mr. Brown's true potassium level was moderately elevated at 6.1 milliequivalents per liter (mEq/L). A normal potassium level was between 3.5 and 5.0 mEq/L. As a rule a low potassium level was not a concern, however a high potassium level was life threatening.

During those critical nanoseconds Mr. Brown's moderately elevated potassium level was loaded onto the hospital's secure computer system. This system was constructed by a legion of Information Technology experts that represented the greatest computer minds of medical technology. Of course the internal hospital computer system then interacted with the hospital's external computer system. This external system then connected to the hospital's internet grid and physician user network. Every physician's home based computer then interfaced with the network. Suddenly by virtue of the world wide web, the lab values of Mr. Brown became available for mass consumption.

Once loaded onto the computer cable Mr. Brown's potassium value traveled at the speed of light through the decaying walls of the old PGH facility. This electrolyte level represented only one of a million bits of data transmitted through the hospital that very day. Then, quietly and without fanfare, a felony crime was committed in cyberspace. The crime occurred at 0025 hours that morning of standard time. For prior to arriving at resident O'Keefe's terminal an internal rogue command rapidly switched Mr. Brown's potassium level from 6.1 mEq/L to 2.1 mEq/L. Unaware of the illegal transgression, Dr. O'Keefe received a routine series of electrolytes with an asterisk next to a bold print low potassium level of 2.1 mEq/L. The tired resident noted the value and made the appropriate knee jerk response that medical training taught him. He keyed into Mr. Brown's order set after logging a secure ID number into the system. He then ordered the SICU nurse to administer extra potassium in the patient's intravenous fluids. He then reviewed the remainder of Mr. Brown's labs noting that a hepatitis and HIV panel were negative.

Veteran nurse Heather Cruise was on duty that evening caring for Mr. Brown. She was in his room when her computer softly purred signifying a new non-urgent order. She clicked on Mr. Brown's order set to see the commonplace order to add more potassium to his I.V. fluids. She always thought highly of Dr. O'Keefe. She noted that Mr. Brown was sleeping comfortably. She forwarded the order to the pharmacy lab one floor below them. Within fifteen minutes an internal delivery shuttle tube system delivered the liter of I.V. saline solution to the waiting arms of nurse Cruise. She ran a bar code scanner across the liter of fluid and the computer recognized the fluid as correct and matching the order and patient. The liter of fluid was marked as Lactated Ringers with an additional 80 mEq of potassium inside. Nurse Cruise removed the patient's prior I.V. fluid bag and replaced it with the potassium rich solution. She opened the stop valve allowing the fluid to run into Mr. Brown's veins, and then left the room to talk to the available young doctor at the nursing station. Dr. Knight's machine was unfortunately operating to perfection that morning. Over the next hour the additional I.V.

fluid pushed Mr. Brown's potassium level to a critical high level known as hyperkalemia.

Potassium is a basic electrolyte in the body. It serves a crucial role in the transmission of electrical signals in the nervous system. It also plays an essential role in the function of all muscle activity including that of the heart. Potassium allows the smooth rhythmic function of a heartbeat that occurs about seventy times per minute in a normal human being. A grossly elevated potassium state disrupts this cardiac rhythm, resulting in an abnormal heart rate called an arrhythmia. Such an arrhythmia is life threatening and when untreated, usually results in death.

Hyperkalemia is clinically difficult to detect. As Willie Brown's blood potassium rose he felt a subtle nauseous feeling in his stomach. He then experienced a tingling sensation throughout his arms and legs. Outside of his room Dr. O'Keefe was flirting with Nurse Cruise as they sat in front of the SICU cardiac monitor screen. This screen constantly displayed every patient's heart rate and EKG. Had they been looking at Mr. Brown's rate that very minute, a noticeable change in his EKG would have been detected.

Then, per the laws of physiology, Mr. William Brown's normal heart rhythm surrendered to the state of hyperkalemia. His heart acutely flipped into an arrhythmic state, setting off every alarm in his room and at the nursing station.

Dr. O'Keefe and Nurse Cruise quickly turned to the monitor screens as their adrenal glands released a bolus of epinephrine throughout their bodies. Mr. Brown's EKG strip was blinking and O'Keefe immediately recognized the dreaded rhythm of ventricular tachycardia or V-tach. His subconscious recalled a basic physiology lecture in medical school describing a V-tach heart as a "bag of worms" all squirming together yet unable to generate any pressure. They both then sprinted into Mr. Brown's room.

O'Keefe looked up to the bedside monitors as Nurse Cruise turned on all the overhead lights flooding the room with brightness. O'Keefe noted Mr. Brown's blood pressure to be nonexistent and his rhythm to remain in V-tach. Mr. Brown was listless at the moment.

O'Keefe quickly looked to Nurse Cruise with bewilderment in his eyes as he rapidly said, "Call a code!"

What happened next can only be appreciated while in a teaching medical institution. Nurse Cruise ran to the center station picking up a designated blue phone, which immediately connected her to the hospital operator. She tersely said, "Code Blue Surgical ICU."

Then as rapidly as Nurse Cruise told the operator a stern female voice came over the entire hospital system intercom system stating slowly and clearly, "Code Blue, Surgical ICU...Code Blue, Surgical ICU...Code Blue, Surgical ICU." At the same time that very operator activated a paging system setting off the pager of all in house medical, surgical and anesthesia residents. Throughout the sleeping quarters of PGH weary house staff members were abruptly awakened to the Code Blue alert. They all jumped out of bed and began sprinting to the SICU floor.

Within seconds a rumbling sensation could be heard throughout the hospital. This rumble was that of young residents sprinting in hallways and down stairwells. Stairwell doors opening and closing contributed to the noise. A subtle shake of the floor could be appreciated in the SICU as the resident mob approached the unit. Nurse Cruise ran back into Mr. Brown's room as house staff sprinted down the corridor leading to the SICU.

"No pressure," yelled O'Keefe. "Open up all fluids," was his next comment as he and Nurse Cruise tried to instill more I.V. fluid into Mr. Brown's body to elevate his pressure. Unfortunately their correct action only supplied more potassium to the problem.

As a group of residents, students and interns ran into the room Mr. Brown's heart function continued to rapidly deteriorate. He appreciated the brightness of light in the room but beyond that appreciated no other external stimuli. His mind settled into a painless and peaceful state as a calm overcame him. While taking his last breath his mind returned to his childhood as his grandmother lovingly hummed a gospel hymn to him. She was tucking him into bed and pulling the tight clean sheets up to his shoulders. It was softly snowing outside. The bed was warm as was his grandmother's hand, as she slowly rubbed his back.

By the time the senior medical resident in house began the first round of CPR, Mr. William Brown was dead. What followed from that point forward was an academic exercise.

Surrounding his deathbed was an anesthesia resident at the head. This resident was responsible for managing Mr. Brown's airway. He unskillfully passed a breathing tube back down Mr. Brown's trachea cutting his lip and chipping a tooth in the process. The anesthesia resident then started ventilating Mr. Brown's lungs. As the room swelled with house staff, the anesthesia resident constantly barked out, "All non essential personnel please leave the room." He looked at all the medical students in the room but no one acknowledged his presence or recommendation.

At the foot of the bed was a nervous chief medical resident who was planning to become a dermatologist. Her role at the moment was to be the team leader of the code. She pulled out a laminated card from her pocket titled "Guidelines for Cardio Pulmonary Resuscitation". As her voice cracked she began reading the card verbatim. It asked a series of questions regarding the patient's vital signs and medications. Surgical resident O'Keefe rapidly answered the questions while providing a history of the patient.

The chief medical resident then ordered a series of IV medications per the card protocol, which was administered by the nursing staff. She also ordered mechanical compressions to commence on Mr. Brown's chest. Stat blood work was then ordered.

Phil Drummer and Rick Polk were present as was medical student Roden. Phil stepped up to Mr. Brown's bedside and began compressions on his chest wall. As he placed his hands on Mr. Brown's sternum he remembered Dr. Knight's antics during that operative case. He then began compressions onto Mr. Brown's chest while keeping his elbows locked straight. As he rhythmically compressed he felt a crackling sensation beneath his hands.

Phil looked at Rick Polk saying, "I'm breaking his ribs."

Polk shook his head as he was busy trying to teach medical student Roden how to draw blood from the inguinal or groin area. With a patient's blood pressure so low drawing blood from a peripheral arm was not an option. Therefore the next viable place to draw blood was from the large femoral artery or vein in the groin. Polk was trying to tell Roden the anatomy of the area as the medical student repeatedly drove a large needle into Mr. Brown's groin. The overall noise in the room made communication difficult but medical student Roden was successful in obtaining two vials of blood from the femoral artery.

The first round of CPR consisted of IV medications, mechanical ventilation and chest compressions. After this cycle the medical resident then commanded a stop to all actions. Everyone looked up to the overhead monitors, which continued to report no pressure or functional heart rhythm. Intern Polk reported no pulse in the groin as he kept his fingers pressed to Mr. Brown's skin. Nurse Cruise reported no pressure as she held her stethoscope to the patient's arm.

"Get the paddles," was her next command.

Before Phil could realize what was happening Dr. O'Keefe pushed him aside and yelled, "Charge!" Everyone quickly stepped back from the patient as he placed two round defibrillator paddles on the patient's chest. O'Keefe looked back at a nurse who quickly pressed the charge button of the defibrillator machine. A rapid pitching tone pierced the room as the unit charged in a second.

"Clear," was O'Keefe's next command as he pressed the buttons on the defibrillator paddles. Mr. Brown's body convulsed upwards as the electrical shock ran through his heart in an attempt to stimulate a rhythm. His heart did not respond and the code continued.

The chief medical resident then continued two more identical cycles of CPR per her guideline card. Mr. Brown did not respond to the efforts. During each cycle fellow interns and medical students took turns compressing Mr. Brown's chest and discharging the defibrillator paddles. Each student gained experience in the aspects of CPR in hopes of a successful outcome at a later date.

At 0237 hours that August morning, Mr. William Brown was officially pronounced dead. A flustered chief resident Larson arrived running into the SICU five minutes later. Living in the suburbs his beeper went off at the code onset. He reported to the hospital as quickly as possible. He was out of breath as he saw a somber code team slowly walking out of Mr. Brown's room. The nursing staff was cleaning up Mr. Brown's bloodied body.

Chief resident Larson looked at O'Keefe saying, "What the hell happened?"

O'Keefe just shook his head, "No warning, just went into a V-tach." O'Keefe ran his trembling hand through his hair saying, "Couldn't pull him out."

Over the next 30 minutes Dr. Larson reconstructed the events surrounding the demise and death of Mr. Brown.

He reviewed his blood work and orders given over the hours preceding his death. He gathered all information regarding his fluid status and management that prior evening. He discussed the case with the nursing staff. Everyone present stated that Mr. Brown was doing well with no obvious concerns present prior to his death.

Then, after careful consideration of all variables, Larson took a deep breath and stood up. He walked away from a dejected house staff team that spoke no further words, and then entered a private room set aside from the SICU proper. He picked up a phone sitting on a desk and brought the receiver to his ear. He hit the zero sign and heard the operator ask, "Yes may I help you?"

"Yes operator, this is Dr. Pete Larson," was he comment as he sat down. He then took another deep breath before quietly saying, "Would you please connect me to the home of Dr. Richard Knight."

CHAPTER 10
The Autopsy

DOCTOR MICHAEL BARNES enjoyed being the Chairman of the PGH Surgery Department. He had been elevated to that post six years earlier. Barnes was a product of the PGH system. Having completed medical school at Harvard he then trained and completed his surgical residency in Philadelphia at the PGH. Possessing a keen mind and an ability to communicate well, he was offered an associate professorship at PGH upon completion of his residency. He accepted the offer and for the next ten years served faithfully on the surgical staff.

Throughout that time he failed to distinguish himself with regards to his surgical skills, being an average surgeon on his best day. However, he did have the discipline and organizational skills that allowed him to generate and publish articles in the surgical literature. Emphasis at a teaching institution was on the ability to perform research, gather data and publish results in peer- reviewed journals. These surgical journals were read world wide and brought recognition, fame and financial funding to the institution. Dr. Barnes was well published in the General Surgery world and therefore well known and well respected, regardless of his average surgical skills. He therefore was destined to become a star at a teaching hospital where he could excel behind the cloak of academia, while only being average behind the secure walls of the surgical room.

Having had a prolific decade of research and publication, Dr. Barnes became a full professor at the age of 44 years old. He then continued on the surgical staff at PGH under the protection of his professorial tenure, becoming acquainted with the rising academic staff of institutions around the country. This inner circle of surgeons then began referring to each other as experts in their field while quoting each other's published works. Before Dr. Barnes knew it he was a leader in his field with a sterling reputation built up over time.

Dr. Barnes possessed positive people skills and was conservative in appearance. At age 53 he was named Chairman of the Department of Surgery at PGH. The selection committee's choice at that time was between Barnes and a younger academic hot shot who actually did exhibit good surgical skills, that being Dr. Richard Knight. The selection committee opted for the safer bet in Barnes. The sting of the committee's selection festered in Dr. Knight's gut ever since. Knight wanted the chairmanship and Barnes knew this well.

Dr. Barnes lived on the Main Line of Philadelphia in the swank Bryn Mawr section. He was married to the same woman for 29 years and had no children. He had no vices. His home was perfectly set on a knoll overlooking a gentle flowing creek below. Each room was pleasant to the eye having been set by a team of interior decorators. No pets lived in the home. A weekly cleaning crew buffed each floor and room to an immaculate and sterile hone. An antique grandfather clock kept time in the foyer and audibly ticked each second precisely away.

Dr. Barnes had a routine that was exact and methodical. No variation occurred. Each morning at 6:20 AM he would walk out of his front door dressed appropriately for the weather. A well paced ten-minute walk would bring him to the Bryn Mawr regional rail station at 6:30 AM. The 5712 train would arrive six minutes later to transport him into Philadelphia. Each trip would find him in the seventh row of the train's third car. Throughout the fourteen-minute train ride, Dr. Barnes would open his briefcase and direct his attention to a folder placed inside by his secretary. The folder listed his daily agenda in detailed fashion. Beneath this itinerary was a collection of priority topics to address. A short hand written note or verbal dictation would address each memo. At 6:50 AM the train would pull into Philadelphia's 30th Street Station. Dr. Barnes preferred to then walk the next four city blocks, allowing him to arrive at the Kirby Pavilion at approximately 7:10 AM. The doctor would then take the steps up to the sixth floor arriving into the surgical department at roughly 7:12 AM.

The morning of Willie Brown's death was no exception to Dr. Barnes' routine. At exactly 7:12 AM he walked briskly into his office to the fresh smell of coffee. After exchanging a quick "good morning" with his secretary Rose, he sensed an instantaneous disruption of routine. Upon entering his office he immediately recognized the disruptive source. Doctor Knight sat motionless with his back to Dr. Barnes, sitting in a chair directly facing the chairman's tidy desk.

"Good morning Richard," said the Chairman of the department to Dr. Knight. "Who died?"

Knight didn't move as Barnes circled in front of him and without pausing sat down in his chair. He looked directly into Knight's eyes with a slight smile and waited for him to speak.

Dr. Knight slowly blinked his eyes and took a slow deep breath followed by an equally slow exhale. Ten seconds passed before he spoke. "A staffer in the SICU early this morning," said Knight then pausing again. Barnes slowly began to rock back and forth in his chair knowing quite well where the conversation was headed. Knight then spoke again while staring at the desk in front of him, "A drunk who just about dropped dead right in front of the hospital. Of course I was the lucky one on call to claim him."

Dr. Barnes then spoke with an uplifting tone, "Well Richard I'm sure you tried your best." The sarcasm of the remark was obvious as Barnes nodded his head slowly up and down. He continued to stare directly at Dr. Knight.

"Don't get smart with me," said Knight with a look directly at Chairman Barnes. "I'm the only one that keeps this department in the black." He shook his head looking down to the right and staring at the carpet. "How this piece of crap patient got to me I have no idea." He then paused and slowly looked back up at Barnes shaking his head side to side, "The numbers are going to be close this year Michael, real close."

"Actually not," said Barnes. "Financially we are doing better than last year. You do realize that nine other surgeons actually work in this department and generate revenue."

"You know what numbers I mean," barked Knight.

"Actually I don't," replied Barnes while knowing quite well what his colleague meant.

"The mortality numbers," said Knight with a whine in his voice. "Remember, the mortality numbers?"

"Oh the mortality numbers," said Dr. Barnes with a feint surprise raising both hands and placing them on his forehead. "How could I forget," was his next apologetic line.

Knight ignored his theatrics and spoke, "This fatality is going to jack up my percentage." Barnes didn't speak and waited for Knight to continue. "One or two more deaths and my numbers will be up and over the region's norm."

"Maybe the Chronicle won't run an article this year," said Barnes.

"Are you kidding me? That report comes out like clockwork every two years," said Knight. "The public eats up those numbers. For God's sake the PR people in this hospital post it on our website." Knight paused and then looked directly at Barnes saying, "Its my damn average with regards to keeping people alive!"

"Calm down, calm down," said Barnes now becoming serious. "The public knows we accept critically ill patients that other medical centers aren't capable of caring for. They make that clear in the article."

"Doesn't matter," said Knight sharply. "The public only remembers the big bold number next to my name, if it's high they pick another surgeon who in their mind won't kill them."

"I don't think it all hinges on one number," said Barnes.

"I do," said Knight. "Its my number stacked up on the front page of the Philadelphia Chronicle compared to every other cardiothoracic surgeon in the region." He paused and continued, "If my practice suffers from this then the whole department will suffer."

Dr. Barnes took a deep breath. He knew that all good surgeons had a great ego. Dr. Knight's ego was no exception. The mortality percentage quoted by the Philadelphia Chronicle fortunately benefited Knight over the past fifteen years. It not only benefitted him financially, but also stroked his ego.

Barnes then shifted gears saying, "Who is going to do the autopsy?"

"I don't know yet," said Knight. "But it better not be that dyke down there again. I wouldn't let her conduct an autopsy on my dead dog. She is out to get me."

Knight was referring to associate professor Jane Falcon M.D., who frequently performed autopsies surrounding a surgical death. She was rumored to be a lesbian. Knight accepted this rumor as fact. In the past both Knight and Falcon argued bitterly with regard to the wording of her autopsy reports, which were then available for public and legal review.

Barnes didn't acknowledge his associates' distasteful social slur. As a department chairman he felt an obligation to uphold a standard of dignity even in private conversation.

"Let's just wait and see what the pathology report says," replied Barnes as he leaned back rocking slowly on his chair. Both men then sat in silence for thirty seconds as Barnes continued to slowly rock back and forth.

"Great," said Knight. "But remember, when my surgical numbers go down, this whole department suffers. And when the whole department suffers, then the hospital system suffers. Tell that to the suits above you that run this place." Knight then shook his head and declined any further comment. He got up and left without saying another word, while heading to the SICU to commence rounds.

Anxiously awaiting in the SICU was the surgical team headed by chief resident Larson. They were unsure what to expect. Phil and the medical students dared not say a word to Dr. Larson who was sleep deprived. They all watchfully peered down the long hallway looking for Dr. Knight to arrive. They then looked into SICU room three which was being scrubbed down by the housecleaning crew.

Knight soon arrived and made no reference to Mr. Brown. Much earlier that morning he released an avalanche of vile onto Chief Resident Larson. He didn't think it was necessary to waste any more energy on the cretins below Larson. The three blue bloods were visited in regal fashion that morning by the surgical team. All patients were doing very well and heading out of the SICU that morning.

Upon the completion of rounds Dr. Knight informed the surgical team that an autopsy would be performed on Mr. William Brown that evening at 5 PM. He fully expected all members of the surgical team to be present for this important step of the medical process. No one spoke as they respectfully nodded their heads in assent.

At exactly 5 PM that evening Dr. Knight confidently walked into the Pathology Department of PGH. He bypassed the secretary staff that was slowly mobilizing to end their work shift. He knew where the autopsy room was and headed directly for it. Upon entering the room he saw the cardiothoracic team talking amongst themselves. The lifeless and nude body of Mr. William Brown lay supine on a stainless steel table in front of them.

"Where's the pathologist?" asked an inpatient Knight.

Before anyone could answer a female voice from another direction said, "Right here." Then entering the room from another door was Dr. Jane Falcon holding a Styrofoam cup with coffee in it.

Knight sighed but before he could speak Dr. Falcon continued, "Good afternoon, or should I say good evening everyone." She smiled and introductions were made. She then looked at Dr. Knight and with a respectful bow asked, "Shall we begin?"

"Yes," said Knight. He then looked at chief resident Larson saying, "Pete, give the good doctor here a summary of this patient's surgical history."

Then with exact clarity Dr. Larson presented the case to Dr. Falcon and a few pathology residents who sheepishly stood behind her. The team looked down upon the body of Mr. Brown who appeared much older then his stated age. The physicians on his left side noticed an iron brand mark over his shoulder area. He also had an amateurish appearing tattoo saying "Willie" on his forearm.

Dr. Falcon then put on a long gown followed by thick surgical gloves. Her eyes were shielded with goggles as she spoke, "Let's start with the chest wall cavity and abdomen." She then took a scalpel and cut a large Y-shaped incision on the ventral or front side of Willie Brown. The incision began at the front of each shoulder and then connected to the surgical incision of Dr. Knight. It then continued down across his abdomen along the midline, ending just above his pubic hairline.

Dr. Falcon made a reference to the wires closing the chest of the corpse. Knight then signaled to Larson who quickly removed the wires holding the chest and ribs together. Within five minutes of commencing the autopsy the entire chest and abdomen cavity of Mr. Brown lay exposed to the team. A stench began to permeate the room.

Dr. Falcon did a quick visual inspection of the chest cavity noting the Mr. Brown's lungs were visibly abnormal. She commented to the team, "An obvious smoker." She looked behind herself at the pathology residents stating, "Note the hyperinflation of the lung and the grey black look. This guy was a two pack a day man." She paused and then continued while cutting away a sample of the lung, "Combine that with living in West Philadelphia for fifty years and you get cancer or emphysema." She then handed the lung sample to a lab tech responsible for generating permanent microscopic slide samples.

Falcon continued, "Now, let's get to the heart of the matter." She then slowly looked up at the group with a slight smile on her face. A sinister short series of laughs then came out of her mouth with a subtle saliva accent.

The pathology residents snickered at her dry humor, the surgical team did not, fearful of Dr. Knight's presence. She then proceeded to inspect the heart.

Falcon then commented on the general enlargement of Mr. Brown's heart, which suggested coronary artery disease. The group noticed at that point that Dr. Knight's body began to slowly sway back and forth. Dr. Falcon then began a short lecture on coronary artery disease directed at her residents. She pointed out other visual factors regarding Mr. Brown's heart that suggested coronary artery disease.

Knight suddenly spoke calmly. "Dr. Falcon, this man dropped dead in front of our hospital because of coronary artery disease. His preoperative cardiac catheterization identified coronary artery disease. I operated on him because of coronary artery disease." He paused and looked sarcastically at Falcon saying, "I can assure you that he suffered from coronary artery disease."

Dr. Falcon maintained her gaze on Knight saying, "Thank you Dr. Knight." She then looked back down on the heart taking a scalpel in her right hand, "Regardless I will take a sample of his nonsurgical artery to confirm that. I will also take a sample of his left ventricular heart to assure that he never suffered a myocardial infarction."

"This man did not suffer a heart attack Dr. Falcon," said Knight. His body began to sway more rapidly. "There was no preoperative, intraoperative, or postoperative indication of a myocardial infarction."

"Yes, Dr. Knight, I understand, but a sample of heart tissue I will take." She then handed the cardiac specimen to the lab tech.

"Now lets take a look at the coronary artery bypass sites," said Falcon.

"Stop!" said Dr. Knight pulling out a pair of surgical microscopic eyeglass loops from his pocket. He put the surgical glasses on and stepped forward to the body. "I'll be the judge of the graft sites since this is my field of expertise."

Dr. Falcon looked up at Knight who towered over her physically. She spoke with a timid tone, "I am capable of commenting on the general appearance of each coronary graft site Dr. Knight." She paused then said, "We have been through this discussion before."

"Make it a quick visual inspection comment Dr. Falcon," said Knight. "I am aware of our prior discussions. We don't have all day here."

Dr. Falcon then pointed out the fact that no internal mammary artery graft was used. She pointed out to the residents that several vein grafts were present, all looking intact.

"Of course they are intact," said Knight who reached inside the chest cavity wearing a pair of gloves. He deftly rotated the heart from side to side inspecting his work. "Each graft is secure and intact Dr. Falcon." He then looked over the top of his glasses at the pathologist saying, "Please put that in your official report, specifically that the pathology team and treating surgeon visually inspected all the grafts and they were intact."

"Yes, Dr. Knight," said Falcon. "I can assure you the official report will comment exactly on that fact."

Dr. Falcon then continued the autopsy heading below the diaphragm into the abdomen cavity. She pointed out a scarred and abnormal liver consistent with alcoholism and cirrhosis. Large sections of liver samples were obtained in wedge shaped fashion. As she spoke and inspected the abdomen the stench in the room intensified. She then proceeded to remove vital organs including the kidneys and spleen, which were weighed by an assistant on a nearby scale. The procedure was moving quickly at this point.

The pathologist then directed her attention to the gastrointestinal system of the body. She deftly opened the stomach commenting on some grossly obvious ulcer disease. An approximate 23 feet of small intestine was then inspected followed by five feet of large intestine. During this portion of the autopsy Dr. Falcon cut a several foot section of large intestine out and walked over to a side table. The entire team followed her. At the side table she took a pair of dissection scissors and quickly cut open the large intestine in longitudinal fashion. Inner bowels were quickly exposed to all releasing a stench that was overwhelming to the uninitiated. The fecal remains of Willie's Brown's last double cheeseburger oozed onto the stainless steal table while gently sliding towards an attached deep sink. Then at that moment a loud thud was heard behind the medical team.

Everyone turned back quickly to see medical student Melissa Bankart lying on the ground. Her head was bleeding from behind. She was overwhelmed by the malodorous stench and passed out. She fell backwards hitting her head on the autopsy table then falling to the ground.

"Smelling salt," said Dr. Falcon.

Knight looked down sneering at the unconscious medical student. "Get her to the E.R." was his comment to Larson while turning his attention back to the bowel dissection. Within three minutes Larson and Phil were wheeling the semi-conscious student to the ER via a wheelchair. She was pasty white in appearance.

Dr. Falcon then asked Knight if a cranial inspection was ordered. "Of course," was his response. "This guy probably blew an aneurism in his head." Knight was looking for any cause of death except the coronary artery system.

The pathologist took a vibrating saw and cut a series of grooves into Willie Brown's skull, then wedging open his cranium to expose the brain. The visual inspection was negative for any obvious hemorrhage as several large tissue samples were then taken for analysis.

The autopsy was then complete. Dr. Falcon then spoke, "My preliminary sense is that a combination of coronary artery disease, emphysema and liver cirrhosis led to the death of this gentleman. Of course we will have to await all the micro slide results." She took off her gloves and gown with a deep sigh.

"Thank you Dr. Falcon," said Knight. "We will all be anxiously awaiting your report."

Dr. Knight then turned and left the room. As he departed Phil returned from the E.R. where Larson remained suturing up medical student Bankart's head laceration.

"Call the morgue," said the pathology chief resident.

Dr. Falcon then spoke, "No. Legal called before the autopsy. His brother signed off on him. We can treat him as a John Doe." Dr. Falcon then left the room.

A morbid grin then came across the pathology resident's face. He looked at his junior resident and said, "Call Boris, tell him we have a John Doe."

Within five minutes a suspicious looking middle-aged man with a limp walked into the Pathology Department. Boris was known only as Boris. His nametag simply said "Boris". His job was to prepare the gift of life cadavers for the first year medical students each year. These cadavers would serve as anatomy specimens for the incoming class in September. He reeked of formaldehyde. Phil had never seen or heard of him before.

Boris slowly limped up to the dismembered body of Mr. Brown on the table and said, "Is this the John Doe?"

The pathology team informed him yes. Boris then walked over to a nearby phone and dialed the hospital operator, notifying her to send out a harvest team alert. He then limped back to the table with a sinister grin on his face, and waited.

What then transpired occurred approximately thirty times a year at the PGH. For whenever a legally identified John or Jane Doe expired, their body parts were coveted for institutional research. With this in mind, each surgical department designated a resident to carry a harvest team beeper. Their responsibility was to respond immediately to a harvest alert, and report to the pathology department. The terminology that "Boris has a fresh kill" was pervasive to the surgical residents throughout the PGH.

Within 30 minutes residents representing all departments began to congregate around the corpse of William Brown. A macabre scene soon unfolded in front of Phil Drummer.

A timid female ophthalmology resident appeared first. She coldly took a scalpel to Mr. Brown's eyes removing both eyeballs in the name of research. She quietly placed them in a small ice bag and left. A soon to arrive otolaryngologist resident removed both ears and the nose placing them in an ice cooler. A young dermatology resident then removed the body's scalp and fingernails. An obviously shaken neurosurgical resident beheaded the corpse in order to depart with the cervical spine from just below the skull to the upper back. Dental residents then took the skull and few remaining teeth. Phil stood in shock as Dr. O'Keefe appeared on behalf of the general surgery department. He took a portion of the small intestine and liver in a matter of fact fashion.

Last and most gruesome to the harvest was the orthopedic resident. A burly appearing young man named Lance appeared on the scene. He had large forearms that were covered in thick black hair down to his fingers. He wore surgical scrubs that were one size too small on him, which accentuated oversized biceps. A forest of hair growing on his back exposed itself on his nape, which was complimented by a unibrow. His job was to secure the extremities for research in the orthopedic department. Lance took a large hacksaw out of a side cabinet and began his work in an orderly like fashion. He instructed Phil to hold each extremity outward with a traction force. He then cut through the humerus bone several inches below the shoulder joint removing both arms. Attention was then paid to the lower extremities. Saw cuts were made through each femur several inches below the hip joints. The old hack saw labored as it loudly cut through each thighbone. After amputating each extremity the resident took the limbs to a side table. He made quick cuts below each elbow and knee joint. Lance then grinned while looking at a fresh set of elbows, hands, knees and ankles ready for the next research project. He quickly wrapped each body part in a plastic bag and then placed them in two large ice filled containers. The remains were destined for a larger cooler in the orthopedic department. Lance departed, leaving only Phil and Medical student Roden in the room.

Medical student Roden looked at Phil in disbelief and said, "I don't believe what I just saw." He stood frozen looking at Drummer. "Like buzzards on road kill."

Phil looked at the torso remains of a human being lying on a cold stainless steel table in front of him. "Neither do I," was his slow quiet response as he shook his head.

Both men were startled when Boris walked back into the room saying, "Help me get this body up to the crematory." Since no one else was around both Drummer and Roden obliged.

Phil then helped Boris lift the remaining stump of Willie Brown's body onto a small metal table with wheels. He was surprised as to how light the limbless and headless body was, while being awkward to lift. Boris covered the body and led the young men down a hall to a steel door that was labeled Crematorium. He then opened the door, which led into a large room with a few tables around the perimeter. Along the far wall was a sparkling clean steel furnace that was supported on four thick posts, having the distinct appearance of an oven in a pizzeria, being much wider than taller. A large exhaust vent exited the oven top while then turning right into the wall. A single handle ran horizontal along the front door of the oven. The door was built to open downward in a fashion like any residential oven.

Boris rolled the cart to the front of the oven and stopped. He then limped to the side of the furnace where a large red switch on the wall was located. Above the switch in bold red letters was emblazoned the word BURNER in capital letters. He then threw the switch firmly from the Off to On position. A power surge was felt in the room followed by a loud blowing noise in the crematory. He limped back to the rolling table on the opposite side of Phil and Roden to open the furnace door.

A blast of intense heat surged out of the furnace causing Phil to wince his eyes and step back. Phil then looked into the furnace and saw four bluish flames rushing out of each oven corner, as they then converged in the middle of the oven floor. The noise of the burners was overpowering making conversation difficult. Boris then signaled to lift the torso followed by a gesture to then place it in the oven. His helpers obliged and the remnant of Mr. William Brown was tossed into the midst of the inferno. Phil and Roden quickly stepped back from the heat. Boris then raised his right hand in appreciation of the help saying a loud thank you. His hand gesture essentially dismissed the services of Phil and medical student Roden, allowing them to step backwards.

For the next three minutes Phil watched Boris slowly rotate the burning torso with a long poker. There was a look of slight satisfaction on his face as he kept the lump of oven flesh spinning. The blue flames danced rapidly around the rotating stump while generating a stench that become overwhelming. The bodily remains of Mr. Brown then began to melt in front of the group, causing Phil and Roden to turn away in respect, and then leave the room.

Five minutes later Phil Drummer left the PGH having finished another overnight call shift. He did not stop down at the Polk Lounge to say goodnight. He needed fresh air. The quick exit outside the hospital confines felt good as he began the walk westward. His mind was trying to register what had just occurred over the past work shift. A collision of emotions swelled up inside him. He recalled the happy smile of Willie Brown calling Knight his "Messiah." He felt the crunch of Mr. Brown's ribs beneath his hands during the chaos of the code blue. Lastly he recoiled at the visual recall of the autopsy and subsequent dismemberment of a human body. He picked up his pace wanting to get away from the hospital quickly that evening.

Then, one block away from the hospital a strange thing occurred. Phil's olfactory senses appreciated a faint but acrid odor. He inhaled again appreciating the scent, now with a briny quality. He soon recognized this to be the vented exhaust smell of William Brown's cremated body. To the unsuspecting students amidst the campus the stench was imperceptible. To Dr. Drummer it was not. Phil appreciated the aroma for the next two blocks. During that time he felt a chill to the bone while reciting a prayer for the repose of William Brown's soul.

CHAPTER 11
The Chronicle

NEARLY THREE WEEKS after Mr. Brown's autopsy, a meeting occurred between The Philadelphia General Hospital and the Philadelphia Chronicle. The venue for the gathering was the classy Three Fives Restaurant. Located on 555 Locust Street the restaurant represented the avant-garde of North Italian cuisine. Originally owned by a chef with an inheritance from a Lusitania victim, it graciously served the well to do in Philadelphia for generations.

It was a warm September night as the parties involved each made their way to the quaint South Philadelphia lane. First to arrive was Doctor Michael Barnes. Doctor Barnes had completed his Wednesday office hours at 5 PM that evening. He then took advantage of the weather conditions and slowly walked downtown to the restaurant. His genetic make up compelled him to arrive twenty minutes early. As a host to many meetings at the eatery he was well known to the staff, who escorted him to a quiet private room on the second floor overlooking the historic street. Per routine they poured him a glass of room temperature spring water.

Ten minutes later marked the arrival of Howard Rineman. Mr. Rineman was the esteemed CEO of the

Philadelphia General Hospital system, having held that position for the past six years. It was a position that he coveted. He was raised in New York City attending the finest prep schools his family could afford. He then attended the University of Pennsylvania as an undergraduate. He completed his training with an MBA from Penn's Wharton School of Business. He relished his job as the kingpin of the largest employer in the Delaware Valley. A true socialite, he excelled in the public arena. His calendar of events featured a community get together nearly every night of the week.

Rineman was also well known at the Three Fives. He was politely greeted and escorted to the upstairs room where Barnes was waiting

"Howard, good to see you," said Barnes extending his hand and standing as Rineman entered. Barnes respected Rineman, always believing his decisions kept the welfare of the hospital staff in mind.

"Good evening Michael," responded Rineman as he shook hands. The two gentlemen then sat down. Without having to ask a young female waitress brought Rineman a glass of Bokma gin.

"Hard to believe it has been two years since the last review article," said Barnes while looking out the window at the historic street below.

"Time flies," said Rineman taking a sip of the gin. "Let's just hope the numbers are favorable again."

"I really don't approve of the emphasis placed on these mortality numbers," said Barnes. "The care of a cardiac patient is complex in nature and cannot be completed represented by a mortality percentage."

"I know," said Rineman. "However accountability and complete disclosure is the standard now. With the Cold War over the government has a surplus of workers sitting around and doing nothing on the taxpayer's dollar." Rineman paused to glance at an oil painting on the wall and then continued, "To justify paying these public servants, attention has focused on the nation's health care system. Once the government gets involved an avalanche of numbers, paperwork and standards follow."

Barnes continued to look out the window as he spoke, "Not like the good old days when a surgeon was a surgeon." He paused then spoke again while shaking his head, "Not a nervous Nellie worrying about his standard of care rankings."

"Ah the good old days," said Rineman. "The days when you and Dr. Knight could knock off a patient and tell the family their loved one just didn't make it," Rineman paused as he finished the gin. "We all miss the good old days."

"There was accountability back in the day," said Barnes turning his gaze back to Rineman. "But it was an internal accountability, within the department, among a surgeon's peers."

"Those days are long gone," said the CEO. "Every external force now demands data available for public consumption." Rineman paused as the waitress brought a tray of cheese. "Like it our not, standards of care must be documented, met or exceeded, and made available to all." He paused to sample some Gouda cheese before saying with a smile, "Hopefully to our advantage."

"It is going to be close this year," said Barnes. "Richard just had a peri-operative death. Per his calculations one or two more will tip the scales in the wrong direction."

"He says that every two years," said Rineman.

"I know, I know," replied Barnes. "Its probably a good idea we didn't invite him this year. He actually took it well."

"After our last meeting with the Chronicle it was a no brainer to leave him off the guest list," said Rineman with an agitated tone. "I mean the guy got drunk right at this very table and a bit ornery with the reporter."

"He is old school," said Barnes. "But a heck of a surgeon."

Rineman smiled in agreement and then asked, "Does he still have that young blonde filly in his stable of women?"

Barnes was impressed by the street lingo from the CEO. However, before he could respond, escorting steps were heard approaching the room. The maître d' was then heard giving a short history on the Three Fives. He soon entered the room with a somewhat disheveled looking middle-aged man. Upon their arrival both Dr. Barnes and Mr. Rineman arose.

Harold Rineman quickly stepped forward extending his hand to the final guest saying, "Mr. Russo, welcome, welcome."

Mr. Anthony Russo was old school. Old school South Philadelphia. He was 59 years of age and a product of first generation Italian immigrants. Italian was the only language spoken in his home growing up. Raised in South Philly he worked in the family bakery as a child. The bakery was located in the heart of the Italian Market on Ninth Street. He attended South Philadelphia High School where he developed a passion for ice hockey. Slight in stature, he used speed and determination to excel at the sport. He relished a good fight in the schoolyard or on the ice. He adored the Philadelphia Flyers and the Broad Street Bully teams of the 1970s. In 1976 his uncle, who happened to be politically connected, secured him a job with the Chronicle as a beat reporter. Since then he rose steadily up the ladder at the Chronicle despite its turbulent relationship with the city's political machine. In 2002 he was awarded an associate editor position, which he held ever since.

Mr. Russo never presented himself well. His hair was thick and wavy and never brushed in any direction. He abhorred fine clothing and physical fitness. He smoked cheap cigars and ate unhealthy foods. He enjoyed strip bars and the clientele that gathered there. He was out of context at the Three Fives when he approached his dinner mates.

"Harold," was the gritty response from the Philadelphia Chronicle's chief medical reporter. "Good to see you again, please, just call me Tony."

Rineman then reacquainted Anthony Russo with Dr. Barnes and the three gentlemen sat down. Niceties were exchanged as Tony Russo then began to run up a bar tab on the health care system's expense. Scotch was his poison. As dinner progressed the reason for their get together became the main topic.

"I can assure you gentlemen, that the report will be fair to all physicians and institutions involved," said Russo. He was enjoying a potato gnocchi entrée.

"Of course, of course," said Rineman. "We have always found your wording to be favorable to PGH." Rineman then paused while dabbing his lips with a napkin. He continued, "That's why we graciously contribute each year to your newspaper's charitable program for intercity kids. We consider it an honor."

Russo understood the comment. His chief editor informed him that the PGH Health Care System was the major contributor to their "Off the Street Program" for underprivileged Philadelphia youth. The medical system was also the top monetary provider to the paper for medical advertisements.

Barnes then spoke, "As usual we need to let the public be aware of the complexity of the cases at PGH. When the community hospitals in the suburbs run into trouble, they immediately ship their critically ill patient to PGH. We are the last stop."

"Of course, of course," said Russo with some pesto sauce on his chin. "But you have to understand that the other major medical centers in town also claim their cases are the most complex." He paused to digest and spoke again, "I met with the Temple boys last week and they said the same thing."

"We understand," said Rineman taking control of the conversation. "As the largest employer in the region we have a commitment to medical excellence. This commitment has been the gold standard for the area and we are confident the numbers will reflect that."

"Any idea how the numbers are looking?" said Russo in a matter of fact fashion.

"No," said Barnes. "We don't worry about them. They are what they are."

"How about Dr. Knight?" said Russo, now starting to stir the conversational pot.

"Dr. Knight is the premier cardiothoracic surgeon not only in Philadelphia, but on the eastern seaboard," said Rineman. "His only concern is each patient's well being, beyond that these numbers don't affect his actions." Rineman paused for credibility sake and then continued, "I can assure you of that."

"They say he is the best," replied Russo. "Always one of Philadelphia's Top Doctors mentioned in that rag of a magazine each year." Russo then finished off his dinner and rubbed his stomach while looking around the room. He then said, "Where is the good Dr. Knight this evening?"

Dr. Barnes went to speak but Rineman cut him off saying, "Prior commitment, but he does send his regards." The three men then smiled at each other.

"His regards," said Russo. "Two years ago at this very table he almost threw me out that window."

"A passionate man," replied Rineman quickly. "A very passionate man."

"That's what makes him so successful," said Barnes. "His passion for life and for the medical profession."

Russo shook his head to try and bring the nonsense to an end saying, "Listen men, this data I publish is available to the public on the internet. They are just too lazy to look it up. The Chronicle just pulls this public information together and publishes it in a fashion that the common man can read while taking his daily constitutional on the toilet. That's it. Its not rocket science, I'm not going to win a Pulitzer for this series."

"The usual timing for the article?" asked Rineman.

"Yep, early January," said Russo. "Possibly New Year's Day. Slow time of the year for news."

"Well we look forward to a well balanced article that accurately tells the region and nation who we are," said Barnes.

"Yes indeed," said Rineman. "An article that will allow both the Chronicle and PGH to continually benefit from the rewards of positive press."

Russo nodded back assuring his hosts of a fair worded report. He then ordered dessert and an expensive bottle of port wine for the group. Anthony Russo then enjoyed a premier cigar offered by the maître d' complements of the house. The group broke up at 9:30 PM. Russo then slowly walked south to a well-known Gentlemen's Club for additional entertainment. Rineman and Barnes headed towards Rittenhouse Square and public transportation.

"That went well," said Barnes as the couple walked through the square.

"Yea, but I don't trust the guy," replied Rineman. "I don't like our system's reputation riding on the wording of a cheesy alcoholic."

"It will be fine," said the trusting Barnes. "And the numbers do speak for themselves."

"Yea, its not like we can control them," replied Rineman while hailing a cab that transported them away from center city.

At that moment, approximately seventeen stories above Barnes and Rineman, sat Dr. Knight. He was visiting the apartment of Jennifer Ranier. It was of course the premier penthouse overlooking the park with a commanding view towards center city. Knight was sitting out on the patio sipping some vodka. Music of Alexander Borodin played softly overhead. It was a peaceful evening with a sky full of bright stars. A warm gentle breeze drifted across the spacious balcony.

Knight had bought the penthouse as a newlywed many years ago. He had strong emotional attachments to it. Ten years ago he and his wife moved several blocks away to Washington Square West. There they lived in a pricey federalist home with an adjacent garden. Mrs. Knight was claustrophobic and hated elevators. She required a home that offered her street access in a posh neighborhood.

Knight kept the penthouse as an investment, for years renting it out to foreign businessmen who appreciated excellence. Then, as his marriage turned into a working relationship, it served as an enticing perk to a string of bedmates. Jenna Ranier was the current concubine residing in the penthouse. She was the holder of the apartments longevity record, having resided there for four years.

Knight was brooding that evening. He was still recovering from the sudden death of his patient. He also was awaiting the final autopsy report from Dr. Falcon. Lastly, he was acutely aware of the fact that Rineman and Barnes were meeting the Chronicle representatives that evening. The fact that he was excluded from the gathering disturbed his psyche. Knight always wanted to be in control of the situation, whether in the O.R. or in his personal life.

He slowly sipped the vodka listening to the city hustle and bustle below. As a rule he only imbibed in spirits on an evening that preceded a nonsurgical day. Tomorrow's schedule did not involve any planned surgery. He sat in a comfortable oversized outdoor ottoman chair. It belonged to a set of furniture he and his wife bought specifically for the veranda. Surrounding the chair was a series of sofas and tables casually placed around a center coffee table. The area was lit by a series of LCD lights running along the floorboards. Some overhead lamps added to the soft ambience of the setting.

Knight was ruminating on the upcoming Chronicle article. Every two years he would become obsessed with his quality control numbers. He understood his place as the self-proclaimed premier cardiothoracic surgeon in the Philadelphia area. Hard work, surgical skills and self-promotion garnered the top spot. The importance placed on the upcoming article was paramount in his mind. An average, or above average ranking would keep him in the top spot. A below average mortality ranking would damage his practice. More importantly it would harm his reputation and ego.

Subconsciously the Chronicle article impacted his medical decisions and patient care. His medical staff micromanaged every patient with the specific goal of discharging a living human being. This was the only criteria for a successful outcome. Other complications such as a blood clot, infection or reoperation did not concern him. Dr. Knight's only conscious concern at the end of a calendar year was his mortality rate. If it was good, then he was a success.

That evening he and Ranier enjoyed a catered meal from a fine French restaurant on Rittenhouse Square. As a rule Jennifer Ranier was an incompetent chef. She fortunately made up for this culinary deficiency with a feminine prowess that captivated Knight. That evening she was mentally and physically prepared to pay her dues to the landlord. She wore her recently highlighted hair straight to the shoulder level with a soft part down the middle. Her skin was lightly tanned from the warm September sun. Sterling silver adorned her neck, wrists and right ankle. She wore a black pullover strap dress that accentuated her toned figure. High heels finished the package that was ready to be unwrapped. The couple had already enjoyed a full bottle of wine with dinner.

As Knight sat in his chair, Ms. Ranier slowly walked out to the balcony in a sultry fashion. She held a glass of wine in one hand as she sat on the sofa next to Knight. She had sensed his uneasiness over the past two weeks, which continued that evening.

"I love September nights," said Ranier. She slowly swept her hair back over one shoulder looking at Knight. Her eyes were welcoming and her lipstick sassy spice red.

Knight just stared forward over the balcony rail saying, "I wonder what those idiots talked about this evening." He was referring to the Rineman and Barnes meeting.

"I'm sure they discussed exactly what they told you," replied Ranier.

"I'm not sure," replied Knight still with a fixed gaze. "I know Barnes well, but I can't completely trust Rineman."

He paused to sip the vodka and continued, "He is just a puppet for that Board of Trustees. I know they hate me."

"No they don't," said Ranier quickly. "You are the main bread winner for the whole health system. The Trustees are only interested in the bottom line."

"I guess so," said Knight. "You know I just worry about this darn article coming out soon." Knight let out a sigh slowly shaking his head side to side. He looked down on the near empty glass of vodka. He slowly twirled the liquid in the glass. He let out another slow exhale.

Jennifer Ranier sensed her opening. She slowly stood up and finished her glass of wine. She walked up to Knight and leaned downwards placing both hands on his knees. As she drifted towards his face, the gentle breeze carried her perfume across his senses. She leaned forward permitting Knight a tantalizing view directly down her dress top. Knight gazed at the breast implants that he paid for three years earlier. He then thought of his wife implants, which she dubbed "the gift that keeps on giving." He wondered if her painting lessons were going well that evening. Knight then recognized Borodin's Nocturne playing over the sound system. It was a favorite of his. At that moment his mind was at a crossroad with his body.

Ranier leaned even more forward and kissed him on the forehead saying, "Lets see if we can put a smile on that face." Her hands then began a slow assault on the surgeon. Alcohol permeated her breath.

Knight's mind and body tried to ease up at the moment. They could not. Despite the combination of cologne, alcohol and willingness he couldn't submit to Ranier's passion. He slowly patted the hips of Ranier saying, "Not this evening." She persisted kissing his neck while pressing her body forward. He had to reiterate the order a second time calling off the attack. His body became rigid as he looked away from Ranier towards the sky. A somewhat rejected

Jennifer Ranier stepped backwards obeying the command. She ran her right hand through Knight's hair apologizing softly. She let out a pouting sigh and then turned away, walking across the balcony to calm her sensuality.

For the next hour some idle chatter occurred between the two. Knight apologized for his lack of interest that evening. He again voiced concern over the pending pathology report and the meeting that evening. At 11 P.M. he left the apartment and headed down to the street below. He gave warm regards to the doorman who respectfully bowed his head to Knight. A ten-minute walk brought him home to his Washington Square neighborhood. Upon entering the home his wife kissed him dutifully before rambling on about her painting lessons. She asked him how the dinner went with the Philadelphia Chronicle reporter. He described to her the meeting in detailed fashion.

Later that evening Dr. Knight went into his study. A message on his answering machine filled him in on the successful meeting with the Chronicle. Dr. Barnes in grand fashion explained to him that a successful outcome was brokered with the medical editor of the paper. He used the term "win – win situation" twice in the message. Knight's spirits improved somewhat.

Then Dr. Knight looked across the study at his fax machine. A message light alerted him to a recent fax. He pulled the paper off the machine noting it to be the final pathology report from Dr. Jane Falcon. He quickly scanned the report noting a description of the surgical vein grafts being secure and intact. Microscopic sections of the heart failed to identify a heart attack occurring. All components of his surgical intervention were normal. The final cause of death was noted to be cardiopulmonary failure complicated by emphysema and liver cirrhosis. He was pleased with the generic terminology and text wording. His spirits improved even more so.

The evening was late and the suddenly inspired Dr. Knight had a choice to make. His final decision was one of a logistical nature. It was a bit too late to walk across town again and his wife was nearby. He therefore quickly went upstairs to find her reading comfortably in bed. She immediately sensed a prowess in his movement as he prepared for bed. He was uncharacteristically talkative in nature. It was soon obvious what he had in mind. Mrs. Knight felt it very uncharacteristic of him on a weekday night. A strong smell of vodka predicated physical contact. She initially rejected his advance, not being in any frame of mind to proceed. However, as usual, she ultimately submitted her will to the unyielding Dr. Knight.

At that very moment Jenna Ranier sat alone on her balcony. The Russian music had been turned off and the city was now quiet below. She was sipping yet another glass of wine. Her blood alcohol level was high and by definition she was legally drunk in the state of Pennsylvania. Her body had calmed down somewhat but her mind began to wander.

Over the past year she began to question her relationship with Knight. The physical novelty had worn off a year or two ago. Job security and material goods now kept their relationship afloat. She tried to feel happy but couldn't grasp any concept of a secure future. A collision of thoughts ran through her mind. She hated classical Russian music, but treasured her penthouse apartment and Mercedes coupe. She despised an inability to display public affection, but cherished her Victoria's Secret credit card. She loathed the gossip behind her back, but adored the Jersey shore beach house.

Then a recurring single word entered her head. That word was mistress. Her subconscious preferred that definition as opposed to prostitute. She was Dr. Knight's mistress and was growing tired of it. The question was where to go next. There was no Plan B in her mind. She needed a Plan B.

Jennifer Ranier then picked up her phone to check for any messages. Outside of the social work girls, she had only a few friends who were mostly married and starting families of their own. Her inbox was empty. She gently held the phone to her lips while tapping the screen with her manicured fingernails. A bold thought struck her. She pondered the idea and suddenly felt like a high school freshman sitting next to the star quarterback in study hall.

Ranier then rapidly typed in a text message on her phone. She wondered whether or not to forward the notation pausing only briefly, until the alcohol in her system helped depress the send button. She leaned backwards and waited, looking upwards into the sky. A smile came upon her lips.

Her message immediately converted to a radio wave and found a local control channel. A quick cell tower relay sent the short message to the recipients enabled cell phone. In a second the transmission crossed the Schuylkill River heading into West Philadelphia. It penetrated the walls of the PGH and found the Polk Lounge with ease. A phone lying on a couch gently delivered a soft tone. A tired Phil Drummer looked down at the phone and then picked it up. He had just finished in the O.R. and was enjoying a piece of cold pizza left over from Polk's dinner. Polk was sound asleep next to him. It was midnight.

Drummer looked at the phone number listed but did not recognize it. He thought it would be another resident asking him to do work. He clicked the OK button to view the text. The message read, "What are you doing tonight? - Jenna". Phil then squinted his eyes again at the phone believing he had misread it. His eyesight was correct. He looked up to see if anyone was playing a joke on him. No one else was near. The room was quiet except for a soft snore from Polk.

Phil picked up the phone and without any further thought typed back, "On call, busy night, why?"

Within 30 seconds Ranier texted back, "Just wondering, thought we could go out for a few drinks."

Phil didn't respond thinking the request was a bit strange so late at night. His phone purred again with a message saying, "How about another night?"

"Sure," was Phil's response.

Jennifer Ranier then typed back a final text saying, "Great, good night." She then shut off her phone and headed back inside, falling asleep quickly that night, with a warm feeling inside her.

Phil put down the phone again not truly believing what had just occurred. He waited for a prank crew to bust through the door laughing aloud. No one entered the lounge. He stared at the phone but no other messages came across. Fatigue settled in as he reclined on the couch while pulling a hospital sheet over his body. He looked at Polk and recalled his bold end of the year prediction regarding him and Ranier. Phil Drummer then soon fell asleep, being completely unaware of his role in Jennifer Ranier's Plan B, which had just begun.

CHAPTER 12
September

SEPTEMBER WAS JENNIFER Ranier's favorite month. She was born in September being the third child of a marriage that was starting to fail. Raised in Baltimore, she grew up in her father's house after his divorce. Their favorite pastime together was watching the Baltimore Orioles play at Camden Yards. The family had season tickets down the third baseline just under the mezzanine section. She once caught a foul ball hit off the bat of Cal Ripken, only to have it chewed to pieces by her dog Earl two months later. Having two older brothers and no sisters, she grew up playing neighborhood sports with the boys. Athletically she was able to run, throw and hit better than the majority of them. Her teammates called her Blondie. Jennifer Ranier was in all aspects a tomboy.

Her high school years brought about a tremendous physical transformation. She retained her father's tall stature yet developed her mother's curvaceous figure. The combination garnered plenty of attention from the upperclassmen. Always the coveted prom date, she deftly handled her beaus one after the other. Her promiscuity led to a dalliance with a young male gym teacher, leading to his dismissal. It was well known throughout her neighborhood that Ms. Ranier enjoyed high school to the fullest.

She shared her parents' intelligence. Always on the honor roll she once thought of being a physician. She entered Villanova as a pre-med major but partied just a bit too hard. By sophomore year an academic counselor steered her into the physician assistant program where she excelled. She possessed an uncanny ability to put a patient at ease. She graduated with honors and was quickly hired by the Philadelphia General Hospital system.

For three years she worked with the Obstetrics team at PGH. However she soon grew tired of childbirth and caring for women exclusively. Her next stop was with the Plastic Surgery department, where she excelled in a field that promoted beauty in everything about itself. However a late evening rendezvous with the newly appointed chairman led to her quiet dismissal. Her next stop was with the General Surgery department where, within three years, she was under the umbrella coverage of Dr. Richard Knight. During this time her social deftness withered away in Knight's orderly microcosm, as she became progressively isolated in his clandestine and materialistic world.

Regardless she always thought September in Philadelphia to be beautiful. The oppressive summer heat was replaced with a warm and soothing sun. The nights became slightly cooler and the change invigorated the city. All the universities came back in session and the populace swelled with youth and enthusiasm. Leaves changed colors and local football teams filled the stadiums. Her birthday was on the last day of the month.

September also marked a confident time at the PGH. Phil Drummer and his fellow interns had settled into a comfortable routine. Having two months of experience under their belts, the four young physicians each began to develop some individual swagger. Phil and Cathy exhibited a quiet confidence in their attitude, while intern Fred Riles personified a nervous and forced assurance. Most notable was the fanfare being generated around Rick Polk, who effortlessly developed somewhat of a cult following at the PGH. He soon began answering to the monikers of King Richard, President Polk and the Lounge Lizard. An early evening in mid September found all four interns uncharacteristically assembled in his self proclaimed Polk Lounge.

"If I knew so many people were coming over I would have cleaned up a bit," said a sarcastic Polk. He was sitting in his recliner chair watching the original M.A.S.H. movie on TV.

"Does the administration know that you actually live here?" asked Fred Riles.

"No, but once they get the room service bill they will," replied Polk. He was off call and sipping a gin martini in an attempt to recreate the M.A.S.H. setting.

"How about we call this place The Swamp," said Cathy Finley as she watched the film also. "That's what Hawkeye called his surgical tent in the movie."

"I'll pretend I didn't hear that," said Polk. "The sign on the door says The Polk Lounge."

"My dad called it The Hole," said Riles. "Its been called The Hole for generations." Riles was turning the pages of a magazine while ignoring the movie of the week. "I think we should call it The Hole."

Polk slowly looked at Riles with a sneer. He then looked at Phil with a slow shake of his head. His right hand turned the volume up a bit on the remote control.

Drummer then spoke changing the subject, "Hard to believe we all switch rotations in two weeks." He paused and then looked up towards the ceiling with wonderment on his face stating, "Now lets see, who is the lucky one going onto the CT team?"

"I'm not afraid of CT," said Polk immediately. He finished off the first martini sucking on the olive. "Me and old man Knight are going to hit it off well."

"I'm not looking forward to trauma," whimpered Riles. "I can't believe I have to sleep in this place every third night." He paused looking around and then said, "For goodness sake there is underwear lying all around."

"Its clean," said Polk referring to his boxer shorts which were stacked up next to Riles. "I do my laundry once a week down in the laundry service department. Good group of guys down there."

"You really do live here?" asked Cathy shaking her head in amazement.

"Why wouldn't you," replied Polk. "The laundry is free and the cafeteria is just upstairs. Every day the bathroom is cleaned and the bed sheets are changed." He paused to get up and mix another drink. He then continued saying, "And you can't beat the commute."

The group burst out laughing except for Riles, who had an annoyed look on his face.

"I'm looking forward to the specials rotation," said Cathy Finley. "Get to sleep home every night for three months." She had a smile on her face looking at Polk. "I'll be checking out of this roach motel you are running Mr. Polk."

"The change will be good," said Phil. "Its time for a switch. CT is starting to get old."

"You bet its time for a change," said Polk with a smirk of bravado. "Time for me to take a crack at climbing Mount Ranier." Polk then put a handful of cheese crackers in his mouth. The group waited for him to digest. He then continued, "Once I flex these guns in front of her its all over." He was pointing to his somewhat flabby biceps muscle.

Phil didn't comment, waiting for someone else to speak. No one did. Rumors were starting to slowly spread through the hospital system regarding Dr. Knights's P.A. and a certain tall, good-looking intern. One week ago Ranier appeared unannounced in the cafeteria and had lunch with a tired post call Phil. Three days ago she just happened to leave the hospital at the same time that Phil was walking home. She claimed to have had business at the bookstore and slowly accompanied Phil on a walk through the campus. It seemed like everything they did together, although innocent, went noticed.

Phil also felt a closer physical presence from Ranier. During each surgical case her body was ever so nearer to his. At times she would lean into him while holding a retractor forcing contact that he couldn't dismiss. Her gaze over the surgical mask frequently caught his and she then held it in an inviting way. He loved her icy blue eyes. She was good at what she did and Phil certainly made no effort to deter this closeness. They both sensed a forward motion that would ultimately bring them together. Of course there was only one big problem, that being Dr. Richard Knight.

"Wow, this is a classic movie," said Polk sensing the uneasiness. "How about that nurse they call Hot Lips in this movie, does she remind you of someone?"

"All right knock it off," said Phil. "There is nothing going on between us." He looked around the room realizing that Polk and Finley were staring at him with a sly smile. Intern Riles looked up from his magazine with a bemused look. Phil continued, "Do you think I'm nuts enough to head down that avenue?"

"I would think not," said intern Finley with a look on her face expecting an agreeing response from Phil.

"The flesh is weak," chimed in Polk. "The flesh is weak."

"I haven't heard anything," said Fred Riles. "What are you all talking about?"

"So I talked to the girl a few times," said Phil. "What's the big deal? She is actually very nice, originally from Baltimore."

"Where will you be honeymooning?" said Polk.

"I love Baltimore," said Finley joining in on the fun, "I hope it's a spring affair. I just love spring weddings."

Drummer gave up and just shook his head. He was quite aware of the great relationship that was formed with Cathy and Rick over the past three months. Each fellow intern worked hard and didn't complain. All three helped each other both physically and emotionally through the first quarter of the internship. Phil knew he was lucky to have them by his side for the next several years. He then looked at Riles and sighed. The first three months of Fred Riles' internship went as expected. His demeanor did not sit well with the upper level residents. His constant reference to his father and the good old days of the PGH didn't help matters. Having started on the specials rotation he didn't have to take call for the first three months. His smug mannerism while heading home every evening just made his perceived persona worse. Riles was not making any friends at PGH and Phil recognized it as an instant replay of his medical school days.

"Oh it's the "Pros from Dover" scene," yelled Polk while looking at the television. "This is my favorite scene."

"I'm going to call you two the Pros from West Philly," said Finley referring to Drs. Polk and Drummer. "The Pros from West Philly."

"Listen up, here is where the nurse calls the surgeons hoodlums," said an excited Polk pointing at the screen.

"What are you talking about?" asked an increasingly bewildered Riles. He had never watched the original M.A.S.H. movie from 1970.

"I like that moniker," said Polk with a proud look on his face. He ignored Riles and continued speaking while sipping his martini, "The Pros from West Philly." He looked at Phil with a smile and raised his glass in salute.

Movie night in the Polk Lounge continued. Phil had a martini since Cathy Finley was on call that night. Each intern settled into a comfortable seat enjoying the flick. Frederick Riles had to drive home and departed shortly after. Phil was so comfortable after the martini that he decided to spend the night there. The three interns spent a relaxing evening together in the Polk Lounge. Finley's call night was quiet and they all slept well through the night, peaceful within the confines of the PGH.

The following two weeks of September were uneventful at the PGH. Before Phil knew it he awoke on the final Friday of his CT rotation. No surgery was scheduled that day and he wasn't on call that evening. Dr. Drummer was in a great mood as he left the Greycliff Apartment complex.

Upon exiting his room he turned left towards the elevators. Immediately walking towards him was floor mate Maria Cruz. A short, handsome man walked next to her carrying a suitcase. He has about two inches shorter that Maria and had a smile on his face.

"Phil," said Maria happily as the group stopped in front of each other. "I would like you to meet Ralf, my good friend from Chicago." Maria stuttered somewhat over the wording of good friend.

The two men shook hands with Phil saying, "Please to meet you Ralph."

"That's Ralf," said the smiling young man with a Teutonic accent. He firmly shook Phil's hand then saying, "A pleasure to meet you Phil." His enunciation was excellent.

"Ralf just took an internship downtown and will be spending the next three months here," said a smiling Cruz.

Phil looked back at her nodding his head with a smile. He couldn't believe how beautiful Maria looked that early in the morning.

"Just got into town on the red eye," was her next line.

"Welcome to Philadelphia," said Phil.

An uncomfortable two seconds then passed between the three without a word being said. The men shook their heads up and down at each other with a smile. Phil then looked at Maria realizing the awkwardness in her position. Ralf was obviously her frequently mentioned boyfriend from Chicago.

"Well enjoy your stay," stammered Phil. "Have a good stay," was his next line as he headed toward the elevator.

"So long," said the couple in unison while turning away to head down the hallway.

Phil gathered his social composure while riding the elevator down to the lobby, realizing that his increasingly frequent visits to Maria's apartment would have to cease. He thought it peculiar that she never mentioned the possibility of her Ralf coming to Philadelphia. The implications of their impromptu meeting occupied his mind during the walk to PGH.

Hospital rounds that morning were festive in nature. The CT team assuredly saw every patient with a happy grin. Medical students Roden and Bankart deftly side-stepped the pulling of chest tubes while Phil was quick to the dressing bucket and stethoscope. Chief Resident Larson even took the time to point out some clinical teaching points to the medical students. Upon exiting their last patient room on the seventh floor they ran directly into a group of medical interns rounding.

"Look," said Larson, "They haven't moved in three months." The medical interns sneered in return having heard the comment.

"To the steps," said Phil. The team then raced down the hall to the stairwell. They rapidly descended several flights of stairs arriving in the cafeteria.

"Widow makers for everyone," said Chief Resident Larson upon entering the cafeteria. "It's on me," was his next comment.

The excitable team stepped up to the cafeteria line where Cookie was working behind the counter.

"Four widow makers," said Phil smiling at Cookie.

"Four widow makers coming up," said Cookie just as excited. He then turned to the grill and rapidly mixed some pre-made egg batter with onions, cheese, mushrooms and bacon bits. The concoction was then placed in a series of preheated omelet pans. Cookie moved quickly and whistled all the while. In the middle of the preparation he sang out a brief song to the attentive crowd. He turned and smiled at the team after the ditty. It was his signature tune from an old jazz album. Phil clapped in appreciation as the dietary worker placed four cholesterol packed omelets, better know as widow makers, in front of the team.

Everyone enjoyed the victory breakfast that morning. The surgical team relived the high and low points of their three-month rotation with gusto. Even medical student Bankart had a smile on her face when Phil described Knight tossing her cell phone across the room in a rage.

"Only one fatality," said Dr. Larson on a more somber note.

"Yea, that was sad," said Phil. "Old Willie seemed like a nice man."

A moment of silent respect passed before medical student Roden spoke. "I still can't believe that autopsy," was his comment shaking his head. "Gives me nightmares."

"I still can smell that horrible stench," said Phil only then recalling that Melissa Bankart had passed out during the autopsy.

"Let's be thankful it was only one," said Larson. Knight took that one kind of hard. "Overall it was a fine three months and everyone here will get my highest recommendation."

"Thank you," said the students in reply.

Larson then directed the team to lay low that morning. Some menial tasks were given to the students. He noted that ICU rounds that afternoon would be earlier than usual at 2 PM. Dr. Knight was heading out of town for the weekend and had to get to the airport. The joyous team then departed ways for the rest of the morning.

At exactly 2 PM Dr. Knight strolled down the long hallway to the surgical ICU. In stride with him was Jennifer Ranier who was dressed to the nines. She had on a tight black skirt and an off white satin blouse with the top two buttons undone. Black stiletto heels complemented the ensemble. Her hair was in a tight bun and she wore a set of black fashion glasses. Atop this outfit was a starched and spotless white lab coat that allowed only her legs to appear below the hem. Her appearance was show stopping to all in the ICU.

"Good morning team," said Knight obviously in good spirits with his exceptional arm candy in tow. "I believe Mr. Charles is the only patient remaining in the unit."

"Yes," said Larson. "Doing well, his incision looks good and he is tolerating foods well. Should be leaving the unit this evening."

"Very good," said Knight leading the team into Mr. Charles' room.

Upon entering the room Dr. Knight's V.I.P. personality went into high gear. "Brett good afternoon," was his vociferous hello to the patient.

"Richard, good to see you," was the patient's response. He extended his hand to Knight who shook it.

Knight smiled as he shook the hand of Brett Charles. Mr. Charles was the partner of a well-known investment firm in Philadelphia. He handled several of Knight's portfolio accounts with much appreciated success. Like Knight he enjoyed Porsches. It was obvious to the team that he also enjoyed young women. While shaking Knight's hand his gaze couldn't help but wander upon the voluptuous assistant standing beside him.

"P.A. Ranier, so good to see you again," was his next comment. He extended his hand, which Ranier shook.

"Everything looks well," said Knight. "Should be out of this unit later on today."

"Great," said Mr. Charles while still gazing at Ranier and holding her hand.

"I'll be gone this weekend but Dr. Larson here will keep a close eye on you." He turned to Larson while still speaking to the patient, "He will give you all the personal attention you need."

"Why thank you Richard," said the patient. "I feel great. Not bad for a 60 year old," was his next comment to the team.

At that moment nurse Cruise entered the room quietly. As the patient-physician conversation continued she approached the IV pole standing beside the patient's bed.

She took off the old IV bag, which was depleted. She then quickly scanned a new bag of IV fluid and hung it up. She opened the fluid valve and left the room.

Knight was wrapping up his dialogue and took a quick look at the IV bag. His motion was merely for show to instill more confidence in his broker.

"Normal saline with a little potassium," said Larson at that moment. "His K is running a bit low," was his next line.

Knight looked back at Larson and paused for effect, "Excellent Dr. Larson, I agree." He slowly nodded his head in approval.

Mr. Charles extended a warm thank you to everyone for their fine care and attention to detail, especially P.A. Ranier. Dr. Knight and his entourage then left the room, as the surgical team gathered for one last time at the ICU nursing station.

"I'll be out of town through Monday morning," said Knight to Larson. "I expect you to keep things tight," was his final comment before leaving. He then failed to thank Phil and the students for three months of hard work, only to rapidly disappear down the hall with Ranier at his side.

"Where's he headed?" said Phil to Pete Larson.

"L.A. for a conference," was his reply. Larson then looked at Phil and the students in front of him saying, "Good job team, until we meet again." He then turned and departed down the hallway. The surgical team then fully dispersed in anticlimactic fashion, committing their months of work to a memory.

Phil left the PGH early that afternoon. He had a quick dinner with Jim Turner who already knew about Maria Cruz's significant other moving onto the floor. The two then traveled to South Philadelphia to watch a Flyers pre-season hockey game.

Dr. Knight's flight was direct from Philadelphia to Los Angeles International Airport. He was traveling alone and enjoyed both a first class nip of vodka and the young perky flight attendant catering to him throughout the flight. He arrived in Los Angeles at 6:30 PM west coast time, feeling uncharacteristically refreshed from the cross-country flight. Upon exiting the ramp an attendant notified him of an urgent call awaiting him.

Knight quickly went to the phone thinking of his wife and her plans for the weekend, which in no way he could recall. A picture of his frail father entered into his mind, as did the last time he saw him months ago. Upon picking up the phone he immediately recognized the shaken voice of Dr. Barnes, who informed him of the unexpected death of Mr. Brett Charles. His subsequent words of consolation didn't register in Knight's mind, as he hung up the phone some three thousand miles away.

CHAPTER 13
Birthday Surprise

THE FIRST SATURDAY of October was sunny and cool in the city. The crisp autumn air was a welcome to all after a long hot summer. Two days earlier Jennifer Ranier turned 33 years old. She celebrated her birthday that day with a visit from her dad and brother, while enjoying a quiet dinner at a local pub. As usual Jennifer had to carefully discuss her social status with the family. Explaining a penthouse apartment and Mercedes Benz was never an easy task. Her father and brother suspected a wealthy companion but played along to keep the peace. They were well aware of Jennifer's historical penchant for relationship intricacy.

Her birthday evening was lonely. After dinner she returned to her apartment and called a few out of town friends. That night found Dr. Knight at a fund raising dinner for the Pennsylvania Academy of Music. The gala was a formal tuxedo and evening gown celebration and included a premier performance of the Russian Ballet Company in the United States that year. Stravinsky's *Rite of Spring* was the feature attraction. Knight certainly couldn't miss this event since he was on the Academy's board of trustees. Ranier knew quite well that a major social function involving Knight and his wife was impregnable. She hated those nights the most.

The only thing Ranier could do that evening was plan. She knew that Knight was leaving the following afternoon for California. Therefore the weekend was free and she declared it her personal birthday celebration. Already in place was a Saturday shopping spree with her two best local girlfriends, Stacey Rickett and Laura Jones, employees of the PGH social services department. They befriended Jennifer upon her arrival to the PGH several years ago. Each girl was single and several years younger than Ranier. All three women enjoyed shopping, followed by dinner and a good night out on the town. It was understood that the financial cost of the junket would be on the tab of the removed Dr. Knight, a perk well appreciated by two girls on a social worker's salary. The Saturday blowout was then followed by plans for a Sunday trip north. The fall foliage was starting to peak and the girls were planning a trip to the bucolic town of Jim Thorpe. More shopping was scheduled, as was a wellness visit to a local spa with a Zen aura. All in all the weekend program personified the adage that when the cat is away, the mice will play.

The only ingredient missing in Ranier's birthday recipe was a male companion. This essential element represented the crux of all the weekend festivities. It was the sine quo non of a successful birthday jubilee. Jennifer Ranier knew that Phil Drummer was that essential ingredient. The question was how difficult would it be to complete the formula? Ranier knew that the groundwork had been laid for a relationship over the past few months. Her contacts with Phil were precise and well calculated. The rumors that followed were expected and part of the whole approach. Most important to the equation was the fact that a reciprocal vibe was appreciated from the young intern.

The question in Ranier's mind wasn't if a dalliance was going occur, rather it was when.

Ranier however knew she was heading out of her safe harbor and into uncharted waters. If her imagined relationship progressed forward in any capacity it would mark the ruin of her lifestyle. Dr. Knight was a man of quick and definite action. Over the years a no tolerance policy was made clear to her with regards to other men. Knight was obsessed with control, possession and dominance. No other competitor was allowed into the arena. On the other hand she did realize that their relationship was growing stale. She couldn't imagine a happily ever after ending to the story between them. Knight was socially committed to his wife despite his documented track record outside the boundaries of marriage. Ranier had tolerated the circumstances for four years to date. It was a time for change and she knew the change would be quick and ugly. She was mentally prepared to move forward despite the expected consequences.

That Saturday morning she confidently picked up her cell phone and called Phil Drummer. Phil had just come back to his apartment from a jog. He ran alone that morning having lost his Brazilian beauty to her boyfriend. He had just exited the shower when his cell phone rang. Running out to his bedroom with only a towel around his waist, he glanced at the cell number realizing it was Ranier calling. He paused a second, then took a deep breath and answered the phone. Phil was also acutely aware of the fact that he was heading into unchartered territory with Ranier.

"Hey, what are you up to?" asked Ranier.

"Just finished a run," replied Phil. "To what do I owe this pleasure?"

"Oh just planning out the day," said Ranier. "I'm having a little birthday celebration with the social work girls tonight, thought you may want to join us."

"Who is having a birthday?" asked Phil in jest.

"You're talking to the birthday girl," said Ranier quite aware of the ploy.

"Wow, so you can legally drink now," said Phil.

"I've been legally drinking for a long time," said a laughing Ranier.

Their conversation then outlined her plans for some shopping and dinner with the social workers. She then mentioned some late night drinks at a downtown bar. An open invitation was given for Phil and whoever accompanied him to join the party.

"Sounds great," said Phil. "My only problem is the Special Olympics program today at Franklin Field. I've been a volunteer at the event every year through med school and I'm trying to continue the tradition."

"No problem," said Ranier with some disappointment in her voice. "How late does the event run?"

"The track events are into the late afternoon. This year we are having an evening banquet to hand out the awards. Probably run until about 9 PM."

Ranier let out a slow sigh accompanied by an "O.K., no problem." She then regrouped and continued, "Well you know where to find us in case you get out early. It would be great to have a few drinks with you. It would make the birthday celebration complete."

The conversation then ended with Phil giving the birthday girl some hope of showing up, depending on how late the event ran that evening. He then ended the call and returned to his morning routine. The phrase of "making the birthday celebration complete" reverberated in his mind.

By noontime that Saturday Phil was having lunch with Jim Turner and reliving the highlights of his cardiothoracic rotation. Turner was shocked by the description of the Willie Brown autopsy. He sat amazed listening to the tales of Dr. Knight and his cabbage patch. During this conversation Phil mentioned Jennifer Ranier's birthday and asked Turner if he wanted to accompany him to the get together. Turner declined keeping in line with his low social profile. Turner was a studying machine and usually hit the books every night of the week. He studied with a single desk lamp on and the remainder of his apartment dark. His desk seat would look over the inner courtyard of the Greycliff. Across the street was a park where locals frequently walked their dogs. Turner loved the view, keeping a pair of binoculars on the windowsill to keep tabs on the park regulars.

After Phil wrapped up his summary of the strange and unusual, Turner took his turn. "I was on call last night," said Turner. "Wait till you hear this story."

"Go ahead," said Phil. "Did it involve an exotic animal?" Drummer enjoyed his on call stories regarding unusual pets such as snakes, ferrets or iguanas. He was amazed at the breadth of knowledge that a vet student had to have.

"A lady calls frantic in the morning saying she was going on vacation and late to catch a plane."

"Yea," said Phil.

"She lays all of her medications out for that morning but in a rush accidentally gives her medications to the dog," said Turner with an amazed look on his face. "She then takes the dog medications for herself only then realizing that the pills didn't taste well and were too large."

"Whoa," said Phil. "Did they survive?"

"Yea. The dog got a bit lethargic but made it through the morning. The lady didn't care about her health as much as she did about the dog. She ended up missing the plane."

"What did you recommend she do?" asked Drummer.

"I told her to drink a lot of water, enjoy a biscuit for lunch and have her husband brush her coat three times a day," said Turner bursting out into laughter.

Phil enjoyed the story and as usual had his tales of medical wonders trumped by the vet student. It was obvious that Jim Turner loved the field of Veterinary Medicine. The goal of returning to central Pennsylvania and caring for the local cattle herds was his sole purpose. Phil knew that Turner would graduate high in his class and return home a hero to the tight knit farm community.

At 2 PM that Saturday Phil volunteered at Franklin Field for the Special Olympics. An awards dinner then commenced in the adjacent field house at 6 PM. The dinner and awards were over at 8 PM when Phil stepped out into the crisp October evening. The cool air felt good on his skin as he stepped towards the intersection outside of the stadium. Then, while standing at the corner of 34th and University Avenue, he became acutely aware of being at a true personal crossroad.

Looking to the left he saw University Avenue cross over the Schuylkill River and run into a brightly lit center city. He knew that Ranier and her troop were downtown at that moment getting ginned up at a local bar. Then he looked right towards West Philadelphia. Shining bright was the entrance to the PGH with the usual hustle and bustle out front. Past the PGH lay darkness and a quiet Penn campus leading to the Greycliff complex. Into Phil's mind a picture of Jenna Ranier flashed as she held a vodka martini wearing a sultry outfit. She looked fantastic and was poised for the taking. Suddenly this vision was replaced by a chilling image of Dr. Richard Knight. Behind him stood Chairman Barnes, both men had a stern and reprehensible look upon their face. They stood staring at Phil with their arms held across their chest. Phil feared for his medical career at that moment realizing that either man could end his internship. Phil then slowly asked himself what would his father do in this situation, realizing that this approach never failed him in a decisive pinch. The answer became obvious as a city cab suddenly sped by Drummer blowing his horn with a frightful shrill, jolting him out of his dream world. He then shook his head in an understanding and positive way and while taking a deep breath, crossed University Avenue and turned right towards home.

Phil Drummer then walked towards the PGH. Near the entrance he decided to visit the Polk Lounge. The evening was still early and he knew nothing exciting was happening back home. Perhaps Rick Polk was showing a movie that evening. Upon entering the hospital he maneuvered towards a side stairwell that took him downstairs to Polk's private lair. Halfway down the stairs he ran into a frantic and quick moving chief resident Larson, who was heading in the opposite direction.

"What's up," asked Phil.

"A lot," said Larson stopping to speak. "Knight is on the warpath."

"Why?" asked Drummer.

"Why?" said Larson raising his eyebrows, "Tell me you haven't heard of his broker's death?"

"What!" said a surprised Phil. "The guy we saw in the SICU on Friday?"

"Yep, he coded about two hours later without warning. Just flipped into a V-tach." Larson just stared over Phil's shoulder shaking his head. "Now Knight wants me staying in the hospital all weekend to keep an eye on his step down unit patients."

"Oh my God," said Phil. "Mr. Charles seemed like he was doing great."

"Yea, that's two in a row for Knight. I'm glad to be off the rotation next week. I pity the chief resident heading onto the CT rotation."

Phil immediately thought of Rick Polk who was scheduled to start CT that Monday.

"Knight's calling me every two hours from L.A.," said Larson. "The guy is freaking out. I wasn't even in the hospital at the time." The two house officers then stared at each other, each shaking their head in disbelief. "Got to go," said Larson who then bolted past Phil heading up the stairs.

"Wait, Pete!" yelled Drummer. "Was there an autopsy?"

"Yea," cried out Dr. Larson as he continued his run up the stairs. "This morning, you missed it."

Phil stood in his place for several seconds trying to digest the info he had just received. He only knew Mr. Charles for a brief period of time but felt a sorry for his demise. He thought of Knight and then Ranier, who was obviously unaware of the death at the time of their last phone call. Oblivious to his movements he continued walking down the stairwell on a path towards the Polk Lounge.

Rick Polk indeed was at home as The Good, The Bad and The Ugly premiered in the Lounge that evening. Phil Drummer walked into the movie about half way through the flick. No other residents were at the showing.

"Of course I knew of his death," said Polk in response to Phil's news. "I live here. I went to the code. What type of citizen do you think I am?"

"Was the guy alive when you got there?" asked Phil.

"No, dead as a doornail. Just like the last code." said Polk.

The two interns then talked about the rotation changes that coming Monday. Rick Polk expressed no fear whatsoever of joining the CT team. Grandiose talk about pitching a perfect game for three months emanated from his mouth. Polk did not fear Knight, and Drummer voiced qualms for his fellow intern's well being.

At approximately 10 PM the door opened to the Lounge. A defeated Frederick Riles entered. It was his first night of call in the hospital. Phil thought he saw a tear in his eye, which Riles wiped quickly away upon entering. Riles' body language suggested a beat down that was occurring that evening. Even more concerning to Phil was the fact that Polk didn't say anything to fellow intern Riles. It was as if he was aware of an ongoing tragedy.

"Hey Fred, how's it going?" asked Phil.

"Don't ask, I'm getting killed," replied Frederick Riles. "I've gotten two hits already and haven't eaten dinner yet. Now they want me in the O.R. for the next three hours." Riles rummaged through a gym bag looking for something while he spoke.

"Sounds bad," said Phil.

"The worst," said Riles. "I hate the junior resident with me on this rotation. I'm not even going to mention his name." His voice crackled as he spoke.

"Take a day at a time," said Phil trying to console Riles and his ever-present black cloud of call.

"Don't let him get to you," said Polk in an attempt to initiate camaraderie with Riles.

"I won't," said a shaken Riles as he headed towards the door. "But I don't know how I'm going to last three months."

"I'll leave the light on," quipped Polk as the door slammed behind intern Riles. Phil and Polk then gave Fred Riles a fifty-fifty chance of making it through the remainder of the internship that year.

The premier of The Good, The Bad and The Ugly finished at about 10:30 PM that night. The two surgical interns watched some ESPN together and then called it a night at about 11:30. Phil then headed home walking slowly through the Penn campus. Some parties were still going on in the fraternity houses prompting Phil to recall his college days with a smile. He arrived home at about midnight and popped open a beer to watch the late night talk shows. Then, at one o'clock in the morning, he heard a thud at his door followed by a knock. Some loud conversation was going on in the hallway.

Upon opening the door Phil encountered Jennifer Ranier being propped up by her social worker sidekicks. She had a broad smile across her face but didn't speak. The two social workers slowly pushed her into the doorway before Phil could speak. She threw her hands around Phil's shoulders and neck.

"Here you go birthday girl," said Stacey Rickett while brushing her hands back and forth signifying a completion of her task.

Phil mumbled out a hesitant and surprised "Hey" and noticed that Jim Turner was peering outside of his door with a smile on his face. He spontaneously reciprocated the embrace that Ranier had initiated.

"We missed you," said Jenna Ranier with a slight slur in her speech. She ruffled her lips while looking at Phil charmingly. Phil was surprised at how tall she was while noticing some spiked heel shoes. She smelled of perfume, alcohol and cigarette smoke from the bar.

Laura Jones then spoke with a shorter tone in her voice. It was obvious that she was the designated driver and the least intoxicated of the three. "We honored her birthday request which was to see you."

"Yea," said Stacey Rickett. "We also saved her from about ten other creeps who wanted to take her home." Rickett was also intoxicated and smiled at Phil while saying, "You are cute," with a gleam in her eye.

Laura Jones then shook her head trying to bring the evening to a close. "Good night Jenna, see you in the morning. We will call you." Then as quickly as they appeared, the escorts turned and disappeared down the hallway. Turner was still looking out his door with a smile on his face.

"Thanks girls," said Jenna as she continued to hug Phil. She looked up at him with a smile as her right leg slowly kicked backwards closing the door on a disappointed Turner. She let out a short giggle and said, "Its my birthday, don't I get a birthday kiss?"

Before Phil could speak she kissed him on the lips. It was a long passionate kiss well worthy of being the first. Phil thought it lasted two minutes and it may well have. Ranier felt good in his arms as she pressed her body closer to his. Their embrace was a perfect fit as her stacked figure entwined into his toned grip.

Ranier then stumbled backwards as her ankle turned one of the high heels. "Whoa," was her response. She held her hand to her head as she shook it, appearing dizzy.

"How much have you had to drink?" asked Phil.

"Oh, just a few," said Ranier as she stepped again forward towards Phil. Her body listed to the left and Phil had to catch her before she fell. At that moment he knew she was inebriated beyond the point of return. Upon recovering her balance she tried to kiss Phil again but missed and pecked him on the cheek. Her hands began to wander on his body.

"Wait a minute," said Phil. "You need to sit down."

"Sure," said Ranier as she stumbled with assistance into the small living room. Phil navigated her towards the couch and she plopped down with a loud out of control thud.

"Let's get you settled in," said Phil realizing that he just had a near comatose female dropped off in his apartment. Ranier didn't argue as she became supine on the couch. Phil placed a pillow under her head.

"I had to see you," said Ranier settling into the settee. She smiled smugly and her head tilted backwards. Phil noticed how beautiful she was even in a drunken state. The combination of lipstick, ruffled hair and glazed eyes furnished a tawdry delight to his senses. However he was aware of her lack of awareness and common sense suppressed his instincts. A platonic tone overtook the conversation.

"Did you have a good time?" asked Phil.

"Yes, but I kept looking at the door to see you walk in." As she tried to continue speaking her eyes began to close. "Where were you? We all missed you." Her last slurred line was, "I only wanted to see you today."

"I was at the Olympics," replied Phil. "Then I stopped up to see Rick at the hospital." As Phil continued to speak he looked back upon Jenna who was rapidly falling asleep as the alcohol toxin took control of her upper level cerebral functions. From that moment onward she was running on basic lower brainstem status. Her respiratory rate slowed as her liver began the long detoxification process that would carry her through the night.

Phil just shook his head in disbelief. There was a definite quality to Jennifer Ranier that attracted him. Her natural beauty was undeniable. She possessed an intangible zest for life that was intertwined with an unpretentious spirit. She was confident in appearance, yet at times displayed an insecure persona. Phil shed a moment of pity upon her thinking of Dr. Knight and her kinship with him. He wondered how two people could function in such a dysfunctional arrangement. His mind then calculated a twenty-two year gap between Knight and Ranier. Phil tried to comprehend being fifty-five years old but he could not. Fatigue began to muddle his thought process as he covered up Jennifer Ranier with a blanket. He carefully tucked her feet under the wrap after removing her shoes. Around her ankle was a gold bracelet with a heart upon it. Phil Drummer then headed alone into his bedroom to fall asleep.

At that very moment Dr. Richard Knight sat at 36,000 feet and 2000 miles away. Outrage prompted him to cut short the conference weekend and return home. The hastily booked red eye flight placed him in coach, sandwiched between two fellow passengers. An oversized woman similar in age sat next to him chewing gum aloud, occasionally laughing at an in flight movie while wearing a set of headphones. Cheap perfume permeated her airspace. To Knight's left was a portly salesman returning from an unsuccessful trip to the coast. He was dead asleep and his head occasionally tilted to Knight's shoulder only to be pushed back forcefully. Lack of personal hygiene filled his breath. Knight was out of his element with these commoners. They were unaware of his importance and this bothered him. Thoughts of Mr. Brett Charles rattled around in Knight's head, as did an uncomfortable condolence call to his spouse. Arrival in Philadelphia was scheduled for 6 AM, which could not come soon enough in the now disorderly world of Dr. Richard Knight.

CHAPTER 14
Deal with the Devil

DR. RICHARD KNIGHT hated cell phones. As one of the leading cardiothoracic surgeons in the country he readily embraced technology. However he was a self imposed exile from the cellular phone communication world. Walking through the Philadelphia airport he frowned upon the hoards staring at their phones and mindlessly pushing buttons. What could they possibly be accomplishing at 6:30 A.M. that Sunday morning? How important could the information be? Why would anyone listen to the hype from a cellular provider that deems your latest and greatest phone obsolete every six months? It was nonsense and a colossal waste of time for him. Knight did own a cellular phone, which he kept in his car. The phone did offer him the convenience of answering a call when away from the home or hospital. He however never carried a cell phone on his person, and proudly never sent a text message in his life. He frequently cited himself as living proof of a human being capable of surviving without sending a text message every minute of his or her waking life.

So when Jennifer Ranier walked into her apartment that Sunday morning at 9 A.M. she had no idea that Dr. Knight was sitting in her bedroom, since he never sent a text to alert her. While approaching her phone machine to check messages she was startled to see Knight sitting with a smirk on his face, staring at her.

"Nice outfit," said Knight. "Just getting in?"

"Richard, oh my God you scared the heck out of me," said a startled Ranier. She quickly searched her mind for an excuse while waiting for a reply. Knight didn't speak and she continued, "You're home early, why?" She paused, "How was the flight?" Her voice was cracking and implied guilt as she ran her hand through a messy head of hair.

"We obviously have some problems," said Knight shaking his head.

"I can explain," said Ranier quickly.

Dr. Knight then raised his hand in a pacifying way to make her stop talking. He waited three seconds and continued, "Have you heard of the death of Mr. Charles two days ago?"

Jennifer Ranier was now mentally backpedaling. Phil Drummer told her of Mr. Charles death over breakfast that morning. Her mind was rapidly searching for another possible source of the info that she knew. Unable to recover in time she responded with a timid and unconvincing "No."

"I didn't think so," said Knight staring at the remorseful woman in front of him. "Why should you bother to check on my patients while I'm away? Its not like I pay you enough to work on weekends."

"Richard, please, it's not what it appears to be," said Ranier. The courteous tone of his voice frightened her.

"Well it appears to me that as soon as I left town my patient, who happened to be my stockbroker, dropped dead," said Knight. "And my physician assistant didn't even know about it. That's problem number one."

Ranier just continued to stare at Knight consciously aware that she was still wearing a tight miniskirt with fishnet stockings.

"Problem number two appears to be your need to tramp around town when I'm away," said Knight.

"Now wait a minute," said Ranier realizing that her goal wasn't truly accomplished the night before. "I went out with Stacey and Laura last night for my birthday and that was it."

"Did you sleep with Stacey and Laura last night?" asked a condescending Knight.

"I did stay at Stacey's apartment last night," replied Ranier quickly.

"Don't lie to me," said Knight shaking his head back and forth as he looked directly into her eyes. Ranier thought it best to remain quiet at that point.

Knight methodically lifted a bottle of water to his mouth taking a slow sip. He then continued, "The main problem is the fact that my patients are dying in the hospital. In one hour I will be meeting with Dr. Barnes and Mr. Rineman to address this problem." Knight paused again, then stood up turning away from Ranier and looking out the window over Rittenhouse Square.

He continued in a lower tone, "My secondary problem is your obvious infidelity. You know my rules. I'll assume this was your first offense." Upon completing the sentence he looked upwards towards the sky in anticipation of a lame response.

Ranier spoke up, "There was no offense, I celebrated my birthday last night with some girlfriends and that was it."

"Regardless," said Knight. "On Monday morning you will report to my good friend Dr. Zalmo in the Gynecology department. I'll have him check you out for any social issues that you may have acquired at the birthday party. If you are deemed clear in two weeks by Dr. Zalmo, I will be willing to continue this relationship letting the good times outweigh some missteps."

"You make me sick," said Ranier who stormed out of the room slamming a door behind her.

Knight continued to quietly look out the window as Ranier left the room. Physical and mental fatigue was beginning to overtake him. His back hurt from being corkscrewed amidst two oversized passengers on the flight home. He wanted to preserve whatever energy he had for the meeting with Rineman and Barnes. Shaking his head he left the apartment realizing what a delicate situation he had just created with Jennifer Ranier. After leaving the apartment high rise he turned west, walking towards the PGH. The pending trek was two miles in distance.

Per his genetic disposition, Dr. Barnes arrived fifteen minutes ahead of time for the meeting. As usual Dr. Knight was sitting in front of his desk silently. Barnes held back on any sarcastic remarks as he offered a sincere "Good morning" to the troubled surgeon. Barnes then circled in front of the motionless Knight and took a seat in his chair. Looking at Dr. Knight he sensed both fatigue and turmoil in his face.

Barnes then let Knight start the conversation. "What the hell is going on here? Two fatalities at the worst time of the year."

"Bad luck," said Barnes, "Just bad luck."

"Its like I'm cursed," said Knight. "Why couldn't they die after the New Year?"

Barnes cocked an eyebrow upwards and looked at the surgeon in front of him. Being a surgeon he knew that a single patient's death, yet alone two, weighed on one's mind. When complications occur the thought process for a surgeon can become cloudy. Barnes knew the best remedy for this was to discuss one's concerns with a trusted colleague. He was one of the few colleagues that Knight trusted.

"They were both doing very well," said Knight. "I just don't understand why they should have coded all of a sudden."

"I'm sure you have looked over every aspect of the first death," said Barnes. "From what I understand everything was appropriate regarding the care of the second fatality."

"That's not what his wife thinks," said Knight. "I could read her mind over the phone on Friday. There is going to be some litigation out of this case."

Dr. Barnes also well knew the second issue that blurred a surgeon's intellect, that being the threat of a lawsuit. He tried to further console Knight saying, "Well that's out of our hands, we will let legal handle that matter if it occurs."

"It doesn't get any easier Mike," said Knight. "I mean this occupation doesn't get any easier. In my younger days a death was just part of the whole occupational package. Now they hang on me like an albatross."

"The faint of heart need not apply for a surgeon's job," said Barnes. "I also think you place too much emphasis on this Chronicle article. The public has a short memory, so don't get too hyped up about it."

Knight looked up ready to reply when CEO Rineman walked in briskly.

"What's the emergency?" said Rineman obviously not happy to be in the hospital that Sunday morning.

"Another one of Dr. Knight's patient's died," said Barnes.

"So what," said Rineman, "This is a hospital, people die every day in the hospital." Rineman then circled around Knight to stand in front of him.

"Not my people," said Knight with an elevated tone to his voice. "Not my people."

Barnes took control of the conversation saying, "Howard, it's just that the timing is bad. Another fatality slants Richard's numbers in the wrong direction for the upcoming Chronicle article."

"For goodness sake, there have only been two deaths," said Rineman. "It's not like the plague wiped out your entire hospital census,"

"That's all it takes," said Knight sharply. "There are still three months left in the year, another death and I'm sunk."

"Well what can we do about it?" asked Rineman. "I mean there has to be an answer."

Five or ten seconds passed in silence between the patriarchs of the PGH that morning. Each man thought of options that their moral compass quickly extinguished.

Barnes then spoke, "The numbers are what they are." He then continued more bluntly, "We can't fiddle with the numbers, they are generated from several different entities that we have no control over."

All three men again sat silently, thankful that no one else pursued this line of thinking.

"There is only one alternative," said Knight looking up at his compatriots with a smile. "I just crank up my numbers."

"What do you mean?" asked Rineman quickly.

"I just operate more, a lot more," replied Knight. The two men looked at him trying to grasp the concept. "I can ratchet up my number of surgical cases over the next three months. Without any other fatalities my mortality number will naturally drop lower."

"That's assuming there are no other deaths," said Barnes.

"That's a risk we will have to take," said an energized Knight.

Rineman wasn't sold on the idea as he spoke, "How are you going to magically find patient's who need heart surgery so quickly?"

"Come on," said Knight. "We are at the helm of the prestigious Philadelphia General Hospital, where more people in the Delaware Valley get their care than any other place. All we need to do is open up the spigot a bit more, convince the patient that the surgical option is a bit more pressing."

"I'm out," said Barnes raising both of his hands up in the air and looking in the opposite direction.

"So am I," said Rineman shaking his head with a look of disbelief. "Do you realize what you are suggesting?"

"Of course," said Knight. "This isn't anything illegal or unethical. I've got a laundry list of patient's on hold for surgery. I'll I need to do is open up another surgery day each week in the OR. That should garner about forty more cases for the year."

"Again, I don't want any part of this line of thought," said Barnes. "I don't feel comfortable even discussing it."

"Then don't," said Knight with a nervous energy. "Just do me two favors." Knight had a slightly maniacal twinkle in his eyes as he spoke, "One is to secure me an extra O.R. day every week. Friday's would be fine. The second is to tell the cardiologists throughout the system that I'm available for all cardiac emergencies, seven days a week."

Barnes pondered the idea and then spoke as he shrugged his shoulders, "I guess I'm O.K. with that, seems like a benign request." He then looked over at CEO Rineman.

"I'll pretend I've never heard this conversation," said Rineman, washing his hands of the whole deal. "If need be I would categorize your decision as an internal surgical department choice based on the best interest of the patients."

All three men then felt at ease with the select and comfortable wording from their health system's chief executive officer. Their conversation then turned onto the upcoming surgical rotation changes.

"Who will be my chief resident for the next three months?" asked Knight.

Dr. Barnes shuffled through some papers on his desk while taking out a pair of reading glasses. "The schedule has Dr. Snyder as your chief resident and Dr. Polk as your intern."

"Snyder!" yelled Knight. "I don't want that incompetent boob with me down the home stretch."

Dr. Barnes didn't speak knowing quite well that chief resident Snyder was the worst resident the program had in a long time. He continued to look at the rotation list as if searching for an answer.

"I'm keeping Pete Larson," said Knight abruptly. "He is good and knows the system well."

"You can't just change the schedule like that," said a concerned Barnes.

"Why not?" asked Knight. "You just heard our CEO call our motives in the best interest of the patient. Do you think Dr. Snyder represents our best interest?" Knight paused and then looked a bit pitiful at Barnes saying, "Just do it Mike. Try to help me out for once."

Barnes stared straight ahead thinking for a moment. In his mind he knew the switch was possible at the upper resident level only. "O.K., I'll let you keep Dr. Larson for another three months. But the surgical intern cannot change."

"Thank you," said Knight with a smile. Despite the two fatalities over the past rotation, Dr. Knight thought highly of Larson. He also realized that Larson was already on high alert. "Who is Dr. Polk?" was his next question.

"Dr. Polk is, let me see," said Barnes then fumbling for a folder in a side drawer. He opened the folder and began to read aloud. "Let's see, Dr. Polk is a graduate of Hershey Medical School. His dad was a surgeon I believe, that's right, a urologist. Good intern, quite the entertainer from what I hear."

"An entertainer, I don't want an entertainer," said Knight. "I want a dull, paranoid intern that checks every detail twice a day."

"I hear he is actually living down in the hole. Stays there seven days a week. Has no actual apartment outside of the hospital," replied Chairman Barnes.

"What?" said Howard Rineman. "Living in the hospital. I'll charge him room and board for that." The three men then burst into hearty laughter appreciating some levity from the executive officer.

"That brings me to another intern that we all know," said Barnes. "That being Dr. Frederick Riles." Barnes paused looking around the room aware that everyone knew intern Riles' father quite well.

"Apparently Frederick junior is having a tough go at it already," said Barnes. "His father has been calling me every other week to complain."

"Like father like son," quipped Knight. "Frederick Riles senior couldn't operate his way out of a paper bag."

"Now, now Richard, we had some good times together back in the day," said Barnes.

"I don't remember good times," replied Knight. "All is remember is his incompetence and covering his lazy behind. Remember that case he botched and we all got sued as residents?"

"I didn't think they had lawsuits back then," said Rineman, now looking at his watch and getting ready to leave.

"Back then you had to really screw up to get sued," barked Knight. "And old man Riles really did. Killed a patient as far as I'm concerned." Knight's face was starting to turn beet red as he continued, "Then he blamed everyone except himself. Real team player," was his final line.

"Richard, Richard, easy. You are going back thirty years," said Barnes calming the discussion. "Apparently Fred junior isn't meshing well with the upper level residents. All I ask it that you don't make it any harder on him. Apparently he is quite the sensitive kid."

"Yea, whatever," said Knight not committing on taking it easy on the younger Frederick Riles. Knight had much larger issues on his mind as opposed to the happiness of an intern.

"Richard, I need assurance that you won't lean on Fred junior," said Barnes pressing the issue. "I've given you my word to open up another day in the O.R. Please help me out."

"O.K., O.K.," said Knight while waving his hand casually in the direction of the chairman. "You have my word."

"How was L.A.?" asked Rineman to Dr. Knight as he changed the subject and began moving towards the door.

"Bankrupt and overrun by illegal immigrants," said Knight. "That's it in a nutshell. Wouldn't want to live there," was his next comment as the three men began to walk out of the office.

Rineman then slapped Knight on the back saying, "I saw you and the wife at the Russian ballet the other night, she looks fantastic. Absolutely fantastic."

"Thank you," said Knight with a smile. "She is a great woman, great woman, really takes care of herself."

"You're a lucky man," said Rineman in return with a smile. "A very lucky man."

CHAPTER 15
M and M Rounds

MORBIDITY AND MORTALITY rounds were held once a month in the department of surgery at the Philadelphia General Hospital. The tradition dated back well over one hundred years. Called M and M rounds by the residents, the meeting represented a gathering of many levels of academia. The purpose of M and M rounds was to discuss in detail a death that occurred recently in the hospital including a review of the disease process, medical management and effect on future patient care. M and M rounds started at 9 A.M. on the third Thursday of each month.

The gathering occurred in the cramped conference room located in the Kirby building. Attendance was mandatory for all interns and residents, and encouraged among all attending physicians. A good turnout was the rule and all attendees filed in according to rank and stature. First to arrive were the confused looking medical students who filtered to the rear of the room. These students were on their surgical rotations in a variety of fields. Medical students were only allowed to wear white coats that came to their waist level, which made their attendance obvious. The students did not speak as a rule during M and M rounds. In the middle of the conference room sat the interns and junior residents. These physicians were allowed to wear the traditional long white coat, which extended towards the knee level. At ten minutes to nine Phil Drummer, Rick Polk, Cathy Finley and Frederick Riles walked in together. They sat side by side throughout the meeting. Several minutes before the hour the chief residents entered the room. They were allowed to have the honorable row behind the attending physicians. Unfortunately the chief residents had to present the cases to the crowd. The task of presenting a case in which someone died was never coveted.

Lastly at 8:58 A.M. sharp a side door to the conference room opened and the grand entrance of the attending staff occurred. The procession was ushered by the department chairman, Dr. Michael Barnes, who walked towards the podium. Behind him was a collection of middle-aged men and women in long white coats. Some were old and some were young, many carried a cup of coffee in their hands. Dr. Knight was third in line, and with a regal aura about his step, marched towards a front row seat. His coat was heavily starched and ironed to perfection. The stage and podium was directly in front on him. The entire spectacle was an awe-inspiring event, as the crème de la crème of the Philadelphia General Hospital entered. The medical students from the rear of the room craned their necks forward trying to connect a famous surgeon's name to a face in front of them. Then at exactly 9 A.M. Dr. Barnes spoke.

"Good morning everyone," said Barnes, "And welcome to Morbidity and Mortality rounds."

At that very moment a hospital switchboard operator could be heard over the public address system stating, "Morbidity and Mortality rounds have begun in the department of surgery conference room on the sixth floor of the Kirby building."

Barnes continued, "I have a few housekeeping items before we begin. First off, thanks to everyone involved in the chief resident rotation shift." Barnes paused, looking up at the second row filled with chief residents. "As you know the shift was necessary to satisfy certain educational criteria that recently came to the attention of the residency director, that being me. I would like to compliment the mature manner in which the news was processed by all."

Phil looked at chief resident Larson who had a look of disgust on his face. The residents were well aware of Dr. Snyder's incompetence and sensed Knight was behind the decision.

Barnes continued, "Secondly, until further notice the chief resident on trauma and cardiothoracic surgery will be required to spend their call night in the hospital." Barnes again looked up at the group of residents in front of him. A look of displeasure was common among all the residents peering back at him. This mandate was passed down to the chief residents two days earlier and had not been well received. The "improvement of patient care" guise was the superficial reasoning for the decision. Keeping Dr. Knight's paranoia of another fatality in check was the true reason. A punitive maneuver to keep the trauma chief resident in house was a smoke screen to balance off the muse. Barnes justified the action in his mind by realizing that in three months it would be reversed.

"Lastly I would like to introduce our esteemed visiting professor for the day," said Barnes with a smile. He motioned to a stately looking physician with a well-groomed manor and shiny white teeth sitting next to the chairman's vacant seat. "Doctor Frederick Riles is a well know colleague of ours, having completed his general surgery training here at the PGH. He currently is a professor in general surgery at the Massachusetts General Hospital. Doctor Riles is well known for his work in liver disease and associated small bowel disorders. He recently published the lead article in Lancet this past month and we are honored to have him here." Dr. Barnes then extended his arm towards Dr. Riles. A polite round of applause followed as the more senior Dr. Riles stood and smiled to the crowd, being quite comfortable in the limelight. Barnes then concluded the introduction with "Welcome Doctor Riles, it's truly a pleasure to have you here for the day."

Barnes continued to smile and clap at Dr. Riles while the guest sat down with a look of content. Barnes paused momentarily to allow a restoration of protocol and then continued, "Now our first case will be presented by chief resident Peter Larson," he motioned to Dr. Larson saying, "Pete." Dr. Barnes then left the podium taking one step down to the first row and sat next to visiting professor Riles. Riles gently slapped him on the thigh and the two friends laughed and whispered to each other as chief resident Larson approached the podium.

Peter Larson then neared the podium with the medical records of Mr. William Brown in his hands. Despite being in the hospital for less than 48 hours, the chart of Mr. Brown was thick with data. The records contained every scrap of medical information generated by the hospital after the collapse of Mr. Brown directly in front of the hospital. Larson positioned the microphone to his height, opened the immense chart and began his medical presentation.

"The first case is that of a 57 year old black male with a history of uncontrolled diabetes mellitus, hypertension and alcoholism, who was followed by the medical residents in the community outreach program." Larson paused and looked up at the room, he had just described the classic staffer patient at the PGH. "He presented to the emergency room unresponsive after collapsing on the front sidewalk of PGH. His vital signs upon presentation were..."

As Dr. Larson continued with the presentation, Phil Drummer looked around the room. The line up of all the attending physicians reminded him of battleship row at Pearl Harbor. Dr. Knight sat calm and motionless in his chair, occasionally sipping a cup of coffee as Larson spoke.

Dr. Larson continued his presentation as he summarized the emergency room physician's analysis, "His chest x-ray showed a small pleural effusion. The working diagnosis by the ER staff was that of 1) rule out a myocardial infarction, 2) diabetes, 3) hypertension, 4) alcoholism...."

Phil then glanced to his right at Rick Polk who was quietly unwrapping a large candy bar. Polk looked at Drummer, and then with a wink and smile, took a healthy bite into the sugar-laced snack. Phil then briefly looked towards the right back row seeing medical students Bankart and Roden. Melissa Bankart had a blank look upon her face as opposed to the intense glare of Charles Roden.

"Any questions on the initial presentation?" asked Barnes to the crowd.

"Yes," said visiting professor Riles, "Was there a family history of cardiac disease?"

"Good question," said Chairman Barnes, "Good question."

Phil noticed that Dr. Knight shifted a bit in his seat upon hearing the question.

"No sir," said Larson. "No family was available to discuss that risk factor. Available records did not support a known familial history of cardiac disease."

Chairman Barnes and Dr. Riles then shook their head up and down in approval looking at each other, acting as if they just discovered the Rosetta stone.

Dr. Larson continued his presentation saying, "A stat cardiology consult was obtained and for this part of the presentation I will turn it over to the cardiology department."

Larson stepped down as a young, attractive female cardiology resident approached the podium. She immediately caught Dr. Knight's attention as he tracked her movements up to the stage. Upon speaking her voice cracked a bit, revealing some nervousness.

Gazing directly down upon a type written note she spoke, "The cardiology consult reviewed the EKG which showed some signs of ischemia...."

Phil noticed that Polk had finished the candy bar and was taking a small bottle of milk out of his backpack. He then looked briefly over his left shoulder at the back row. A standing room only crowd was present. Then, two bodies in the rear slightly shifted their stance, revealing the presence of physician assistant Ranier. Her gaze caught Phil's eye and she smiled at him. Phil was unaware that Polk was looking backwards at the same time. Upon returning his gaze to the stage Polk tapped him on the side and gave a thumbs up sign. Polk then whispered to Phil, "I move my prediction up to Thanksgiving."

The cardiac resident continued, "And now we will present the video of the cardiac catheterization." A screen came down from the ceiling above and the lights dimmed. After fumbling with some buttons on the podium a short video of Mr. Brown's cardiac cath appeared on the screen. The attractive physician then walked up to the screen pointing out several critical arterial blockages. She had the utmost attention of battleship row. "The blockages were considered non-amendable to stent placement and a stat cardiothoracic surgery consultation was placed." Then, the relieved resident left the stage, having completed her presentation.

Dr. Larson returned to the podium asking, "Are there any questions up until this point?"

Again, as if trying to justify his paid trip to the city, visiting professor Riles arose and spoke, "It's obvious that we have a very sick man in the ER at this point. He has severe multi-vessel cardiac disease. The only fortunate factor is that he nearly dropped dead in front of one of the best cardiothoracic surgery departments in the nation." Riles smiled brightly as he clasped his hands together. He looked at Dr. Knight expecting a response, which did not occur. Then, like all good public speakers, he recovered quickly, slowly looking at Dr. Larson and saying, "Please, continue."

"His status was deemed stable for the night and he was prepped for surgery the following day. The next morning he presented to the O.R., on a ventilator but in stable condition. He underwent coronary artery bypass surgery times four in an uneventful fashion." Larson then paused as he looked up to the crowd. "Are there any questions at this point?"

No one spoke except Dr. Riles, who again was just playing the obligatory role of a visiting professor, "Was the IMA used in one of the grafts?" He was referring to the internal mammary artery that Dr. Knight had to tie off after it bled uncontrollably. Phil recalled this bit of info since it occurred after the needle stick and cell phone event. Phil sat more erect in his seat as chief resident Larson began to fumble through the chart. Larson knew that the IMA wasn't used but couldn't come up with an excuse to cover the fact that Knight botched the harvest. Larson paused as long as he could, hoping that Dr. Knight would chime in. He didn't, as he remained quiet in his chair.

Dr. Larson then pulled out the operative report, and then appeared to read it for affect, only to say, "No, the IMA was not used." He looked up at the group waiting for something to happen.

"Why not?" asked one of the junior cardiothoracic staff surgeons.

At this point Larson was at the end of his rope. He started to speak not sure what he was going to say. As he mumbled through a reason the eminent Dr. Knight arose, turned, and faced the crowd.

Knight cleared his voice, and began speaking to the group with authority, while extending his arms outward in an explanatory mode, "Our honored guest from Boston has asked an excellent question. For the students in the room an IMA is short for Internal Mammary Artery. It's a vessel on the inside of the chest wall that we commonly use to hook up to the heart. Unfortunately, in this case, the patient's arteries were ravished by arteriosclerosis. He had one of the hardest arterial walls I've ever seen. Hard enough to bend a suture needle tip. Therefore using the IMA was out of the question in this case." Knight paused looking away from the crowd and in the direction of Barnes and Riles saying, "We therefore utilized four excellent vein grafts to complete the case, without complication." Dr. Knight then calmly sat down confident of his words and ability to move the presentation along.

"Thank you for that explanation Dr. Knight," said Chairman Barnes. "Would the chief resident be kind enough to continue?"

Pete Larson then continued as he outlined the patient's trip to the recovery and uneventful night in the SICU. In rapid fashion the presentation progressed to the early morning cardiac arrest suffered by Mr. Brown in the SICU. Larson wrapped up his presentation by saying, "After three rounds of standard Advanced Cardiac Life Support, the code was called and the patient was pronounced dead at 0237 hrs. that day." Larson then paused and looked upwards to let the discussion begin.

Chairman Barnes stood up saying, "An interesting case involving a patient with a lot of medical issues, who appeared to be doing well, and then unexpectedly expired." He paused and looked at the elder Riles saying, "Dr. Riles, any thoughts?"

Dr. Riles again rose to speak, "Interesting indeed. To my understanding it appears that everything was done appropriately in an attempt to treat a gravely ill man." It was apparent to Phil that Dr. Riles had nothing of importance to say at that point. Riles however continued, "Was an autopsy done?"

Chief resident Larson then spoke, "Yes, an autopsy was done the evening of the event. We have members of the pathology department present to now report their findings." Larson again relinquished the podium as a slightly balding and robust pathology resident approached. Phil looked towards the back of the room searching for Dr. Falcon, who performed the autopsy. He spotted her drinking her never-ending cup of coffee, sitting on a folding chair. She wore her hair in a ponytail with little make up on, a woman not concerned about appearance.

Over the next ten minutes the resident went over multiple pathology slides ad nauseam. It was apparent that Mr. Brown had an ongoing disease process in every possible bodily organ. Phil's mind wandered during the dry presentation. He went over dinner plans for the following night with Jennifer Ranier. Over the past week she voiced pending doom with regards to her relationship with Knight. Her refusal to concede to a gynecologic exam was paramount in the demise. Ranier took a moral stand on the subject knowing quite well what occurred during her birthday celebration. However she was quite aware of Knight's phobia regarding the possibility of contracting a sexually transmitted disease. Regardless she felt the need for some trust in their relationship, which did not exist.

Phil was aware that the dinner represented a definite date between them. The pending consequences were obvious as he stared at the majesty of battleship row.

Upon completion of the pathology resident's dissertation, chief resident Peter Larson returned to the podium. "Are there any questions on the autopsy?" was his comment.

"Did the patient suffer a myocardial infarction?" asked the junior cardiothoracic attending.

"No," said Dr. Larson. "The final pathology report confirmed no damage to the heart." Phil noticed a slight smile on Knight's face as he turned towards his junior partner.

Then, like any good attorney, Chairman Barnes asked a question to which he knew the answer, "What was the status of the coronary bypass grafts at the time of the autopsy?"

"All grafts were secure and intact," responded Larson proudly. Phil again noticed Knight nodding his head up and down in the affirmative as he looked to his left at the department chairman.

Professor Riles then stood up and spoke, "Well, I guess the question is why did he die?" He slowly stepped forward, apparently gathering thoughts for a winded speech, when Dr. Knight arose to face the crowd.

Dr. Knight then spoke, "This unfortunate gentleman died because of an unhealthy lifestyle that decimated his system and deposited his body on the front steps of this institution. Despite expert care, the shock of his heart malfunction set off a cascade of events that led to a multiple system shut down. Simply stated he didn't have the cardiac reserve or strength to survive his brush with death."

"Very well put Dr. Knight," said Chairman Barnes closing ranks on the case. "Very well put. I would agree that I see no serious issues in regards to the medical care provided."

However, deep in the cranial recesses of Dr. Frederick Riles, sat a tasteful dislike for Dr. Knight. Riles recalled the cocky confidence that Knight constantly brandished throughout their training together. He was acutely aware of having Knight in the precarious position of explaining the death of his patient in front of the department staff. The opportunity was to good to pass up as he spoke, "This case intrigues me and I believe it requires more academic discussion. What was the official cause of death?"

Dr. Riles looked around the room as if someone was going to answer. No one spoke. He then looked toward Dr. Knight who was still standing and facing him. Phil thought he saw Dr. Knight's left eye twitch. Riles then spoke again, "Is the pathologist who performed the autopsy here? Maybe he or she can shed some more light on the matter."

Dr. Knight did not speak knowing quite well that he couldn't deny this simple request.

Doctor Larson responded in the affirmative and identified Dr. Jane Falcon in the rear of the room. He asked her for a comment regarding the autopsy itself. Doctor Falcon invited herself up to the microphone. Phil noticed she was wearing sandals without socks as she walked by him.

Dr. Falcon adjusted the microphone to speak, as Dr. Riles and Knight took their respective seats. "Good morning," said the pathologist. "Let me start off by saying the official cause of death was cardiopulmonary failure that was complicated by emphysema and liver cirrhosis. The staging of the emphysema and cirrhosis was quite high." Phil sensed a nervous tension in the room as she continued to speak, "However I would like to make one comment regarding some of the cardiac muscle slides." Dr. Falcon requested a series of slides to be returned to the overhead screen.

"Stop right there," said Falcon pointing to the projector screen. "Here we go. Here is a cross section slide of the heart with standard stains, notice the disruption of the cell membranes themselves." Dr. Falcon then looked up at the audience realizing that their knowledge of molecular structure was limited. She took a laser pointer and again emphasized a portion of the slide saying, "See here, there is complete disruption of the cardiac cell wall, not common to come across in a post operative patient."

Dr. Knight quickly said, "Please, Dr. Falcon, we are not pathologists. What does that mean and what can cause it?"

"It means that some imbalance occurred across the cell membrane causing a disruption of metabolic flow." She then looked up above the bridge of her nose at the audience saying, "What ever it was, it destroyed the cell membrane and may have contributed to the cardiopulmonary failure."

There was an immediate rumble throughout the room.

Knight stood up and stared at Dr. Falcon. "What are you trying to say Dr. Falcon?"

"I'm saying that this is a peculiar pathologic finding, one that I can't explain."

Chairman Barnes then stood up to speak, "Dr. Falcon, can you give us any idea as to the etiology of these findings."

Falcon shook her head again looking at the slide. "I looked at these slides repeatedly with my colleagues. Our only guess, based upon published reports, is some sort of gross electrolyte imbalance. The disarray of the cell wall is suggestive of this."

"That's hard to believe," said Knight. "This patient's blood profile was within normal limits."

Professor Riles then spoke again, trying to delve further into Dr. Knight's fatality case, "Can the chief resident please review for us the patient's electrolytes prior to the code." A coy smirk arose upon the face of the visiting professor as he directed everyone's attention back towards Pete Larson.

Dr. Larson ruffled through the immense chart as a cacophony of discussions filled the room. Upon locating the patient's laboratory data he identified the cardiac arrest date saying, "Here we go, approximately two hours prior to the cardiac arrest the patient's electrolytes were normal except for a low potassium level." He paused and continued, "The potassium level at midnight was 2.1 mEq/L."

"Nothing out of the ordinary there," said a relieved Dr. Knight. "A low potassium level cannot injure the cardiac musculature."

"Interesting," said Dr. Riles holding his hand to his chin.

"Wait a minute," said Dr. Larson now fumbling through more lab values. "I'm getting a bit confused on the dates since it occurred just over the midnight hour." Knight and all of battleship row stared at the chief resident as he visually scanned and then methodically rechecked two pages. Phil noticed visiting professor Riles standing more erect while awaiting the news.

Larson then continued in a slow tone, "Blood was apparently drawn during the code itself, lets see, at approximately 0155 hours." Larson again rechecked the report to assure accuracy and carefully spoke, "This set of lab values however notes the potassium to be high, very high."

"How high would that be?" asked Chairman Barnes.

"8.1 mEq/L," said Larson who continued saying, "That's impossible, I've never seen a potassium level that high before."

"8.1 is nonsense," said Knight. "A draw just two hours previously was low. That must be a lab error."

"Or clotted blood," said Dr. Barnes. "I've seen blood drawn from a vein and then not sent to the lab quick enough. It clots, which can elevate the potassium level."

Knight's blood pressure was starting to rise. He was losing control of the conference and had a sense of being in damage control mode. He looked at Larson saying, "Who drew the blood? It wasn't you since you weren't at the code."

Dr. Larson took the snide remark in stride saying, "I'm not sure, perhaps we can ask Dr. O'Keefe who ran the code itself."

Before Dr. O'Keefe could be questioned a voice from the back of the room cried out, "I drew the blood."

Dr. Knight and the fellow attending squinted towards the back row. Throughout all of their years they had never heard a voice come from so far in the rear of the room. Phil heard the voice and immediately knew it was medical student Charles Roden.

Knight put his right hand above his eyebrows to block the overhead light as he peered into the back of the auditorium. "Who is speaking?" was his comment. "Please identify yourself."

Third year medical student Roden stood up and all eyes focused upon him. "I drew the blood sir, and it was definitely from the femoral artery."

"Who exactly are you?" asked Knight.

"Third year medical student Charles Roden," was the confident response.

Dr. Knight was now on the verge of erupting. He spoke loudly saying, "This is why we are having the chief resident stay in the hospital overnight when he takes call." He turned back to Larson and continued, "By my understanding a junior resident ran the code along with a dermatology resident. To top it off a medical student was drawing blood at a most critical juncture of medical care."

"Young man, are you sure it was blood from the artery?" asked Dr. Riles.

"I can attest to that," said Rick Polk as he stood up next to Phil. "Surgical intern Polk here," was his next line looking around the room and giving a slight wave. "I was teaching the student a femoral blood draw and it was definitely bright red blood from an artery. Actually pulsating into the vial with each chest compression."

"How quickly was it sent to the lab?" asked Knight.

"Immediately," said Charles Roden. "I placed an I.D. sticker on the vial and sent it to the lab via the tube system, as the code was going on."

Silence filled the room as Roden and Polk sat down. All heads turned towards the front of the room. Dr. Richard Knight was deep in thought as were his colleagues.

"8.1 is impossible," said Knight shaking his head and looking at the floor.

"I agree," said Dr. Barnes. "It surely must be a lab error."

"I would tend to agree," said Dr. Riles. "A potassium swing from 2.1 to 8.1 doesn't seem possible in a two hour period." Silence then gripped the room for several more seconds as the attending physicians all pondered further comment.

Dr. Riles then pompously continued while sensing the moment was his, "This is the importance of M and M rounds. Only in this environment of academia can so many wonderful minds gather to discuss a case. Not just any case, but a case that results in death. Remember that death is a mythical creature that we try ever so hard to defeat. But in the famous words of William Shakespeare, "all that live must die, passing through nature to eternity." Visiting professor Riles then held his chiseled jaw upwards towards the ceiling, as a sense of awe filled the room.

"Very well put," said Dr. Barnes as he arose and approached the revered Bostonian. "Very, very well put." Barnes allowed a few more seconds of adoration to occur from the crowd, which was appreciated by his long time friend. He then looked at his watch saying, "Now lets get to the second case presentation today." Upon doing so he sat down next to the exalted Dr. Riles, allowing surgical Morbidity and Mortality rounds to continue that Thursday morning.

Throughout the remainder of the conference Phil noticed a somewhat catatonic posture to overtake Dr. Knight. It was obvious that he was paying no further attention to the cases being presented, as he stared somewhat distraught at the floor, with a series of deep furrows across his forehead. He failed to speak throughout the remainder of M and M rounds and cancelled his office hours that afternoon. His demeanor remained uncharacteristically reserved throughout the following day, which was obvious to all personnel around him.

That Friday evening Phil Drummer and Jennifer Ranier went out to dinner together. They sat at a corner table, in a quiet restaurant, in downtown Philadelphia. The meal was simple, as was the conversation. A bottle of red wine was shared between the two. Topics varied from high school memories to favorite sports teams. Ranier had a physical attraction to Phil that she had not felt in years. The young surgical intern was overwhelmingly smitten by his stunning date. Each of them sensed an indescribable force that had collided their young lives together. A momentum

that could not be denied, despite the obvious risks it en-
tailed. They spent that October night together in the one
bedroom apartment of Phil Drummer. Throughout the
entire evening, the name of Dr. Richard Knight was never
mentioned.

CHAPTER 16
The Knight Prowler

DOCTOR RICHARD KNIGHT was a Russophile. His 50th birthday was celebrated in Saint Petersburg, Russia, with his wife. While visiting the Resurrection of Christ Church, the good doctor claimed that a personal religious experience overtook him. The church was built on the spot where Tsar Alexander II was mortally wounded, and therefore Knight sensed the Tsar's presence. While offering a prayer on bended knee, Knight claimed the Tsar's spirit entered his body, thus changing his bloodline to Russian. His wife however assured him that the local vodka was the only deity speaking to him on that junket. Regardless, from that point forward, Dr. Knight's devotion to Russia intensified.

He loved Russian culture, specifically music and literature. Knight was capable of reciting lengthy verses from Alexander Pushkin's *Eugene Onegin*. The greatest love story ever written, according to Knight, was Tolstoy's *Anna Karenina*. In an academic pursuit of self-discipline, he had just reread *War and Peace*. However Knight's most beloved gem of Russian literature was Boris Pasternak's *Doctor Zhivago*. He felt a kinship to Dr. Yuri Zhivago and his struggles with the utter chaos surrounding him. Knight drew strength from Zhivago's uncompromising pursuit for medical knowledge and excellence. Likewise, he personified Zhivago's passion for marital infidelity and lust. To Dr. Knight, Zhivago was an icon, despite only existing in literature.

The weekend after M & M rounds was mentally tumultuous for Dr. Knight. A recent visit to the director of laboratory services was met with disdain. The director informed Knight that no possible laboratory reporting error existed. He was tersely schooled on the exactness of blood testing, including a constant internal monitoring and calibration of the system. Absolute assurance was given to Knight that all blood values were accurate. A reason for the potassium level discrepancy therefore did not exist. Dr. Knight could not accept this fact, which contributed to his angst.

Also occupying space within Dr. Knight's cranium was the pending autopsy report of Brett Charles. An uneasiness regarding the record existed since Knight was unable to attend the autopsy. Visions of Dr. Falcon authoring a report while high on caffeine danced in his mind. Her sinister laugh permeated his senses as he occasionally glanced at the fax machine, which faithfully awaited her report.

Lastly, the situation with Jennifer Ranier resonated within his skull. She had boldly refused submitting her body to a gynecological mission of discovery. Repeatedly she had proclaimed her innocence and allegiance, which Knight was beginning to believe. Most disturbing however, was a recent phone call from a good friend, who espied his mistress having dinner with a "young stallion" that Friday night. Knight thought of Dr. Zhivago and his tumultuous affair with Lara. He pondered the future possibilities with Ranier that Saturday night, alone in his home. He had begun drinking some vodka immediately after dinner that evening. This was a warning sign to his wife, who smartly remembered and departed for a social date across town that night.

Sitting in his study he opened a chart on his desk containing the records of Mr. Brett Charles. With surgical eyes he poured over every detail of the case. The surgery itself was textbook in nature with no complications. All was well in the recovery room and throughout the immediate SICU care. Knight then paged to the day of Mr. Charles death, including the brief note that he wrote after seeing the patient. The note was scribed as "Doing well, no complaints. Exam stable. Plan transfer to floor today." Knight then remembered his bedside conversation with the patient and the prolonged handshake that Ranier had received. His memory banks then pictured a nurse hanging an IV bag and chief resident Larson mumbling something about a low potassium level. Knight's senses peaked at that moment, like a cat hearing a noise behind a wall. He quickly paged to the patient's morning blood work, seeing a low potassium level. Subsequent physician orders were reviewed which appropriately instructed nurse Cruise to hang a bag of potassium. Knight then rapidly forwarded through the chart to the cardiac arrest section. There was no written record of any blood being drawn during the code. This was not an uncommon event, depending on the chaos of the code and the ability of the team to obtain blood. He checked the exact time of the code and returned to the laboratory section, trying to identify any blood results obtained during that time frame. There were none. The last potassium level drawn was several hours before the demise of Mr. Charles. An empty feeling now entered the cluttered mind of Dr. Knight.

As he closed the chart he noticed a legal document adhered to the front inside cover. It was a subpoena from a well know law firm in Philadelphia. Knight immediately recognized the law firm name and the attorneys involved.

Their names instantly matched those of mean looking, ambulance chasing faces seen on T.V. commercials, asking the populace to call if they or a loved one had been injured. Injured by negligence, defective devices, motor vehicle accidents, workplace mishaps, nursing home abuse, or medical malpractice. The subpoena requested the complete chart of Mr. Brett Charles, per the request of his widowed wife and his estate. It was the first sign of a pending lawsuit against the hospital system and Knight himself. The law firm used a childish jingle that rhymed in all of their ads, offering a free consultation in order to right their wrong. Without prompting, the jingle added to the cacophony of noise in Knight's head, signaling the success of a local advertising firm's marketing campaign. *"In legal need, call S.R.T. – In legal need, call S.R.T."* The lonely drinking of Dr. Knight continued well into the morning hours of that Sunday.

Fortunately, like all great Russian czars, Knight was a tenacious man. Over time he had developed a well-disciplined intellect that allowed him to process and categorize multiple pieces of information. Once placed in a tidy corner of his mind, the data would be available for immediate recall and processing, therefore allowing forward and purposeful progress to continue. As Knight dozed off alone that evening his sights were set upon the week ahead, which was already burdened with a noticeable increase in surgical cases.

That week saw an invigorated Dr. Knight assault the cardiothoracic program with a vengeance, with an extra hop in his step. This hop included an additional day of surgery that the residents took in stride. The resident team of Drs. Larson and Polk adapted well to the upswing in surgical case volume. By the Friday of their first week, the cardiothoracic team was in good spirits as they started their final case.

"This is Stravinsky's *Petrushka*," said Knight to intern Polk who was assisting him at the head of the table.

"I find Igor Stravinsky fascinating," said Polk. "Do you know that he spent the majority of his years in Los Angeles?"

Knight stopped his work and looked up at Polk. The room went quiet. Knight then said, "No, I was unaware of that fact young man." He returned to his trade looking down into the chest cavity saying, "Please continue Dr. Polk."

Polk did indeed continue with a polite discussion of Stravinsky's life including his sordid affair with Coco Chanel. During his off call nights Polk drained the internet of all information regarding Russian classical music. Knight was therefore quite impressed with the young intern. To Knight, the portly image of Dr. Polk was omnipresent throughout the PGH system. Wherever he turned, it seemed Polk was there.

"Dr. Larson, are you aware that this intern actually sleeps here in the hospital?"

"Yes I am sir," replied Larson knowing where the conversation was headed.

"Just like the old days, when a house officer meant the intern actually lived in the house," said Knight shaking his head. "Reminds me of my residency days." He continued, "By the way, how is taking in house call going over with the chief residents?"

"Great," said Larson, lying to the elder surgeon. Larson and all the other chief residents despised the decision to make certain chief residents sleep in house during their call nights. They considered it punishment for the recent death of Mr. Charles.

"The way it should be," said Knight. "The way it should be. Don't you agree Dr. Polk?"

"Of course," said Polk. "And besides, I get free internet and cable T.V. down in the on call lounge."

Knight erupted into laughter as he continued the operation. The remainder of the surgical team joined in laughter. Polk, in a twisted way, pacified Dr. Knight, and they all appreciated the fact.

The case soon finished with Dr. Knight stepping back and breaking scrub. He took off his surgical gloves and arched his back saying, "Good work team. That was our ninth case this week." He stretched downwards to touch his toes continuing with, "I believe this Friday O.R. date will work out well. Don't you agree?" No one else spoke.

Dr. Knight then instructed the team that he had to leave town after he spoke to the patient's family. An order was given to the team to round on all patients that afternoon. Larson would then call Knight with an update on all the patients. Knight instructed Jennifer Ranier to please round with the team to assure continuity of care. He specifically noted that the current patient on the table was a member of the hospital board of trustees. An emphatic plea was given to monitor her closely. He then left the room.

"You're like his svengali," said a fascinated Ranier to Polk. She was amazed of the soothing effect that the physically unappealing Polk had on Dr. Knight. "Somehow, someway, he enjoys having you in the room."

"Did you say svenjolly?" asked Polk.

"No, I said svengali," answered Ranier.

"I think you said svenjolly," said Polk. "In fact I'm sure you said svenjolly."

"Don't let him continue," said Larson jumping in. "He is just trying to relive another Seinfeld moment."

Polk smiled at Ranier as she sneered back at him. Polk was well aware of her interactions with Dr. Drummer, yet somehow didn't broadcast it all over the hospital.

He considered Phil a friend. One who requested that he keep their recent actions quiet. Rick Polk, like Drummer, found Ranier quite fetching. However, he was aware of his standing with Ranier, which was low on her totem pole. Therefore he relished his newly christened role of svengali with a particular zest.

Later that afternoon the official autopsy report of Brett Charles arrived in the office of Dr. Michael Barnes. As chairman of the surgical department, Dr. Barnes reviewed the autopsy report of all in house fatalities first. It was a routine that the prior chairman instilled upon him years ago. Barnes methodically read through the report authored by Dr. Jane Falcon. The official cause of death was acute cardiac arrest. No other contributing factors were listed amongst the final diagnosis. It was noted that all surgical venous and arterial grafts were intact. The usual terminology within the report appeared routine to Barnes. Wording of Dr. Falcon regarding a concerning breakdown and disruption of orderly cardiac cell membrane did not appear unusual to him. Dr. Barnes smiled and placed the report on a stack of papers for his secretary. He wrote atop the report, "Please fax to Dr. Knight." His secretary Rose went home early that day, therefore allowing the report to sit on his desk over the weekend.

Just as Dr. Barnes placed the report down on the desk, he looked up to see CEO Rineman enter the room.

"Michael, just passing by," said Rineman.

"Sit down, sit down," said Barnes motioning to the chair in front of his desk.

Rineman did sit down while saying that he was in a hurry. He then asked, "How is it going with Richard?"

"O.K.," replied Dr. Barnes. "We got him another day in the O.R. and he is filling it up." Barnes looked at Rineman with amazement just shaking his head. Both men wondered where Knight was able to find surgical patients on such short notice.

"How did it go with Mrs. Hine?" was Rineman's next question. He was referring to the board of trustee member that was operated on that day.

"From what I hear, excellent," said Barnes. "Lets just hope it stays that way."

"I agree," said Rineman, "No more excitement for this year at least."

"I think we will be O.K.," said Barnes. "Again, I think too much emphasis is placed on that darn article."

"Any other contact from the *Chronicle* reporter?" asked Rineman. Before Barnes answered, he continued with, "Maybe we should send him a bottle of scotch for the holidays."

"Nothing since our dinner," replied Barnes. He sensed that Rineman had more important questions in store for him.

A moment of pause occurred before Rineman spoke again asking, "How is Richard doing overall?"

"I'm not sure what you mean by overall," said Barnes.

"Overall, you know, professionally, socially, mentally," said Rineman.

"Why do you ask?" said Barnes, "Is there something I should know?"

"Well I was out with a client for dinner last Friday night," replied Rineman. The CEO then leaned forward towards Dr. Barnes and in a lower tone said, "And I saw his blonde hottie out with a young man." Rineman paused momentarily as he shifted position in the chair before saying, "Boy, that girl is smokin' hot."

"So what," said Barnes, "Probably her brother or friend."

"Not the way they were acting," said Rineman. "They were sitting too close for comfort."

"Don't worry about Richard, he can handle himself when it comes to matters of the heart," quipped Barnes.

"I know, I know," said CEO Rineman. "Just want to make sure that our prize surgeon isn't under any undo stress."

Barnes laughed at the terminology used in describing Dr. Richard Knight.

"The young man, or should I say boy that she was with, looked quite familiar," said Rineman. He looked to the right of Barnes with a pensive frown saying, "I know I've seen him around before."

Dr. Barnes realized that Rineman always expressed an interest in the extracurricular activities of Dr. Knight. His lifestyle fascinated the CEO, as did his distinct taste for women, especially Jenna Ranier. Barnes however thought the private life of Dr. Knight was somewhat of a taboo subject as he said, "Don't worry, I'll keep an ear to the ground for any more info."

"Keep an eye on him," said Rineman. "And please, keep me posted."

"Of course," said Barnes now fully understanding why the CEO stopped into his office that Friday afternoon.

That Friday evening a freakish sleet storm hit the greater Philadelphia area, cancelling Dr. Knight's travel plans. Begrudgingly he caved into his wife's demands to go out to dinner that night. Mrs. Knight complained recently of her husband's mood swings, while voicing concern over his accelerated drinking and lack of interest in their sham marriage. Having nothing else to do that evening, and with the 76ers out of town, he conceded to a dinner date with his wife of twenty-nine years.

They dined at a swank new restaurant located in the Philadelphia suburb of Manayunk. A good friend of Mrs. Knight had recently opened up the eatery to rave reviews. The food was delicious as was the wine selected by the chef himself. The couple sat at a cozy side table with a small adjacent window overlooking a terrace. A single candle lit their faces as they spent quality time together. Mrs. Knight rambled on throughout the dinner while covering a wide range of topics ad infinitum. She informed her husband of the latest gossip amongst the fine arts committee. He was shocked to hear of a pending divorce between their good friends of thirty years. Updates were given on their three children and their respective career progress. A donation to the Philadelphia zoo was decided upon, being quite generous in nature.

Doctor Knight enjoyed seeing his wife with a smile on her face. He thought of the difficult situation that he had cornered her into over the years. She took his pandering in stride, never displaying public discord. Knight envied at times her pure lifestyle, always finding the best in everyone, including him. The candlelight complemented her silhouette and the artistry of the plastic surgeon he had entrusted it to. Knight felt a physical attraction to his wife that evening, grinning warmly as she continued to babble on.

Upon completion of dinner the seemingly reconnected couple arose. Compliments were given to the maître de and chef. A close friend of Mrs. Knight was recognized and niceties were exchanged by the well to do couples. Knight then escorted his date towards the exit, aware that their public persona together was quite striking.

Their track proceeded down a short hallway turning right into a posh barroom area. Dr. Knight put his arm around his wife, steering her through a crowd of patrons. He greatly appreciated several men in the room visually checking out his wife, who looked divine that evening, dressed in a smart black dress. Then, while approaching the end point of the bar, Dr. Knight immediately noticed a young couple staring directly at him. He then appreciated some rapid arm movements and quick discussion between the bar patrons. Within five steps more, Dr. Knight and his spouse stood directly in front of the couple who, sat rigidly in their barstool seats. Phil Drummer and Jenna Ranier were shocked to see Dr. and Mrs. Knight out that evening, being previously sure of his travel plans. Despite the abrupt social collision, Jenna was quick to recover and commented first.

"Dr. Knight, so good to see you," was her energetic line. Phil sat silently next to her, quickly taking his hand off her shoulder.

"P.A. Ranier and Dr. Drummer, a pleasure," said the unflappable Knight. Mrs. Knight paused looking at the two, expecting an introduction.

"Dear, you've met my P.A. Jennifer Ranier before, I believe at a hospital fund raiser," said Knight.

"Of course," said Mrs. Knight who was always cognizant of any bombshell that was within twenty feet of her husband. She immediately remembered the then intoxicated and shapely Ranier well. "So good to see you," was her next comment extending a handshake to Jennifer Ranier.

Before Dr. Knight could speak his spouse extended a hand to Phil saying, "And who is this fine looking young man?"

"Philip Drummer," was his response. "I work with your husband, a, I mean Dr. Knight that is. I'm an intern at PGH."

"They get younger every year," said a now smirking Mrs. Knight to her husband. "He looks like our young David," was her next line.

"No, we get older every year," said Knight with a faint chuckle. He was dismayed to see how young Jennifer looked next to his wife.

Mrs. Knight then went on to summarize how delicious the food was that evening. She gave a short recap of the recent restaurant history, mentioning the name of her owner friend, while imploring the couple to spread the word among the "young crowd" regarding the new eatery. Throughout the discourse ire began to rumble within the soul of Dr. Knight as he stared at Ranier. Years and years of opulent pampering ricocheted throughout his mind. Ranier sensed his anger while smiling attentively at chatty Mrs. Knight. Throughout the dialogue Phil sat quietly with a pitiful feeling in his stomach, allowing Ranier and Mrs. Knight to carry on the majority of the conversation. As their social collision came to an end the couples then parted ways, after somewhat clumsy goodbyes were exchanged.

"What a lovely young couple," said a whimsical Mrs. Knight as they exited the restaurant, "To be that young and carefree again. They don't know how lucky they are." She then smiled and looked back at her husband saying, "Don't you agree dear?" Dr. Knight just nodded his head in consent as the couple stepped outside, both almost falling on a patch of ice. Their return trip home to center city was quiet, only interrupted by the classical music playing on the radio. Throughout the trip Mrs. Knight maintained a sarcastic smile upon her face, confident in their cruel affair called marriage.

That night Jennifer again stayed at the apartment of Phil Drummer. A mutual shared fear made the evening platonic in nature. Their conversation centered upon Dr.

Knight and his powerful demeanor. Jennifer thought it truly unsafe to return back to the penthouse apartment that evening. Phil agreed fully, now quite aware that his internship was about to become much more difficult.

Mrs. Knight's suspicions regarding Ranier were immediately confirmed upon the couple's arrival home that night. Knight feinted a headache, saying some fresh air would do him well. He abandoned his wife for a walk through the neighborhood. As he then prowled through center city Philadelphia a rage churned over and over in his stomach. The orderly intellect of Dr. Knight placed all the blame on the infidel from Baltimore, as opposed to the naive intern that had fallen under her spell. Rapid plans for social disengagement were formulated while the penthouse apartment above remained quiet and dark, atop the Rittenhouse Square skyline.

Early the following morning Jennifer returned downtown to her apartment. A concern overcame her as the doorman inexplicably failed to respond to her nervous hello. Apprehension filled her heart as she rode the elevator to the penthouse level. The glass mirrored Otis conveyor car reflected a fatigued look upon her face. Upon exiting the elevator she turned right, down a hallway towards her apartment. Directly outside of the locked penthouse door was a collection of stacked moving boxes, each having been professionally packed earlier that morning. Each box simply had the word "Ranier" written upon them in black, bold marker print. Jennifer was surprised and saddened as to how few personal items she actually owned. Jennifer then recognized a female who approached from the opposite hallway direction. She appreciated a smug look on the elderly face of her social elite neighbor, realizing that her stroll was well timed in order to take a final look at the now homeless tart. No goodbyes were exchanged as the snobby resident feinted displeasure while having to navigate around the boxes that cluttered the hallway. Words could not describe Jennifer's shame as she tried to quickly phone her social work friends. A "No Service Available" message blinked on her cell phone as a harsh sense of doom took hold of her senses. Jenna Ranier then turned around to begin a slow, somber walk back to the elevator. During her ride down she tried to recall if a public phone was available for use in the lobby.

CHAPTER 17
Information Technology

THE RAPIDLY EXPANDING field of Information Technology plays a crucial role in the daily function of a tertiary care medical center. This process, which involves gathering, storing and disseminating private information, is enormous in scope. Nowhere else within the hospital setting has the impact of Information Technology, or I.T., been more pronounced than within the Medical Records Department. Gone are the days of massive patient charts stuffed with paper reports from a multitude of providers and ancillary services. Present are sleek desktop computers that communicate with a mainframe unit capable of storing an unimaginable amount of information on a single hard drive. Information that is available to be retrieved and shared faster than the human hand can turn a page. The entity of a patient electronic medical record, or EMR, was born over time, in response to a series of federal mandates and the technology revolution. Although superficially seamless at the PGH, an enormous infrastructure lay beneath the EMR surface allowing the process to function on a constant basis.

Management of EMR involves a professional team whose training and experience rivals that of any other department within the medical center. The I.T. department at the PGH occupies the ground floor of the old east wing. One hundred and twenty five employees make up the department, growing in size each year. The purpose of the I.T. department is to ensure the smooth 24/7 function of the hospital's information network. The system involves over 5,000 computer terminals throughout the hospital. Over sixteen miles of computer cable run through the hospital's recesses to connect the behemoth complex. A never-ending series of routers, Ethernet cables and power grids litter the medical center, and the I.T. department is responsible for every single computer connection throughout the system.

The hub of the storage system resides within the I.T. department building. This control center receives a continuous flow of real time information that needs to be processed every second. Incoming data includes all patient blood work, nursing reports and physician orders. Adding to the mix is a never-ending avalanche of reports from the departments of radiology, pathology and surgery. Every scrap of patient information, no matter how trivial, has a dedicated and assigned file within the system. The end product of this collective process represents a patient's EMR, which is a dynamic snapshot of their state of health. Within the PGH medical system sits over five million electronic medical records, securely stored and backed up for medical legal purposes on a daily basis. Maintaining security amid this wealth of data is paramount, both to the patient and the PGH.

Mr. James Asher is the head of the I.T. security division at the PGH. Conservative and serious, he represents the type of persona necessary to protect such a variety of sensitive information. Asher has been with the PGH system for the past thirty years. Growing up in the sixties, he caught the computer wave early in his career. An original *Star Trek* fan, he was fascinated with Mr. Spock and his use of the starship's computer system. His first computer program course in high school was an after school club, consisting of only three members. During these sessions, Asher and his fellow "Trekkies" would build and dissect early computer prototypes, inspecting their inner workings. Texas Instrument calculators served as common sacrifice to the gods in their laboratory. The club grew yearly, while enduring taunts and "nerd" labels from classmates. Casual group discussions were carried out regarding the futuristic role of computers in their lifetime. In retrospect, even their most grandiose forecasts failed to predict the impact of computer technology over their lifespan. The ability to store data was clear to the young team. However, the rapid development of computer processor speed, power and size was unpredictable. Even the most forward thinkers of the club never imagined a computer superhighway of information. No members, in their wildest dreams, ever envisioned the words and actions of Mr. Spock coming to fruition. Certainly, they thought, it would never occur in their lifetime.

Asher was of average size with a portly, pot bellied physique. Strands of grey streaked through his jet-black hair and goatee beard. He wore thick black wire rimmed glasses that, along with his clothing, were outdated. A necktie always adorned his wardrobe, being consistently short in length, never touching his belt line. Jim Asher did not own a sports coat. His image was solidified by a habit of wearing white socks. A high school gym teacher once warned him of the possibility of blood poisoning from a colored sock and blister combination. This falsehood anchored the color wheel of Mr. Asher, dooming him from any semblance of fashion.

The Monday morning following the banishment of Jennifer Ranier from her roost found Asher lecturing to a group of college students at the University. Present in front of the technology guru was a collection of students from local universities majoring in Information Technology. Asher had just completed a lecture titled "The Development of EMRs and Their Role in Health Care." He opened up the lecture to questions from the audience, having just pointed to a front row student with a raised hand. The student was awkward in appearance and reminded Asher fondly of his early years.

"Yes young man. A question?" said Asher.

"Mr. Asher," said the student while standing up respectfully. "I am a bit confused on your description of accessing the EMR from a remote location outside of the hospital."

Asher smiled at the student as if aware of the pending question. He noticed that several other students shook their heads in unison as if meaning to ask the same question.

"Can you please explain to me the process again?" asked the student.

"Of course," replied Asher. "Accessing the system within the hospital is quite simple. Any medical provider just has to log onto a hospital computer station and type in their name and password. This permits immediate access to any patient EMR, as long as a patient medical record number is known."

"Does the password change frequently?" asked the student.

"Yes," said Asher. "The system prompts the user to change his or her password every four weeks. This is a standard security action for a closed computer system, which is the case for the terminals directly connected to each other in the hospital proper."

Asher paused while looking around the room prior to answering the student's question regarding remote or off site access into the EMR system. This topic was his forte, having spent the better half of his career developing the technology allowing such access, which was now the standard across the nation. Asher knew that the group in front of him was aware of this fact, so he paused for effect. He then ran his hand through his hair as if in thought, prior to launching the response that everyone came to hear.

"A most excellent question from our student here in the front row," said Asher. "As you may or may not be aware I have devoted a significant amount of energy over the past several years in developing a secure entry portal into the hospital EMR system from anywhere throughout the city or country. I would like to preface my answer by stating the technology that we have to store and retrieve massive amounts of medical data is first rate. Computer speed, power and memory are expanding in an exponential fashion. Our PGH private "cloud" is the Cadillac equivalent of storage technology, capable of handling ten times the available data that we have."

Asher paused and looked around the room, realizing that audience interest was at a peak. A few hands were raised to ask further questions but the I.T. maven continued uninterrupted.

"Unfortunately the computer superhighway outside of the hospital proper is a poorly developed dirt road, riddled with potholes," said Asher. "And this is where potential security breaches my occur."

Hands shot up throughout the room and Asher pointed to a young female towards the rear of the auditorium.

"Dr. Asher, I've read that EMRs can be retrieved from home computers, laptops and smart phones. How can a system be secure with so many portals of entry?"

"The answer is simple," said Asher with a smile. "The token. The authentication token is the key." He then

reached into his pocket and pulled out a rectangular token that was attached to a key chain. The token was the
size of a house key and fit unobtrusively on the chain.
Asher held the token up high for all in the room to see.

"Allow me to go a bit more into detail regarding the
token," said Asher. "As you know, the amount of computer access portals outside of the hospital proper is endless, which allows great freedom to our physicians in accessing data necessary to treat patients. However, as you
know, lurking around any major information system is
the potential hacker trying to obtain some sort of adrenaline rush in penetrating the system. This cannot occur,
especially when strict patient confidential information is
at stake."

"Has the system ever been knowingly penetrated?"
asked a voice from the middle of the pack.

"No," said Asher quickly and with confidence. "To re-
pel such an external assault we developed a two-staged,
trusted authentication system which guarantees absolute
identity assurance of the system user. This proven meth-
od requires every health care provider given EMR clearance, to carry an authentication token." Asher paused to
look up before continuing in a professorial tone. "Each
token produces a visual six digit number code that changes every sixty seconds. The token itself contains a factory
produced random key that triggers the numerical change.
Therefore an outside user wanting to log onto the network would need to type in their name, password and the
number being displayed at that very moment in time, on
their token. Our system would then compare the provider's password against their authentication token number,
only then deciding to allow or deny system access." Asher
then walked close to the first row with a smile saying,

"This combination creates a unique, one time password, assigned to each user at the time of their system access."

"A system that therefore changes a user's code every sixty seconds," said the student in the first row.

"Correct," said Asher.

"Where is the weak point of the system?" asked the woman from the rear.

"Slip shod handling of the token and passwords," said Asher without hesitation. "We constantly stress to all EMR users not to write down their computer IDs or passwords as a reminder. As you all know it's too easy to write down a password on a notepad next to the computer. This haphazard practice potentially surrenders one key piece of the puzzle that allows access."

"Is the system expensive?" asked the man in the front row.

"Horribly expensive," said Asher. "But the downside of a major penetration into the system would be financially catastrophic to the system. So its money well spent."

James Asher then invited all members of the group to come forward for a hands-on demonstration of the system, which was a treat for the technology savvy group. Within thirty minutes the lecture ended, allowing Asher to head back to his office. Outside of the lecture hall he was met by the chairman of the hospital's laboratory services, who sat in for the second half of the lecture.

"Nice lecture Jim," said the chairman to Asher.

"I love having young minds around me," said Asher. "So full of energy and ideas. Can you imagine what the future holds for them?"

"I can't imagine," said the department chairman as he began walking down the hallway with Asher. The two had known each other for years, having worked together to coordinate the exact handling of laboratory results within the PGH system. As their conversation continued the chairman brought up a recent discussion he had with Dr. Knight, who approached him regarding the possibility of a laboratory reporting error occurring within the computer system.

"He claims it happened to one of his patients," said the chairman. "Regarding a shift in potassium that couldn't be explained from a physiologic standpoint. He was blaming the computer system."

"Did you explain to him the constant calibration of the system?" asked Asher. "I mean it is tested weekly by an independent lab to assure accuracy."

"Yes I did," said the chairman. "And I gave him the name of the company that performs the weekly check, just to appease him."

"We've been through this discussion before," said Asher. "With today's technology a computer reporting error regarding blood work is next to impossible. I mean there is no human step involved in the process."

"I know that Jim, but he kept talking about a recent discussion at a department M and M meeting that brought up the possibility of a lab error. The guy had an uneasy look in his eyes when talking to me," said the chairman.

"Give him my name if he has any other questions regarding the process and overall security," said Asher. "I've met him before but he may not remember me."

"Sounds good," said the chairman with relief. "If I had to guess he will be calling back soon. The guy appears to be a bit overbearing."

"He once asked, or should I say ordered me, to come over his house and hook up his personal computer," said Asher.

"Did you do it?" asked the director.

"Of course I did," replied Asher. "That guy is like God around here." The two men continued down the hall with Asher again saying, "He hates technology with a passion. Nice house though, and I must say his wife was most pleasant and welcoming."

"It's his age group, they hate technology," said the laboratory director immediately realizing his faux pas.

"I believe I'm older than him, young man," replied Asher as he jokingly grasped the back of the director's neck.

The two men then turned right towards an elevator. The director spoke again, "He must use the hospital system, at least the EMR? Nobody can function here without using it."

"Not Dr. Knight," replied Asher. "He has his nurses and staff use the computer." Asher then hit the elevator button for his friend. The door opened as he continued to speak, "I would venture to say that he doesn't even know his password." The two men then stepped quietly into the elevator car, being confident in the reliability of the system they created.

Asher was right. Dr. Richard Knight had no idea what his password was into the system. He relied on his support staff to access the computer system. This team, which included Jennifer Ranier, performed whatever mandatory EMR tasks the administration mandated. Therefore his computer code and key token were the virtual property of his trusted employees. Knight wasn't even aware that a token existed for his computer use, and never accessed hospital computer information on his own. So while sitting in front of Chairman Barnes that mid October afternoon, the whereabouts of his token wasn't even a thought.

"Your surgical case load has risen significantly Richard," said Dr. Barnes with a smile. "Feeling young again?"

"Don't be a smart ass Michael," said Knight with a broad smile. "If this plan succeeds I may someday be Chairman of the Surgical Department."

"You can have the job if you want it," said Barnes. "It doesn't pay well." Both men smirked at each other realizing that Knight still coveted the position.

"I actually like operating on Friday," said Knight. "I love to see the misery of the O.R. staff, realizing they won't be getting home early for the weekend." Knight paused while looking at a new paperweight on Barnes desk. While picking up the crystal weight he continued saying, "What's the rush to get home?"

Dr. Barnes appreciated the cruel truth in his colleague's statement. Surgeons loved being in the hospital, it was their domain. The world made sense within the confines of the surgical theatre. Late weeknights and weekends meant absolutely nothing to a surgeon. Simply put, a surgeon's life is strung together by an uninterrupted series of interruptions. Peace lived within the walls of the PGH, where the outside world rarely reached in. So while socially sane employees looked forward to Friday night and a weekend, surgeons did not. Spending a weekend in the hospital was a mental vacation for surgeons. If success was measured by how happy a person was on Monday morning, then Barnes and Knight were successful beyond one's imagination.

Barnes continued, "What did you think of the Brett Charles autopsy report?"

"Not much considering the source," said Knight looking to the right and shaking his head. "When are they going to weed out that incompetent pathologist?" was his question in reference to Dr. Falcon.

Barnes noted an immediate mood change but continued in the Brett Charles direction. "Legal notified me that a lawsuit is going to be filed within weeks." He paused, allowing Knight to speak. A long ten seconds passed between the two surgeons. Barnes then continued, "I don't see a problem, everything was in order. That's why the surgical consent includes the word "death"."

"I did everything correctly," said Knight. "I looked over the chart a hundred times. That verdict is in God's hands."

"Remember we can always settle before the press gets a hold of the case," said Barnes.

"I know," said Knight, "But that decision is years away. The brutal truth is that when someone dies post op, someone is going to get a cash payout." Knight then paused only briefly before saying, "Did you think anything was peculiar about that autopsy report?"

"No. Looked over it quite well," was Barnes response.

"That boob downstairs keeps putting in terminology about cell wall destruction and disorder. I can't figure that out," said Knight.

"Didn't notice that," replied Barnes.

"Well you should," said Knight. "If was the same terminology she brought up in M & M rounds."

"Oh yes, M & M rounds," said Barnes leaning back in his chair. He smiled and continued, "Our visiting professor, Dr. Riles was well received, don't you think?"

"Well received by who?" said Knight. "The psychiatry department? That guy is a buffoon. How he got on the Mass General staff is a wonder to me." Knight paused then spoke after recalling Riles pedigree, "Oh yea, his father was a surgeon there. No wonder. It's a whole family tree of hackers."

"Now Richard you are not suggesting that nepotism played a roll in the generational success of the Riles family. Are you?"

"Sure I am," barked Knight now completely forgetting about the death of Brett Charles and the autopsy report. "I hear his son, who by the way is our problem now, is all thumbs in the O.R." Knight smirked looking at Barnes then saying, "A real chip off the old block."

"Give him a chance, give him a chance," said Barnes realizing that he pushed one of Knight's emotional buttons. Then trying to change the subject he said, "On the brighter side, I'm glad Mrs. Hine did O.K. with her surgery."

Knight waited a few seconds to recalibrate. "I'll give him a chance, just one chance," was his first response regarding intern Riles. "And yes, I am glad that Mrs. Hine made it through quite well. It would have looked bad for a trustee member to die post op."

A discussion then occurred regarding the internal politics of the hospital's Board of Trustees. The name of Howard Rineman surfaced in the conversation. Dr. Barnes voiced his admiration of Rineman in controlling the board, realizing that he treated the medical staff well, with an even hand. By and large he thought Rineman was good for the PGH system in a time of nationwide medical and economic uncertainty. Knight somewhat agreed although still not fully confident of where Rineman's true allegiance stood.

Barnes again spoke regarding Rineman, "Howard stopped by my office last week, was asking about you."

"Why me?" asked Knight.

"Wanted to know how our prize surgeon was doing," quipped Barnes with a smile. He loved Rineman's description of Knight as a prized surgeon.

"Prize surgeon, what is he talking about?" said Knight.

"Just wanted to see if you were holding up to your self imposed increased case load," said Barnes.

"Did he happen to mention anything about a certain P.A. that previously worked with me?" asked Knight.

Knight was well aware of Rineman's longstanding infatuation with Jennifer Ranier.

"Yes he did," said Barnes then following quickly with "And did I hear the phrase *previously* worked with you?"

Knight shook his head in the affirmative and frowned while looking at his long time colleague. He then said, "That's right Mike, previously. I let her go earlier today."

Chairman Barnes nodded quietly wondering about the cause of the dismissal. Certainly from the mouth of CEO Rineman, it appeared that another man was involved. He then asked Knight a simple question, "Why?"

"It was time," said Knight. "It was just the right time." He stared down at the floor saying, "Nothing from an employee standpoint, she was a great physician assistant."

Barnes went to speak but Knight continued, "I've contacted the marketing department to post a job position for another P.A."

"No problem," said Barnes.

"I'll need one quickly to keep up the pace," said Knight.

"No problem, no problem Richard. We can hire one immediately from the P.A. program."

"She was hired right back by the Plastic Surgery department," said a dejected Knight referring to Ranier. "Go figure."

"The Plastics team!" said a surprised Barnes. "She nearly destroyed the chairman's marriage when she worked there."

"I know," said Knight. "But four years have gone by. Surely the chairman's marriage must be in worse shape by now. It will be a more satisfying experience for him this time around."

Both men burst into laughter at the humor, realizing the truth of the matter. Yet within the laughter Chairman

Barnes sensed a hurt and sorrow in Knight's feinted bravado. He watched Knight's eyes drift to the floor in a somber moment of reflection.

"Its definitely over?" asked Barnes leaving the conversation open for more discussion.

"Definitely," said Knight still staring at the ground. "Definitely. Had to end."

Knight then rose to leave. "Good conversation as usual Michael. See you in the morning. Thank you."

"Always a pleasure," said Barnes as he watched Knight turn towards the door. "My door is always open."

Knight headed towards the door but before he left Dr. Barnes spoke again, "Oh yes, Richard, I almost forgot."

Knight pivoted back towards the chairman with a questioning look on his face.

"I see that a Mrs. Katherine McDuff is on the schedule next week," said Barnes. "Is that the Katherine McDuff of the McDuff Food empire?"

"Yes it is," said Knight. "The matriarch of the family." He nodded his head while still staring at Barnes. Both men stared at each other with the same thought running through their minds.

"Keep her healthy Richard," said Barnes with a smile. "For the sake of us all, please keep her healthy."

"I plan on it," said Knight confidently as he sighed and then turned to exit the room. "I do plan on it."

As Dr. Knight left the room Dr. Barnes leaned back on his chair, slowly rocking back and forth. His mind was digesting the recent information regarding Jennifer Ranier. He wondered if Howard Rineman was aware of her dismissal. The emotional impact on Knight was obvious to him. He then thought of Knight's plan to increase his surgical volume over the next several months. The McDuff name entered his mind, as did the catchy commercial song for their nationwide food empire. Then, deep within his cranial vault, he heard a pleading voice saying, "Keep her healthy Richard. For the sake of us all - please keep her healthy."

CHAPTER 18
The McDuff Empire

KATHERINE MCDUFF WAS the 80-year old matriarch of the McDuff Food Corporation. Her great grandfather started a food distribution business in New York City during the late 1800s. Her father took the regional business to national fame during the early 1900s. Katherine and her late husband solidified the corporation as an international player over the past fifty years. McDuff Foods was a conglomerate that owned hundreds of smaller corporations, employing over 30,000 people throughout the world. The McDuff logo was ubiquitous throughout every supermarket in the country.

Katherine McDuff was an articulate, chain smoking, pepper pot that weighed 110 pounds soaking wet. Years of summer vacation and tobacco addiction produced a wrinkled and leathery face. A short grey mop of hair was always held tight together in a characteristic bun. Her clothing was plain, yet from the finest shops of London. She always wore flat brown shoes and walked with a quick pace. Her height was five foot two inches. An entourage of four assistants always trailed a few paces behind Mrs. McDuff. This cadre included two attractive females who cared for her womanly demands. Two thin and balding males managed her daily calendar and logistical needs. Katherine never carried a purse or cell phone. A lit cigarette lived between the second and third finger of her left hand, while her right hand remained in constant motion with her mouth.

Katherine was a philanthropist. No one else in the Philadelphia area gave away money like Katherine McDuff. Her father always told her that a successful corporation had three generational stages of development. The first generation was characterized by hard work, brutality, greed, and at times deceit. The second generation was blessed with success yet carried the burden of constant denial for past crimes of business. The third generation was to be universally adored and hailed as a community treasure and philanthropist. Katherine McDuff was that third generation Good Samaritan. She donated money on a weekly, if not daily basis. A keen marketing department tastefully displayed her generosity, which benefitted all genres of the needy. Beneficiaries included homeless soup kitchens and local foster homes. More cultivated recipients included local high schools and universities. Of course the crème de la crème of Philadelphia could not be denied access to the McDuff purse. This local hierarchy of successors included the Philadelphia Art Museum, Academy of Music and Philadelphia General Hospital. It was within this milieu that the grand world of Katherine McDuff crossed the comparatively pedestrian life of Dr. Richard Knight.

Dr. Knight befriended the McDuff family decades ago while serving on the Philadelphia Fine Arts committee. He graciously accepted their monetary generosity on a seemingly constant basis. The socially striking Dr. and Mrs. Knight were commonplace at the McDuff mansion, rubbing elbows with local and national power brokers. Katherine loved to refer to Dr. Knight as her "young heart doctor" with a grin and puff of cigarette smoke. Unknown to Dr. Knight, she was quite aware of a mutual encounter the young heart doctor had with a cocktail waitress in the McDuff mansion library. Knight considered it one of his greatest scores during a New Year's Eve party in the late 1990s. During his fit of adultery and passion he was unaware of the family matriarch, who wandered into the library that evening. Katherine was momentarily caught off guard by the spectacle, but ultimately appreciated the young doctor's verve. The act of fornication reminded her of an illicit encounter she participated in some fifty years earlier, in that very room. From that moment forward, a twisted bond of connection existed between Mrs. McDuff and her young heart doctor.

Of course when Katherine's cardiologist recently suggested she see a surgeon, her choice was obvious. That October she arrived with much fanfare and a trailing cloud of smoke in Dr. Knight's office. A one-hour consultation with the esteemed surgeon resulted in a decision to proceed with surgery. Katherine pinched Dr. Knight on the cheek as she left his office with the utmost confidence in him. Her logistical team deemed that early November would be the best time to proceed, based on her calendar of worldwide events. Knight planned on a quadruple bypass surgery to counteract sixty years of smoking and a family history of high cholesterol. Katherine McDuff represented a moderate surgical risk, a risk that Knight gladly accepted in the social eyes of Philadelphia. Knight ultimately left no stone unturned in the preoperative planning of her surgery.

From the moment Katherine McDuff arrived in front of the Philadelphia General Hospital, every step was well orchestrated. Her convoy of stretch Mercedes stopped directly in front of the hospital, ignoring traffic regulations and hustling valets. A porter opened the door to her car allowing the spry octogenarian to step out into the crisp, sunlight November morning. Awaiting her arrival was CEO Rineman and a team of hospital dignitaries. The welcoming committee smiled and bowed as they followed the patient into the lobby named after her husband. Smoking was temporarily allowed in the lobby that morning as Katherine stormed through a parting sea of onlookers. She bypassed the admissions office and was led to a private elevator, which took her to the seventh floor. Howard Rineman then escorted her to a reserved suite occupying the corner of the hospital wing. The suite had recently been repainted and decorated in preparation for the hospital's most gracious donor.

Upon entering the suite her entourage quickly set up a laptop computer and communication center. Female attendants began unpacking several suitcases of clothing and personal items. Mrs. McDuff threw the floral pattern shades open, peering out across the Schuylkill River. The sunlit skyline of Philadelphia looked her directly in the eye and she smiled. Then, over the next six hours, a constant stream of physicians and dignitaries flowed through the room.

Her medical team formed the "McDuff Nucleus", which was a term coined by Dr. Knight. Each doctor played a specific role in the medical care surrounding the surgery, having been picked personally by Dr. Knight. The Nucleus consisted of a cardiologist, internist, anesthesiologist, and pain management physician. Also included were a pulmonologist, physiatrist and catholic priest. Knight was well aware of the McDuff family's Irish Catholic roots and their love for religion and a strong Sunday sermon. One by one the dream team of the PGH medical staff entered the McDuff suite. Katherine was repeatedly palpated, probed, pampered and reassured by the medical squad. In between physician visits she answered questions from her business staff over internet connections. She only paused for a short lunch and routine mid afternoon tea. By five o'clock in the afternoon she was seen by every necessary medical provider except her treating surgeon, Dr. Knight.

At exactly seven o'clock in the evening Dr. Knight appeared at the entrance of the McDuff suite. Wearing a starched long white coat he was accompanied by chief resident Larson and intern Polk. Both young physicians stood stoically behind Dr. Knight. Lastly a tall, thin young woman of striking beauty accompanied the group. She was nearly six foot tall with high heels on, and wore a long white coat. Her complexion was dark by nature as was her straight black hair. Holding a clipboard in her hand she trailed somewhat confidently behind the three physicians.

Upon entering the McDuff room all of the matriarch's assistants stood up and stepped to the side. Katherine was on a cell phone looking out over the night skyline of the city. She quickly told her caller that she had to go and terminated the call. She then turned to her surgeon with a smile while throwing her arms widely overhead. She stepped towards the entering team.

"My young heart doctor," was her cry as she strongly shook the hand of Knight. "So wonderful to see you."

"Good evening Katherine," was the polite and calm reply by Knight. "Its very good to see you."

Before Knight could go any further the patient peered around him saying, "Who are these fine young men behind you?"

Knight then introduced Peter Larson and Richard Polk to the head of the McDuff Food Corporation. He explained the role of each resident and the fact that they would constantly be monitoring her progress. Dr. Polk then informed her that he always enjoyed eating the companies crème filled cup cakes that were universal to any convenience store. Katherine McDuff then promised a whole carton of cupcakes would be delivered to him as her assistants jotted down his name. They were later shocked to discover that his home address was in the basement of the hospital complex.

Lastly, Katherine McDuff sidestepped the male entourage and stood directly in front of the young female who accompanied the team. She then said, "And who may this young, beautiful woman be Richard?"

"This is Olivia Casey, my physician assistant," said Knight in a proud, fatherly tone.

"Olivia Casey," said Katherine looking the young female in the eyes. "What a beautiful name to match such a beautiful and intelligent young girl."

"Thank you," said Olivia extending her hand, "It's a pleasure to meet you."

"My pleasure indeed," said Katherine with a handshake and coy look at Dr. Knight. "I know that Casey is Irish but your beautiful dark complexion is not from the Emerald Isle."

"I'm half Irish," said Olivia with a smile. "My mother is from Spain."

"Ah, thus the reason for your beautiful dark complexion, you are blessed," said Katherine as she gently touched the cheek of Knight's new assistant. "You are truly blessed."

"Thank you," said the twenty four year old recent graduate from the hospital's physician assistant program.

McDuff then turned toward Dr. Knight saying, "Richard, you are a lucky man to have such young, handsome and energetic people working with you."

"Yes I am," said Dr. Knight with a smile and glancing look at Katherine McDuff's female attendants.

Knight and his team spent the next full hour in the McDuff suite. An explanation was given for every step of the surgical and postoperative process. All of Katherine McDuff's questions were answered in detail. The discussion was exhaustive in scope. At exactly eight o'clock a tired, yet satisfied Katherine McDuff, excused the medical team from her room with appreciation. She would spend the next two hours getting her affairs in order, preparing for surgery the following morning.

At exactly seven o'clock the following morning, the scalpel of Dr. Knight hit the skin of Katherine McDuff. Knight had moved up her surgical time to magnify the importance of the case. At his side was nurse Ella Frey. Across the table was intern Polk who was slowly establishing himself as a trusted assistant. At the lower half of the table was chief resident Larson and P.A. Casey, harvesting a vein graft. It was understood by all physicians that the inexperienced Casey would stay away from the chest cavity and play a minimal role in the case. No medical students were allowed in the room. The chairman of the anesthesiology department, along with a more competent assistant professor, managed the airway of the patient. Dr. Knight was at his surgical best, completing the case with perfection. No other cases were scheduled that day, allowing the team to micromanage her SICU care that day. Her postoperative course was unremarkable over the next 24 hours. Word then spread throughout the hospital that the surgery was a success. The passionate matron of the McDuff family had done well and was resting in stable condition.

The following morning found Mrs. McDuff alert and strong. Knight and what appeared to be the entire surgical staff evaluated her at 7 A.M. A decision was made to remove her from the ventilator at eleven o'clock that morning. Katherine tolerated this well and by lunchtime was breathing on her own and asking for a cigarette. This demand was her only request not permitted up until that point. When the clock struck noon an army of caterers entered the hospital with a lavish lunch provided by the McDuff Corporation. The honorees were the physicians and nurses of the cardiothoracic program. Katherine's attendants had arranged the luncheon at her specific request. Occupying the center of the gourmet table was a delicious array of cheesecakes, which made her company famous over the past century. It was a cherry topped cheesecake that Rick Polk went for first.

"That's right, a whole crate of Creamy Cup Cakes was outside the door of the Polk Lounge this morning," said Polk. He was loading a huge chunk of cake on his plate. "Like Santa Claus appeared the night before with it."

Phil was layering his tray with a hot entrée of chicken potpie and a garden salad. He responded to Polk saying, "Did it have your name on it? If not it's the property of the entire intern team."

"No way," said Polk, "Katherine said it was for me. I have witnesses."

"Katherine? I see," responded Phil. "On a first name basis with Mrs. McDuff?"

"As a matter of fact yes," smiled a proud intern Polk. "When you caress someone's broken heart in your hand, you earn the right to call them by their first name."

Intern Fred Riles then stepped into the conversation saying, "Glad the old dame is doing O.K." He was placing a vegetarian wrap on his plate.

"I agree," said Phil Drummer. "The old man has been uptight regarding this one."

"Tight as a gnat's behind," said Polk starting off the feast with his dessert.

Phil was acutely aware of Knight's relationship with Katherine McDuff. Jennifer Ranier had the good fortune of attending a McDuff mansion social event under the cardiothoracic department umbrella. Her description of the mansion's opulence and grace was stunning. Ranier also described Knight's passion for the McDuff family with all of its fortune and fame. She truly believed Knight would suffer a mental breakdown if anything bad occurred to her during the hospital stay.

"How's the new P.A. doing?" asked Phil while looking at Polk.

"Incompetent but gorgeous," replied Polk.

"Wasn't that the case with his last one?" asked a constantly unaware Fred Riles.

Both interns looked at their colleague realizing the limits of his social I.Q. level. By November of that year it was common knowledge throughout the institution that Ranier and Drummer were an item.

Just then upper level residents Pete Larson and Randy O'Keefe appeared at the banquet.

"Wow, the whole department is here," said O'Keefe looking around at the crowd.

"A beggar's banquet," said chief resident Larson with a smile. "Thanks to the expert skills of our super intern," was his next line as he patted Polk on the back. "The old gal really loves you."

"What's not to love," said a proud intern Polk rubbing his stomach. The group broke into laughter, which unfortunately was to be short lived that early November afternoon.

"Code Blue, Surgical ICU," pierced over the hospital public address system. "Code Blue Surgical ICU."

"Oh no," said Larson as he dropped his plate and bolted out the conference room door. The remainder of the residents and interns rushed behind him.

"Code Blue Surgical ICU," continued as they raced down the hall towards the ICU.

"Anyone but Mrs. McDuff!" rang collectively through their heads as they turned the corner into the ICU.

"Code Blue Surgical ICU."

As the herd of physicians entered the SICU proper they saw a frantic nurse Cruise rushing a cardiac crash cart into the room of Katherine McDuff. The grand dame of the McDuff Corporation was in full cardiac arrest. It was 1:23 PM.

"What happened?" yelled Larson as he entered the room.

"Was doing fine," said Nurse Cruise. "Just flipped into a V-tach and the alarms went off."

Larson then looked down at Mrs. McDuff who was turning a deep pale blue. He glanced at the overhead monitor, which displayed a dysfunctional heart rhythm. A blood pressure reading was incompatible with life.

"Start the code protocol!" yelled Larson. The surrounding team then jumped into action. Polk applied an oxygen mask to her face as Phil began cardiac compressions. Randy O'Keefe opened up all of her IV fluid bags and directed intern Riles to draw some blood. Nurse Cruise rapidly opened the code cart to begin drawing up the appropriate medications. At that moment the hospital cardiac arrest team arrived in the room.

The arriving anesthesia resident then rushed to the head of the bed saying, "All non essential personnel please leave the room." He repeated his demand watching a few confused medical students leave the room. Within two minutes he had a breathing tube down the patient's airway to provide oxygen.

An intelligent looking medical resident soon appeared, declaring responsibility for running the code. He calmly said, "Can someone please give me a history on this patient and a list of her medications?"

"I'm running the code," said a frantic Pete Larson. "I know the patient well."

"Not according to protocol," said the medical resident.

"I said I'm running the code," was Larson's response. He then ordered the appropriate IV medications for the patient. Nurse Cruise rapidly administered the drugs into Katherine McDuff's veins. Larson then asked Phil to stop his compressions. The team looked up at the monitor hoping for a spontaneous cardiac rhythm from the patient. There was none.

"Continue CPR," yelled Larson. Phil started the chest compressions watching intern Riles struggle to draw blood from the patient's groin area."

"I am responsible for this code," said a defiant medical resident. "I demand responsibility or my chairman is going to hear about it!"

Larson turned quickly to the resident at the end of the bed saying, "Listen hear you little piece of…" His voice suddenly seized up, as did his body. Behind the slightly framed medical resident stood Dr. Richard Knight with a scowl on his face.

"I'm running this code," yelled Knight stepping past the medical intern. "Get out of my room," was his last response to the intern. Knight then dispensed the young physician with a backwards shove of his arm.

Knight peered up at the monitor in disbelief. He then looked around the room seeing nurse Cruise administer drugs and Phil continue with the compressions. The anesthesiology resident rhythmically applied pressure to an oxygen bag with his hand.

"What have you given her so far?" said Knight to Larson.

"Round one protocol," was his response.

"Stop compressions," was Knight's next demand directed at Phil.

The room again went quiet as everyone looked up at the monitor. No heart rhythm was seen.

Knight then looked at Nurse Cruise saying, "Open the chest cart!" He looked back at Phil saying, "Continue compressions!"

Within sixty seconds Nurse Cruise returned to the room with several other SICU nurses. They were pushing in a large cart filled with surgical gowns and instruments. Chief resident Larson then began pouring betadine antiseptic solution all over the chest wall of the patient. Knight turned towards the nursing team seeing that O.R. nurse Frey was now present. Surgical gloves were quickly placed on Knight and Larson as they began applying sterile sheets across the chest of Katherine McDuff. The nursing team rapidly hooked up suction tubing to a canister connected to the wall. Phil and his fellow interns realized that Knight was about to crack open the patient's chest right there in the SICU.

As Knight reached for the scalpel he noticed a commotion under the surgical sheets in the patient's groin area. It was intern Fred Riles still trying to draw blood. His attempts were unsuccessful up until that point.

"What the hell is going on under there?" barked Knight.

Fred Riles slowly lifted his head up from above the sheets. At that moment nurse Frey hooked up a portable head light atop Dr. Knight's surgical cap. The light peered into the frightened face of the young Dr. Riles.

"Just trying to get blood, sir" was his timid response. Knight noticed that his hand was trembling.

"Get out of my room," was his terse demand to the intern. Riles quickly obliged bolting out of the room to join the crowd of bystanders in the SICU center.

"Polk, draw that blood and make sure you get it," snapped Knight. Rick Polk took to the task immediately finding the femoral artery and sending several vials of blood to the lab.

Dr. Richard Knight then quickly took a scalpel and re-opened Katherine McDuff's sternal incision. Within seconds Larson was suctioning up blood that oozed from the wound. The surgical wires holding the sternum together were rapidly cut and removed. The click, click, click of Knight's sternal retractor was heard by all as the chest cavity became visible to everyone. In the rear of the room a concerned Chairman Michael Barnes and CEO Howard Rineman appeared. Rineman had never seen an operation and soon had to leave the room.

"No bleeders," said Knight to Larson. The chief resident nodded his head in agreement. "All the grafts look good," was Knight's next line as he rapidly rotated the heart from side to side.

"Get me the paddles," was his next request as he looked up at the monitor. No functional heart rhythm existed.

Nurse Frey then produced a long sterile set of cardiac paddles. The two paddles were connected to a defibrillator next to the bed. Knight applied a paddle to each side of the patient's heart and then instructed the nurses to discharge the device. A thump could be heard throughout the room as the matriarch's heart was jolted by the electrical charge. The team peered at the heart muscle, which did not respond. Knight then again applied the paddles to the heart sending a second charge through it. Again, there was no response.

Knight then began massaging the heart with his right hand saying, "C'mon Katherine, C'mon Katherine. Don't leave us."

The cardiac massage continued for two minutes with no response. Sweat began to pour down his brow.

"Epinephrine," was his next demand.

Nurse Frey then handed the doctor a large vial of epinephrine. Knight took the syringe and inserted the tip of the attached needle directly into the heart wall of Mrs. McDuff. He rapidly injected a large dose of the adrenaline directly into the cardiac musculature, attempting to energize it into action. Upon withdrawing the needle he continued a direct heart massage for several more minutes. Unfortunately there was no response.

For the next 30 minutes Dr. Knight frantically continued to cycle through a series of electrical defibrillations and cardiac massage. Nurse Cruise drained her supply of emergent intravenous medications. Throughout the ordeal Knight spoke to Katherine McDuff as if she could hear and respond to his pleas. He implored the Gods above to spare her life and respond to his demands. His prayers went unanswered. Approximately one hour after he entered the room, Knight suddenly felt a hand holding his right forearm down from behind. Turning backwards he saw Dr. Michael Barnes staring directly at him with a stern face.

"She's gone Richard," was Barnes comment. He continued to hold the heart surgeon's forearm in an attempt to stop his actions. After a silent pause Barnes continued by saying, "She's dead."

Silence gripped the crowded room. Knight looked first at Larson who shook his head up and down, agreeing with the surgical chairman. He then looked around the room at all of the faces refusing to make direct eye contact with him. No one moved. Knight then looked up at the monitors one more time and then back into the chest cavity of his deceased patient.

"But that's impossible," was his sorrowful comment as he continued peering downward. "Impossible."

"She's dead Richard, you did all you could," was Barnes reply. He paused for five more seconds holding the surgeon's arm, only then saying, "I'm going to call the code. Time of death is 1432 hours." He then released the forearm of his colleague.

Silence gripped the room.

Knight slowly blinked his head as he continued to stare down towards the floor. Next, he stepped back away from the patient's bed. Nurse Frey unhooked his head light from a power box, allowing the cord to swing freely from the back of his head. He turned towards the doorway without removing his gown, gloves or head lamp. Blood covered his surgical gown and shoes in a blotchy pattern. He then looked up towards the door, pausing to orientate himself, and walked towards it. The crowd of faculty members, residents and interns parted to the side, clearing a path for the surgeon. Knight slowly left the confines of the room only to encounter an even larger group of hospital personnel outside. A silent and mournful crowd gave way to the doctor as he slowly walked through the intensive care unit. Turning to the left he headed alone, down the hallway, leaving the SICU. He sadly passed the conference room containing the complimentary luncheon sponsored by the deceased. An aroma of freshly baked goods engulfed Knight as he continued his exodus. A cluster of McDuff Corporation employees frightfully peered out of the room, staring at the dejected physician walking by. He did not acknowledge the group in passing. The despondent surgeon then turned right into a stairwell exit, vanishing from sight.

Later that evening Dr. Knight sat alone in his residence. The clock on his study mantle slowly clicked away each audible second. The chart of Katherine McDuff sat atop his antique desk. He had just completed a detail review of her treatment during that unforgettable day. While looking outside a window he noticed some fine snow flurries starting to fall. A fir tree in front of a brick wall peacefully gathered snowflakes upon its frozen branches. Knight's mind began to churn through a long list of personnel associates and medical colleagues. He wondered what Jennifer Ranier was doing at that very moment. A grim picture of Phil Drummer compressing the chest of Katherine McDuff entered his mind. The snickering face of pathologist Falcon peering over the lifeless body of Katherine McDuff only added to his mental angst.

Knight reached for a phone to the right of his seat. He slowly picked up the receiver and methodically dialed a number jotted down in front of him. The time was 11:50 P.M. After hearing a sleepy voice politely answer his call, Knight identified himself with a late night apology. Mr. James Asher was startled and surprised by the urgent call from the physician. He did however agree to meet with him early the following morning.

CHAPTER 19
A Matter of Security

THREE DAYS PASSED before Mr. James Asher walked into the office of CEO Rineman. Asher had arranged the meeting and requested that an attorney for the hospital system be present. Waiting in the office with Rineman was Dr. Barnes. Sitting along side them was an attorney from a prestigious and expensive Philadelphia law firm. The legal counsel was a close friend of Rineman, and like the CEO, was the figurehead of his firm. The parties had predetermined not to invite Dr. Knight to the discussion. Knight was completely unaware of the gathering that morning.

Introductions were made and Asher was invited to sit down in a plush chair facing Rineman's massive desk. Behind his desk was a large window overlooking the city. The desk was littered with photographs of his family and high profile dignitaries in his presence. A photo of the CEO with his arm around the president of the United States caught Asher's eye. Sitting to the right of Rineman was Dr. Barnes and the legal counsel for the hospital system. Behind their antique Chippendale chairs stood a massive oaken grandfather clock. The timepiece expectedly announced nine o'clock with a calculated series of sharp, yet pleasing pings.

As soon as Asher sat down he sensed power in the room. Despite being in the hospital complex itself the office was comfortable and deathly quiet. The hustle and bustle of a major medical center surrounding the confines had somehow been kept out of the quarters. A soft hum surrounded the room. Asher suddenly felt as if he was on the bridge of the Starship Enterprise. His favorite Star Trek episode titled *Balance of Terror* entered his mind. An exact star date of 1709.2 arose from his memory banks. The computer genius could remember the snowy December day in 1966 when he first watched the episode. As Rineman began to speak Asher tried to picture the CEO as Star Trek's Commander James T. Kirk. Unfortunately, Rineman had the physical attributes of the crafty Romulan leader who met his death in that memorable episode.

"To what do we owe this pleasure?" said CEO Rineman after introductions were made.

"Thank you for meeting with me," said Asher. "I will try to make this brief since I know we all have busy schedules."

The pricey Philadelphia attorney shifted in his chair rather hoping for longevity. Despite charging a thousand dollars an hour he was glad that his firm included travel time in the fee. He noticed a picture of Rineman teeing off at the Augusta National Golf Club. He wondered how the CEO was able to get on the course while his efforts three years ago failed. The word "unfair" registered in his wealthy mind.

"As you may know I spoke at length with Dr. Knight about two days ago," said Asher. "Dr. Knight had some troublesome concerns that I believe warrant your attention."

Doctor Barnes then stared out the window. It was a blustery November day in the city. A group of pigeons rapidly flew with the wind in a downward direction just outside. Barnes was still getting over the shock of the McDuff death. Grave concerns about the well being of his cardiothoracic colleague occupied his mind. A sorrowful feeling entered his gut while thinking of Knight and the upcoming Philadelphia *Chronicle* article. Looking at CEO Rineman he wished he had washed his hands completely of Knight's plan to ramp up the surgical volume.

Asher continued saying, "First of all, Dr. Knight raised concerns about the validity of our blood testing laboratory." Asher then proceeded into a detailed description of Knight's discussion with the head of laboratory services. Asher confidently assured the group that all laboratory values were valid. After answering a few questions he then informed the group that this was not the main reason for the meeting.

CEO Rineman then spoke again saying, "We all know that Dr. Knight has been under an immense amount of pressure lately." He paused to look at the attorney and chairman next to him, then continued, "Certainly this can explain his intense concerns regarding patient care." Rineman then again looked at his legal counsel hoping that the I.T. guru was not wasting his precious legal time. The attorney reflexively shook his head in agreement while still stewing over Augusta National's rejection of him.

Rineman then looked back at Asher and while cocking his head to one side said firmly, "Well then please tell us Mr. Asher, what is the urgent topic that prompted you to gather us together?"

"Dr. Knight is convinced that some computer virus is altering the laboratory values of his patients," said Asher bluntly. His comment was followed by silence in the room.

"What do you mean?" said Rineman with a wrinkled forehead and frown, "I don't understand."

"He stated to me that several of his patient's have died unexpectedly over the past few months," replied Asher. "Two of these patient's had rapid changes in their electrolyte levels that he couldn't explain from a medical standpoint."

Barnes immediately thought back upon the M & M rounds discussion regarding a patient's potassium level. The pitiful feeling in his stomach became more intense.

Asher paused to look around at the now very attentive group. He then continued, "Simply put, he could not explain to me the rapid change in lab values from a scientific standpoint. He told me that no known law of pharmacology or medicine could explain the sudden shift in lab values."

"What are you suggesting?" asked legal counsel.

"I'm not suggesting anything," said Asher. "I'm just bringing a serious concern to your attention."

"Let me get this straight," said Rineman. "Knight thinks that something or someone is altering the lab values of his patients while they are in the hospital?"

"Correct," said Asher.

"There must be a logical explanation," said Barnes. "Do you realize what you, I mean he, may be implying?"

"That someone is trying to harm his patients," said the Philadelphia attorney now with a very serious look on his face. "Some illegal entity I presume," was his follow up line.

"He didn't put it that bluntly," said Asher. "But that was the concern that I took away from the conversation." Asher paused to look around at the puzzled faces surrounding him. He then said, "His speech was very rapid during the conversation. He looked as if he hadn't slept all night."

The attorney continued, "I mean, I'm assuming that when laboratory values come back erroneous, subsequent medical care can be detrimental."

"Of course it will be detrimental," said Barnes. "All of our treatment protocols are centered upon objective laboratory and clinical findings. For every action occurring on the surgical floor, this in an appropriate reaction." Barnes paused, then continued saying, "Assuming the original information is accurate."

"What proof does he have?" asked the attorney.

"None that I am aware of," responded Asher. "Just a rash of deaths with unexplained lab shifts." Asher paused and continued while recalling additional facts, "Oh yea, he threw in some talk about pathology reports and peculiar cell wall findings. Lost me a bit on that stuff," said Asher with a quirky grin.

"We need to call the police," said Chairman Barnes.

"Whoa, whoa!" said Rineman holding the palms of his hands up to Dr. Barnes. "Let's not go crazy here." Rineman looked at the group and then continued, "We don't want mass hysteria here. Certainly not based upon the hunch of a surgeon who frankly in my opinion, is overworked and overstressed."

"This whole thing is going to far," said Barnes staring directly at Rineman. "We need someone with experience in this type of matter involved."

"We do have someone with experience in this matter Michael," replied Rineman as he held his arm out in the direction of the attorney. "Our esteemed friend sitting next to you is the head of the most storied law firm in Philadelphia." Rineman paused to gather his composure. He did not like Barnes' terminology of "this whole thing." Once settled he continued saying, "That's why we invited him to this meeting. Now lets hear what he has to say about the matter."

The legal eagle stared at the floor gathering his thoughts. All eyes in the room were upon him. He then spoke in a calculated fashion saying, "Mr. Asher, have any other physician's or department chairs voiced a similar concern?"

"No" was the response.

"Has there been any known breach into your information system?" was the next question addressed to Asher. "I mean a breach from a computer security standpoint."

"No" was his response once again.

"I see," said the attorney, again pausing for effect while formulating his next expensive question. "Can you please explain to us how each physician or medical worker accesses your system?"

"Surely," said Asher who then proceeded to succinctly summarize the process of logging into the EMR system. A brief tutorial was given regarding the two-step log in process required from outside the confines of the hospital. The crucial role of the authentication token was then explained. Asher kept the terminology simple, yet soon travelled beyond their level of comprehension.

The medical system proxy then spoke again, "The way I see it is that we have a state of the art EMR system that is the gold standard for hospitals around the country. The system has never been knowingly violated. Our I.T. department is top notch and they constantly monitor the system. Our only concern at this point is the belief of one, and only one surgeon, that the entire system is being breached solely for the purpose of harming his patients." The attorney looked at the party and then asked, "Is that a clear description of the scenario at hand?"

"That's the way I see it," said Rineman.

"I would agree," said Barnes.

"How knowledgeable is Dr. Knight with computers and the EMR?" asked the attorney.

Some subtle chuckles went through the crowd. "No knowledge whatsoever," said a smiling Asher with a grin on his face. Asher recalled setting up Knight's home computer system being amazed by the absolute lack of technological savvy displayed by the surgeon.

"Then I agree that we have to proceed slowly here," replied the attorney. "Very slowly. To release any portion of Knight's concerns to the press would be poison to the system." He paused, then spoke again, "I mean Dr. Knight may be a bit over paranoid at this point in time. Allowing his concerns to run out of control would be Armageddon to the PGH system."

"I fully agree," said Rineman. "But we do need a plan."

"Why didn't he come to us?" asked Barnes still skeptical of the entire situation. "I mean we are his most trusted confidants."

"Pride, anger, disappointment," said Rineman. "Take your pick. You know Richard, he is a bit of a rogue. Once he sets sail in a certain direction an unalterable course is usually set."

"Here is what I recommend," said the PGH head attorney as he checked the time on his Rolex Day Date Presidential watch. The medical system's lead attorney then proceeded to formulate a plan in response to the concerns of Mr. Asher. He firstly informed CEO Rineman that several other members of his legal team would need to be involved. Rineman readily consented to this blunt warning of a future financial plunder. Next, he asked Asher to immediately commence electronic and computerized surveillance on all of Dr. Knight's patients. Asher agreed to personally supervise this task, which sent his mind into a frenzied state of energy. He then requested that all parties in the room meet once a month to discuss the progress of this matter of security.

"All agree?" asked counsel.

"Agree," said Rineman and Asher.

"Agree with one caveat," said Barnes. He then looked first at Rineman, then at legal counsel before saying, "That we immediately notify the police if any known unauthorized trespass of the system occurs."

"Of course," said counsel. "Dr. Barnes, let me be clear. We aren't trying to cover up anything. Rather we are making an appropriate response to a concern brought to us by the hospital's I.T. team. If, at any moment an illegal action is suspected, the authorities will be notified at once."

Dr. Barnes then agreed to the plan. A brief exchange occurred regarding paralegals and secretaries responsible for lines of communication. Asher assured the team that an internal alarm system would be in affect by one week at the latest. Legal counsel then questioned Rineman on Augusta National and his contacts there. A series of handshakes transpired as the group broke up and headed towards the door. Asher told Rineman to "live long and prosper" but received no Trekkie response to the comment.

"Oh, one more thing," said Barnes. "What about Dr. Knight? Shouldn't he be aware of this plan?"

"I was wondering who would ask that question," said legal.

A brief pause occurred as everyone gathered a measured response to the question. Then, a unanimous decision was made not to alert Dr. Knight of the surveillance plan. The consensus being that Knight was under enough duress at the moment. All agreed that Knight would be made aware of the plan if he ever voiced direct security concerns to either Rineman or Barnes. Then the meeting ended, sending each man in separate directions.

James Asher headed directly to his office to commence his assigned task. By Monday of the following week the entire EMR system, as it related to Dr. Knight, was under his surveillance. Anyone logging into the data of a Knight patient would be tracked with regards to their actions. This included floor nurses, laboratory personnel, interns, residents and ancillary services. All EMR access from outside the hospital setting would also be monitored. Specifically, the access token used to enter the system would be documented alongside any patient care orders given. Lastly, Asher installed sophisticated antiviral software linking the laboratory data on all of Knight's patients to his personal communication network. This spyware would identify any external corruption attempting to alter the blood work values of Knight's patients. He specifically adjusted the software to be vigilant in relation to the electrolyte values transported through the system. This tweak of the system was based upon Knight's original conversation with Asher. The entire system was set to trigger a personal alarm to Asher immediately upon sensing a breach. This included Asher's work computer, home computer and smart phone. James Asher was the only employee within the I.T. system aware of the settings. It was his brainchild.

Fortunately, for all involved parties, Asher failed to detect any paranormal activity throughout the month of November. The month was marked by a somber mood on the cardiothoracic team. Dr. Knight took three full days off after the death of Katherine McDuff. Considering the fact that he only took one day off for the birth of each of his children, this was a major event. The McDuff name was never again mentioned to Knight directly. However, upon his return the surgical volume remained heavy. The team of Larson and Polk became one of Knight's favorite combinations and their efficient work was well appreciated by the demanding mentor. Knight never lost sight of the fact that a Philadelphia *Chronicle* article would hit the newsstand in January of the following year. He remained obsessed with surgical numbers and a soon to be published mortality rate. A cold, surgeon's mentality allowed him to churn without emotion through a heavy surgical load. Thanksgiving week was marked by a flurry of so called emergency cases. The ramped up volume prompted three surgeries to be performed the Friday after Thanksgiving.

"How was your Thanksgiving," asked Nurse Frey to Dr. Knight.

"Pathetic," said Knight as he finished the first case of that Friday morning. "Absolutely pathetic. Another wasted work day for the American laborer." Knight then looked around at his staff saying, "Thank God we are all back to work. Normalcy has been restored."

No one dared to interject. The O.R. staff in general was upset about being there that morning. No other surgical rooms were running that Friday morning. A skeleton crew of employees was originally scheduled for the day, which was not open for elective surgery. However a phone call from CEO Rineman mandated duty for the C.T. team that Friday. His reasoning was based on the best interest of the public.

"I love Thanksgiving," said nurse Frey realizing that her good will with Knight allowed her to speak. "Mmmmm, turkey is my favorite."

"Why don't you try the hospital's turkey dinner," said Polk as he helped suture close the chest. "That will change your mindset."

A collection of light laughter followed Polk's line. Polk knew that Knight appreciated him living downstairs in the hole. It reminded Knight of happier days as a resident himself. Whenever possible he hinted to his current PGH residence in conversation. Over the past month Dr. Polk had solidified his position on Knight's very short A-list.

"My wife cooked dinner for the first time," said chief resident Larson. "I'm lucky to be here alive."

The room burst into laughter at the line. Knight had to step back from the table to gather his senses. A tear ran down Polk's eye as he laughed a hearty laugh. Beneath his scrub gown a belly could be appreciated jiggling.

"Shame on you," said nurse Frey.

"Shame on me, shame on her," said Larson. "Shame on her mother who taught her how to cook."

"Go ahead, blame the mother-in-law," said nurse Frey with a smile. "When in doubt, always blame the mother-in-law."

Nurse Frey just shook her head and then looked at Olivia Casey who quietly stood at the foot of the table. "What about you P.A. Casey, did you cook yesterday?"

Olivia Casey just shook her head in a negative fashion. She didn't verbally respond to nurse Frey's question. Her mood was depressed that morning and Knight sensed it. Her reasoning was obvious in that she didn't want to be there that Friday morning. Knight knew that her family lived in Boston and she had to cancel plans to travel home that holiday. With three cases on Wednesday and then three more on Friday, time didn't exist for the back and forth travel.

"You should have joined me," said Polk to P.A. Casey. "Cookie wasn't much company at the cafeteria table yesterday. Nothing like Thanksgiving with your loved ones."

Olivia Casey didn't respond. She blinked her eyes as they started to well up with tears.

"Leave the girl alone," said a raspy voice from the back of the room. It came from circulating nurse Warner who also didn't care to be working that day. Nurse Warner was a veteran general surgery nurse of fifteen years. Knight's regular circulating nurse called in sick that morning. Nurse Warner was subsequently required to report to duty. Longstanding Black Friday shopping plans were cancelled and her daughters were not happy. She did not like Dr. Knight.

"The poor girl is upset, can't you see?" was her next line. There was quiet in the room as Knight continued to operate, unfazed by the rebel. She continued saying, "Who in their right mind wants to be here today? It's a family holiday for God's sake, we should all be with family."

Pete Larson looked back at Nurse Warner who was behind Knight. His eyes pleaded for her to stop. She smirked at him and continued, "I had to cancel shopping plans today on short notice. I certainly do not want to be here."

Knight continued working but calmly said, "Consider yourself lucky nurse Warner. Your hard earned money won't be spent on the latest marketing scam of Madison Avenue." Knight looked up with a smirk then said, "Gotta get the designer boots! Don't forget the matching hand bag, they're on sale!"

Polk began laughing. No one else in the room did. Knight continued, "Besides, what's going on back at home? All of America is asleep on the couch today."

"Tryptophan," said a Seinfeld obsessed Polk. "It's from the turkey, makes you sleep. Season nine, episode number six."

Knight continued, "Every TV across our land is on loud and louder. Fathers will occasionally open their eyes to watch yet another hour long *Sportscenter* on ESPN. Mothers continue to bake and cook despite trying to kill their relatives with overconsumption the prior day. All the kids are in the basement staring at their gaming consoles. Rock music is blaring while they talk on their cell phone and shoot up their video screens. The only thing that can stop their addiction is a power outage or epileptic seizure." Knight was now starting to warm up. He stopped suturing the chest and stepped back. Larson recognized this as a harbinger of badness. "Their parents can't stop their demise. What we need is discipline, austerity and structure," said Knight. He paused and then slowly turned to nurse Warner and finished his retort with, "And what better structure than work? Good old-fashioned work. That's an ethic we all need." Knight then paused and stared directly at the circulating nurse as he said, "Don't you agree nurse Warner?"

Per protocol the anesthesia attending surfaced from above the head sheet. He had been listening to the exchange, yet held his position until the final tragic act was about to begin. To fuel the fire he said, "Well said Richard. Very well said. Kudos." Knight nodded his head in acceptance of the praise, while continuing to stare at Nurse Warner in a dare to respond. Larson stood behind him shaking his head, imploring her not to continue.

"I'd rather be shopping," said a defiant nurse Warner with an attitude. "And besides, only emergencies should be done on a day like today."

No time elapsed before Knight roared forward at Nurse Warner. "You lazy incompetent ninny. Are you suggesting that these cases aren't emergencies? How dare you question my decision making!" Warner stepped backwards as Knight's assault continued, "You're making time and a half for sitting on that chair and complaining about a shopping trip. That's what's wrong with this country. Nobody wants to work. Just stand in line and get a hand out from the government. You should be working at the V.A. Hospital!"

Warner went to respond but never got the chance. Knight continued by screaming, "Get out of my room you ungrateful socialist! Get out right now before the sale ends at the shopping mall!"

Nurse Warner was flushed in the face and turned quickly for the door. She bumped into the doorjamb while exiting without saying a word, not to be seen for the remainder of the day.

Knight turned back towards the table with anger in his eyes. He stepped up to the patient and placed his hands back on her chest. Looking to his left he said to the anesthesiologist while shaking his head in disgust, "Do you believe it? Lord save us all."

"Unbelievable," said the anesthesiologist as he slowly disappeared below the head sheet. "Absolutely unbelievable."

Thus the Friday after Thanksgiving continued. A backup nurse soon received a call to report to duty. Knight added on a fourth case that day for good measure. The surgical team finished operating that evening at 8 o'clock. The Big Knight Machine was firing on all cylinders as it continued its run down the home stretch.

CHAPTER 20
Vacation

By December of that year Jennifer Ranier had moved into Phil's apartment. After her eviction, she split time evenly with Phil and the social work girls. At first Jennifer would only spend weekends with Phil. Then, as their hospital schedules overlapped, midweek stays became commonplace. Slowly but surely more and more of her personal belongings ended up in the Greycliff apartment. Then, as their intimacy solidified, the well-rounded girl from Baltimore began calling West Philadelphia her new home.

Her relationship with Phil Drummer blossomed. Despite being several years his elder, they had much in common. Both enjoyed sports, physical fitness and city life. They spent weekends socializing with friends, and weekdays carrying out the mundane aspects of life. Their presence together seemed to make everything that occurred special, no matter how trivial.

As the halfway point of internship approached, Phil had trouble recalling what life was like without his current roommate. His life was completely different as opposed to six months ago. Gone was the tentative intern worried about his first call night. Present was a talented intern who was somehow revered within the PGH system.

Polk tabbed him with the moniker of Romeo, which seemed to stick, at least amongst the interns. Life on the surgical floor was also different for Phil. He noticed that nurses paid more attention to him, while frequently catching their gaze and whispers around him. Within the O.R. setting the attention was more blunt among the nurses. Phil was constantly bombarded with coy questions about his current girlfriend. He deftly managed all of the attention with a smile and well put answer, only creating more gossip and interest concerning the two. As the end of the year approached he was reaching a cult status within the confines of the PGH. This status was noticeable to all, including an ever appreciating Jennifer Ranier.

As the second week of December approached, Phil and Jenna prepared for a short vacation together. The vacation schedule of an intern was a marvel of simplicity. During the first week of July each intern was given two assigned weeks for vacation by the Department of Surgery. It was that simple, take it or leave it. There would be no complaining, bargaining or special requests. An intern lived at the bottom of the academic food chain. The most undesirable weeks of the year would subsequently fall on their laps. Phil was assigned a week in December and a second week in the middle of February. Fortunately for Phil, Jenna was able to take a week off and join him as well. They planned a short trip North to visit Phil's family and then travel to the town of Eagles Mere for some cross-country skiing. After a hectic week of work they gathered up their travel supplies in the Greycliff complex. It was a cold Friday night in Philadelphia that December.

"Are you sure your dad won't mind me staying there?" asked Jenna.

"No problem," said Phil. "As long as we stay in different rooms and you keep your hands off me in public."

Jenna smiled with a nod of her head. It was amazing to her how happy she was with Phil. Her time with Dr. Knight seemed so far ago.

"Who's going to take care of Goldie?" asked Ranier. She was referring to a plump goldfish with buggy eyes resting in a large bowl sitting on the coffee table. Jenna won the fish at a local festival then spared him or her a ride down the toilet as recommended by Phil.

"Jim said he will watch him," replied Phil. "He's a vet student, couldn't be in better hands. If needed he can perform CPR on Goldie."

"That guy gives me the creeps," said Jenna referring to Jim Turner.

Phil came out of a closet holding some folded clothes saying, "Give him some time, he is a nice guy. Smart as can be."

"He just looks at me funny," said Ranier. "Does he have a girlfriend?"

Phil smiled. "No. He is an eligible bachelor." He then stuffed his clothing into a duffle bag. "Maybe you can hook him up with one of the social work girls."

"Are you kidding me," said Ranier. "He is a choir boy compared to them. Their antics would burn a hole in his retina."

"That's what your girlfriends said about me, right?" asked Phil.

"No. Not right," was her reply.

At that moment there was a rap on the door. Phil opened it up to let in Jim Turner from across the hall. He was holding a cold piece of pizza in his hand.

"When are you leaving again?" asked Turner as he walked in past Phil. Phil did notice that Turner usually walked directly towards a visual of Jennifer. He stopped while staring at Ranier and taking a bite out of his pizza.

"Hi Jim," said Ranier smiling as she continued to pack a bag.

"Greetings," said Turner with a slab of pizza in his mouth. He locked his gaze upon the woman in front of him. Her perfume was a sensual pleasure to him.

"Soon," said Phil. "Will be gone through next Saturday."

"No problem, I've got you covered," said Turner.

"Remember to feed Goldie," said Ranier.

"Check," said Turner. "Anything else?"

"No," said Phil as he slung the travel bag over his shoulder. "Remember, I'm an intern, I have nothing of importance in my life." Phil headed towards the door saying, "Adios, amigo."

"Ready," said a smiling and perky Ranier zipping up her bag. "Let's head north to wherever the heck you came from Dr. Drummer."

"Vaja con Dios," said Turner raising his right hand in the air as the couple slip passed him. "Remember to write."

Turner then watched the happy couple head down the hallway to the elevator. His gaze was fixed on the backside of Jennifer Ranier. A picture of fellow floor mate Maria Cruz entered his mind. Suddenly Turner realized that Phil Drummer had an impeccable taste for beautiful women. He spent the next hour thinking of Jennifer and Maria, trying to make a difficult fantasy league first round draft pick. After much internal debate he choose the sensual blonde from Baltimore. Her lingering smell played heavily into the decision.

The ride North to Phil's hometown took the couple up the Pennsylvania turnpike through the Lehigh Valley. Further north they passed beneath Blue Mountain and headed directly into coal country. Jennifer was educated about the vast culm banks that surrounded towns named Carbondale and Miners Mills. She learned what a coal cracker was and discovered the difference between anthracite and bituminous coal. Mercifully, her informational tour was over when the couple arrived at the Drummer homestead.

Phil's home sat on a quiet street across from an elementary school named after a local congressman. Phil pointed out that the street was a dirt road when he grew up. He also alerted Jenna that the school originally was a combination dump and culm bank, which sat adjacent to now abandoned and partly sealed off mine shafts. Despite this final tidbit of historical information, she agreed to spend the weekend in Phil's childhood home.

Jennifer was amazed at the small, double block home where Phil grew up. How everyone coexisted in such a small home was difficult for her to comprehend. Adding to her wonderment was a single bathroom that sat directly off the kitchen, just a few steps from the kitchen table. Certainly a sister would have never survived in this household. Shortly into her stay she also realized two distinct traits of the Drummer household. One was a male dominated décor that was obviously not funded by a wealthy benefactor. Phil's dad kept the place clean to an extent, but it was obvious that no beautification budget existed. Secondly, and more tangible, was the lingering effect that Phil's deceased mother had on the household. Photos and memories of the matriarch adorned the household. To the unknowing one would think that Mr. Drummer was living with his spouse, who just happened to be physically away from the premise on that day. In conversation, Mrs. Drummer was constantly spoken of in the present tense, as if she was going to turn the corner and walk into the kitchen that very moment.

"Mom loves Eagles Mere," said Mr. Drummer as the three sat in the family room. Mr. Drummer was just sitting in a chair looking forward at the two sitting in front of him. He nervously tapped his fingers on his thigh, still not completely comfortable with the elder beauty sitting next to his son.

"Always did dad," was Phil's response. "It's her special spot."

"What time do you want to leave tomorrow?" asked Jennifer to Phil. She was trying to wrap up the conversation that could only be appreciated by small town folk.

"Lets try to be on the road by 10 AM," said Phil. "Its about an hour and a half ride from here."

"How is that crazy heart surgeon treating you?" asked Mr. Drummer out of the blue. He was aware of Dr. Knight from the weekly phone calls from his son.

"Not bad now dad," said Phil. "Fortunately I'm off his rotation now, so I don't run across him very much."

"From your phone calls he sounds a bit maniacal," said the elder Drummer. "Do you work with him Jennifer?"

Jennifer briefly looked down at the ground with a pensive gaze saying, "No, not any more." After a pause she then looked up with a smile at Mr. Drummer saying positively, "Not any more. I'm working with the Plastic Surgery department now. It has been a welcome change in my life."

"That's good," said Mr. Drummer. "That's very good. One thing I learned from mom is that life's too short." He paused and smiled a reflective smile saying, "If you don't like where you are in life, then make something happen. It may seem scary but it is usually for the better."

Jennifer Ranier smiled at Phil's dad. She then looked at Phil while responding, "That's exactly what I did Mr. Drummer. I surely made something happen." She paused and continued, "And it has been a definite change for the better."

The conversation then lasted into the night before the group broke up. Jennifer spent another lonely evening in Phil's old room, sleeping on a mattress that was twenty years past prime. She pictured the bed and breakfast that was awaiting her and Phil the following night. The vision was the only thing that gave her solace. A clanking radiator pipe kept her up on a regular basis through the cold night.

Eagles Mere is a bucolic resort nestled at 2100 feet in the beautiful Endless Mountains of Pennsylvania. It became popular in the 1800's among well to do Philadelphians seeking out a cool summer refuge. Large Victorian style cottages were erected along a mile long lake that was known for its beauty and serenity. A quaint village soon arose adjacent to the water. Over time the town somehow managed to maintain an amazing pastoral flavor. Hence the local motto declaring the resort "the town that time forgot."

Fortunately for Phil and Jenna an early winter storm had coated the area with a foot of snow several days earlier. Jenna was happy to be out of coal country. Her stay at the Drummer home was delightful, but by that Sunday morning it was time to move on. Both she and Phil looked forward to some quiet time together. The two nights apart made Jennifer realize how much Phil's presence meant to her. Despite his provincial upbringing, she realized that this up and coming surgeon was her very own diamond in the rough.

Their next 48 hours were spent in constant contact. A bed and breakfast with a fireplace served as home base for their respite. Beer, wine and whiskey primed their hepatic system while fueling their familiarity. Daytime hours found the couple out skiing across the frozen lake. Dinners were spent in the surrounding cozy inns, which were not crowded during the midweek. Evenings found the young couple together, reading and watching movies underneath a woolen blanket. The rustic ambience provided the ultimate hideaway for the two companions. Phil couldn't recall a more satisfying vacation up until the moment his cell phone rang out that early Wednesday morning.

"Sorry to bother you Romeo," was the opening line from Rick Polk. "However, all is not well here in Disneyland."

"What was the last thing I told you Rick," said Phil rubbing his eyes. Jennifer was lying next to him as she shook her head and rolled over, pulling the covers tight to her neck.

"I know, I know," said Polk. "Only call in an emergency. Well this is an emergency."

"What is it?" asked the disbelieving Phil.

"Riles quit the internship program yesterday," said Polk in a serious tone. "Had a major run in with Knight and couldn't handle it. Apparently turned ugly."

"Oh no," said Phil. "I know he didn't take it well when Knight tossed him out of the McDuff code."

"Well his dad charged down from Boston, caused a big scene. Chairman Barnes got involved. Apparently old man Riles and Knight despise each other," said Polk.

"What happens now?" asked Phil hating to hear the answer.

"The call schedule is all messed up," said Polk. "Knight is going ballistic about not having enough in house staff to care for his patients." Polk paused, then continued saying, "The guy is operating like a madman. We are all having trouble keeping up with him. Now this with Riles, it couldn't have happened at a worse time."

Phil cringed at this news. He knew quite well were the conversation was headed. He felt a momentary sadness for the Riles clan, remembering the overpowering shine of the elder Riles' teeth.

"Word has it that all intern vacations are being cancelled until the end of the year," said Polk. "Not that I was planning on going anywhere next week."

"How does that involve me?" asked Phil. "My next vacation isn't until February."

"I've got a funny feeling the higher ups will be trying to contact you today," replied Polk. Both he and Phil paused before Polk continued, "They may want you back now, like today."

"Oh no," said Phil as Jennifer now raised a concerned head toward his direction. "What gives you that idea?"

"Both Barnes and Knight asked me where you were, and how to get in touch with you," said Polk.

"What!" yelled Phil. His outburst immediately garnered Jennifer's full attention.

"I didn't cave," said Polk. "Held my ground. But you know satellites and communication nowadays. The cell phone can find you anywhere if you wish to carry it."

"Oh boy," said a disgusted Phil now realizing that he drank too much wine last night.

"Got to go," said Polk. "Three more heart cases today. I'll play dumb regarding your whereabouts. Remember, keep the faith," was his final line before hanging up the phone.

Phil tossed down his cell phone in disbelief. He looked at the fireplace which still held a few smoldering embers. A partially drawn shade over a window let in some morning sun. A light snow was starting to fall outdoors.

"It's him," said Jennifer. "I know it has to do something with him. Please tell me I'm wrong."

Phil just shook his head while staring at the fireplace. His gaze then turned to Ranier. He couldn't believe how good she looked so early in the morning.

"Yep," said Phil rubbing his eyes. "Fred Riles quit and Rick said they, or should I say he, wants me back."

"Control freak," said Ranier in disbelief. "When do they want you back?"

Just then the cell phone rang again. Phil looked at the caller I.D. while cringing. He gazed turned back to Jenna as he sadly whispered, "Now."

The ride back to Philadelphia that day was somber at best. Jennifer briefly pleaded with Phil not to answer the call, but he did. Both knew that the barrage would continue until Phil was tracked down. Chief Resident Larson notified Phil that all intern vacations were being rescheduled to a later date, and that his services were immediately needed back at the PGH. The Riles situation was briefly mentioned, as was the urgent nature of the mandate. No option was given to contest the demand and Phil begrudgingly obliged. The vile name of Dr. Knight was never mentioned throughout the long car ride home.

CHAPTER 21
The Fat Lady Sings

THE NEXT SEVERAL weeks were a blur in Phil Drummer's mind. Upon returning to PGH he was informed that an additional intern was needed on the CT team, due to the increase in surgical volume. Phil then rejoined the Big Knight Machine, working side by side with Rick Polk and Pete Larson. Despite Knight's disapproval of his extra-curricular activities with Ranier, he knew that Phil was a trusted intern with a good set of hands. The surgical department then abruptly released physician assistant Casey. Her dismissal was largely due to inept skills and partly due to lack of willingness. With Phil back in O.R. four there was no room at the table for a timid and inexperienced helper, at least not in December. Lastly, the call schedule for all interns became every other night, for the remainder of the year. This was compliments of Frederick Riles III, who along with his father, threatened legal action against Knight on the way out the door.

None of the above seemed to bother Dr. Knight. His persona became larger than life that last month of 2010. An amazing influx of cases poured through the PGH. Knight had primed the pump of every cardiologist over the past two months, and his grease job was paying off.

He was performing ten to fifteen cases per week. The SICU had to hire more staff and open up an adjacent wing to accommodate the overflow patients. CEO Rineman was all smiles, as he saw a bump up in hospital revenue. Chairman Barnes was very uneasy, as he saw a somewhat possessed Dr. Knight carrying out his twisted plan. Knight was revitalized as he operated at a frenetic pace, rarely going home to face the music of his sham social existence. In essence Knight had reached the earthly equivalent of a surgical Valhalla, enjoying the spoils and life of a warrior, while being revered by his underlings.

Despite the élan of their leader, the surgical support team beneath Knight was on the verge of collapse. Every other night call meant nothing to Rick Polk who lived in the hospital. However it meant a lot to the remaining interns, Phil and Cathy Finley. Each intern was fatigued yet kept the pace. The pace unfortunately affected their lives outside the hospital. Phil would come back to the Greycliff every other night and collapse on the bed after dinner. Jenna was convinced that Knight was methodically trying to break his morale in an attempt to have him quit the residency program. Phil disagreed while maintaining a respect for Knight, who thirty years his elder, was the leader of the charging brigade. When Phil arrived at the hospital, Knight was there. When Phil left the hospital, Knight was still there. An unconfirmed rumor spread that Knight was actually seen in the Polk lounge late one evening. Rick Polk was confident in his unwillingness to confirm, nor deny this report.

Although the holiday season soon appeared on the Philadelphia streets and through the commercial airwaves, it did not exist within the walls of the PGH. There was no time for holiday cheer and holiday joy. Sick patients needed surgery to save their lives, and that was the drumbeat. Knight even managed to put on an emergency case that Christmas morning, securing his position as the most hated surgeon amongst the staff. Nurse Warner tabbed him with the "Grinch" moniker that snowy morning of the twenty-fifth. The crusty nurse however dared not question his authority this time around. As the last week of December approached, no one within the PGH system dared question Knight. He had become larger than the whole, sitting atop a fatigued infrastructure that was being pushed to its physical limits.

As the last Tuesday of the month approached, a weary surgical team hustled down the steps to the operating room. Knight had three cases on that morning, as the final push to end the year was on.

"What's up with next week?" asked an out of breath Polk as the team ran down the stairwell. "There are no cases." He was referring to the first week of January, the following year.

"Weird," said Larson. "Knight must be going away, but he hasn't said anything."

"That guy is going to be the richest surgeon in the cemetery," said Phil Drummer. "He is going to kill himself and all of us at this pace."

"Its gold Jerry, gold," said Polk to the unappreciative audience.

As the team rushed down the corridor to the OR they soon heard a strange sound coming from the surgical holding area. At first they thought a catfight had broken out amongst the nurses. High pitched whining and screaming was heard from a distance. Then, as they approached the doorway of the surgical suite, a more distinct Italian based clamor was appreciated. It soon became apparent that someone was singing opera in the holding area.

The bemused house staff turned the corner to see an adoring Dr. Knight standing in front of a portly female who had just checked in. The nursing staff had gathered around the surreal event in appreciation of the ongoing performance. For in front of Dr. Knight stood the world renowned Helga Cox, soprano for the Dallas Opera Company. The diva had met Knight after a sold out performance at the Philadelphia Academy of Music several years ago. Since then, they had befriended each other. Cox had flown in the previous day from Texas, and was scheduled for an aortic valve replacement that day by Dr. Knight. At that very moment she stood in front of Knight with one arm across her chest and the other pointing to the heavens. Her gaze was beyond the audience as her fateful aria went on.

The lyrics continued as they bellowed out of her robust body, "Nell'ora del dolor, perche, perche, Signor," Phil looked at Knight who had a tear in his eye. He was sure at that moment that the pitch of her voice was going to shatter the glass in the room. Her heavenly voice was intoxicating to all who listened. It was as if an angel had descended upon them that joyous morning.

Then, while looking directly at Knight with a smile, the Dallas diva emphatically ended her highlight with an ever so softly, "ah, perche me ne rimuneri cosi?" The final words were riveting, and lasted an eternity to everyone present.

"Bravo, Bravo!" yelled the medical crowd. "Bravo!" The applause was thunderous as Knight approached the starlet with open and extended arms. He reached forward and, while bowing, kissed her hand. Knight then patted her on the forearm while expressing his personal thanks for the aria. He then turned to the crowd, while gently lifting Ms. Cox's hand in appreciation. His other hand gestured towards her, fueling the applause and festivity that morning.

"Wow," said Pete Larson. "Wow."

"Girl's got some pipes," said Polk.

"Beautiful, absolutely beautiful," said Phil in amazement. He was in such awe that his colleagues' comments failed to register in his mind. "What a beautiful song."

Knight then personally escorted Helga Cox to the check in area through a throng of well-wishers. The VIP from Texas was then turned over to an adoring nursing staff that began prepping her for surgery that very morning.

Knight then turned away and approached the team. He walked by quickly saying, "Now that's talent gentlemen, real talent." The team nodded in agreement and then quickly followed their honorable leader down to O.R. room number four.

The knife hit the skin ahead of schedule that morning. Knight was on his A-game while roaring through the first case without a glitch. Soon, the opera star from Dallas was on the table being put to sleep by the anesthesiologist. Knight then uncharacteristically stood next to the prima donna as her breathing tube was being inserted. He wanted to specifically put some pressure on the anesthesia attending that was passing the endotracheal tube down the patient's windpipe.

"Careful with the vocal cords doctor," said Knight. "Very careful with the vocal cords. They are worth some money."

"No problem," said the gas passer who slid the tube skillfully down the airway of Helga Cox.

Within minutes Ms. Cox had her chest prepped and draped by the resident team. Knight returned to the room with a skip in his step, humming a tune as Nurse Ella Frey gowned and gloved him. As he stepped to the table he looked up while taking the scalpel from Nurse Frey. Knight then announced the start time and nodded to circulating nurse Warner who hit the switch to the overhead speakers. Immediately overhead roared the opening music to the opera Tosca. The roar of the orchestra caught the team off guard, as they expected the obligatory Borodin symphony.

"Anyone, anyone?" asked Knight as he cut his way down to the sternum. "Anyone know the composer?" A rush of bright red blood followed the scalpel's path.

The faces around the table were blank. Polk was quiet not knowing an opera star was scheduled for the day. Otherwise he would have studied internet opera basics in hopes of impressing the senior surgeon.

"I thought not," said Knight smugly. "The answer of course is the incomparable Giacomo Puccini." The music roared as Knight took handle of the power saw to split the diva's sternal bone. "When in doubt on an opera question, always guess Puccini," said Knight.

"Anyone know his birthplace?" asked Knight again.

"Italy," said Polk.

"Of course Italia," said Knight slowly rolling his head back and forth to the music, "But where in Italia?"

"Tuscany," said Larson with a guess.

"Bravo," said Knight cranking open the retractor to expose the beating heart of Ms. Cox. "Bravo. But I need a city name, a city name."

"Anyone remember the Seinfeld episode regarding the house in Tuscany?" said Polk.

"The answer is Lucca," said Knight in a professorial tone. "That's L-U-C-C-A, Lucca. They have a statue erected to him in the town square. Image that, a statue erected in your honor, to stand as a memorial, forever and ever."

No one answered as the roar of the music continued. Soon, male and female voices were signing Italian operatic verses, foreign to all ears except Knight. Knight appeared to be overcome by the music, which was incorporated into his every bodily movement. He was picturing a statue of himself, but couldn't decide on the exact hospital placement for the monument.

"Now for the bonus round, can anyone name the opera?" asked Knight as he started the process to put the patient on the heart-lung machine.

"I'll give you a hint, the woman whose heart lies before you just sang the most famous aria from the opera hours ago," said Knight. "Do you remember this beautiful women singing to you earlier today?" A minute went by before Knight again spoke, as if talking to himself saying, "Vissi d'arte, means I lived for my art." His body continued to slowly sway back and forth to the foreign cacophony.

Faces around the table remained blank as Knight briefly looked up at them. He shook his head in mock disgust saying, "Gentlemen, you should all be ashamed of yourselves. To be treated to such operatic excellence and have no knowledge of the history is inexcusable. What do they teach you in college these days?"

"The Barber of Seville," said Polk.

"No," said Knight immediately. "Don't be an idiot."

"Remember the Seinfeld episode centered around the Barber of Seville?"

"Time has run out gentlemen," said Knight. But before he could utter the correct answer, a promiscuous voice from beyond the table spoke out.

"Tosca," said circulating nurse Warner with an Italian dialect.

Knight stopped cold in his tracks and lifted his head up. The surgical team froze as a high-pitched operatic voice screeched from above. Without turning around to face the nurse he said, "What was that?" The face of the anesthesiologist suddenly arose from the head of the table.

"Tosca," said nurse Warner, again with a defiant snap in her voice.

Knight turned around from the table and looked directly at the circulating nurse. He lifted his head slightly upwards to shine his headlight into nurse Warner's face. He then spoke very slowly saying, "Magnifico, nurse Warner, magnifico. I am impressed." He then spun back around to the patient to continue his trade as the high-pitched voices sang overhead.

"Most impressive," said Knight again. "Are you an opera aficionado nurse Warner?"

"Yes, I love the opera," was her matter of fact response. "My parents introduced me to it at a young age."

"A woman of culture," said Knight. "Why don't you educate these imbeciles about Tosca? Which by the way is my favorite opera."

"If you insist Dr. Knight," said nurse Warner as she took two steps towards the table. She stood right behind Knight with a smirking smile that could be appreciated behind her mask. Chief resident Larson looked at her and immediately sensed trouble. The anesthesia attending ominously kept his head above the surgical sheet, a subtle sign appreciated by Drummer and Polk.

"Tosca was a beautiful woman, a singer who was beloved by her fans," said Warner.

"Most beautiful," replied Knight. "An angel with an angelic voice."

Nurse Warner continued saying, "She loved a young, romantic painter named Mario. He was a handsome and very young man."

Knight continued his trade while cutting through Helga's heart muscle to approach the leaky valve. His body swayed back and forth as if possessed by the music. "True love," was his only response.

Larson looked at Phil as an uncomfortable feeling started to arise between the two.

"However, their love was spoiled by the older and ruthless police chief Baron Scarpia, who lusted the younger Tosca," said Warner. "Baron Scrapia was an old geezer who couldn't keep his hands off young women."

"Sounds good so far," said Polk.

"A love triangle," said the anesthesiologist while looking at the group.

"This valve is really shot," said Knight upon first inspection of the aortic valve. He had temporarily lost track of the conversation. A surgeon's concern arose in his eyes as the cardiac inspection continued.

"Baron Scarpia had the younger Mario imprisoned and sentenced to death," said Warner who now had the attention of the entire room except for Knight. "Only Tosca could save his life."

"But how?" asked Nurse Frey.

"I've got a good idea," said Polk.

"We are going to struggle with this valve," said Knight shaking his head in disgust.

"She had to submit to his passion and sleep with him," said Warner. "A tough decision," was her next comment. "Either submit to the dirty old man's desires, or watch your true love die."

"Power is the ultimate aphrodisiac," said the anesthesiologist. "The ultimate."

Knight looked up at the anesthesiologist saying, "What are you talking about?" It was apparent that he had not been listening to nurse Warner's operatic summary.

"Tosca," was the anesthesiologist's response as he reoriented Knight to the conversation.

Nurse Warner sensed that her time was now limited and rapidly continued, "With a heavy heart she agreed, and old man Scarpia proceeded to immediately manhandle the beautiful young girl."

"What are you talking about nurse Warner?" said Knight again with a concern in his voice.

Then, while continuing to describe the scene, nurse Warner said, "But Tosca had a hidden knife, and stuck it into the old fart's gut, killing him." She then acted out Tosca's lethal forward lunge with a twist of her hand saying passionately, "Here is a kiss from Tosca." Her theatrical thrust was directed straight towards Knight, who suddenly realized the implied parallels between Tosca and physician assistant Ranier.

"Bravo," said Polk, "Magnifico."

Knight then turned around to face nurse Warner who continued to twist her wrist back and forth in his direction. She had a smile in her eyes.

"That will be enough nurse Warner," said Knight in a calm and stern voice. "That will surely be enough."

"But what happened to Tosca and Mario?" asked nurse Frey.

"He was shot by a firing squad and she committed suicide," said Warner rapidly. "Jumped off a cliff." She then turned quickly away from Knight and walked away. Her mission was accomplished.

"Good God," said the anesthesiologist. "Love stinks."

"Great ending," said Polk. "Everybody dies. I could have written that one."

"Enough with Tosca!" barked Knight now fully aware of the tragic opera's similarities to his life. "Enough! We've got a surgical problem on our hands everyone. Lets act like professionals people."

Knight then turned back to the damaged heart valve in front of him. He paused to regain his composure, then saying in a somewhat tragically sad tone, "Let's get this thing replaced. Turn the music down. In fact, just please, turn the music off."

There was no verbal response from the surgical team. Everyone was trying to mentally register the exchange that had just occurred. Polk looked at Phil noting a very serious and uncomfortable tone in his face. Larson looked back at nurse Warner who stared directly at him with a smile, her head nodding up and down in victory.

The remainder of the case was uneventful. The soprano's damaged aortic valve was replaced with difficulty. Knight's experience and technical skill led to a successful outcome. Helga Cox's vitals remained stable throughout the case. She was then transported to the recovery room in good condition. Upon completion of the procedure, Knight left the room without saying a word to anyone. Fatigue and sorrowful emotion engulfed his body as he plodded out of the surgical theatre. The tension in the air was palpable.

Helga Cox sailed through the recovery room that day. Her postoperative course during the next twenty-four hours was unremarkable. Knight brought the starlet a large bouquet of roses the morning after surgery. The Philadelphia *Chronicle* ran a short article in their society section regarding her successful surgery. Rave reviews surrounded Knight and his cast of characters in reference to the principle vocalist. Knight was convinced the success would land him the coveted chairmanship of the Academy of Music next year.

Unfortunately, the Dallas diva was murdered per protocol, on postoperative day number two. The cursed team of Dr. O'Keefe and nurse Cruise were again unsuspecting witnesses to the event. A code was called that afternoon after an iatrogenic dose of potassium was administered to Ms. Cox. Her heart responded in physiologic fashion, triggering a fatal arrhythmia.

Throughout the code, Dr. Knight and his surgical team were in the operating room, completing the final case of the day. Shocking verbal reports were constantly relayed into the room, updating Knight on the progress of his superstar. With a patient's heart exposed directly in front of him, the distraught surgeon stoically held his post. All news was bad news that fateful day. Soon afterward, a saddened Chairman Barnes entered the room, announcing the death of Helga Cox.

Sorrow and disbelief seized the head surgeon. He instructed nurse Warner to immediately play the second movement of Beethoven's Seventh Symphony in honor of the maven. No other words were spoken throughout the remainder of the case. Sadness gripped the team as the angelic voice of the deceased echoed through their minds. Knight turned the closure over to the resident team and wandered unsteadily out of the room. All eyes were upon him as he slowly walked down the hallway towards the locker room. The eerie sound of a violin section trailed behind him. No one dared turn off the music until Knight had left the floor, heading to the deathbed of his patient.

Upon entering the room of Helga Cox a single white sheet covered her entire body. A representative of the cleaning staff was present in the room, amid a sea of debris generated by the code. The mere presence of Knight sent the cleaning lady scurrying out of the room. All was quiet as Knight approached the bed. He slowly lifted the sheet off the head of the patient, exposing the peaceful, blue face of Ms. Cox. Knight laid the back of his hand upon her cheek, which was ice cold. A tear slowly worked its way out of his left eye, as he wiped some clotted blood off the split lip of his patient. He then whispered words of solace to the deceased, who lay motionless in front of her beloved surgeon. Knight then recited a solemn prayer prior to gently placing the white sheet back over the head, seeing her for the last time.

He looked up, dazed. Signs of a chaotic cardiac resuscitation abounded. A nearby garbage can was filled with once sterile gloves and dressings sponges. The cardiac crash cart was in disarray with drawers opened, and supplies depleted. Vials of epinephrine and cardiac stimulants lay empty atop the cart. Above the patient sat several monitors, each turned off with no signs of life. Knight's mind automatically reenacted each step of the unsuccessful resuscitation. Questions immediately arose as to who ran the code, and where were his fellow attending surgeons? Why did she die so suddenly? Someone surely had to be held accountable for this death.

His gazed then centered upon an I.V. pole near the head of the bed. It was supporting multiple bags of I.V. fluids that were hung haphazardly during the event. Knight reached his hand up to inspect the content of each bag of fluid, slowly rotating every liter in order to expose its label. Standard mixtures of saline and electrolytes were noted. All fluids were appropriate, except for a single mixture hidden in the midst of the larger fluid bags. Knight's hand grasped the empty fluid container and lifted it off the pole, bringing it to eye level. A label, generated by a computer, identified the patient's name and medical record number. Below the bar code read Potassium 80 mEq. The time registered on the sticker was noon, of that fateful day.

A collision of thoughts then roared through the mind of Richard Knight. Immediately, the deceased names of Katherine McDuff and Brett Charles came to light. The trusting face of Willie Brown appeared, as did his voice, calling Knight his "Messiah." The snickering laugh of Dr. Falcon and her band of morbid pathologists arose, as did the wording of her reports. Knight then pictured the smug Dr. Riles, sitting in the front row during M & M Rounds, instigating doubt amongst the surgical department. The seemingly rational plan to ratchet up his surgical volume resonated in his cranium. Lastly, and most oddly, a picture of Jennifer Ranier entered his mind. It was a sad Jennifer, leaving her penthouse apartment in squalor and disgrace. She slowly carried a small moving box in her hands down the hallway towards the elevator. She appeared very pale. Ghostly music from Tosca then sang out, freezing the premier surgeons cognition, immediately bringing him to a physical and emotional standstill.

A voice from behind broke the gridlock saying, "Richard, Richard."

Knight turned around to see Chairman Barnes standing in the doorway. A solemn look was upon his face.

"Michael," said Knight while still holding the empty bag of potassium. "Someone is killing my patients."

"I know," said Chairman Barnes. "I know."

Chairman Barnes then escorted the beleaguered surgeon to the office of Howard Rineman. The CEO of the hospital system awaited their arrival, having been earlier alerted by Dr. Barnes. Over the next thirty minutes Rineman and Barnes described their previous conversations with the hospital's Information Technology department. They tactfully explained to Dr. Knight the monitoring system set up by James Asher, who just hours ago alerted Rineman of a breach into the system. Dr. Knight was initially caught off guard with the description of the covert operation. His bemusement slowly turned to anger as the discussion continued.

"How dare you monitor my patients without informing me!" screamed Knight.

"Richard, calm down," said Rineman. "A concern was brought to our attention by the I.T. department, and we made an appropriate response."

"That was my damn concern! I brought it to the attention of Asher," said Knight in disbelief. "How long has this been going on?"

"About six weeks," said Barnes while shaking his head in disgust. "This whole plan of yours was a bad idea Richard. Just a bad idea."

"Don't change the subject Michael. We all agreed to the plan a few months ago. Do you remember, we were sitting in this very office?" said Knight.

"I'm not sure I technically agreed," said Chairman Barnes.

"Gentlemen, please," said Rineman. "The problem at hand is an identified breach into our seemingly secure hospital computer system. This is a very serious matter."

"Who else knows about your monitoring setup?" asked Knight.

"Legal counsel for the hospital was present when we talked to Asher," said Rineman. "Counsel agreed to the plan, and thought it was an appropriate response to a concern raised by a single surgeon."

"You're all a bunch of idiots," barked Knight.

"A surgeon who quite frankly, has been under a lot of self imposed stress," said Rineman calmly.

"Your obsessed with the *Chronicle* article," said Barnes.

"Don't call me obsessed," yelled Knight. "Somebody is killing my patients! Don't you understand?"

"Hold on you two!" said Rineman. "Please, settle down."

All three men then took a deep breath while trying to gather their composure. Knight leaned forward on his chair, holding his head between his hands, while looking at the floor. Rineman was staring directly at Chairman Barnes shaking his head in disgust. Chairman Barnes appeared pale, realizing the consequences of his passive agreement to Knight's warped plan.

"Now," said Rineman after a sense of order was restored. "Let's not jump to conclusions about patients being killed."

"What else can explain the deaths of four of my patients?" asked a dejected Knight.

"What we know is that someone has breached our computer system," said Rineman ignoring Knight's question. "We are also aware of your recent string of postoperative fatalities."

"We need to call the police," said Barnes, who appeared ready to vomit.

"We just can't haphazardly connect a computer security leak to a series of deaths within the hospital," said Rineman.

"Where is Asher?" asked Knight. "Where are the overpaid attorneys that you call legal? I mean, shouldn't they be here in the discussion."

"Asher is in California," said Rineman holding his hands up in a calming fashion towards the two surgeons. "I just got off the phone with him, he is heading back as soon as possible, will be in town early afternoon tomorrow."

"He did alert you to the system breach?" asked Barnes.

"Yes, the alarm was triggered around noon time today," said Rineman.

"Well, who is killing my patients?" asked Knight. "He must know the identity of the intruder."

"Apparently its not that simple," replied Rineman. "He got into a lot of technical jargon, saying the trail had to be followed a bit more." Rineman then looked at his two friends staring at him in disgust. He then methodically said, "He assured me by tomorrow he would have the identity code of the intruder, at least that's a start."

Rineman then began to inform the duo of a planned meeting for the next day. He had already alerted legal of the matter, who agreed to be present. The CEO then assured the surgeons that prompt action would be taken under the guidance of the legal department. A lengthy discussion then occurred between Rineman and Barnes regarding the pros and cons of alerting the local authorities.

Throughout the discussion, Dr. Knight's thoughts were consumed by the realization that someone was methodically murdering his patients. A single question arose in his mind - "Who?" His memory spontaneously imported and exported the names and faces of hundreds of people. Who had he wronged so badly in the past, that their retribution would be so severe? Certainly his demeanor and demand for excellence had stomped on the ego of many a medical colleague and resident. Could it be another physician? Over the past twenty years he had been part of multiple business ventures, some successful and others not. Had he ever knowingly brought financial ruin to a fellow investor? He recalled thirty years of womanizing, along with the peculiarities of each tryst. Was it a jolted lover or jealous husband? Family members and close social acquaintances from Philadelphia entered the thought process. Who had he rubbed wrong within the upper crust of society? To the disturbed doctor there was no obvious answer, only a recurring question -"Who?"

"Richard, are you with us?" asked Rineman. "Do you agree?"

"Agree with what?" asked Knight snapping out of his fog.

"That we hold off on notifying the local authorities until after our meeting tomorrow afternoon?" said Rineman, aware that Knight had no knowledge of the discussion that just occurred.

"Yea, yea, that's fine," said Knight while reorienting himself. "What time tomorrow? Isn't it New Year's Eve?"

"3 PM" said Rineman. "And yes, it is New Year's Eve, but this matter cannot wait."

"No problem," said Knight without recalling the long-standing reservations that he and his wife had for the night. "No problem, we all have to be there, and get to the bottom of this."

The three heavyweights of the Philadelphia General Hospital system then dispersed in solemn fashion. Knight spent the next three hours consoling the grieving family of Helga Cox, who remained sadly unaware that their loved one was murdered on that very cold December day.

CHAPTER 22
The Token

DR. KNIGHT SUFFERED a fitful night of sleep that evening. The Cox family was distraught over the loss of their loved one. A close relative of the deceased was a pathologist from the Dallas area, who demanded an independent autopsy be performed, outside of the PGH system. Knight obliged to the request, and the body of Helga Cox was transferred to Jefferson Hospital in downtown Philadelphia. The autopsy report and final wording were therefore out of the hands of Knight and his PGH machine.

Adding to his angst was the fact that Chairman Barnes called him late that night with news regarding the *Chronicle* article. Barnes informed him that Associate Editor Russo had completed his article, which was ready for public consumption on New Year's Day. The *Chronicle* always released this series on New Year's Day, realizing that the majority of the populace was at home and therefore more inclined to read the article. Russo was calling for an update on the numbers and data from the cardiothoracic department. His statistic department was tallying the final percentages for each hospital and physician. The deadline for the final numbers was that very night. Incapable of telling a lie or stretching the truth, the chairman's update was accurate, and included the fatality of Helga Cox on that very day. Russo was only capable of saying that Dr. Knight's numbers were running "right in line" with the others. Of course this was prior to receiving the update, which included another fatality. Beyond that wording, Russo would divulge no further information regarding the ranking of Dr. Knight or the PGH cardiothoracic department.

Lastly, the news that her New Year's Eve plans were being disrupted did not sit well with Mrs. Knight. To offset the pretense of their relationship, Mrs. Knight courted personal satisfaction outside of the physical realm. She enjoyed society and everything about it, including her perception within society circles. Over the past three months she served as the planning co-chairperson of a benefit gala supporting breast cancer research. The confirmed guest list for the event included the Philadelphia elite. The "must be seen at" gala was scheduled for New Year's Eve and included a formal dinner and orchestral band. The thought of not having her husband next to her at the head table was unacceptable, the equivalent of social suicide. She made every effort to avoid this scenario. As a veteran wife of a surgeon, she repeatedly notified every scheduler in her husband's chain of command in regards to the event. Constant reminders were personally given to her spouse over the past several weeks, all met with an incredulous sense of insult, and absolute commitment to attend. Then, twenty-four hours prior to the event, she received a terse notification from her morbid husband that his attendance was in jeopardy. Upon hearing the news the usually reserved Mrs. Knight went berserk, verbally abusing her spouse to the fullest degree. Even the calloused surgeon was taken aback by the malice and disdain in her words, prompting him to compromise a bit. He promised to wrap up the critically important meeting at the hospital by 4

PM and then, meet his wife at the event, dressed in full tuxedo by 5 PM. The timing would be close, but possible if all went well. Mrs. Knight begrudgingly agreed to the plan, yet still protested the whole situation, in order to stress the social magnitude of the dinner.

To make sleeping matters worse, Dr. Knight had a bizarre dream that night. He dreamt being rolled into operating room number four as a patient, then being placed on the surgical table by the nursing staff. The disdainful nurse Warner helped to shift his body onto the table, smirking at a seemingly comical view of his partially exposed genitalia. The table was cold and the atmosphere unwelcoming, as the bright overhead surgical lights shined in his eyes. Loud, heavy metal music was being played over the stereo system. Then a surrounding cast of surgeons appeared on each side of the table. Behind their surgical masks Dr. Knight was able to identify interns Polk and Drummer. Chief resident Larson was present and standing strangely next to CEO Rineman, who appeared frightened. Knight tried to speak and argue the fact that he didn't need surgery, but the head of the anesthesiologist peered over a sheet with a smile, asking him to relax. Knight tried to recall why he was being operated on, and what led to this surgery. However his mind was blank, only finding solace in thoughts of Jennifer Ranier, and the good times they had spent together. Her carefree and spontaneous nature warmed his heart, as did the momentary belief that they were still together and heading away for the weekend. Certainly she would care for him throughout the post-operative state, easing his expected pain. Then nurse Frey's voice could be heard welcoming a surgeon with dismay. Knight looked up to see visiting professor Riles step up to the table as the others stepped aside. He then asked his exiled son to stand beside him in preparation for surgery. The youngest Riles then took a scalpel and began to incise the chest of Knight, causing an intense pain. Knight let out a vile scream, which awoke him from the nightmare. Spontaneously he then reached for his wife who was not beside him, choosing to spend the night in a separate bedroom of dissent. Suddenly the surgeon felt completely alone. The room was dark and the walls seemed close. A realization that Jenna was no longer with him occurred. Howling winds rattled the shutters of the historical house as a cold chill blew through the antique windows. The frightened surgeon then spent the next hour trying to morally examine his conscience, in a way that his father taught him as a young boy. Unfortunately, he self graded the attempt a failure.

The following morning was bitterly cold in the city. Despite being New Year's Eve, there was no festive atmosphere surrounding the PGH family. The death of Helga Cox cast a mournful spell upon the entire surgical department. Phil drew the short straw amongst the interns and was on call that night. Rick Polk was planning on hosting a New Year's party in his lounge that evening. However the only confirmed guest for the event was Phil himself. Jenna had wanted to attend, but after much discussion declined, in light of the recent events at the hospital. Rick invited a select group of nurses from the floor, but there were no takers.

By noontime, Dr. Barnes had arrived in his PGH office in preparation for the afternoon meeting. Like Dr. Knight, he had suffered through a restless prior evening. He was distraught over not alerting the legal authorities earlier with regards to the whole matter at hand. Like his associate, he had also received heat from his wife, regarding a social event supporting the Bryn Mawr Hospital that evening.

CEO Rineman appeared in his hospital office two hours later. Rineman was unaccustomed to working a holiday, and it felt strange to enter the hospital that day. Absent was the usual hustle and bustle outside the facility. Rineman had slept well through the night, not concerned about the series of events. A true businessman, he was comfortable with the earlier recommendations from the legal department. As a matter of protocol he had documented their advice in a series of internal memos, thus protecting his role in the matter. His wife didn't care about the meeting, since he was always at some important meeting or affair every night of the week.

Twenty minutes prior to the meeting, the two men met as Dr. Barnes arrived early in the CEO's office.

"Good afternoon my friend," said a smiling Rineman to the arriving Barnes. "Plans for tonight?"

"Good afternoon and yes" said Barnes. "Hor d'oeuvres at 5 PM sharp with the wife, otherwise our marriage is in trouble," said Barnes with a forced smile. "Hopefully the predicted bad weather will hold off until I get home."

"I agree," said Rineman as he looked out the window. "From what I hear a nasty storm front is headed into town." Rineman paused while continuing to peer out the window towards the sky. He then continued, "Tough time for a meeting but we have to hear from Asher with legal present. He didn't get into town until just recently, and promised to head right over to the hospital."

Then, at that very moment, James Asher walked into the room. He was disheveled, having just taken a taxi from the airport. In tow was a roller suitcase with a broken rear wheel that rhythmically clicked behind him. Wearing his trademark white socks, the I.T. guru carried a laptop in his right hand.

"Salutations," was his hello to the team.

Greetings were exchanged and superficial chat occurred regarding the great weather on the West Coast. All three men had a deeper sense of concern about the meeting, albeit at separate levels of gravity. Asher excitedly discussed promising updates to the computer world that he had heard about at the national meeting.

Ten minutes later, legal arrived at the meeting. The figurehead of this entourage again included Rineman's close personal friend from the downtown firm. However this time he was accompanied by four junior attorneys, each dressed in an obligatory dark suit with conservative shirt and tie. The group of understudies included three males and one female, each billing time and a half in honor of the holiday. A smile was on legal's face as he shook Rineman's hand in preparation for the financial plundering about to be performed.

As the grandfather clock within the office chimed three times, there was not a sign of Dr. Knight. No concern arose until fifteen minutes later when legal, in a show of expense, checked his wristwatch directly in front of Rineman. The CEO then went to call Knight on the phone, only to be told by Barnes that he never carried a cell. Rineman then suggested the meeting start without Dr. Knight.

"Gentlemen, thank you for meeting here today," said Rineman in opening. "We have gathered to discuss a matter of critical importance that has come to our attention."

Dr. Barnes then spoke saying, "Yes, this is a follow-up meeting to our earlier discussions regarding the possible breach of our computer systems by an unauthorized entity."

"We have asked our I.T. expert, Mr. James Asher to again be present with regards to this topic," said Rineman as he looked towards the legal team. "Earlier this week we did experience an apparent illegal entry into our system."

There was a pause in the room as CEO Rineman looked around at the group slowly. Suddenly the room was very quiet and only the methodical tick of the clock could be heard. Rineman continued with, "This activity was then followed by the sudden and unexpected death of a hospital patient."

A sudden rustle occurred amongst the pack of attorneys. Several of the younger members were writing down notes on a yellow pad, not daring to speak. The head legal eagle then cleared his throat to speak, and then said, "This violation was picked up by the monitoring system that we agreed to just last month?"

"Yes," said Asher. "At approximately noontime yesterday, east coast time, my alarm tripped. I was in Los Angeles at the time."

"What exactly triggered your alarm?" asked the attorney.

"A malware that through a series of corrupt commands entered the blood laboratory pathway of the PGH. This penetration seemingly altered the blood value of a patient within the hospital."

Again, silence engulfed the room as all eyes were on the head proxy. No one moved in his amen corner behind him. Legal then spoke asking, "Did the blood value involve one of Dr. Knight's …?"

"Yes," answered Asher quickly.

"Was it the patient that expired after the infraction?" asked legal.

"I don't know," said Asher. "I am unaware as to who died, but I do have the patient's name whose blood work was altered."

"What would be that name?" asked legal.

Asher scrolled down on this screen and squinted a bit. He then said, "The patient's name, or should I say her name, was a Helga Cox."

"That's who died," said Dr. Barnes shaking his head back and forth with a suddenly pale face. "Richard was right. He was right all along."

Suddenly the door to the room burst open and in walked Dr. Knight. He was wearing a black tuxedo with a bow tie and his cheeks appeared reddened, as if he ran up a few flights of steps. Subdued anger was upon his face, as was an ever so slight stench of vodka on his breath. He approached the group in a frenzied fashion, as if he were already late for another meeting.

"Sorry I'm late," was Knight's feinted apology. "Troubles everywhere, what did I miss?"

"We were just discussing with Mr. Asher the recently identified computer intrusion within the hospital," said Rineman immediately realizing that he had a bull in a china shop.

"You were right Richard," said Barnes in disgust, "Somebody altered Cox's labs right before she died."

CEO Rineman tried to respond but was cut off by the still charging Dr. Knight.

"Of course I was right!" screamed Knight. "I knew it months ago when I talked to this fool from the computer department." The irate surgeon was pointing directly at Asher when speaking.

"Gentlemen, lets discuss the facts rationally," said legal.

"Who the hell are you?" said Knight in anger looking at the group of suits from across the Schuylkill River.

"Richard, take it easy," said Rineman. "Present besides me are the attorneys who have skillfully represented this institution since I have been chief executive officer."

"Have they been a part of your little secret society monitoring my patients over time?" said Knight. "The same patients that have been getting murdered right under our noses?"

"Howard, we need to settle this down or I'm afraid this meeting will be adjourned shortly," said legal.

CEO Rineman then successfully calmed down Dr. Knight for the time being, as he begrudgingly took a seat. As order was restored more detailed questions were presented to James Asher. While Asher responded, Knight listened attentively while staring directly at the floor, not making eye contact with anyone in the room.

"The value that was altered was the potassium level," said Asher.

"I don't understand," said legal. "Please explain to me how someone changing a lab value within a computer system then results in the death of a patient?"

"Its quite obvious now," said Barnes. "If someone, or should I say some twisted person, decided to change the potassium level of a patient, it would immediately alter their care." Barnes then looked at Asher asking, "What exactly happened to the potassium level in this case?"

Asher again stared at his computer screen and typed in a series of commands. While scrolling down a column of numbers all eyes in the room were upon him, except Knight's.

"Here it is," said Asher. "The true potassium value was 6.1 mEq. The corrupt value which the computer system relayed to the floor was a lower number. Lets see, that number was 2.3 mEq."

"Oh my God," said Barnes. "Oh my God."

"Explain your concern," asked legal in a matter of fact fashion.

"Don't you see?" said Barnes. "A low potassium is no big deal, it won't kill a person. However, a high potassium level is a medical emergency, it can kill a patient in a matter of minutes if given rapidly."

Silence again gripped the room as the nonmedical attendees tried to digest the information.

Dr. Barnes then continued, "If a resident identifies an elevated potassium level over the computer, he or she will take actions to lower it, not increase it. However if the information provided identifies a low potassium, then the knee jerk response of the house staff is to pour more potassium into the patient."

"I see," said legal. "So in this described scenario a patient with an already elevated potassium level, gets even more potassium pumped into their system by the unsuspecting resident."

"Exactly," said Barnes. "Because the resident received the corrupt lab value stating the potassium level as low, instead of high."

"So the dangerously high potassium level goes even higher," said Rineman, "Even that is clear to me."

"Right," said Barnes. "It will rise rapidly, to a point of triggering a cardiac arrhythmia."

"Dr. Knight, what are your thoughts?" asked legal.

Knight slowly looked up from the floor and scowled at the group of hospital advocates in front of him. He despised attorneys of all walks of life, regardless of race, color or creed. He looked down again to seemingly gather his thoughts but did not speak.

"Richard, we need your input," said Rineman. "This is a problem that we all share, not just you."

"Don't give me that crap," said Knight sharply looking up at Rineman. "Someone has been methodically executing my patients over time. This is my problem. A vendetta against me."

"You're right," said Dr. Barnes. "I mean you are correct with the execution terminology. Potassium is what they give prisoners that are executed."

"What are you talking about?" asked Rineman.

"I've had the pleasure, or should I say displeasure of being a former advisor to our northeast regional court system. Our committee was responsible for helping the judges with decisions involving medical matters. One such matter involved the medications used to execute a prisoner."

"A lethal injection?" asked counsel.

"Exactly," responded Barnes. "I quickly became an expert on the medicinal cocktail that the state gives a prisoner during an execution."

"And potassium is in that mixture?" asked legal.

"Yes," replied Dr. Barnes. "An execution by lethal injection involves three separate medications given sequentially in a particular order. The first drug administered is sodium pentothal, which renders the condemned unconscious. The second medication given is pavulon, which causes whole body muscle paralysis."

"How are the medications administered?" asked legal.

"Intravenously, directly into the patient's vein. The medicine is mixed into a liquid solution so the effect is immediate," said Barnes.

"Where does the potassium come in?" asked Rineman.

"Potassium chloride is the final medication administered intravenously," said Barnes. "It is actually the one that kills the patient, or should I say prisoner."

"How does it work and how fast does it take effect?" asked legal again.

"A bolus, or concentrated dose of potassium immediately affects the heart muscle. It disables the heart at the cellular level, making it unable to generate an impulse," replied Barnes.

"Therefore I'm assuming it cannot pump blood to the body," said Rineman.

"Exactly," said Dr. Barnes. "It cripples the heart on a molecular level."

A pause again overcame the room as everyone tried to gather their thoughts. During this time Dr. Knight stared at the floor, occasionally shaking his head slowly back and forth with a scowl on his face. His right knee bobbed nervously up and down in rapid fashion. He appeared anxious and ready to leave at a moment's notice.

"Richard!" said Barnes quickly, "It now all makes sense." Everyone in the room stared at Dr. Barnes. "Remember the pathology report from M & M rounds, nobody could explain the pathologist's findings regarding the heart musculature. Don't you see? It was from the potassium overdose!"

"Of course I see," said Knight with an incredulous stare at his colleague. "As usual you have a keen grasp of the obvious," was his next slur directed at Barnes. "Thank god you are the department chairman," was his final vile comment.

Dr. Knight then turned his gaze upon James Asher saying, "Mr. Asher, can we cut to the chase. Will you please tell us who is the culprit of this crime?"

"Not an easy answer," said an unfazed Asher to the group.

"Why?" asked Knight quickly.

"I can only give you the authentication token that was used by the perpetrator," replied the I.T. expert.

"I don't know what that means," said Knight in a more agitated tone. "Give us a name. With all the technology at your disposal are you telling me you can't come up with a name?"

"Exactly," said Asher in defiance. "I can only give you the token that was used."

"But from what I understand, every token is specifically authorized to a PGH employee," said Rineman, recalling their earlier meeting.

"Yes," said Asher. "Each employee is administered an exact token, which is used to securely and legally enter the system." He paused before continuing in a lower and more professorial tone saying, "The system is secure, with the assumption that the token not be shared with others, who also have knowledge of the physician's password. This has been a strong warning our department has made clear from the beginning."

"Just give us a name to the token," rumbled Knight. "Do you think we are playing games here? Somebody is killing my patients, and may be doing it again as we speak."

"All right," said Asher with a look of disgust at Dr. Knight. He shook his head slowly back and forth to non-verbally voice his disdain for the CT surgeon. Then, as if savoring the moment, he spoke again, while staring directly at Knight, "The authentication code used to violate the system was your token doctor. It was the token administered to one Dr. Richard Knight, from the Department of Surgery."

Knight only paused momentarily before speaking with an incredulous tone, "What are you talking about? I don't even know what the hell a token is."

"You have a token," said Asher. "Its under your name. That was the token used to alter the potassium value."

"Are you insane?" said Knight standing up in front of the physically slight I.T. master. "Are you suggesting I'm killing my own patients?"

"No he isn't Richard," said Rineman standing up and walking around the desk. He was trying to ease Dr. Knight who appeared to be one step away from assaulting Asher.

"Richard, calm down," said Dr. Barnes while also standing up. "Of course you are not the perpetrator, but someone is obviously using your token to enter the system."

"The question is who?" said legal.

"Someone you must trust," said Rineman. "Someone within your inner circle that currently has, or had access to the token."

"Does anyone immediately come to mind?" asked legal. "Anyone that you trusted so well that they had access to your token and password?"

Knight turned slightly away from the cowering Mr. Asher. He looked down towards the ground with a frown upon his face, while his eyes blinked rapidly. Subconsciously a suppression of his memory banks occurred, not allowing him to tally a list of possible offenders. Despite his best efforts to create a list of top candidates, only one name was allowed to escape from his cerebral cortex. That name was Jennifer Ranier. Jennifer Ranier, the beautiful blonde, carefree girl from Baltimore that he loved so much. The name screamed into his skull, resonating with an echo that was both deafening and blinding. The shrill caused Knight to look up at the faces surrounding him, staring and waiting for an answer. Jennifer Ranier, it was Jennifer Ranier! Despite the utter shrill of the name, he was incapable of saying it to the group surrounding him.

"Richard," said Dr. Barnes, "Can you help us? Does anyone come to mind that would do such a thing?"

"I recommend you notify the police department immediately," said Knight who then turned and bolted towards the door. "Tell them that someone has killed four of my patients," was his exiting cry. While rushing out he was unaware of the shouted questions from his colleagues and legal advisors, who were all left behind in disbelief. Only one thought registered in his mind as he rushed down the hallway towards the stairwell exit. He needed to see Ranier immediately. Only she held the answer to his questions, certainly she would have an explanation.

The startled group remaining in Rineman's office then agreed to notify the authorities. An immediate call was placed to the Philadelphia Police Department, who requested Rineman and his legal team report to their headquarters. Detectives from the homicide division would be awaiting their arrival. Dr. Barnes then requested Asher to disable Dr. Knight's token, which he rapidly accomplished. Then as the team rushed out of the CEO's office, legal checked his watch while smugly looking at his posse. He grinned, knowing from past experience that it was going to be a long night, a long, but very lucrative night.

CHAPTER 23
New Year's Reunion

DR. KNIGHT RACED out of the hospital heading across the street to the adjacent parking lot. His black Porsche sat poised in its reserved slot. Upon entering the vehicle he fumbled into the glove compartment, searching for a knowingly hated device. Then, from the depths of the compartment, his hand pulled out a cell phone. The instrument was outdated by three generations of technology, yet still held a charge. The doctor turned on the phone and scrolled down a list of stored numbers. Only two phone numbers existed in the cell's call list, representing the only two things that actually mattered in Knight's life. Listed in the top spot was a number titled "O.R. PGH." Below this number in the second slot, was simply a name, that being "Jenna." Knight quickly clicked on this number and held the phone up to his ear as the Porsche's engine revved to life.

Jennifer Ranier was three blocks away from the parking lot, fighting a stiff head wind while walking back to the Greycliff. The temperature was rapidly dropping that day, with an icy cold rain starting to fall. She had just completed assisting in a plastic surgery emergency case that afternoon. Her workday was over, with no plans set for that evening's New Year celebration. Phil was on call at the hospital, and the social work girls had some "boy toys" well lined up in advance for the night. The only thing registering in her mind at that moment was a hot shower, warm meal and good book under a blanket.

The ring of her cell phone barely reached her auditory canal as the wind howled down the streets. Jenna reached for the device wishing she had worn gloves that chilly day. While peering at the cell's screen, she had to wipe some raindrops that had obstructed her gaze. Then, as the caller number came into view, she stopped dead in her tracks, suddenly unaware of the elements. A moment of hesitation occurred as a myriad of thoughts raced through her mind. Then, curiosity overcame her, prompting her to receive the call and place the phone to her ear.

"Jenna, it's me," was the reply to her hello.

"What do you want?" asked Jenna with a tone that matched the weather conditions. She slid into the confines of a bus stop shelter to ease the whine of the approaching storm's wind.

"I need to talk to you, where are you?" asked Knight.

"What's there to talk about?" said Ranier. "I got all my boxes out of your place by myself, thanks for the professional pack job."

"Jenna, what I need to talk to you about is much bigger than that," said a hurried Knight. "Trust me, we need to talk now."

"What's so important?" asked Ranier with a peaking interest. A cold tone was maintained in the response.

"We need to meet in person," said Knight. "The whole matter is just to unbelievable to discuss over a cell line."

"I really don't have anything to discuss with you," said Ranier as she waved off a city driver that was looking at her impatiently through an open bus door. The drone of the bus pulling away muffled Knight's next line. Jenna was however able to hear Knight asking her where she was at that very moment. Unaware of his near presence, she looked up at the city intersection and recited the street names.

"I'm nearby, will be right there," was Knight's rapid response.

"Don't bother," said Jenna as she heard the call being terminated. She then put the phone away while pulling her collar tight to her neck. Upon exiting the shelter the groaning wind of the developing tempest caused her body to shutter. She proceeded to walk briskly west in a homeward direction, wondering what possibly could be the matter of such extreme importance.

Then, just one city block later, Jenna was able to appreciate the familiar whine of the overpriced Porsche approaching from behind. While looking to her right the vehicle screeched to a stop along the curbstone, several feet in front of her. The window rolled down to expose a squinting Dr. Knight peering out against the wind.

"Jenna, we need to talk, please get in," was the yell of Knight over the howl.

"I have nothing to say," said Ranier. "Nothing." She continued to walk up the avenue.

Knight then jumped out of his car, running towards Ranier, while leaving the car door open. The rain pelted his tuxedo, soaking him quickly to the skin with a chill. Ranier continued to walk forward as Knight approached her from the side, keeping pace with her every step. She glanced sideways noticing the tuxedo and frenzied look upon his soaked face.

"Jenna please," was his plea as he reached out to hold her right arm. "Please, I can't tell you how important this matter is."

Ranier stopped and turned towards Knight. He looked pathetic with a somber frown upon his face. Icy rain pelted their faces as they momentarily stared at each other. She then shook her head sadly saying, "What Richard, what can possibly be this important?"

"Jenna, a series of events have occurred at the PGH that are beyond belief," said Knight above the noise. He then placed his other hand on her right shoulder, while staring directly at her. The rain continued to pepper the two as a chill physically shook Dr. Knight's body. "Can we get into the car?" asked Knight. "I'll explain it while driving you home." He held her ever so carefully, realizing she was on the precipice of a fateful yes or no. "Jenna, please, it will only take a few minutes. I'm searching for answers," was his plea. The flower on his lapel was now drooped and soaked.

"You are really nuts," said Ranier in disgust as she turned backwards towards the waiting Porsche. "This better be good," was her next shout as she headed towards the passenger side of the vehicle.

As Ranier jumped into the car the warmth of the heated leather seats felt wonderful. Knight slammed the door against the wind and ran his hand through a soaked mop of hair. Reaching forward he turned up the heat in the car, then checked the rear view mirror for traffic. The 911 turbo then lurched into traffic in a manner that brought back good memories to the passenger.

"Thank you," was his heartfelt line as he shifted into gear. The windshield wipers cleared a view forward as the vehicle headed west.

"I'm only three blocks up," said Ranier unaware as to whether or not Knight knew her current residence.

"Jenna, do you remember my stockbroker Mr. Charles?" asked Knight, unaware of her directions.

"Yes."

"How about the staffer, Willie Brown that coded and died in the SICU?" asked Knight.

"Of course," said Ranier. "He called you the Messiah."

"Well since then two other deaths have occurred," said Knight. He then looked over to Ranier saying with a slow and emphatic tone, "Two more unexplained deaths."

"What's the point?" asked Ranier.

"Jenna, its come to our attention that someone has been methodically killing my patients," said Knight in matter of fact fashion.

Ranier quickly looked at Knight whose eyes remained on the road. She became unaware that the vehicle passed the intersection of the Greycliff apartments. Her mind was trying to decipher the magnitude of what she had just heard.

"What are you talking about?" was her incredulous reply.

Knight then rapidly began to blurt out the series of events that had occurred over the past two months. He briefly described the computerized alarm system and deaths of Katherine McDuff and Helga Cox.

"You passed my apartment five blocks ago," was her numb response to the described scenario.

Dr. Knight then turned left crossing over two city blocks to catch the one-way avenue back east. While negotiating the route he continued to update Ranier on the bizarre series of events, including the bogus potassium values.

"Who would do such a thing?" said Ranier now unaware that they were traveling again past the Greycliff intersection, heading towards the PGH. "Are you sure about this whole matter?"

"Absolutely," said Knight as he darted through traffic. He proceeded to quickly tell her about the trap set by Asher, and the role of the authentication token.

"Does anyone else know about this?" asked a bewildered Ranier as she stared directly ahead, beyond the rapidly moving front windshield wipers.

"Barnes, Rineman and a few attorneys," said Knight. "They all seem to believe the killer's identity will hinge on some computer token needed to enter the system." Knight then rapidly glanced at his passenger saying, "Do you know what they are talking about?

"Of course," said Jenna. "Everybody needs a token to enter the medical record system."

"Who has my computer token?" asked Knight, explaining that he was unaware that it ever existed.

"We all shared it," said Ranier. "In fact you had two tokens, remember? Your office manager always complained that we needed two, just to keep up with the log on demand for your patients. Everyone in the department used them to log onto your patients." Ranier then proceeded to rattle off a list of the token users, including Knight's office manager and nursing team along with the residency staff. She ended the list by including her name.

"Where are the tokens now?" said Knight rapidly.

"Who knows," said Ranier. "I mean it's been a few months since I was rudely released by the department."

"Jenna, please, I did what I had to do," said Knight. "You were making a mockery of me."

"Untrue," replied Jennifer. "I was never unfaithful to you. Never!" An uncomfortable moment passed between the two before Ranier continued saying somberly, "And that's the truth."

"What was the password associated with my token?" was Knight's next query as the vehicle sped past the PGH complex.

"Richard, where are you going?" asked Ranier upon seeing the hospital pass by.

"The password, what was the password?" asked Knight as he unexpectedly turned left onto a Schuylkill Expressway entrance ramp. "Who knew the password?"

"I hope you're not thinking I harmed your patients," said a shocked Jennifer Ranier as she looked directly at him. "Please tell me that's not the reason you tracked me down."

"I don't know what I think," said an increasingly agitated Knight. "The token used to alter the potassium level was my token, that's what I know," barked Knight over the roar of the Porsche's engine. "Someone used my token and I need to know who was aware of the password." He again peered into the rear view mirror, while slipping deftly into traffic.

The sports car moved quickly into the Schuylkill passing lane, roaring up river. The sparkling lights of the city reflected off the window of Jenna's passenger side. Despite the onset of darkness, ominous black clouds hovered just above the skyline. Knight was quiet, giving his former mistress the opportunity to respond to his question. He was confident that she would possess information to expose the culprit.

"You think I killed your patients," said Ranier looking downward at her feet while shaking her head. "You actually think I killed your patients." She then looked at Knight saying, "What kind of person do you think I am, don't you trust me? After all we have been through together, don't you trust me?" Tears began to well up in her eyes as the magnitude of the perceived accusation settled in. "For God's sake, we spent four years together. Did you ever doubt me?"

"What was the password and who knew it!" yelled Knight realizing that his passenger had no available escape option while traveling at 70 miles per hour.

"Everybody knew it!" yelled Ranier back at him. "Everybody, absolutely everybody including the interns, residents and office staff. Take your pick. Your token was passed around the entire hospital system on a daily basis." A brief silence ensued followed by Ranier saying, "Take me home, now."

"The password," said Knight sternly. "Why won't you at least tell me that?"

"Do you want to know the password?" asked Jennifer. "It was no secret. We all knew it. The password was Borodin, that Russian composer you always talk about. What does that tell you?"

Knight was then silent as a list of suspects ran through his head. A collision of facts, dates and possible motives rattled through his cranium. With two tokens under his name the situation became more confusing. A full, thoughtful minute went by as Jenna blankly stared out the window at Boat House Row passing by along the opposite bank of the Schuylkill River.

"Who kept the tokens?" said Knight in a hurried tone. "I mean who physically kept them? Were they kept in the hospital, the office, did they go home with people."

Jennifer continued to stare out the window while responding dimly, "I shared one with the house staff. We all carried it and each one of us would occasionally take it home. It all depended on the day, hospital census and case load."

"What about the second one?" blurted Knight.

"Don't know, they kept it at your office," said Ranier with some bitterness. "I stayed out of there, you know they all hated me."

"Nobody hated you," snapped Knight. "We had a great thing going until you started tramping around with the intern staff."

"That's not true!" shouted an angry Jenna. "Not true. You had no reason to humiliate me the way you did."

"That's not the way I saw it," said Knight with a frown and slow shake of his head. "You were embarrassing me. I had no other option."

"Slow down, you're going 80 miles an hour!" pleaded Jennifer as the rain pelted the windshield.

"Did you kill my patients?" asked Knight bluntly while continuing to stare forward with an unexpressive gaze. "Just answer yes or no," was his next morbid line. A deep darkness now surrounded the speeding vehicle. "Please Jenna, I will believe you, just a simple yes or no."

"You're sick in the head," said Ranier. "Take me home now," was her next demand as she pulled out her cell phone. "I'm going to dial 9-1-1 immediately if you don't exit now."

"Who is killing my patients?" screamed Knight.

Jennifer went to dial 9-1-1, but as she did Knight fiercely slapped the phone away from her hands, sending it down to the floor. She froze while looking forward at the seemingly stationary traffic being passed by. An innate cry for safety seized her body while she reflexively grabbed onto the edge of the seat. Fear overcame her and she dared not move.

"Who is killing my patients?" said Knight again with threatening groan. "You must know. Tell me now."

"I'll tell you who!" screamed Jenna in a panic as she looked back at her captor. "Someone who has hated you with such a passion over time it makes them bleed," screeched Ranier.

Knight then turned to the right with a monstrous gaze over his passenger. A scowl came upon his face as he slowly lifted his clenched right fist up into the air. "Who? God damn it, tell me who?" Passing headlights created an eerie camouflaged pattern across his face.

Before Jenna could answer, Mother Nature intervened in unison with the laws of physics. While speeding at eighty miles per hour the exterior temperature gauge on the vehicle's dashboard read twenty-seven degrees Fahrenheit. Sleeting rain fell around the perimeter of the vehicle in a manner unappreciated by the driver. Over the Porsches muted radio, a winter weather advisory from KYX News Radio was unheard by the occupants. Then, as Jennifer was about to answer, the vehicle entered the notorious ninety-degree Conshohocken curve of the Schuylkill expressway. In a split second the car's radial tires attempted to maintain contact with the icy road. Despite three generations of German innovation and technology, the complex safety system of the Porsche could not respond, permitting the vehicle to slide out of control. A buzz and flashing warning lights alerted the doomed occupants of the dire situation while the vehicle became airborne. Jennifer screamed as Knight unsuccessfully attempted to regain control of the speeding trajectory. Initial impact was with a concrete side road barrier, which in turn ricocheted the vector back onto the median, causing it to rapidly turn over in a side-to-side counter clockwise fashion.

The initial barrier impact caused the most brutal damage upon the occupants. Jennifer's right knee hit the dashboard as the airbags deployed, sending a tremendous upward force through her thighbone. As the main ligament tore in the back of her knee, the femur bone of her thigh cracked along its mid portion. The jagged edge of the fractured bone then sliced through her quadriceps muscle prior to exiting the skin. Her right hip nearly dislocated, barely remaining in socket, as the force vented through the thigh gash. Jennifer appreciated the snap of the bone and a fearsome pain before the airbags hit her face, rendering her unconscious.

Dr. Knight was much less fortunate. The angle of impact transmitted an excessive amount of energy onto the driver's side of the vehicle. Despite front and side air bag deployment, the excessive nature of the force transferred across his abdomen contents. His spleen and liver ruptured, immediately sending blood pulsating out of control into his abdomen. A portion of his small bowel was also lacerated by the sheer dynamics, adding fecal material into the peritoneal cavity. The exiting force then cracked a total of seven ribs while bursting two thoracic vertebral bodies. His spinal cord was spared, but his brainstem was not. The ferocity of the impact placed a sheer force across the arterial supply to his brainstem area, just below his cranium. An acute brainstem bleed occurred, which shut down his most basic life functions, including the ability to breath. Ten seconds after impact, Dr. Knight was in critical condition, having been rendered incompatible with life.

A dispatched EMT squad arrived on the scene ten precious minutes later. Both occupants were extricated and stabilized while being placed onto separate ambulances. A breathing tube had to be inserted in Knight's airway to assist in ventilation. Jennifer became aware of her surroundings, however did not recall the impact of the collision. An incoming alert was put out to the nearest trauma hospital, that being the PGH. Each ambulance then sped back towards center city, rushing their patient to the awaiting medical teams.

Up until that point, it had been a quiet night of call at the PGH. Rambo III was being premiered in the Polk

Lounge when Pete Larson's beeper went off. He called the E.R. and spoke to the trauma triage nurse, who alerted him that two patients from a motor vehicle accident were three minutes away from arrival, one being critically injured. Upon hanging up the phone he gestured to Phil to accompany him to the E.R. immediately. Not wanting to be left out of the action, Rick Polk jumped off the couch to volunteer. All three then began the sprint upstairs to the trauma bay, dawning gloves and gowns upon arrival. Along with the nursing staff they anxiously awaited the two ambulances that were simultaneously backing up into the trauma bay.

"Adult male and female arriving," cried the triage nurse over the ambulance engine whine. "Male in critical condition, blood pressure low with a tense abdomen," was her next line. "Female stable with an open femur fracture."

The rear ambulance door carrying Dr. Richard Knight burst open first, followed by a rush of exiting EMTs hoisting a gurney out of the vehicle. Pete knew by the frenetic action of the transport team that the patient was unstable.

"Adult male, high speed MVA," said the head EMT to the awaiting trauma team. "No blood pressure or spontaneous breathing at the scene. E-tube inserted to assist ventilation. Pressure low, I.V. fluids running wide open."

The fast moving gurney was then transferred to the nursing and physician team. The patient was rushed into an awaiting trauma bay. Phil was the first to recognize the victim as his chief resident was inspecting an increasingly expanding abdomen.

"Oh my God," said Phil. "Its Dr. Knight!" was his next cry as Pete quickly looked up at him. The breathing tube partially blocked his bloodied face, but the profile of his esteemed mentor was undeniable as he was wheeled into the trauma room. A team of orderlies began to cut the tattered Brioni tuxedo off his torso and extremities. Trauma nurses deftly hooked up EKG pads and secured a blood pressure cuff across his upper arm.

Chief resident Larson was suddenly rendered speechless as the reality of the situation set in. Lying in front of him was the most respected and vilified attending in the department of surgery, who was dangerously unstable and now under his emergent care. Overhead monitors triggered alarms as their readout displayed grossly abnormal values. Knight's blood pressure was 80 over 30 and dropping. It was obvious to the team that severe internal bleeding was occurring, causing the drop in pressure. Within seconds an anesthesia resident arrived to maintain control of his airway and ventilations.

"Open up all the fluids," yelled Larson. "Type and cross for stat blood, hang two units," was his next order. "Stat x-ray of his cervical spine and pelvis. Get his abdomen prepped for a tap."

Phil immediately responded by opening a sterile tray behind him in preparation for the abdomen tap. While pouring betadine over the blotted abdomen of Dr. Knight, Phil suddenly heard his name cried out by Rick Polk, who was behind him, peering into the chaotic scene from the adjacent trauma bay.

"Phil, get in here," was Polk's cry. "Now!"

Phil briefly looked at Polk with an incredulous glance, then shaking his head in the negative, returning to the task at hand. With each passing second the clamor in the room increased, both by volume and personnel.

"Phil!" was his cry again. Polk was waving his arm frantically at his fellow intern. Drummer looked up again now concerned as to why Polk was making such a demand at such a time.

"Go Phil," yelled Larson, "He needs your help next door."

At that moment Phil appreciated another body pushing him to the side, away from Knight's body. It was medical student Roden, who was on an emergency room rotation that month. Roden was dressed in a trauma gown with protective glasses on. He rapidly began to arrange the peritoneal tap instruments for Larson. Phil again looked up towards Polk who by then vanished back into the adjacent trauma bay. Stepping backwards he bumped into the portable x-ray unit being positioned by the technician for an x-ray. A trauma nurse then slid between him and Knight, further pushing him towards the back of the table. Turning to his left he maneuvered himself through the mob towards the exit. The kinetic energy within the room then catapulted him towards the adjacent trauma bay. Upon entering the adjoining room, the young doctor was unprepared for the shocking scene that was unfolding.

He immediately recognized Jenna lying on the trauma table with a hard cervical collar on and frightened look upon her face. She was moaning in pain as an anesthesia resident administered narcotics into an intravenous line connected to her right arm. Surrounding her head was a gaggle of nurses, adjusting tubes and wiping blood from her face and earlobes. Radiographic technicians were positioning an x-ray unit above her pelvis, while bumping into a team of orthopedic residents. Junior resident O'Keefe was examining her abdomen, which appeared soft and nondistended. Lance, the muscled orthopedic resident stood beside her damaged right thigh, wearing his trademark tight green scrub outfit. Surrounding him was a team of junior orthopedic residents and interns, all with seemingly chiseled jaws and athletic builds. They were formulating a plan for the open gash in Jenna's thigh that exposed her jagged femur. Phil then looked down at the end of the table where Rick Polk was holding axial traction on the extremity, per the direction of the chief orthopedic resident. Phil rushed into the room while visualizing the remainder of her body, thankful to see no other obvious visual deformities. He fought his way towards the head of the bed, noting that her face was spared the bane of any trauma.

"Jenna!" was his cry, "Jenna!"

She looked up with a glaze in her eyes and recognized the approaching intern. Pain prohibited her from speaking but she was able to hold up her left hand as Phil approached.

Phil grabbed her bloodied hand and held it as he stood to her left side. He squeezed it tightly and appreciated her warm responsive grip.

"Jenna, you're O.K.," said Phil while looking up at the overhead monitors. Her vital signs were all stable.

"Phil, I'm sorry," was her weak response.

"Just try to relax Jen, breath in and out slowly," was his reply while looking down towards the orthopedic team. Lance had knocked Polk out of the way and was now holding Jenna's angulated extremity while looking at the anesthesia resident, who had just administered more intravenous narcotics. The anesthesiologist then nodded in assent, prompting the bone doctor to pull forcefully down on the crooked extremity. The reduction maneuver straightened out the thighbone, causing Jenna to scream in pain. The remaining orthopedic interns then placed heavy sandbags around the damaged bone, maintaining its corrected alignment. A smile came upon Lance's face as he approached the head of the table with a swagger.

"Ma'am, you broke your thigh bone and it came out of the skin," was Lance's introduction to Jennifer. A deep voice matched the physicality of his body. "We need to go to the operating room, wash it out and place a steel rod down the bone."

Jenna was in near shock from the pain, unable to speak. She nodded her head in no particular direction while continuing to squeeze Phil's hand. Sweat was beading up around her forehead. Her hand suddenly became a bit cooler.

"Do you have any questions?" was Lance's next blunt line.

There was no response from the patient as Lance looked up at Phil, asking him his role in the matter. A brief exchange occurred as Phil was able to provide information to contact Jennifer's family, in order to obtain consent for the surgery. Lance then left the room to call Jenna's father, while the medical team prepped her for emergency surgery. Phil continued to comfort Jenna as the narcotic medication finally took effect, rendering her near unconscious.

At that moment a shrill cry came over the hospital's intercom system: "Code Blue, trauma bay one, Code Blue, trauma bay one, Code Blue trauma bay one!" Phil looked up to see Rick Polk dart into the adjacent room. A compassionate nurse tapped Phil on the shoulder while telling him Jenna was fine, prompting him to following Polk. The doorway into the adjacent room was suddenly blocked, causing Phil to detour into the hallway. He was overwhelmed by the swell of people amassing outside of Dr. Knight's room. Present in the crowd was a concerned Dr. Barnes and CEO Rineman. A squad of Philadelphia police officers was strangely adjacent to them.

For the next twenty minutes an all out resuscitation effort occurred over the damaged body of Dr. Knight. The frantic endeavor was successful in returning a cardiac rhythm. Once temporarily stabilized, the critically injured surgeon was then rushed to the operating theatre, in an emergent attempt to stop the abdomen bleed.

Then, as quickly as the mob amassed, it dispersed. All medical personnel involved with the efforts accompanied the injured parties to the operating room. The trauma bays were in disarray as a cleaning crew arrived on the bloodied scene. Outside of the rooms remained a distraught Howard Rineman and Dr. Barnes. It was 6 PM when Dr. Barnes looked down at his watch, suddenly wondering if anyone had notified Mrs. Knight of the mishap. The answer to his question was an inexplicable no. The shock and chaos of the past sixty minutes had crippled the hospital's standard communication protocols. Barnes was irate as he picked up a hospital phone, calling Mrs. Knight. There was no answer at her home, but a second call to a cell number did garner a hello.

When her cell phone vibrated, Mrs. Richard Knight was in the lobby of the swank Rittenhouse Hotel, greeting the rich and famous to her evening fundraiser. The vibration bitterly reminded her that her esteemed spouse, who promised to be there, was not. She fully expected yet another pathetic reason from her husband regarding his tardiness or absolute inability to attend the event that evening. Initially she was shocked by the news given to her by Dr. Barnes. The chairman explained the magnitude of the event, yet settled her concerns with words of encouragement and confident expectations. However, shock suddenly turned to anger as the forthright chairman mentioned injuries to his passenger and former physician assistant. Her memory quickly flashed back an image of the sultry blonde sitting with her legs crossed in the Manayunk restaurant, being so young and inviting. Mrs. Knight then politely thanked the chairman for the call while coldly consenting to all medical care. She then terminated the call and graciously returned to the gala's receiving line.

CHAPTER 24
The V.I.P. Patient

DOCTOR KNIGHT SURVIVED his emergency surgery. Three hours in the surgical suite cost him his spleen, left liver lobe and four feet of small bowel. Most devastating of all was his nonoperative brainstem bleed, which by CAT scan criteria was extensive. Postoperatively he was admitted to the surgical intensive care unit in critical condition. Unable to spontaneously breathe, he remained attached to a mechanical respirator, with a breathing tube down his trachea. A combination of narcotic analgesics and sedatives dripped into his veins, easing the pain and swelling throughout his damaged body.

New Year's morning found Dr. Barnes and Mrs. Knight besides his SICU bed. Barnes was fatigued, having assisted in the lengthy surgery that saved his colleague's life. Mrs. Knight was also physically spent, now gravely aware of the injuries her adulterous husband had sustained.

"He will survive the abdomen injuries," said Barnes. "The question is the brainstem bleed, that will take time to declare itself."

"Is any more surgery necessary?" asked Mrs. Knight.

"No," replied Barnes while arching his stiff back.

"Can he hear us?" asked Mrs. Knight. "I mean does he know we are here?"

"Its difficult to say," said Dr. Barnes looking up at the above bed monitors. "We have him on a lot of medications to keep the brainstem swelling down. He is also being sedated. If he is able to hear us, he wouldn't be able to respond."

Their conversation continued at the bedside that bleak and somber holiday morning. Through it all, Dr. Knight was partly privy to the discussion. His cerebral cortex intermittently collected short bits of voice recognition and information. He briefly heard that a Philadelphia police officer was stationed outside his room that morning. A discussion of brainstem injuries and their prognosis registered in piecemeal fashion. Strangest of all was his acute olfactory awareness, which appeared heightened by the trauma. An aroma from a single rose in his room was bursting in his nasal passages. His wife's perfume, once thought old and stale, was now overflowing with life and pleasure. The intermittent nearness of ICU nurse Cruise penetrated him with a pheromone rush. Despite the pain, sedation and neurologic injury, the smell of life invigorated the subconscious of Dr. Knight. Then, like a supernova, an image of Jennifer Ranier exploded into his mind, capturing all of his emotions. Her perceived presence saturated every cell of his being, providing comfort in a time of need. Certainly all would be well thought Knight, as long as Jennifer was at his side.

Dr. Barnes then stepped closer to the bed saying loudly, "Richard, just want to let you know the *Chronicle* article came out this morning." Barnes paused and looked back at Mrs. Knight with a proud smile, then leaned closer to his patient's ear. He continued saying with a grin, "You beat everybody else in town, terrific numbers."

"He would be so happy," said a tearful Mrs. Knight dabbing a tissue to her eye. "So very, very happy."

"Congratulations Richard," said Dr. Barnes loudly. "Your numbers are the best. You are the best darn CT surgeon in all of Philadelphia. I'm so very proud of you."

"It meant so much to him," said Mrs. Knight with a sob. "So very, very much."

Both visitors then paused and continued to look at the body lying in front of them, hoping for a gesture of understanding. There was no physical response whatsoever. It was unclear to them as to whether or not the long anticipated news registered in Dr. Knight's mind. Silence engulfed the room in wait, only broken by the exact tone of overhead monitors, which closely recording the situation. Sadly, they turned away, leaving the room to continue their conversation out of earshot.

Earlier that morning Dr. Barnes informed Mrs. Knight of the series of unexplained deaths within the hospital setting. Due to the magnitude of all the recent events, he failed to use the term "murder", not wanting to further burden the surgeon's grieving wife. Mrs. Knight did however agree to meet with the Philadelphia police detectives, along with Dr. Barnes, that afternoon. As they parted company that morning, words of condolence and hope were exchanged, bringing solace to each party.

The atmosphere in Jennifer Ranier's room was not as grim. Her medical status was stable, and her prognosis good. Several bouquets of flowers already adorned her room on the orthopedic floor, which had a spacious view of the city below. Lance and his crew of musclemen had already rounded on their postoperative patient that morning, expressing great success with regards to their surgery. Jennifer's femur bone was stabilized with an internal rod, and her thigh gash was repaired and loosely closed together. Physical therapy would help to get her out of bed that morning in order to sit in a chair. She would require intravenous antibiotics over the next 48 hours and then be discharged from the hospital. Her father and brother had already visited and set out for breakfast, allowing Phil to enter the room in his post call state. Jennifer had a vague memory of the motor vehicle accident from the night before. However she had no specific recall of the events or conversation leading up to it, a product of her traumatic concussion.

"Why the policeman outside?" asked Phil as he approached Jennifer.

"Don't know," said Jennifer as she received a soft hug from the intern. "I'm having a little trouble remembering the crash and everything about it."

"Probably a good thing," said Phil sitting next to her bed. "A picture of the car was on the news this morning, you're lucky to be alive."

"All I remember is the cold rain, darkness and an awful noise from the crash," said Jenna. "Then you holding my hand in the E.R., that's it."

"It sounds like everything went well in your surgery," said Phil. "I was in the room next door working on Dr. Knight."

"Oh my god, how is he?" asked Jennifer abruptly. "Was he badly hurt?"

"Pretty beat up," said Phil unaware as to how much Jennifer knew about his condition. "Ruptured spleen and liver but he will bounce back. Fortunately he is a hard headed surgeon who is trained to take pain."

Jennifer smiled at Phil and held his hand. The lingering effects of her concussion made conversation choppy that morning. Phil didn't inquire as to why she was in the car, or where they were headed. He thought these questions best be answered over time, in more private circumstances.

The reasoning for the police guards outside of their rooms however did trouble him, as it did the rest of the hospital. Rumors were already abuzz throughout the facility regarding the ill-fated couple and their New Year's Eve crash. Of course the most popular theory had them reunited, being in route to an illicit tryst, in celebration of the holiday.

Fatigue then set upon the couple. Phil again hugged and gently kissed Jennifer on her forehead, wishing her comfort. He mumbled the day's plan for some college football on T.V. and much needed sleep. The possibility of a return visit that evening was discussed. The intern left the room with a serene post call attitude, despite the horror of the night before. Upon exiting the room a burly Philadelphia police officer looked up from his chair while lowering the newspaper he was reading. Phil caught a glimpse of the headlines from page two regarding the crash and injuries sustained by the premier Philadelphia surgeon. A picture of the mangled Porsche accompanied the article. All eyes were upon the young intern as he slowly walked down the hallway, before taking a stairwell exit to the street below.

Drummer returned to the Greycliff complex at noontime. Heading towards his apartment he met Jim Turner in the hallway. The two made plans to watch the Rose Bowl that evening, with a pizza and some beer. Phil wandered into his apartment, finding it strange that Jennifer was not there to welcome him. He fed Goldie, had a peanut butter and jelly sandwich and fell soundly asleep on the couch. His post call night slumber was deep. During the next three hours his body did not move as it recovered from the most memorable of all call nights at the PGH.

At 3 PM that afternoon Dr. Barnes and Mrs. Knight walked into the sixth district headquarters of the Philadelphia Police Department. The couple was escorted down a series of stairwells to a room several floors below ground level. An overweight clerk with a holiday attitude led them through the cold hallways of the structure. Already awaiting their arrival was CEO Rineman and his cadre of attorneys. Their gathering was in a small, windowless conference room within the inner quadrant of the secure bunker. Drab walls surrounded the uncomfortable group as they sat in the foreign environment, awaiting the law enforcement team arrival. Soon afterward, a team of two male detectives entered, with a young female assistant. Both detectives were middle aged, sporting mid waist paunches and dressed in an unkempt fashion. Each lawman wore a dress shirt and tie, with a leather pistol holster sitting awkwardly across their torso in an oblique fashion. Their faces portrayed an "I've seen it all" attitude, with both lawmen smelling of cigarette tobacco. The female assistant dressed in a standard policewoman black pants and shirt outfit. A short ponytail held together a crop of badly dyed bleach blonde hair in place. The two bar chevron sewn on her left arm sleeve identified her rank insignia as corporal. She held a manila folder that contained the preliminary investigative information regarding the PGH case.

"Good afternoon everyone," said the slightly older detective as he sat down on a dented and somewhat rusty metal chair. "I am Detective O'Brien, and this is my partner, Detective James."

Introductions and handshakes were exchanged between the group members, and everyone settled in around a long rectangular conference table as the police corporal passed out bitter coffee in plain Styrofoam cups. Mrs. Knight kept her coat on against the cold dampness of the subterranean lair. An old fashioned clock adorned an otherwise blank wall. The time was 3:15 PM.

Howard Rineman and his legal team commanded the first fifteen minutes of meeting time, laying out all the information known to them. The legal squad spoke with exactness while reporting dates, times and details of the suspected four hospital incidents. The law enforcement team listened attentively to the information while sipping on their coffee. Dr. Barnes thought it strange that no member of the police team wrote down or recorded any of the information being provided. A frightful look settled in on Mrs. Knight's face as she became aware of the apparent criminal information regarding her husband's patients.

"Thank you counsel," said Detective O'Brien upon completion of the legal department's statement of known facts.

The detective then looked at Howard Rineman while asking him what steps have been taken to secure the hospital system up until that point. A brief discussion occurred regarding the authentication token used by the perpetrator, along with its subsequent deactivation.

Detective O'Brien then stood up and began to pace along his side of the table while slowly repeating the facts. He then looked at Mrs. Knight asking, "Mrs. Knight, is this the first time you have become aware of these allegations?"

"Yes."

"Mrs. Knight, did your husband ever express to you any concerns regarding his patient's being harmed, or quite frankly being killed?" was the detective's next question.

"Absolutely not," was her rapid response.

O'Brien then shook his head in acknowledgement while slowly returning to his seat. A several second pause passed amongst the group before the lead detective again spoke asking, "Mrs. Knight, does anybody immediately come to mind who would possess a passionate hate towards your husband? I mean a vengeful hate that can lead to the crime of murder?"

"Oh my," said Mrs. Knight caught off guard by the blunt question. "That's a very difficult question to answer under the current circumstances."

"Take your time Mrs. Knight. Please take your time," said the detective while holding up his coffee cup for a refill. "No one here is in a hurry."

A very pensive look came upon Mrs. Knight's face as she began to churn through decades of faces and time. Scattered throughout her brain was an endless list of incompetent physicians, businessmen and acquaintances that her husband berated on a nightly basis. Shattered marriages involving unknown jealous husbands and their cheating wives entered the equation. All eyes in the room where upon Mrs. Knight as her lower lip began to slightly tremble. A stunning recall of Jennifer Ranier flashed through her mind, as did a series of other suspected tramps from the not so recent past.

"Again, anyone that immediately enters your mind?" asked Detective O'Brien in a slow and methodical fashion.

"I mean, it is so hard to just come up with a name," said the doctor's wife. "So many people, over so much time." Another quiet minute passed as retrospection covered her face. Mrs. Knight then looked up saying cautiously, "Well I guess one or two people do come to mind."

"Who may they be?" asked the detective.

At that moment the shrill of Dr. Barnes' beeper echoed through the stark room. The chairman kept the beeper on his body for emergency purposes, in case his cell phone didn't connect. The depths of the underground conference room prohibited any penetration of a cell phone signal, however it allowed the pager to connect. The doctor excused himself as he stood up, walking to the corner of the room where a single phone sat on a table. The phone was an old fashioned desktop, with a dial face. Dr. Barnes then dialed the pager number, which was unknown to him.

James Asher answered the call on the first ring with a rapid hello. Dr. Barnes immediately sensed an urgent tone in his voice.

"We had another breach of the system," was the hurried line from Asher.

"What!" yelled Barnes. "When?"

His sudden excitement caused all the room occupants to suddenly turn towards him. Detective O'Brien got off his chair and approached the doctor and his ongoing conversation.

"About 30 minutes ago, my alarms went off," said Asher. "I've been keeping the monitoring system on just is case."

"I thought you turned off Dr. Knight's token," said Barnes.

"I did," said Asher. "He actually had two tokens, both of which are disabled."

"Well then who's token was used to enter the system?" asked Barnes. "And what was done by the violator?"

"I can't tell you as of yet who was the violator. Should know within about twenty minutes," said Asher. "Whoever it was changed the blood values again."

"Oh no," cried Barnes looking at the crowd that was now standing around him.

"Michael," said Asher with a pause. "The patient involved was Dr. Knight. Someone altered his potassium value. His life is in danger."

Dr. Barnes held the phone to his ear as the news penetrated into the core of his being. Looking up he saw a concerned and confused group staring at him anxiously. Still sitting at the table was a pale appearing Mrs. Knight with a tissue up to her eyes, gently sobbing.

"Keep me posted," said Barnes to Asher, "I'll be in cell range momentarily."

Dr. Barnes then hung up the phone, immediately notifying the group of the news. A decision was made by Detective O'Brien for he and Barnes to travel at once to Knight's bedside crime scene. The remainder of the party would stay behind, allowing them to complete a statement of fact. Prior to their hasty departure Dr. Barnes again picked up the phone and rapidly dialed a number.

After answering the phone in the SICU proper, nurse Cruise put Dr. O'Keefe on the line. O'Keefe was personally monitoring Dr. Knight's care that afternoon.

"Randy," yelled Barnes over the phone, "Did you see Dr. Knight's recent blood work?"

"Yea," said O'Keefe wondering what the concern was. "Labs looked good."

"What about the potassium?" said Barnes.

"A bit low, but we corrected that as soon as the results came across," said O'Keefe somewhat proudly.

The answer was exactly what Dr. Barnes feared. He suddenly realized that his infirmed colleague was about to become a casualty of his own coldly efficient ICU team. "Is the potassium bolus in?" asked Barnes.

Randy O'Keefe paused and peered into Dr. Knight's room before saying, "Yes sir, just about complete."

"Randy, listen to me," said the chairman with intensity. "This won't make sense to you but we need to rapidly reverse the potassium. Do you understand?"

"Not exactly," said the now confused resident.

"Just do as I say and do it STAT," said Barnes emphatically. He then proceeded to rattle off a series of emergent drugs to be administered intravenously. The list included calcium gluconate, dextrose, insulin and sodium bicarbonate.

"Are you sure?" asked the bemused Dr. O'Keefe. "I mean I've never heard of this combination of meds given before."

"Do as you are told!" yelled the department chairman over the phone. "Get the crash cart to his bedside and call the cardiac arrest team immediately."

"But he is fine," said O'Keefe. "Rock solid."

"That's an order!" screamed Barnes. "I will be there in about fifteen minutes. Do you understand?"

"Yes, yes I do," said Dr. O'Keefe in disbelief. "I'll do exactly what you said."

Doctor Barnes then hung up the phone while asking the detective how fast he could get to the hospital. The duo then ran out of the building to an awaiting police car. They proceeded with sirens blaring to the hospital, arriving on the ICU floor within twelve minutes. Upon turning the corner into the ICU proper a sea of chaos unfolded in front of them. It was immediately apparent that Dr. Knight was in full cardiac arrest for the second time in the last twenty-four hours.

As Dr. Barnes rushed towards the crowded room his cell phone rang aloud. He immediately looked down at the cell, noticing the incoming number to again be that of Asher's. The recognition caused him to divert backwards towards the less crowded central nursing station. He flipped open the cell and quickly held it to his ear.

"I've got the token I.D!" yelled Asher.

"Who? Who was it?" screamed the chairman over the loud commotion.

"The token belonged to Philip Drummer," said Asher sharply. "A doctor Philip Drummer."

CHAPTER 25
A Person of Interest

THE SHRILL RING of the phone awoke Phil with a sudden fright. Initially confused, he thought he was in the Polk Lounge receiving a call from the chief resident. While peering at a clock across the room he soon became oriented to person, place and time. It was 4 PM on that fateful day. Rolling to his left side, he picked up the phone, which sat atop a night table. While rubbing his eyes the weary intern then mumbled "hello."

"Hey, what are you up to?" asked Jenna with a voice that immediately voiced concern.

"Oh, just woke up from a nap," said Phil while blinking his eyes and sitting up on the couch. Looking outside he saw a bleak January day, with an overcast sky and a threat of rain. Dark clouds were rapidly moving across the skyline. "Wow, I was really out."

"Phil, I'm starting to recall some of the events from last night," said Jenna. "Including the conversation just prior to the accident."

A chill ran down Phil's spine from the comment and dampness that seemed to grip the room. "What do you remember?" was his question. A siren below raced down the street, away from the apartment complex.

Jennifer then proceeded to recall the series of events leading up to the crash. Her memory recapped a frantic phone call from Dr. Knight and the reasoning behind her getting into the Porsche. A description of the surreal ride and conversation through West Philadelphia was given, causing Phil to stir uneasily. As Jenna continued, the surnames of Brown, Charles, McDuff and Cox echoed through his mind. She then described the final argument and scream exchanged between the two prior to the crash.

"He thought I was killing his patients," said Jenna sadly. "Can you believe that?"

"What?" shouted Phil, "That's crazy. Why would he think that?

"I don't know," replied Jennifer. "He was screaming at me, asking who could possibly be killing his patients."

Phil paused to digest the information, wondering who else was aware of Knight's concerns. "How sure was he about these alleged events?"

"He was sure," said Jenna. "Darn sure."

"Seems a little far fetched, doesn't it?" asked Phil. "Was he drinking?"

"No," said Jenna now getting a headache. "He seemed sober." She paused, "But he was wearing a tuxedo for some reason."

"Have you told anyone else this Jenna?" asked Phil.

"No," was her response. "But they must know, I mean the police. They plan on talking to me this afternoon."

"That explains the police officer outside your room," said Phil. "There was also a policeman stationed outside of Knight's room."

Before Phil could continue, Jennifer abruptly informed him that a group of men entered her room. He was able to hear a muted exchange of greetings with the word detective and attorney intermixed. He heard Jennifer asking the parties to sit down.

"Phil, I have to go," said a concerned Jennifer, "They are here to talk to me."

"No problem," said Phil quickly. "Just tell them what you know." He paused in expectation of a response from Jenna, which did not occur. He then said quickly, "I love you Jenna." His parting words were followed by a click on the other end of the line, which terminated the conversation.

Phil hung up the phone and stared out the window, trying to make sense of the unfolding events. Storm clouds outside were getting thicker and lower as the wind began to howl. A sudden gust of wind rattled a window with an audible force. Phil walked over to his desk and sat down slowly. He then turned on his computer. As the desktop device churned to life he glanced up at a corkboard hanging on the adjacent wall. Amongst the hodgepodge of postings was an old laminated article from his hometown newspaper. It was titled, "Pennsylvania's Finest." Slowly he read the article that described his academic and athletic career, and ultimate acceptance to the University of Pennsylvania Medical School. At the bottom of the article was his dad's scratchy penmanship stating, "Congratulations son, mom is very proud of you." Thoughts of his mother began to race through his head, including the sound of her guiding voice, and the calm of her gentle hand. It disturbed him that these fond memories were becoming more and more difficult to recall over time. He reached upwards towards the corkboard and pushed aside a collection of papers, exposing a picture of himself with his parents. It was the final picture they took together at his mother's bedside. Despite the obvious pain and sickness in her face, a proud smile burst through as she held Phil's body close to her own. She died peacefully, three days after the photo was taken. Tears began to well up in Phil's eyes.

The ping of the computer suddenly signaled to Phil that he was on line. Pausing for a moment he stared at the screen, which beckoned him for a command. Looking downward he rapidly began to hit the keyboard, logging his code name into the Philadelphia General Hospital system.

At that moment, ten blocks away from the Greycliff apartment, rode Philadelphia police car number twenty-nine. Operating the cruiser was Corporal Weaver, a five-year veteran of the force. Riding alongside him was Private Jones, a rookie who just completed his first year on the force. Until that point it had been an uncharacteristically quiet New Year's Day. The officers were discussing upcoming weekend plans when their radio came to life.

"Central units and 1A29, 187 suspect there now, 42nd and Spruce Street, Greycliff Apartments, seventh floor, apartment number 734. Suspect male/white 24 years old. Black hair, tall, answers to Doctor Drummer. Code 3, Incident 4531, R.D. – 153."

Corporal Weaver raised his eyebrow while looking at his partner. Officer Jones quickly picked up the radio unit and brought it to his mouth saying, "1A29 roger, responding from 1st-Philadelphia."

The dispatcher's voice again crackled over the airwaves saying, "1A29 is responding Code 3 from 1st Philadelphia to 42nd and Spruce Street."

"Let the games begin," said Corporal Weaver as he flipped on the vehicle's overhead lights and siren.

Private Jones' heart began to beat rapidly, as the police car sped towards the Greycliff complex. He looked straight ahead while saying to himself, "Time to make a house call."

The sudden knock on the door jolted Phil with a scare, diverting his attention from the screen. A second knock followed that was more of a thud than a knock, followed by a series of rapid thuds. Phil jumped up from his seat and rambled towards the door, wondering why the knock was so strange and out of sync.

He swung the door open only to see Jim Turner attempting another kick on the door. He was holding a pizza pie, Stromboli and six-pack of beer. A happy grin was upon the veterinary student's face.

"The granddaddy of them all," yelled Turner referring to the Rose Bowl game scheduled to kick off soon. "Sorry I couldn't knock," was his next line.

"No problem," said Phil as Turner walked past him with the pizza aroma trailing. Phil grabbed the six-pack from his friend as he walked by. The two then headed into the galley kitchen.

"Where's Jenna?" asked Turner as he put the pizza and Stromboli on the table. He then looked into the living room, fully expecting to see Ranier.

"Not going to be here," said Phil rubbing his eyes and then sliding them down his face. "Just not going to be here today." Phil then began to walk towards the cold supply of beer that was just delivered.

"You look like crap," said Turner. Before Phil could respond he again spoke saying, "Hey was that your mentor in the crash last night? I just read the *Chronicle*."

"Yes," said Phil while putting the beer in the refrigerator. "My esteemed mentor was the driver of that rocket."

"He survived that crash?" said Turner in disbelief. "How is that possible?"

"I don't know? It was a miracle," said Phil. "That's why I'm beat, we were up all night operating on him."

Phil briefly described the tremendous internal injuries suffered by Knight, along with his amazing survival. In great detail he relived the chaos of the emergency room scene, followed by the intensity of the prolonged surgical intervention.

"The article said a passenger also survived. That's hard to believe," said Turner as he started to assault the pizza.

"Did it mention the passenger's name?" asked Phil.

"I can't remember," said Turner as he walked into the adjacent living room. "Where's the remote? I love the granddaddy of them all. I'm going with U.S.C. as usual, love the Trojan fight song."

"The passenger was Jenna," blurted Phil not realizing why he had even said it.

"What!" yelled Turner, "Is she O.K.?"

"Yea, she will be O.K., just a bit banged up," said Phil. He then went into more detail regarding her injuries and care. Throughout the description of events Turner sat mesmerized, as he listened to the account with an incredulous stare.

"What was she doing with him on New Year's Eve?" asked Turner. "I mean that seems kind of strange Phil."

"I have no idea," said Phil sitting down and popping open a beer. "Did the article give any details about their evening or plans?"

"I can't recall but I just skimmed the article," said Turner. "Now you got me all riled up," was his next response as he then headed rapidly towards the door. "I'll go and get the paper."

Phil instinctively got up and followed Jim towards the door. The duo then walked into the hallway towards Turner's apartment. Midway across the hall they both appreciated the characteristic ding of the elevator car arriving on the floor, followed by the opening sound of the Otis doors. Both men continued their course while peering down the hallway. Two Philadelphia police officers then stepped outside the elevator car, looking at the numbers on the apartment doors facing them. They looked left, and then right, to orient themselves. Each officer then turned to the right, and commenced to walk briskly down the hall towards the two.

Their sudden appearance stopped both Drummer and Turner in their tracks, as the appearance of two police officers on an apartment floor characteristically does. Phil noticed the officers checking the apartment numbers and then sequentially calculating a predetermined number down the hallway. Concern overtook him when their gaze fixated on his end of the hallway. The pace of their cadence picked up as the officers now rapidly approached. From that moment forward events unfolded in Phil's mind in a peculiarly slow motion.

Phil noticed the lead officer was short and mildly obese, with a face scarred by acne. This officer wore a corporal's rank on his sleeve and appeared to be a bit out of breath. While approaching Phil he tilted his head to his shoulder and spoke into a microphone that was clasped to his uniform. The second officer was much younger, with a wiry build and uniform that seemed a bit oversized for his stature. This second officer seemed physically fit in comparison to his partner. Each lawman wore a characteristic policeman's hat, with a short brim slanted downward, per academy training. Phil heard the squeak of their spit shined shoes garbled amongst Turner question of "What's this?" A voice was heard coming across the corporal's radio signifying a backup unit on the way. It was obvious to Phil that his apartment was the destination of the officer's visit. The recent conversation with Jenna entered his mind, as did the word "murder."

Phil's heart rate delivered an adrenaline rush through his body, triggering a physiologic "fight or flight" mechanism. His pupils immediately dilated while his respiratory rate increased. A rapid flush of blood warmed his extremities as his mouth became suddenly dry. Tunnel vision focused on the policeman while his auditory sense lessened.

During the final approach Corporal Weaver placed his right hand on a service weapon that was attached to his utility belt. Phil noticed that he unsnapped a safety strap across the top of the weapon. The younger office behind him followed suit in a much more inexperienced fashion. Each lawman maintained a stern, serious look across their face. They were approximately twenty feet away when officer Weaver spoke.

"Doctor…" was the first word expressed with slow clarity and conviction by Weaver. Both officers then stopped dead in their tracks, freezing their pose, while cocking their heads ever so slowly to one side. Phil noticed that both policemen maintained a firm grip upon their weapons.

Police officer Weaver then went to speak again. "Doctor…"

Then, before he could continue, Phil appreciated a forceful shove to his right shoulder that propelled him into the direction of the officers. The unexpected impact caused him to stumble forward towards officer Weaver. Phil suddenly realized that Jim Turner had knocked him forward. He peered backwards only to see Turner bolt around the corner in a sprint, heading down the back hallway of the apartment complex. Before Phil could respond he felt officer Weaver expertly apply a straight-arm bar take down maneuver upon him. Phil did not resist the submission hold. Then, upon looking upwards, he peered directly into the 9 mm Baretta pistol that Private Jones had drawn during the event.

"Freeze!" yelled officer Jones while continuing to direct his weapon at Phil's head. A slight tremble of the policeman's hand caused the barrel of the weapon to teeter ever so slightly.

Phil did not move, nor could he. The plodding trot of Turner could be heard racing away down the back corridor of the Greycliff.

"Identify your self," said Corporal Weaver with a hint of shortness in his breath.

"Phil, Philip Drummer," was the response.

"Doctor Drummer?" asked officer Weaver.

"Yes, Doctor Philip Drummer," was Phil's reply. Then, for whatever reason he continued to speak saying, "Surgical intern, Philadelphia General Hospital."

Policeman Weaver then stood Phil upwards with the arm lock maintained behind his back. He then turned Phil towards the wall while bringing his other hand backwards. Before Phil could realize what had happened, he was handcuffed and turned towards the officers. Officer Weaver was red in the face and panting, his breath smelled of stale coffee. Phil then appreciated the stench of Old Spice cologne on the officer's body.

"I've got him," said Weaver with a pant to his partner. "Get the other guy."

Officer Jones then quickly turned the corner with his weapon drawn not knowing what to expect. He peered down the long hallway to see the portly body of Jim Turner slip through an emergency stairwell exit. Placing his revolver back into his gun belt, he proceeded to race down the hallway. Officer Jones remembered his collegiate track days as the sprint began. Being the local star of the Penn Relays just three years prior, Turner didn't have much of a chance on that momentous New Year's afternoon.

Phil was informed of his Miranda rights by officer Weaver. The officer refused to answer any questions from Phil as to why he was being arrested. The policeman honored Phil's request to close his apartment door prior to being led down the hallway towards the elevator. Several neighbors peered outside their doors with concern upon their faces. The wait for the elevator seemed like an eternity to Phil, as the hallway chatter behind him increased. Upon exiting the Greycliff courtyard below, a police cruiser car awaited, with overhead lights flashing. Phil looked about, but there was no sign of Turner. He was lowered into the rear seat of the police cruiser with his head protected in standard fashion. A uriniferous stench permeated the rear seat of the vehicle, which was filthy and littered with debris. The officer then slammed the door behind Phil, which automatically locked with a mechanical clunk. Phil looked forward to see a thick screen separating him from the officer driving the car. The second patrolman then slid into the passenger's seat with a thud, while picking up the radio receiver to speak into. The vehicle suddenly lurched forward away from the Greycliff complex. Phil noticed some neighborhood children staring blankly at the patrol car as it passed by. The return chatter over the police radio disclosed their destination to Phil. He was being taken handcuffed, to police district headquarters, in downtown Philadelphia.

CHAPTER 26
Surgical Closure

DOCTOR PHILIP DRUMMER was now the principal suspect in the alleged killing of four patients at the Philadelphia General Hospital. After arriving at police headquarters, he was unceremoniously escorted to a stark second floor room by an elderly policeman with a limp. Above the room entry was a chipped painted sign, simply spelling the word Interrogation. A single metal table graced the center of the facility, with four dented metal chairs surrounding it. An ashtray and yellow legal notepad sat upon the table, next to an urn filled with stale coffee. Opposite the entry sat a solitary table with a phone, surrounded by a mess of papers. A single corkboard hung upon a wall, with police propaganda and several Most Wanted posters upon it. Otherwise, all of the walls were bare except for the obvious two-way mirror that Phil recognized from cop shows on television.

Phil was asked to sit down by the thirty-five year veteran of the force. Upon declining an offer for coffee, he was informed that a detective was on his way to speak to him. The policeman then turned away politely, and walked with an unsteady gait towards the exit. Phil imagined that the officer was once shot in the line of duty, landing him an office job for the rest of his career.

No one entered the room for the next fifteen minutes. Throughout this time Phil appreciated the presence of a seated policeman just outside the door. Silence commanded the room as his fatigued mind tried to place the pieces of an eerie puzzle together. Questions collided in his brain, with seemingly no obvious answer or connection between them. Why would someone be killing Dr. Knight's patients? Was Jennifer truthful in her reasoning for being with Dr. Knight the prior evening? Why did Jim Turner shove him forward and run away? What had happened to Turner in the pursuit? A subtle headache began to take hold of Phil as the ultimate question then entered his mind. Why had he, Phil Drummer, been handcuffed, arrested and taken to a police station for questioning? Details regarding the death of Willie Brown arose, as did his morbid dismemberment. He recalled the wandering eye of stockbroker Charles as he blatantly undressed Jennifer in his bedridden mind. Phil pictured Mrs. McDuff's wealthy and lifeless heart, not responding to her despondent surgeon's pleas and massage. Lastly, the angelic voice of diva Cox echoed in the artless room, rendering a tear in the intern's mind. Four completely different people, four very separate walks of life, all now deceased. How was that possible, thought Phil, and why?

Detective James entered unobtrusively. He wore a wrinkled shirt and outdated tie, with several stains upon it. Brown, unpolished shoes failed to complement a black belt and gray trousers. The detective cleared his throat as he approached Phil while extending a handshake.

"Doctor Drummer, I'm Detective James," was his introduction as a puff of recently inhaled tobacco smoke exited his mouth.

Phil shook hands with the detective, appreciating a cold and callused palm. Each man then sat down, across from each other at the table. The detective gathered some papers in front of him, and then turned the top page of the legal pad over, in an apparent gesture of note taking.

"Doctor Drummer let me start by saying that this conversation will be recorded and you have a right to an attorney being present," said James. "Do you understand?"

"Yes," said Phil.

"Do you wish to exercise your right to legal counsel," asked the detective while drawing a bold line forcefully across the top of his pad.

"No," said Phil. "I have nothing to hide, or should I say be concerned about."

"Good, then lets get started," said the officer. "Mr. Drummer, I mean Doctor Drummer, are you aware of the names William Brown, Brett Charles, Katherine McDuff and Helga Cox?"

"Yes," said Phil.

"Are you aware that each of these victims, or should I say patients, have since died within the confines of the Philadelphia General Hospital?" was his next question.

"Yes I am," replied Phil as he adjusted his seat and sat up straighter in the chair. "I assisted in their medical care at the PGH," was his next line. Phil then uncomfortably glanced at the two-way mirror, wondering who was on the other side of it.

"Thank you," said the detective. James then looked up at Phil stating, "Dr. Drummer, you have been detained and brought to police headquarters for questioning regarding the deaths of these four patients. Do you understand?"

"Yes," replied Phil.

"Very good. Then let me continue," said an unemotional Detective James staring down at his notepad. "It has come to our attention that each of these patients may have been purposefully harmed during their stay at the hospital. To be more exact, we have information suggesting that each of their deaths may have been orchestrated by an outside person or persons, resulting in their rapid demise." Detective James then looked directly into Phil's eyes stating, "Doctor Drummer, are you aware of any truth to this grave matter, which if proven true by a juror of peers, constitutes a crime of capital murder?"

"Yes," said Phil sharply to an immediately amazed officer of the law.

"I see," said Detective James with an obvious glance towards the two-way mirror. "Please explain your knowledge of the situation."

"I became aware of this possibility just prior to the two Philadelphia police officers appearing at my apartment," said Phil. "By a phone conversation with physician assistant Jennifer Ranier."

"I am aware of Ms. Ranier, please continue," said James.

"She called me from the hospital, telling me that Dr. Knight believed that someone was harming his patients, specifically the patients who you just mentioned."

Detective James then proceeded to dissect the conversation that occurred between Phil and Jenna just minutes before his arrest. Exact details of the conversation were fresh in Phil's mind, which generated precise answers to the officer's broad questions. Phil then relayed Jennifer's description of the frightful events leading up to the automobile crash that hospitalized both her and Dr. Knight.

"What is your relationship to Ms. Ranier?" asked the detective.

Phil paused and shook his head, wondering how he had gotten into this seemingly confused mess. He then spoke saying, "She is my girlfriend."

Detective James immediately sensed that proceeding upon a more exact line of questioning regarding their relationship would be harmful to the interrogation. He paused, while jotting down some information on the notepad. Phil noticed that his penmanship was shaky and illegible.

"Do you believe that Ms. Ranier was in any way responsible for the alleged deaths of the previously mentioned patients?" asked James.

"No," said Phil quickly. This response was then followed by a more pensive, "No sir, I do not."

"Can you tell me your understanding of the relationship between Ms. Ranier and a Doctor Richard Knight?" asked Detective James, realizing that he was pushing the envelope of discussion.

Phil looked up at the sleuth with a blank face, and then stared back down at the table before responding. "No I cannot. Not with any accuracy," was his response. "I suggest that you ask P.A. Ranier and Doctor Knight that question for a more exact description of their relationship."

"Thank you," replied the detective while then crossing out a series of questions on a separate piece of paper that accompanied him. "Doctor, can you think of anyone within the Philadelphia General Hospital System that would wish to bring harm upon the patients of Dr. Knight? Or for that matter, wish to harm Dr. Knight himself?"

The question caught Phil off guard, immediately causing him to wonder how Dr. Knight was doing that day. He then began to mentally construct a list of people who hated Knight, soon realizing that such a list was long. Sitting atop this mental laundry list of suspects was the revered Riles family from the Boston area. The bleached, overpoweringly white smile of Frederick Riles Sr. arose in the doctor's mind. Jennifer had informed Phil on many occasion of the longstanding hatred between the senior Riles and Knight. Phil was also well aware of the younger Riles' hatred of Knight prior to his resignation from the internship program.

"Anyone?" asked Detective James again.

"No," said Phil disbelieving that the Riles family was capable of murder. "No one that I can be definite about."

"Doctor Drummer are you aware of what an authentication token is?" asked Detective James.

"I believe so," said Phil.

"Please explain your understanding of this device," said James.

After first clarifying that he was no computer expert, Phil proceeded to describe his understanding of the token. A superficial discussion occurred between the two regarding computer systems and associated technology. It was apparent to Phil that Detective James had limited knowledge of the subject.

"Dr. Drummer, it is our belief that the perpetrator of the alleged crimes had changed the blood report values of the victims, thus altering their treatment in a dramatic and fatal fashion." Detective James then looked at Phil while continuing, "Are you aware of this possibility?"

"No."

"Let me be perfectly clear regarding the next statement," said James who sat up more erect in his chair while clearing his throat. "It is a fact, that the last illegal entry into the system was just several hours ago, and that violation entered the system under your token. The token of Dr. Philip Drummer."

Silence gripped the room as Detective James stared at Phil, who in return cast his eyes down upon the floor in thought. "Are you aware of that fact?" asked the detective.

"No," was the quiet reply of Phil Drummer. "No I was not." Phil immediately tried to recall the whereabouts of his token but the rapid line of questioning continued.

"Doctor, have you in any way, shape or form, ever altered the lab values of Dr. Knight's patient's during their hospital stay at the PGH?"

"No."

"Have you knowingly ever brought harm upon Dr. Knight's patient's at the PGH?"

"No."

"Have you knowingly ever conspired with someone to harm Dr. Knight's patients? Specifically, did you knowingly provide your authentication token to another person or persons to illegally enter the hospital computer system?"

"Of course not," said Phil now starting to get a bit annoyed at the accusations from the police official. "Why would I do such a thing?"

"Doctor what is your relationship with a Mr. James Turner?" was the next rapid fire question.

Before Phil could answer the two were surprised by the sudden and unannounced appearance of Detective O'Brien who stormed into the room. Walking briskly behind him was Chairman Barnes with a grim look upon his face. Dr. Barnes held a folder in his hand containing records from the Philadelphia General.

"Detective James, a moment please," said Detective O'Brien to his colleague. Phil noticed that Detective O'Brien nodded his head up and down in a positive fashion as he spoke, while looking directly at him.

Detective James arose from the metal chair as it gave a sharp screech upon the floor. He then approached Detective O'Brien and Doctor Barnes to discuss the matter in private. The two detectives then excused themselves from Chairman Barnes and carried on a brief conversation alone. They quickly began nodding their heads together and turned back towards the two physicians. Detective James was apparently in charge from this point forward as he walked up to Phil and took a deep breath before speaking. Phil's heart beat rapidly in anticipation of his remarks as he sensed his medical career about to end in dramatic fashion. A sudden thought of his father entered his mind.

"You're free to go," said Detective James in a relieved fashion. "Thank you for your time."

Phil sat still, shocked by the abrupt end to the meeting. Thoughts raced through his mind as to a reason for the obvious finality of the situation. He stared in disbelief at the two detectives and his department chairman, who stood uncomfortably in front of him. His facial expression pleaded for an answer as to why he was suddenly allowed to leave.

"But, I don't understand," said Phil slowly while looking at the detectives. "Why all of a sudden am I allowed to go?"

His confused stare was met by silence.

"Please, can someone explain to me what is going on?" said Phil. "I mean I was just handcuffed and brought down here for a reason."

Detective James then looked at his colleague before speaking, as if seeking permission to talk. Phil noticed that Detective O'Brien nodded in apparent consent to respond.

"It was Mr. James Turner," said Detective James to Phil. "He just gave a full confession at the hospital."

"What!" said Phil in disbelief, "Jim Turner!"

"Yes," said O'Brien. "Mr. Turner orchestrated the murder of each victim, via the internet."

"What, I mean why?" said Phil in disbelief that his good friend would be in any way responsible for the deaths of four patients. "Why would he ever do such a horrible thing?"

Detective James then sat back down in his metal chair with a pensive look upon his face, having just heard of the confession himself. He sat with his hands clasped together in front of his face, as they supported his protruding jaw. Then, while looking up at his partner, he said, "The young doctor has raised a good question regarding Mr. Turner's motive. Please, help us connect the dots." Detective James again paused while turning his gaze to Phil in saying, "Certainly Dr. Drummer will become privy to all of this information as the investigation continues."

"Here is your motive," said O'Brien who then pointed to the chart that Dr. Barnes held in his hand. The doctor opened the chart, pulling out a two-page record that he immediately handed to the still seated Detective James.

James then studied the document intently for a very long minute before looking up at his colleague saying, "This makes no sense to me. It's a medical record from 1980."

"A surgical record to be exact," said Dr. Barnes.

"I see your name on it, and Dr. Knight's," said the detective. "Otherwise I don't recognize anyone else listed."

"Doctor Barnes will explain the meaning of this record," said Detective O'Brien looking at the Chairman. O'Brien then noticed that Phil was physically trembling while trying to still decipher the news. He then asked that a copy of the report be given to the young intern prior to any further discussion. Barnes obliged as he gave a second copy of the 1980 operative report to Phil.

Phil immediately scanned the report dated July 6th, 1980. The attending surgeon was listed as Dr. Fox, one of the many famous names that Phil recognized from tales of the past. Dr. Fox was a true academician at the PGH, well published yet all thumbs in the operating room. It was rumored that he was an alcoholic in his later years, commonly sleeping in the surgeon's lounge while the residents performed his elective surgeries. The residents adored him for this cavalier lack of presence, since it allowed them to practice their future trade on unknowing patients.

"This is a surgical record from 1980," said Dr. Barnes. "As you can see both Dr. Knight and I were involved in this case."

Phil's eyes then rapidly scanned to the next line below that of Dr. Fox's. There, listed as the chief resident overseeing the procedure, was the name of Dr. Frederick Riles, II. The proceeding line recorded the names of the junior resident and intern involved in the case, Dr. Michael Barnes and Dr. Richard Knight. Phil realized that it must have been the first week of Knight's surgical internship year.

"The procedure being performed was that of a cholecystectomy, or gall bladder removal," said Dr. Barnes. "Believe it or not, I do remember this case quite well."

Phil then scanned the remainder of the report summary that sat above the detailed description of the operative procedure itself. Next to the heading of Blood Loss was the term: "Massive". Adjacent to the category of Complications was a singular word: "Death."

"This was a complicated case involving a very scarred down and chronically inflamed gall bladder attack," said Barnes. Phil noticed that the chairman's dialect had suddenly switched into a professorial tone of unapproachable excellence, which was only spoken at a tertiary care medical center.

While the chairman continued to pontificate upon the case, Phil scanned down to the written text of the surgical procedure. Here, contained within the report, was the most exact description of what occurred in order to cause such a massive bleed and subsequent death. Phil was underwhelmed by the vague description of tissue scarring and chronic swelling. Inexact sentences failed to connect together any exact description of what may have gone wrong. A single line described pulsatile and uncontrollable bleeding from the cystic and adjacent hepatic artery. A cardiac arrest was documented in the final line of the nondescript report, stating that all attempts to revive the patient were subsequently unsuccessful.

"I'm still lost," said Detective James after hearing Dr. Barnes' tight synopsis of the surgical case gone wrong. "How does this report, from thirty years ago, help me understand why a veterinary student named James Turner would murder four patients in the year 2010."

"Look at the patient's name on the report," said a solemn Detective O'Brien. "That will explain it all."

Phil quickly scanned to the top of the report, realizing that he never read the name of the ill-fated patient operated on that July day. A pitiful sense of sorrow overwhelmed him as the patient's name immediately registered in his mind. The name was that of Nancy Turner, the mother of then three-year old James Turner, who was innocently playing at home that sunny July day. Playing at home, unaware of the tragedy that had stricken his loving mother, thus altering his childhood in a cruel and unforgiving fashion.

"Oh my God," said Phil. "It was Jim's mother." Phil's mind immediately unleashed a flood of emotions bringing into play thoughts of his own mother and her demise. He slowly lowered his head into his hands, instantly recalling Jim's prior description of a PGH surgery gone bad that resulted in the death of a family member. Jim never mentioned that his mother was the victim of the July event. Tears began to well up in his eyes as he stared blankly at the floor beneath him.

"Turner had been illegally entering the hospital archives," said O'Brien "Apparently roaming through old records. The detective paused while clearing his throat before continuing, "Naturally he retrieved the complete medical record of his mother, including the operative report." Several seconds of silence then passed among the group as each member gathered their composure. "Apparently it was this report that triggered his vengeance towards Dr. Knight," said O'Brien.

"Why Dr. Knight? Why not me?" asked Barnes.

Phil immediately thought of all the discussions that he and Turner had regarding Dr. Knight. He immediately recalled the long conversations that the two had regarding the inner workings of Knight's machine. A cruel pang of sorrow overtook him as he recalled the then seemingly innocent references to Knight's blue bloods, including Charles, McDuff and Cox.

"Don't know why he choose Knight first, but you were probably next," said O'Brien looking at Barnes. "Consider yourself lucky."

"Did he act alone?" asked the never assuming Detective James.

"Yes, per his confession," said O'Brien. "He would secretly use the available tokens of Dr. Drummer and Ms. Ranier that were kept in their apartment. Apparently he had a computer savvy mind that allowed him to execute such a brazen plan."

Phil immediately thought of the relatively free access that Turner had to his apartment, including a recently shared key to provide care for Jenna's goldfish. His mind flashed back to Turner's original help in connecting Phil to the PGH system, via the laptop computer.

"Were you aware of this?" asked James to Phil.

"No. Absolutely not," replied Phil in a somber tone. "Jim was a brilliant student and good friend, who I trusted completely."

"Mr. Turner was adamant that he acted alone," said Detective O'Brien. "He specifically exonerated Dr. Drummer and Ms. Ranier. In fact he expressed some deep personal emotions for Jennifer Ranier in particular."

"I remember that case so well," said Dr. Barnes, who was equally shocked by the magnitude of the situation. "Dr. Knight never forgave Riles, who quite frankly botched the surgery that morning. Unfortunately, Dr. Riles turned the whole situation into a blame game that haunted the two throughout the remainder of their years together. A very tragic event."

"A tragedy that has unfortunately claimed the lives of several innocent people thirty years later," said Detective O'Brien.

"What happened to Jim Turner?" asked Phil.

"He jumped off the fire escape attempting to allude the officer pursuing him," said Detective James. "Dislocated his ankle in the fall."

"Needed it set by some bone doctor that looked like Hercules up at the hospital," said Detective O'Brien. "He won't be walking for a while."

"You're free to go," repeated Detective James. "Of course as the case progresses we will need further comment from you and Ms. Ranier."

"I understand," said Phil standing up to depart. He felt a bit lightheaded as he began to walk towards the door. "Thank you very much for the explanation."

"One last thing Dr. Drummer," said Detective James, "This is an ongoing investigation, so please do not discuss this freely with anyone."

Phil agreed as handshakes were exchanged among the group members. Phil headed down the hallway unescorted towards an exit stairwell. As he walked away the voice of Dr. Barnes called out his name. Phil waited atop the stairwell as his Chairman approached him, unsure as to whether or not an internship still existed for him. The approaching footsteps of Dr. Barnes echoed loudly through the vacant halls of the building.

"Doctor Drummer, I would like to compliment you on the mature way you handled yourself over the past twenty four hours," said Barnes.

"Thank you," said Phil. "It was a bit nerve racking at times."

"Nerve racking for all of us," said Barnes. "No one expected such a series of events to occur."

The chairman then discussed with Phil the uncertainty that lay ahead for the surgery program and hospital system in light of the recent revelations. A public outcry was sure to follow once the news hit the streets. He then congratulated Phil on his performance over the past six months, saying that his internal grading as an intern has been one of the best. Phil appreciated the candor expressed by Barnes who made it quite clear that his internship would continue uninterrupted by the recent events. Phil again shook his chairman's hands and then began his descent down a stairwell.

Phil suddenly turned around saying, "Doctor Barnes, how is Dr. Knight doing?" Up until that point he had been unaware of the recent murder attempt on his life.

Doctor Barnes paused and took a deep sigh before looking at Phil, obviously attempting to maintain his composure. "The old dog is just fine," said Barnes with a sudden smile. "He has been to hell and back, but he is going to make it."

"Wonderful," said Phil as he turned away and headed towards the exit. "Absolutely wonderful."

Upon stepping outside a magnificent blast of cold winter air struck Phil's face. Looking overhead he appreciated bright sunshine that commanded a presence over the city. Phil inhaled deeply to fill his lungs with the icy chill of the day. Gazing downtown he recognized the statue of William Penn perched atop city hall, and a jolt of freedom, true Philadelphia freedom, energized him. With a skip and renewed sense of purpose he blissfully began the long walk back to West Philadelphia. Peace and quiet engulfed the city that afternoon, as it recovered from a previous evening of raucous celebration.

Phil walked briskly out of center city, and then crossed the Schuylkill River onto the hospital campus. While looking up at the approaching medical center he immediately felt the power and awe of the institution. Despite the holiday, the usual hustle and bustle of activity abounded at the corner of 34th and University Avenue. Patients of all ages, race and creed bypassed each other in a haphazard fashion while accessing the front lobby. Only then did Phil completely understand the importance of this esteemed medical center. He understood that eternal hope and knowledge anchored the institution, offering each patient the possibility of a medical cure. He also realized that the great PGH held generations of knowledge passed down by word of mouth and action. Knowledge that was available to all students in their quest to join the most noblest profession of all – medicine.

Looking upwards Phil quickly located Jennifer's room high above the city street. The sun shone brilliantly upon her window, creating a peculiar reflection against the afternoon sky. A warm comfort overtook Phil's heart knowing that Jennifer was safe within the walls of the Philadelphia

General. A smile came upon his face as he pictured her triumphant return back to the Greycliff apartments.

Upon completing his walk home Phil entered the courtyard of the Greycliff Apartments. His overhead gaze focused on the window of Jim Turner's apartment where the shade was partly drawn. A sense of disbelief and confusion cluttered his mind as he rode the elevator alone to the seventh floor. Upon entering his apartment he walked over to his computer, which was still on, and sat down. He stared at the screen for several seconds before his gaze took him beyond the computer to a framed picture on the desk. The photo was that of Phil and his dad taken seven months ago on graduation day. They were standing in front of a statue of Benjamin Franklin shaking hands while Phil held up his medical diploma. The photograph caused Phil to pause and smile, being aware that he fulfilled a promise to work hard and remember his roots. He knew that his mother and father would be proud of him, and that's all that mattered, at least where Phil Drummer came from. He then reached behind the computer screen to touch the power button, ordering the machine to go silent.

THE END